All Jackson wanted to do was kiss away her fears. No, that wasn't true. That wasn't all he wanted to do. But first, he'd kiss away her tears.

"I'm not crying!" Erin protested, turning her face toward the rumpled pillow.

Jackson caught her chin. "No one said you were, kid."

"And I'm not a kid."

That could not possibly be more apparent to him. The thin material of her camisole did little to separate him from the feel of her soft and feminine curves.

"Are you going to kiss me on the mouth?" she whispered.

"It's crossed my mind," Jackson admitted.

Erin's pulse leapt at the thought. She recalled vividly the last time those lips had wreaked havoc with her senses. "Would you mind just holding me first, Tyler?" she asked softly. And maybe the room would be still, she thought, giving in readily to the arms that enfolded her.

The room stayed still, and Erin felt warm, wonderfully warm, and, oddly enough, safe. She entwined her legs around one of his and tucked her head under his rough-shaven chin.

His lips found hers, and she found herself yielding to his passion, clinging to his broad shoulders for support, her defenses crumbling. No, the room was not still, it was reeling . . . for his kiss had deepened. She closed her eyes and gave herself up, floating. It was pure rapture.

# LINDA WINDSOR

# DELTA MOONFIRE

**ZEBRA BOOKS**
**KENSINGTON PUBLISHING CORP.**

*To my family*
*and the memories we shared*
*on the Mississippi.*


ZEBRA BOOKS

are published by

Kensington Publishing Corp.
475 Park Avenue South
New York, NY 10016

Copyright © 1992 by Linda Windsor

First printing: October, 1992

Printed in the United States of America

# Prologue

The saloon was filled with smoke; the single fan over the bar, pulled by a young boy in the corner, had little effect on it. The noise level was inordinately high, considering that a corpse was lying in a pine box shoved against the back wall. Raucous feminine laughter sometimes broke out from one of the tables or drifted down from the upstairs rooms. At the bar a boy in his teens stared starry-eyed at a saloon girl as she counted the night's earnings, trying to muster the nerve to approach her about an evening's entertainment.

He was handsome, Giselle Devareau thought, her sharp mind keeping track of the coins she counted while she assessed the young man. But if he was a day over seventeen, she'd be fooled. She wondered if the boy's father knew he was in Under the Hill. Robert Tyler would have his hide, she'd wager, and Auralee Tyler would be mortified. But then, boys would be boys and young Jackson Beauregard Tyler was no exception. Judging from the way he'd been tossing his money up on the bar, he'd be lucky to have enough to get out of the saloon alive, let alone spend the night with her. It was clear from the lusty speculation glittering in that silver gaze of his that he'd made the mistake of thinking she was one of the

5

ladies for hire.

She shifted her gaze to where a few of the locals were sizing Tyler up. It was just a matter of minutes before they'd spring the trap on him. Lord, she'd seen it done a thousand times and those that didn't have enough money left from their spending suffered a terrible beating at best. Still, like their fathers and their fathers' fathers before them, those Over the Hill boys strained at the bit to get a taste of the wild side of life down at the cluster of shabby buildings along the waterfront that made up Natchez Under the Hill. But there was something about this one . . .

"Hey, boy, you been swillin' our liquor and flirtin' with our women most of the night now, but I swear I don't recall you payin' your respects to the dead."

The youth drew his silver-gray gaze from Giselle, his face a picture of confusion as he faced the man addressing him. "I beg yer pardon?"

Bless him, he was so drunk he could hardly speak the very proper English Giselle was certain he'd been tutored in from an early age.

"I said you haven't paid your respects to the dead!" the longtime patron of the bar repeated in a raised voice that caused the noise to dwindle instantly.

"Oh." The youth shifted his open collar ineffectively, his tie having come undone at one of the other establishments on the low side of Silver Street. "Well, where is he . . . or she," he finished with a subdued hiccup.

"Back there against the wall, my friend."

Giselle nearly chuckled as the youth pivoted and saluted the back wall with a, "Sorry to see you go, friend!"

"Not like that, you drunken fool," the patron snorted, catching the boy by the collar and ushering him over to the pine box that was usually empty. The only time anyone lay in it was when an unsuspecting stranger stumbled into their midst.

6

"Now be a sport and give the corpse a kiss to send him off."

Jackson Tyler swayed unsteadily on his feet, his dark brow knitted at the unsavory turn of events. If there was any kissing to be done, he was hoping it would be with the barmaid, not a bloody corpse.

"Go on, boy, Clancy won't bite. The soul never had tooth in his head, s'long as I know'd him!" his escort exclaimed, exacting howls of amusement from the crowd.

Taking a deep breath, more to steady himself than to sustain his lungs, the youth leaned over the corpse and placed a hasty and reluctant kiss on his cheek. The first thing that struck him was that the dead man was warm, but that fact did not have time to register before the same reached up and seized the loose ends of Jackson's tie. Startled, Jackson stared bug-eyed at the man who yanked his face down so close that their noses nearly touched.

"You been had, boy!" the corpse snickered, his foul breath making it difficult for Jackson not to turn away. "That'll be drinks around for everybody at your expense."

"You're crazy!"

"You be the crazy one, boy, if you don't do as I say."

"And you, sir, be the one who's really dead, if you don't unhand me this instant!"

"Oohwee, ain't we got us a young banty here . . ." Clancy O'Day broke off at the sharp jab of a knife blade against his ribs, his red-eyed stare bulging on his ruddy cheeks. In all the years they'd been hustling greenhorns and strangers, this had never happened. The blokes usually paid up or took a beating, providing entertainment either way.

"Do we have an understanding, sir?" the youth grated out, fully prepared to drive the knife he'd drawn from his boot between the blackguard's ribs.

Giselle stiffened, realizing something was going wrong with the worn-out ruse. She saw the man who had ushered Tyler to the coffin quietly raise a chair over his head, but before she could cry out a warning, it smashed down over the back of the boy.

"Christ's sake, he's stuck me!" Clancy bellowed, rolling the unconscious youth away to climb, very much alive out of the coffin.

The other man bent over Tyler and rummaged through his pockets, emptying them of anything of value. The booty that consisted of a few small bills and a gold watch was hardly worth the trouble. Angry, he kicked the boy in the ribs viciously as Clancy dumped the remains of a stale drink over his face to revive him to receive his due.

Giselle watched as they hauled the half-conscious young man to his feet. "Hold it, boys!" she shouted over the hoots of laughter and shouts of encouragement. Reaching into her pocket, she clutched the small purse she kept tied to her waistband. "Here's the money for a round of drinks."

"We ain't takin' your money, darlin'!" Clancy exclaimed indignantly.

"But it's his, isn't it, love?" she cajoled upon reaching the dazed youth. "Remember the down payment on a night to remember?" She tossed the purse to Clancy and slipped her arm under Tyler's to help steady him. "It doesn't look as if he's going to need it for what he intended," she remarked wryly, "but be a love and help me to my house with him anyway."

Coleman would be furious when he heard she'd bailed out the young man. He hated the Over the Hill crowd with a passion she never understood. If that was not enough to spark his fury, the fact that she'd been saving money would set him on his ear. He wanted all his girls indebted to him for as long as they were young and attractive. And when they no

8

longer possessed their youth and desirability, he cast them aside like the trash society dubbed them.

Unlike the others, Giselle could handle Coleman Horsey. She not only managed his saloon, but possessed the Creole beauty to go along with her intelligence. She looked at the blood seeping into the collar of the youth's tailored jacket. Yes, she would take on Coleman Horsey for the sake of the heir to the Tyler dynasty . . . not just out of charity of a heart known to be kind and generous by those who knew her, but for Erin's sake.

# Chapter One

The whistle of a steamboat sounded off the Natchez riverbank and the sleepy landing jumped to life. The roustabouts who had been whiling away the afternoon under the shade of the catslides of the various shacks and shanties that made up Natchez Under the Hill shoved away from their benches and sauntered down to the shoreline to watch the gangway of the arriving vessel come down like a giant tongue ready to spill out its passengers and cargo. From the top of the hill, the answering whistle of the Bluff City Railroad heralded its descent to receive them. Carts, drays, and wagons of all description sprang into motion, eager to handle their share.

From the roof of the saloon, Erin Devareau watched it all with the same fascination that always followed the arrival of one of the floating palaces. From her vantage, she was able to get a good look at the boat and what she saw brought a frown to her pixielike features. Sure it was the *Delta Moon*, if she knew a thing about riverboats, but something was different. The whistle blew again with a black puff of smoke from the fluted stacks, smudging the clear blue sky, and green eyes just as clear widened in surprise. Saints be damned, the whistle had been

11

cleaned, which explained the reason the boat hadn't
announced its arrival with its customary shriek; and
sure enough, the main and texas decks boasted a fresh
coat of paint!

So it was true, Erin reflected with more than a little
satisfaction. Coleman Horsey had lost the *Delta
Moon!* Whoever the new owner was, it was clear he
had a greater respect for the majesty of the vessel than
Horsey. But then, Coleman Horsey had little respect
for anything. There was very little the man touched
that did not suffer in some way.

"C'mon, Erin, there's fresh pickin's from N'aw-
lin's!"

Erin lifted her folded arms from their rest on her
knees and nodded reluctantly. "I'll be ready soon
enough," she told the young man who was a year her
senior.

Erin didn't particularly like this way of *earning
her keep,* as Cready and his papa called it, but it sure
beat the alternative for a young girl raised in the den
of iniquity known as Natchez Under the Hill.
Besides, she'd soon have enough money to earn her
way to New Orleans where she could be with her
mother again. Together maybe they could start a new
life where folks wouldn't look down their noses at
them. After all, her mother was educated and could
play a piano as fine as any Erin had ever heard in her
eighteen years. Giselle Devareau could give music
lessons and Erin could get some sort of job that was
respectable. She could read and write and do figures
as good as any man. Sharp as a tack, so her mother
had called her.

Too sharp to be working with Cready, Erin mused
grudgingly. It wasn't that she disliked the boy and
his family. When her mother took sick and moved to
New Orleans to stay with Aunt Elly, the MacCreadys
had taken Erin in and given her two meals a day and a
cot in the kitchen. For that, she washed dishes and

glasses at Mac MacCready's saloon and worked the streets with his son.

"Erin!"

Erin wrinkled her nose and pulled her cap down over the thick mass of short dark hair that curled around her collar. "I'm coming, for the love of Mike!"

Anyone that saw her emerge from the alley with her little bench under arm would have sworn she was a boy, which was just what she intended. Boys had less trouble than girls in places such as this and she and her mother agreed to take advantage of the mistake the midwife who had delivered her had made on her birth papers, naming the baby girl Aaron, instead of Erin. They hid her ripening figure beneath boy's togs and kept her hair cut to her collar. Besides, boy's clothes were much more practical than all the paraphernalia women had to wear. And boys had more freedom. Erin was particularly fond of that aspect of her disguise.

"It's about time!" Cready derided, his brown eyes flitting over to where a host of passengers were disembarking. He snatched the bench from Erin and plopped it down in front of her. "Hop to it, wart!"

Erin gritted her teeth at being ordered about, but dropped to her knees and fished three thimbles and a pea out of one pocket of the oversized vest she wore. From the other pocket she produced a handful of pennies and dimes. She only put up with Cready's superior manner because Giselle had asked her to be polite to the MacCreadys. And Cready really wasn't that bad. They'd been playmates for as long as Erin could recall.

When her mother left, he sort of took her under his wing and tried to help her understand why Giselle hadn't taken her along to New Orleans. He convinced her that it wasn't because Giselle Devareau didn't love her anymore and managed to assuage Erin's fear

13

that her mother might not come back. It was a retreat, he'd said. Just like those that the rich folks take to recover their health. If that was a fact, then it made sense that her mother hadn't had the money to take the two of them.

That was six months ago. Erin pasted on a bright smile for the group of passengers making their way toward her. Bejesus, she'd missed her mother—the talks they used to have while she helped Giselle close up Horsey's gambling house, her gentle smile and sense of humor that persisted, no matter how desolate things seemed at times. Sure, Erin was eighteen, well old enough to have made her own way by now and was educated to boot. Giselle had seen to that. Still, the little three room cottage at the edge of the respectable side of town still dominated the dreams she'd shared with her mother. It even superseded Erin's secret ambition ... to captain one of the floating palaces and ride the muddy Mississippi from tip to top.

"Here we go, folks, have a bit of fun and try your luck at guessing which thimble the pea is under. Place your bet and watch carefully, you can double it!"

Erin sought eye contact with one of the ladies peering out from under a ruffled parasol. "Come along, ladies, just a harmless way to pass a bit of time till your ride comes."

"Oh, Mother, you can't really call this gambling," one of the younger ones cajoled. "Even if I lose, he looks like he could use the decent meal he'd win. Call it charity."

"Call it what you will," the older woman huffed haughtily. "It's gambling."

"I call it charity. Here young man," the younger version of the same female spoke up, condescending to drop a dime on the bench. "I'll give it a try."

Erin felt the color flush up from her neck. For

14

people supposedly brought up right, some had no thought whatsoever for those who had to work for a living. That made relieving them of their money easier. After all, they had plenty of it by the look of the fancy dresses and all the trappings. Erin would bet ten dollars a private coach was on its way to pick them up, and when it arrived the driver would get a proper redress for being late.

Like Cready always said when she balked at baiting the unwitting passenger while he lifted their wallets and purses, it was a matter of us and them. No matter how much Erin thought Giselle Devareau transcended those barriers, for her mother was as much a lady as the one standing in front of her as far as Erin was concerned, when the raw truth emerged, it was a battle of survival between the haves and the have-nots.

With deft hands, Erin made certain the young woman won the first two times. Exactly as expected, on the third, she doubled her bet. Not caring for Cready to be the only source of income this time out, Erin managed to slip the pea out from under the thimble, hiding it between her fingers.

"Drat!" the young lady exclaimed in wide-eyed wonder as she viewed the unproductive thimble Erin held up for her to examine.

"Aw, give it another try," Erin encouraged, her voice tinged with the soft brogue she'd unwittingly picked up living in the Irish section of town and with the MacCreadys.

"Here you go, lad, try this."

Erin was temporarily distracted by the silver dollar that rolled on its rim to the small pile of coins she'd stockpiled before raising her startled gaze to a pair of mercurial eyes just as bright. They looked right through her, she thought nervously, as if their owner knew what she was about. Inadvertently, she took note of the silver-tipped cane he sported in one hand.

Where in the name of bloody hell was Cready?

"I . . . I don't have that much to bet if you win," she managed huskily.

"But you'll see that I don't, won't you?"

Erin's gaze moved from the pile of coins she assessed, back to the man innocently. "I aim to try, sir. It ain't like I can afford to sit here and let you win."

She took in the fine cut of his suit, steel-blue gabardine and cuffed. A ruffled shirt failed to disguise the muscled chest and wide shoulders that had surely given the tailor a task and a half in fitting him. And that vest! She'd never seen a silver brocade like that or the diamond breast pin and the watch chain that adorned it. They matched his eyes . . . and the color of his money. For all the finery, there was a certain raw strength Erin could sense, and a certain instinct much like her own, one that made her wary. If she lost it all, she dared not try to trick him.

He doffed his hat and bowed to the young lady who had lost her coin. "I will be satisfied to attempt to recover this lovely lady's losses."

Erin's victim tittered in delight. "Why how gallant, Mr. Tyler!"

*Tyler.* Erin mulled the name over in her mind. She knew most of the names of the area, both reputable and not, just as she knew every steamboat whistle and the name that accompanied it. Surely not Black Jack Tyler! She chewed her lower lip as the man lifted the lady's gloved hand to his lips. Smooth as good whiskey, she observed, the outrageous thought flitting through her mind of how it would feel if a man did the same to her. She glanced down at her work-reddened hands and dirty fingernails and smirked. Not that that would ever happen. Where in the . . . ?

Erin started at the sound of a shrill shriek, followed by scuffle. Before she knew what was happening, she

16

was smothered in mountains of perfumed ruffles. Sprawling backward, she shoved the young lady's crinolines out of the way in time to see Cready pick himself up from the ground and take off, shouting an apology over his shoulder. A puzzled expression settled on her face as the silver-eyed gentleman relieved her of the lady's crushing presence. Something was wrong. Cready hadn't snatched her purse as planned. Unless . . .

Green eyes widened as she saw the man called Tyler start to reach into his pocket. Sweet Mary, she was done for! Erin didn't wait for him to discover his wallet missing. Instead, she scrambled to her feet and darted into the alley. As she rounded the corner, his enraged shout erupted above the din of the cargo being unloaded. She didn't need to look back to know that she was being pursued. Instinct told her that. Tyler was not a man to be toyed with and this time Cready had overstepped his bounds.

Her lungs threatened to burst as she slipped into a warehouse built on pilings along the dock. She looked around frantically, realizing her mistake. There was no way out, and if she was any judge of character, Tyler would not leave until he'd literally pulled the building apart to find her. No escape, she thought, raking in a ragged gasp of air that seemed to burn in her aching chest. Unless . . .

There was no time to think, for Erin could hear the thunder of booted footsteps on the planked walk. There was only time to do. Without so much as a second thought or backward glance, Erin leapt through the open window, cutting smoothly into the muddy water swirling below. Too intent on escaping to congratulate herself on the cleanness of her dive, she kicked furiously, allowing the current to assist her. Until her youthful body had started to round out with the onset of womanhood, she'd boasted that she could dive deeper, stay down longer, and come up

17

drier than any of the other river rats, and thank the Lord, her prowess still served her. In no time at all she was concealed under the branches of the trees that grew low over the water down river.

It was only as she recovered her breath that she realized she clutched Tyler's silver dollar in her hand. A smile tugged at the corner of her lips as she recalled the words Cready had spoken after the first time their little scam had paid off. "You're a natural scalawag, wart . . . a bloody damned natural." Erin turned the coin in the sunlight, her smugness wavering with the onset of the conscience Giselle Devareau had instilled in her since she was knee high. A man like Tyler wouldn't miss it, she told herself in a stern attempt to thwart her second thought.

After making sure that her pursuer had given up the chase, Erin climbed out of the muck and made her way through the back alleys to the saloon where Cready's father worked. Some of the whores were out back hanging out laundry on a line strung between two trees, sheer frilly things Erin wouldn't be caught dead in. As she passed, a buxom redhead she recognized as the woman who had taken the saloon over after Giselle left called out to her, inquiring about her mother's health. Erin slowed her pace long enough to let them know that there was no change since the last time she'd spoken with them and hurried on before they started questioning her as to her sodden, muddied state.

There was a stack of glasses in need of washing waiting for her, so there wasn't time to change as she'd initially planned. There always was when a boat pulled in and unloaded a passel of thirsty businessmen and travelers. By nightfall, most of the rooms at the boarding houses would be taken and Erin's *aunts* wouldn't get a wink of sleep till sunup.

It would be almost that before Erin would turn in as well, but it would be from keeping the bar in clean

18

glasses rather than entertaining gentlemen friends. Cready would show up from picking the pockets of the drunks that staggered from the gambling and whorehouses and walk her home. Erin looked forward to that time, for they would share their adventures and count their loot, speculating on what they were going to do with it.

"I'm going to put it in the jar for my trip to New Orleans," she said, producing the silver dollar proudly for Cready to see.

"You always say that," Cready snickered. "Tell you what, how about adding these to it?"

Erin stopped dead in her tracks as Cready pulled out a roll of bills and peeled off a few of the smaller ones. "Sweet Mary, Cready, did you rob a bank?"

Cready's half-grown mustache twitched. "Damned near. You know who we took down today?"

"Black Jack Tyler," Erin said, lowering her voice, as if the tall gambler might materialize from the shadows.

Her companion made a face at her. "Damnation, wart, how'd you know that?"

"He's got silver eyes and a silver vest, just like folks say." Erin scowled suddenly, recalling the near miss she'd had in escaping the long-legged gambler. "And damned your ornery hide, why didn't you snatch the purse like usual? I could have got my neck broke by the likes of him!" Taking the balled up fear that had not yet left her insides out on her companion, she delivered a well-placed punch into his unprotected stomach.

Cready bent over double, cursing. "You little wart, I'll . . ." Before he could finish his threat, Erin brought a foot up and sent him sprawling out on the ground behind the house that was their home, his since birth and hers since her mother left. "Sonova-bitch, damned if I'll give you a cent now!"

Erin was on him like a fly on molasses, grabbing

Cready's wiry arm and trying to twist it behind him, but before she could get the upper hand, he shifted under her. With a startled squeal, she hit the ground. Suddenly his arm was pressed against her head, driving her face into the dirt.

"When are you gonna learn, you just ain't big enough to take me on anymore, wart?"

Erin spat out the dirt and blessed him with the foulest of the considerable vocabulary she'd picked up in her years at Under the Hill. To her dismay, he pushed her face down even harder.

"Say uncle!"

Another torrent of curses streamed from her mouth through lips distorted by the pressure her companion exerted.

"Just won't give up will you . . . hey!"

Erin froze in spite of the fact that Cready's weight was suddenly lifted free of her, for a pair of highly polished black boots commanded her attention. Before she even saw the cane come swiping down to flay Cready's backside, she knew their owner. Those silver eyes had haunted her all day, causing her more than one time to look over her shoulder, as if expecting to see Black Jack Tyler ready to . . . what? Run her through with the knife reputedly hidden within that fancy cane of his?

"I take it you've tossed my purse, but I see you haven't had time to spend my money," the man was saying, holding Cready by the scruff of the neck as he retrieved the wad of bills her companion was boasting earlier.

"We was goin' to give it back, sir, but we didn't . . ."

"Don't add lying to our growing list of vices, son." The cane whipped again, smacking Cready soundly and causing him to dance around like a puppet. Erin couldn't help the grin that tugged at the corners of her mouth, in spite of her circumstances. Besides,

Tyler was so busy admonishing Cready, he'd hardly noticed her.

"Please don't call the law, sir. I was just tryin' to support my widowed mother . . ."

"Widowed mother, is it? It's a damned shame the woman'll soon be childless as well, though from what I've seen to date, she'll be better off."

Cready put his hands together, his eyes almost wider than his face. "Bejesus, don't kill me!" he sobbed, dropping to his knees.

It was one thing to see Cready taken down a peg and get the beating he was well overdue, but murder was something again. Without second thought, Erin sprang from her crouched position and latched on to the arm bearing the death-dealing cane. Clinging like a leech as the man tried to shake her off, she bit into his shoulder. Instead of making him drop Cready, the assault only seemed to worsen her companion's lot, for now Cready was pinned to the ground with a booted heal at his throat.

"Unhand me, you ungrateful brat, or your brother dies here and now."

Erin shrunk under the piercing eyes, her hold loosening so that she slid down his lean and hard frame to her feet. Self-consciously, she wiped the dirt from her mouth and nose as she backed away. "You kill 'im and I'll witness against you!"

The eyes lessened in their intensity for a moment and a dark brow shot up. "Less than a moment ago he was grinding your face in the dirt and threatening to break your arm."

"We was just havin' fun," Erin mumbled huskily. She looked at the wad of money the man had managed to retain. "Why don't you just take your money and leave?" She reached in her pocket and withdrew the silver dollar. "Here, here's all of it."

Tyler looked from Erin's begrudging face to the silver dollar, as if he'd totally forgotten the boy under his foot, and hooted with laughter. "So you *were* in it with him. When I found you two fighting I'd thought . . ." He laughed again, his eyes never leaving Erin's face. "I need some information. You two cooperate and I'll forget I've ever seen you."

A shiver of foreboding ran up Erin's spine. This man was bad news, she just knew it. The less they had to do with him the better. "What do you want?"

"I'm looking for a young man named Aaron Devareau."

Erin's stomach twisted. She knew it! She knew the minute she saw him something bad was going to happen. "What do you want with him?" she managed.

"That's between me and the boy."

Unaware of the panic that betrayed her, she glanced down at Cready nervously. "We don't know any Aaron Devareau."

She flinched at Cready's strangled cry. "'At's him," the young man rasped, an incriminating finger pointing at her.

Erin felt the color leave her face, temporarily draining her of strength. It was bad. Whatever Black Jack Tyler could want with her, it had to be bad and she wasn't going to stay around to find out. She'd outrun him once today and she could do it again. With a fearful, "No!" she twisted away and darted over an empty crate and into a dark alley. What she didn't see was the second one hidden in the shadows. Feet tangling with the brittle pieces of lumber and wire, she plunged forward, arms in front of her, but just as she was about to dive facedown in the muddy pathway, she was hauled upright by the rope that held up her trousers. Her startled protest was cut off sharply.

Kicking and swinging wildly, Erin found herself being carried just above the ground toward the main street like a blasted carpetbag. Where was Cready?

22

Why didn't the tattletale at least call for help? Erin tried that herself, but her wind was cut off and it was all she could do to breathe.

In desperation she reached over and pinched the hard flesh of the thigh that stretched the fabric of the fitted trousers. Suddenly a pain exploded across her buttocks, giving her the added incentive she needed to cry out. The bastard! Infuriated by his condescending treatment and her own helplessness, Erin resorted to one last effort. She balled up her fist and with all her strength, twisted to land it at the apex of the long legs that jostled her with each stride.

# Chapter Two

"Why the hell don't you just kill me and be done with it instead of hacking my ass off a little at a time with that blasted cane of yours!"

God in heaven, she'd thought he was going to kill her then and there on Silver Street, right before God and all those whose sleep or amusement had been interrupted by the commotion she made. Erin backed against the corner of the lamplit room, careful to keep her bruised buttocks away from the wall. Surely she'd never sit down again in her life!

Jackson Beauregard Tyler ignored the most proper of the string of curses and names that had been constantly coming at him since he took the whelp into hand and closed the door to his lavish stateroom. It was almost impossible to believe that this cocky thieving little heathen could be related to the lovely and gentile lady who had once saved his life.

Giselle Devareau never should have been in a place like Natchez Under the Hill. Jackson had been around ladies long enough to recognize one, even in the sinful trappings in which they'd met. She was someone with a past, she'd told him mysteriously when he'd asked her about it. Instead of robbing him blind, like her offspring and his cohort had tried to do, she'd let him sleep off his overindulgence of liquor in her little shack near the base of the hill and sent him off to the reputable cliff where the wealthy and successful dwelled with the money he had not gambled away. In lieu of taking the reward he offered her, she'd told him that the favor might be returned at a later date. Never in his wildest dreams did he expect this.

He looked at the boy crouched in the corner, glaring at him with contempt. How in the name of all the saints was he going to educate this foul-mouthed little beggar and give him the start in life Giselle had asked of him in her letter? If the boy hated him now, the news he had to relay to the lad would not improve their relationship.

"If you think you can carry on a conversation without the use of vulgarity, I will attempt to explain our business." Yes, it was Giselle Devareau's child. He'd never seen eyes like those glowering at him now before or since he'd met the mother. They surely wouldn't make life any easier for the lad. With those small features and sooty thick lashes, he was too pretty to be a boy. "How old are you?"

Erin crossed her arms in front of her obstinately. "What's that got to do with business?"

Jackson grimaced. The kid wasn't going to make it easy, but somehow, after that little affair on the dock, he supposed it was foolhardy to think it would be otherwise. "Sixteen?" he guessed.

"Eighteen."

"Not much of you for eighteen years," Jackson observed matter-of-factly. "You think you can chop and haul wood?"

"What for?"

"For three dollars a week and room and board."

Erin's face went blank. She couldn't believe a man like Black Jack Tyler had hunted her down to offer her a dream job on a riverboat. It would be like getting paid to have fun. And if they went to New

Orleans . . . "What's the hook, Tyler?"

Jackson turned to the rich mahogany locker containing his clothing and selected a less distinctive attire. He would have to spend the day at the plantation. His sister Jennifer's fiancé was coming for dinner to go through the formality of asking for her hand in marriage and as head of the household, Jackson was obliged to be there. A change of clothes and the gambler known up and down the river as Black Jack Tyler would become Master Jackson Beauregard Tyler of Retreat. He removed his jacket and vest and began to unfasten the ruffled shirt that was tailored to his narrow waist.

"The hook is," he explained, tongue in cheek at the boy's impudence, "that I expect you to do an *honest* day's work. That should be something of a novelty for you."

"Why?" Erin asked warily, ignoring the jibe. Surely there was something else. "I mean, why did you look for me?"

"I knew your mother . . . do you always growl when you talk?"

Color flamed in Erin's cheeks. "I don't make fun of you 'cause you talk so blamed fancy." She'd tried to maintain a low voice for so long that it was habit. "Have you seen her?" Her excitement over news of her mother was too much to hide, in spite of her intention to appear disinterested.

At the sudden rise of her voice, assessing silver eyes sought hers out again, quelling the light that brightened there. Jackson supposed it was natural. Eighteen for some, if he could believe that was how old the lad was, was still an age where the voice wasn't exactly stable. His cousin had squeaked until he was nearly twenty-one, a disturbing hindrance for an aspiring young lawyer. "I received a letter from her," he answered awkwardly, stripping off his shirt and laying it atop his other clothes.

Erin was about to ask if she might see the missive, but the sight of a naked chest padded with muscle and furred with dark crisps of hair silenced her. It wasn't that she hadn't seen a man stripped to the waist before. Many of the dockworkers doffed shirts under the hot Mississippi sun. It was just that those men were not nearly as handsome as the one working at the fastens of his trousers. She moved out of the corner, suddenly ill at ease. "When do I start work?"

"When I tell you. Now have a seat."

Shrugging noncommittally, Erin walked over to the wide berth and eased down on it. She'd tried to do the decent thing, but if he was bent on stripping down mother-naked, she wasn't too proud not to look. Just about once a week she'd get a peek at some nude soul scampering across Silver Street with his britches over his shoulder and a jealous husband or boyfriend on his tail. Sometimes she and Cready would whistle, just to watch the mortified Romeo move all that much faster. But she'd never seen the likes of this. Her bottom lip slipped under her teeth as her breath whistled softly through them.

Until now Jackson had coped with everything this unpredictable young man had thrown at him, but the curious eyes fixed on the hands about to slip off his trousers left him discomfited enough to turn his back. Damnation, it didn't occur to him that the boy's effeminate build and features might mean . . . That would be all he needed! he thought irritably. He doffed the pants and snatched up a towel, wrapping it about his waist securely. Well, if he is affected in any way, the crew will straighten him out in short time or drown the little rat.

"What did Mama say?"

"Hmm? Oh . . ." Jackson walked over to his desk and took out the letter that had caught up with him on the Delta "O" Line in Memphis. His irritation faded as he handed it to the boy. Until now, Aaron

Devareau had been pure leather and hellfire, but the unexpected vulnerability in those lucid green eyes of his touched Jackson. Accused of being a silver-tongued devil, the gambler could not find the words to tell the youth of Giselle Devareau's death. Instead he chose the coward's way out.

When Erin read the letter through the first time, she was confused. First, it wasn't her mother's neatly penned hand. Furthermore, even she could tell the grammar was horrid. From what she could make of it, her mother had written this man about a debt that he owed her. She wanted him to help Aaron make something of himself, since she was not going to be around to do it. A chill crept up Erin's spine. Why? Surely her mother wouldn't leave her again unless she was referring to . . .

"My mother didn't write this!" she challenged the man watching her reaction.

"I would assume that she was unable to write it herself, Aaron. But she did send this with it."

Erin shook her head, refusing to believe what this man and the letter intimated even as she took the necklace Tyler handed her. It was a fascinating piece of work, a gold locket inlaid with a silver rose. On the back was inscribed, *To my one and only love, J.* Inside was Erin's baby picture, a chubby little cherub in a long white gown. Her mother had once told her that she'd never part with that locket. Erin's father had given it to her and he had been her one and only love.

She turned her delicate inheritance in her hand, fighting to keep from admitting what it meant. Why hadn't anyone told her her mother was so ill? Why hadn't her mother given her some hint? And the MacCreadys, did they know all along? Is that why they always dismissed Erin's notion of going to New Orleans to live with her mother?

Erin's chin began to quiver threateningly. She

28

crushed the poorly penned and written letter and threw it on the floor, focusing on anger to keep from spilling the tears that welled in her eyes. Why? she moaned silently. Why didn't somebody tell her so that she could have been with her mother? They were all each other had!

"Here, drink this. My engineer will be here soon to show you where to bunk."

Caught off guard, Erin met the surprisingly sympathetic silver gaze of the man offering her a glass of fine bourbon. She mustn't cry, she thought, steeling her jaw to thwart her traitorous chin . . . at least not in front of him. A brisk knock on the door announcing the engineer's arrival gave her the strength to hold on just a little bit longer. Once she was alone, she would be able to deal with this unbearable hurt in her chest. She needed to think . . . and maybe, if no one was within earshot, to cry.


A shout interrupted Jackson Tyler's work as he pondered over the ledger accounting for the tentative repairs that had been done to date on the newest ship to the Delta "O" Line. Since the ship was underway, he thought perhaps he'd imagined it until a member of the engine crew burst into his cabin without taking the time to knock. It was obvious from the panicked look on his face that something was indeed wrong after all. "What is it, boy?"

"It's de new kid! He done passed out in de heat!"

Just when he was beginning to think his task of guardian wasn't going to be so difficult after all, Jackson mused wryly, closing the book in front of him in resignation. He guessed that one day on the river without incident was too little to judge from. Reds said the boy had done well for his size, although he was bit peculiar, keeping pretty much to himself.

"Where is he?"

"Mr. Reds is takin' 'im to his cabin."

Jackson pushed himself up from the desk and followed the frightened boy out into the corridor leading to the crew's quarters. Maybe he'd given the kid more than he could handle, he admonished himself as he passed the brass numbered doors in the heart of the vessel. Aaron was slight of build, although Jackson had thought the hard work with the crew might toughen him up after being raised around women and without a father. A crimson-faced Reds Jones met him at the door of the cabin where the boy had been assigned a berth.

"How is he?"

*"He,"* Jones enunciated strongly, "ain't a bit good. See for yourself."

Puzzled by the strange inflection in the engineer's answer, Jackson pushed past his hulking figure to the bunk where the unconscious boy lay, thick black lashes fanned against ashened cheeks. "For the love of God, man, it's no damned wonder! I told him to shed some of these clothes." Aggravated with the youth's obstinacy, Jackson seized the top of his shirts.

"I wouldn't do that if I . . ." Reds' warning came too late.

The sound of ripping fabric filled the small room followed by an astonished, "What the . . . ?"

Jackson's shocked reply fell short at the sight of two perfect globes, small and compact, but nonetheless quite feminine. As if stung, he hurriedly threw the rented fabric back over them and looked up at the engineer, seeking affirmation of what he'd just seen.

"I tried to warn you," Reds told him with a helpless shrug. "I found out when I hauled him . . . uh, her up and over my shoulder to get 'er up here." He met Jackson's gaze evenly. "Now what?"

Jackson shook himself from the angry shock numbing his thoughts. "Damned if I know," he replied as he slipped his arms under his charge's shoulders and knees. "But we can't leave her down here with the men." Now things were beginning to make sense. It was no wonder the boy didn't socialize or bunk in with the crew. *He* was a *she!* "And go get Mariette and send her to my cabin."

The girl was feather light and never stirred as he carried her up the stairwell and on to his stateroom. Her skin was cool and dry which further supported his theory of sunstroke. A girl! What in the name of creation was he going to do now? His experience with women was hardly what Giselle Devareau had in mind for her daughter . . . of that he was certain. Damn it, he'd known something was amiss!

It was to the touch of a cool cloth over her forehead that Erin began to struggle out of the limbo that had taken her over. She was no longer hot, but chilled. She pulled the sheet draped over her closer around her shoulders and shifted on the plump pillow under her head. She'd been hauling fuel for the firemen. Then she was falling and the wood crashed with her on the deck . . .

Her eyes flew open and with a brush of her hand, the cloth covering them was slung aside. One glance at the richly papered walls and gilded edged paneling was enough to tell Erin where she was, but how she got there remained a mystery. She pushed herself into a sitting position on the wide bed, her legs dangling over the side. As she did so, the sheet fell away, drawing her attention to her scant attire.

Confused, she rolled the fine linen of the shirt that fell past her hips between her fingers. Considering that it was her only garment, her charade as a boy was surely over. She tried so hard. After their first day on the river, she'd dragged herself away from the window looking into the salon where fancy dressed men and women laughed and danced and slipped under the lifeboat kept on the bow of the observation

31

deck where she'd found a place to sleep away from the male crew members. All she could remember was that horrible heat and the way the passing scenery began to wave dizzily before her eyes before she collapsed on the deck.

Bejesus! she thought, drawing the sheet around her miserably. Her gaze roamed the room more thoroughly this time, searching for the clothes she'd been wearing. Jackson Tyler might have seen her in the altogether, but he needn't think that she was going to warm his bed! Her lifeboat was all she needed.

Her color reaching an all time high, Erin slid off the bed and was surprised that her legs were not as sturdy as she had thought. She ran her tongue around the inside of her mouth as she pushed herself upright. Her mouth was so dry, she'd need scissors to spit!

The search for her clothes taking a second priority to her need to quench her thirst, she made her way to the washstand. The hand-painted china washbowl was nearly filled with dingy gray water making her swear under her breath. Beside it were soiled damp towels rolled up in a ball. The sonovabitch had not only stripped her down, he'd given her a bloody bath! Mother Mary, it was hard to say what else he'd done to her!

She'd had no direct experience of an intimate nature with men, but she'd heard plenty about them. The one thing that all her advice had in common was that they were not to be trusted, especially ladies' men like Tyler. She seized the pitcher and peeked down inside to see a small remnant of clear water left in the bottom. Lifting it high over her head, she started to drain it when the door of the cabin opened suddenly, startling her so that she lost her hold.

The pitcher crashed to the floor and broke into a dozen or so pieces as she came face to face with the owner of the ship. Her first reaction was to apologize for breaking it, but there was something in his gaze that made her feel like a witless ninny, unable to summon an intelligible word. "What the hell are you looking at?" she demanded at last, mustering enough resolve to break the charged silence. "It ain't like you never seen the like, I'll wager."

Jackson snapped out of the surprise that had taken him upon entering the cabin and seeing much of what his young charge had been so painstakingly determined to hide. She was not voluptuous in build, but the firm upthrust breasts that filled out the good shirt Mariette had put her in when he'd left the girl to her care and the long shapely legs peeking out from beneath it were so pleasantly unexpected that he could not help but stare. Under other circumstances . . .

"What the hell do you think you are doing?" he countered angrily, dismissing the thought before it could even take root.

"I . . . er . . . was thirsty and . . ." Erin broke off as he came to a halt in front of her, forcing her to look up into his accusing gaze. Of all the nerve, she thought, indignant at being put on the defensive. Who is he to come in and accuse her of doing anything after the way he'd taken advantage of her. Unabashed by his superior height and size, she poked her finger at the open vee of his shirt. "Where are my clothes, you lecherous polecat!"

"Lecherous!"

"I'd say that about sums you up after you've had your bloody way with me and *me unconscious!*" she challenged, her voice rising to an unmistakably feminine high.

"I *what?* Just what exactly did I do?" he exclaimed, making an obvious effort to keep a straight face.

Somehow the fact that her adversary saw humor in what she was saying did little to assuage Erin's growing resentment. She threw up her hands. "How the hell am I suppose to know, you braying jackass? But I'll tell you one thing straight," she added, stepping forward to seize his shirt threateningly. Instead of the ultimatum she intended to deliver, a sharp cry emerged from her lips as a piece of glass entered her heel. "Sonovabit—" Her curse was cut off by the shoulder that plowed into her middle, lifting her free of the floor.

"You," her assailant declared emphatically, landing a loud smack on her buttocks, "have a filthy mouth and a mind to match, it seems."

Her muscles barely recovered from the abuse of the man's cane, Erin howled and broke into a string of expletives the likes of which managed to turn the gambler's ears as red as her face as he dumped her unceremoniously on the bed. Ignoring her stinging heel, she swung at him and swore profanely as he sidestepped her fisted blow and raised a warning finger to her.

"Enough!" Jackson demanded, his initial amusement at her absurd accusation giving in to temper that flared to the full limit of his control. The little witch had disrupted his crew and work, broken a collector's piece, accused him of molesting her, called him names he'd take any man to account for and by thunder, he would take no more.

"You common whoreson! Touch my ass again and I'll . . . I'll knock your bloody balls loose," Erin finished uncertainly as Jackson spun on his heel with a muttered oath and stalked away from her, his boots crushing the broken pottery underfoot.

When he turned back toward her there was a bar of soap in his hand and a diabolical glint in the gray eyes taking note of her balled fists. "One would think you'd learned your lesson where my anatomy is concerned, but another can be arranged just as soon as I finish this one."

"What's that for?" she asked warily, a decided dread settling in her chest. A smirk formed on Jackson's lips and Erin guessed quick enough. The man was crazy, she thought, crouching at the edge of the mattress to spring out of his reach without thought to the blood soaking the white linens. But before she could leap from the berth, he was in her path, catching her and thrusting her back to the bed with his full weight.

Erin fought him furiously, but Jackson managed to wedge himself in a position so that her flailing legs and fists fell ineffectively against his hard frame. With an arm braced across her collarbone, he held her helpless and proceeded to force the bar of soap into her mouth. She clenched her teeth, only to have him grate small pieces against them until her mouth was filled with its bitter taste. She tried spitting them out at him, only to be rewarded with more of the same until, at last, she was too spent to fight any more.

Sensing her weakening, Jackson lightened his attack and stared down into eyes that glowed like emerald fire. "From this point on I expect complete compliance with my wishes, since your mother saw fit for me to keep you under my wing until you are twenty-one. I will treat you according to your behavior."

"I ain't sharing your bed!" Erin averred vehemently with what wind she could muster under the full weight of the body pinning her to the mattress.

"What a relief!" Erin felt the impact of his sarcasm, color rushing to her face as he chuckled derisively, "Madame, I have no inclination whatsoever to share my bed with an ill-bred, unkempt, verbally abusive little wildcat whose only course of action when in disagreement with a man is to assault his male anatomy with her fists."

His cynical assurance should have pleased her, but for some odd reason, Erin felt humiliated. Of course he was right, she realized, recalling the way that woman in the ruffled gown had fawned over him the night before. Like as not, a man like him could have his pick of women without fooling with the likes of her. Still, she hid her feelings under a false bravado. "Then get off me and let me rinse this da . . . darned soap out of my teeth!" she corrected swiftly.

Jackson breathed a sigh of relief at the small victory. This girl gave the word stubborn a whole new meaning. For a moment, he'd thought he'd really have to hurt her to make her listen, something he was averse to doing. He didn't believe in striking women, no matter what walk of life they came from. But this one . . .

"As I said, I will treat you according to your behavior. If you curse, you will have your mouth washed. If you do not do as I expect, I shall tan your hide until sitting becomes a torture. Are we understood?" At Erin's grudging nod, he turned and made his way to his desk. "I've arranged to have the cabin across from mine removed from the guest accommodations. You'll move in there."

"And I can keep my job?"

"Not hardly," Jackson replied sourly. "But I'll think of something you can do."

"What?"

A fist slammed on the desk. "Damn it, Aaron, or whatever the devil your name is . . ."

"Erin."

"Erin," he conceded stiffly, "I don't know what I am going to do with you yet. I suppose you can clean the cabins. That would be suitable," he mused aloud.

"I ain't no cleanin' woman!"

His patience exhausted, Jackson raised a warning finger. "You'll do any damn thing I tell you and be grateful I just don't toss you out on your lying little . . . ear," he finished, catching the rise of an imperious brow.

"How much?"

"How much what!"

Erin settled back on the bed, a pillow drawn to her chest. "*If* I clean, how much will you pay me?"

The ungrateful little twit! "The same as before!" he exclaimed in exasperation.

"And afternoons and evenings off?"

"Of course, your majesty," Jackson derided with a sweeping bow. "Will there be anything else?"

Erin glanced down at the cut that had made a wide scarlet stain on the bed and her stomach turned threateningly. "A bandage would be nice."

"Good God, woman!"

The broken pottery on the floor was further reduced to smithereens as Jackson rushed to his bed, producing a clean handkerchief from his trouser pocket. As he grabbed the bleeding foot, Erin yelped and would have pulled away but for the solid hold he had on it.

"I can't work if you cripple me!"

"There's something still in it, you simple idiot!" Jackson shifted her heel toward the light coming in through the porthole and spied the very tip of offending material protruding from the ugly gash. "Now be still!" Using the knife he fished out of his pocket, he gently scraped over the bleeding cut, the grip of his other hand tightening as the girl curled on his bed jerked instinctively. "I won't hurt you, Erin," he cajoled, his voice softening like it used to when he'd take a splinter out of his little sister Jennifer's finger when she was a child. "Trust me?"

Gray eyes met green in question. Once again that childlike vulnerability was there, the kind that could worm its way into his conscience and tug at his heart. Child? Jackson mused, distracted by the snow-white length of thigh revealed by the disheveled shirt. Hardly. But then, there was something in her eyes that told him she was not quite a woman either;

37

that and the fact that she naively thought he had taken certain privileges with her. "Well?" he asked, consciously diverting his thoughts to the matter at hand.

Erin nodded, intrigued by the sudden change in her companion. One moment he was shouting at her and threatening her, and the next he was hovering over her foot in concern and speaking in such a gentle tone that her distrust wavered dangerously. She clenched her teeth as he probed with his knife until he produced the shard of pottery that had caused so much trouble.

"And now for a little disinfectant," he announced brightly, turning to fetch the bottle of bourbon that she'd sampled her first time there from his desk.

The moment the whiskey fell into the open cut, they both began to blow frantically to assuage its medicinal sting. Confident the job was well done, Jackson picked up the clean handkerchief from the bed and proceeded to wrap the wound. He tried not to notice the shapeliness of the long legs twisted at a provocative angle or the somewhat impressed look that met his when he finished tucking the edge of the bandage in a fold.

"How am I supposed to get to my room?" Erin asked, leaning over to examine the glass-littered floor.

Jackson followed her gaze in a conscious effort to avoid the temptation to seek out the swell of the bosom he'd accidentally discovered earlier. This was absurd, he chided himself sternly. Erin Devareau was little more than a child standing on the brink of womanhood. His taste ran to the more sophisticated of her species. Nevertheless, he was becoming increasingly aware that while his head had certain preferences, a more primitive part of him did not.

Almost irritably, Jackson seized the sheet and threw it over her. "I'll carry you," he told her shortly.

"I need my quarters to finish my work and the last thing I need is you interrupting me."

"I didn't ask to be brought here," Erin rallied, somewhat ruffled by the abrupt dismissal.

Eager to rid himself of this most disconcerting distraction, Jackson paused at the door to look for anyone who might be in the corridor and then quickly dashed across and into the open stateroom one of the maids had prepared. Without ceremony, he took the girl to the amply wide turned-back bed usually set aside for the wealthier clientele or his personal family and associates, and deposited her abruptly.

"There!" he averred in relief. "Now stay off that foot until tomorrow."

Erin tucked her feet under the linens that carried the clean scent of lemons. "Could I borrow a book then?"

Surprise registered on Jackson's face. "You read?"

"Of course!" Erin exclaimed indignantly. "Why shouldn't I?"

Thinking better of starting another conflict by telling her, Jackson shifted his tact. "I don't have many romances, if any, but . . ."

"I'd like one on navigation, if you please," she announced sweetly.

Too bewildered to question at this point, Jackson crossed back over the hallway and selected two books on the subject from the bookshelves built in at the head and foot of his bed. But when he handed them to her, he could not contain his curiosity. "Why are you interested in navigation?"

Erin looked him squarely in the eye. "Because someday I want to be the captain of one of these boats, even if I have to make beds and clean to start with." She wanted to ask him if she could spend her free time in the pilot house, but somehow she thought this was not the right moment. She'd give

39

Tyler time to digest her announcement before pushing him further. Once he saw that she was serious, she could make her move then. "You think I'm silly, don't you?"

Jackson put his hand on the knob of the door and looked back at the girl sitting upright on the bed. If nothing else was clear, it was apparent that he was going to have to get used to surprise from this enigmatic creature. "It is a rather odd ambition for a young girl of . . . eighteen, isn't it?"

"Eighteen and two months," Erin informed him proudly.

"Ah, of course. Well, whatever your pursuits are on your time are your own concern. But I expect you to give Hannah and her girls your fullest cooperation."

Erin read the label of the first book, her active mind already eager to delve into its contents. "Of course," she quipped absently. "Close the door when you leave, please."

For a moment Jackson stared at the hand that brushed him aside as neatly as her tone did. "As you wish, your majesty," he retorted, his acerbic reply falling ineffectively on the girl's ears, for already the book was open and she was propping herself up on her elbow and settling comfortably in her new berth.

He should have been irritated, but an ironic smile tugged at the corner of his mouth as he closed the door as commanded. He'd counted his laurels too soon in supposing that his task concerning Giselle Devareau's offspring was turning out easy. Something told him the days ahead were going to be anything but, and this time he was listening to his instincts.

# Chapter Three

New Orleans! Erin stood at the rail of the *Delta Moon* as the steamboat maneuvered up to one of the docks lining the crescent-shaped shoreline and marveled at the city she'd so often pictured in her mind from her mother's description. Over the tops of the warehouses she could see the slate roofs of its buildings and the spire of a large cathedral. It was surely the grandest place her eyes had ever seen! Not even the cloud cover moving in overhead could spoil the prospect of seeing it close up, which was exactly what she was going to do.

"So there you are!"

Erin turned to see Mariette peeping over the rail of the steps leading up from the boiler deck. "Are you ready to go in town and get yourself measured for some new clothes?"

Nodding eagerly, Erin abandoned her post to join her friend, her hand flying to the loose ribbon Anita had tied in her hair to match her faded green dress. She'd even let the girls talk her into wearing stockings to cover the bare leg that was exposed most of the time and a pair of shoes that, like the dress, were too large. They were, however, nicely wedged on Erin's feet with a perfumed hankie wadded in each toe to keep her foot from sliding down into them too far.

Her first weeks' wages jingled in her pocket as she hopped down the steps behind her friend. Jackson Tyler told her first thing that morning that Mariette was going to take her into town to a seamstress to be fitted for clothes suitable to a girl her age and Erin supposed since he'd given her a decent job, not to mention burned her old clothing and forced her to wear a dress two sizes too big, she'd humor him and stand for the fittings the women told her about.

In fact, after their argument over his burning her clothes, she was astonished that he hadn't decided to throw her off the boat. How was she to know when she barged into his cabin that he was entertaining that Hispanic casino girl who followed him about like a pie-eyed hound in his bed! It was enough to make her sick, the sight of the two of them mother-naked. Upon seeing her error, she'd retreated to her own quarters, wondering how her mother could have left her in the care of a pervert, for it took no genius to figure out what they'd been up to.

She'd heard Cready and the boys talk, plus she'd stumbled on it by accident once in one of the rooms over the saloon when she'd gone up to fetch the jacks she'd been playing with one of the saloon girls that afternoon. From all the carryings-on she'd witnessed, it was no wonder it was done behind closed doors and she'd told Jackson as much when he raked her over the coals for barging in unannounced.

That was when she forgot herself. The cuss words just came as natural as her own anger at having her clothes burned. Somehow in the fracas another pitcher was broken and she had another taste of soap. It was getting to the point that she hated to use it, even for bathing.

There was just something about Jackson Tyler that brought out the worst in her, no matter how she was determined to make her way aboard the ship.

Maybe dressing better would help. As for his intimate affairs with the casino girl, she didn't give two hoots what he did. He was no different than any other man, she thought, once again distracted by the activity on the wharf.

The *Delta Moon* was going to be in New Orleans longer than its normal stopover because of additional carpentry being done to the ship, but three days didn't give Erin much time to do the things she needed to do. As soon as she was finished with the fitting nonsense, she intended to see to her own affairs. Her mother had told her to never look back, but there were some things she just needed to know before she could go on with her life.

As they did in every port, the crew waited until the passengers departed before those who had leave to go left for shore. Erin stood impatiently, fingering her coins through the thin material of her dress and strained on tiptoe to see over the plumed bonnets and beaver hats of the gentry hailing carriages to take them to their destinations in the city. It would take a good while just to walk past the warehouses and scattered stacks of crates, barrels, and sacks before they would even see the city itself!

When the last of the passengers cleared the gangway, she was the first to lead the way for the steamboat staff. It was beyond her what Anita and Mariette found to talk about that delayed them. Unable to stand the wait a moment longer, Erin turned in mid-skip to urge them on and plowed head-on into a well-dressed gentleman who was making his way aboard. Between the ill fit of her shoes and the momentum that bounced her off the man's chest, she would have sprawled at his feet, but for the quick hands that caught her arms and righted her.

"Whoa there, missy!"

"Bejesus!" Erin swore, eyes full of wonder as to

where the dandy devil materialized from. "Sure and I'm sorry, sir!" Certain that those expensive clothes meant he was someone important, she brushed the lapel of his coat free of unseen dust.

"Good day, Mr. Davenport!" Mariette called out, brandishing a winning smile.

"And good day to you, ladies . . . miss," he added, tipping his hat a second time to the girl admiring the gold watch chain sparkling on his vest. "It's an heirloom from my great-grandfather."

Erin blinked. "What?" His words sunk in and her cheeks colored to a becoming rose. "And a fine one, it is, sir! Why I could watch it all day, but me 'n the ladies here have to go shoppin' before the bottom drops out of them clouds sneakin' up on us."

With a patronizing smile that stretched a perfectly waxed mustache, Davenport pointed to the locket hanging on the chain around her neck. "That's an interesting piece as well."

Erin fought the urge to draw away as he turned it in his fingers curiously. A man that smelled like he'd just climbed out of a whore's bath surely wouldn't snatch the first and only jewelry she had, she reasoned, unaware of the suspicion clouding her face. "It's an heirloom, too," she mumbled, her fingers flying to it the moment he let it fall against the thick gathers of her ill-fitted neckline.

"And a fine one it is," he averred, catching her eye with a mischievous wink. "Good shopping to you, Miss . . . ?"

"Erin Devareau," Erin supplied quickly, tiring of the small talk.

"Erin is a newcomer to the *Delta Moon*," Mariette informed him, taking Erin under the arm. "Jackson has turned her over to Nita and me to outfit her with a whole new wardrobe."

A thick reddish-brown eyebrow, the same color as the hair winged in silver at the temples, shot up.

"Then you must have a gown done in ice-green silk to compliment the gemlike color of those beautiful eyes." To Erin's astonishment, a gloved hand sought hers and raised it to his lips. He brushed her knuckles and met her startled gaze evenly. "Although I can't imagine her more lovely than she is right now."

The moment he released her hand, she backed against Mariette, self-consciously wiping her hand on her skirt. "I think he's been drinkin' some of that sweet stuff he's doused in," she whispered under her breath.

Mariette threw back her head and howled, making Erin painfully aware that she'd spoken her thoughts aloud. The fact that Davenport and Anita joined her, only made it worse. She wished the gangway would just open up and let her drop into the water to staunch the heat flaming from her neck.

"By the saints, she's witty, too!" the man snorted, fighting to master his amusement long enough to tip his hand once again. "Ladies, good shopping."

Jackson Tyler watched from the deck above as Erin bolted for the street, her long legs taking strides that made her friends protest as they trotted to catch up. He was ready to send one of the crew after his wayward charge, but once she reached the other side of the thoroughfare filled with carriages for hire and wagons, she stopped and waited. It wasn't until he glanced down to see the white of his knuckles that he realized how tightly he was holding the rail. Damnation, that girl had a way of keeping him in knots!

"Where on earth did you find her?" his business partner exclaimed, coming up the last of the steps leading to the boiler deck.

"In an alley at Natchez Under the Hill and I haven't had a minute's peace since!" Jackson retorted, adding in a barbed tone, "and don't you think she's a little young for you?"

Four years ago he met John Davenport in a game of blackjack at one of New Orleans' finest gambling dens. Although there were three others in the game, the contest hung between the two of them. As the dawn was breaking through the stained glass window behind their table, the night's winnings lay piled in two stacks, one in front of John and one in front of Jackson. Jackson won with a straight flush, but just as he was raking in his money, Davenport challenged him to one more hand. He had a steamboat in mint condition he was willing to put up in exchange for what was on the table. Instinct told Jackson to let it be, but the man had been such a good sport, he agreed.

In what seemed less than the time it took to deal the cards, he found himself staring at the king, queen, and jack of spades. Grinning cockily, he spread them on the table and asked for the papers to his new acquisition. But when he realized that his opponent was grinning with equal arrogance, he studied the three cards put down over his own—an ace, king, and queen of hearts.

"Remember, my friend, luck is a lady, unpredictable, but oh so favorably impressed with the suit of love."

The gambler proceeded to admit that he'd won a steamboat the night before and had no idea what he was going to do with it. Somewhere between the opening and the emptying of the finest house bourbon, they became partners. He put up the boat, Jackson the brains. Within two years, the line was doubled and then tripled.

Then two weeks ago, Jackson pulled the same deal with a drunken and obnoxious Coleman Horsey and found himself using his friend's favorite quote as the lady luck placed her heart into his hands. Except that he knew exactly what he was doing. The *Delta Moon* was shabby, but there was an elegance about the older ship that, properly treated, would make her a queen among her peers. The fact that it belonged to Coleman Horsey, a man Jackson detested for his general lack of gentility and morals and who seemed for some odd reason to consistently cross his path, just made the pot sweeter.

"I was going to say the same about you, friend." At Jackson's incredulous snort, he pointed out, "After all, it is you who is dressing up such a lovely little doll at your own expense."

"Don't lower me to your level, Davenport! My intentions and expenditures are perfectly honorable. That little ragamuffin you found so breathtaking down there is my . . . *ward*, I guess you'd call it, for lack of a better name."

For the first time in his life, Jackson Tyler saw his partner lose his poker face. Incredulity flashed across his handsome features, followed by disbelief. "You?"

"For the love of God, John, it could be worse! She might have been left to your care. From what I saw down there, you both looked like you'd met your match."

His dour remark was meant to elicit a laugh, but to Jackson's surprise, his friend became quite serious. "This, my friend, you must tell me about . . . but not out here. In the gambling parlor over a glass of good whiskey."

By the time Erin, Mariette, and Anita stepped out on the tiled banquettes in front of the shops lining the street, Erin felt like running. It had been a trying experience for her to stand still for so long while the woman with pins in her teeth fitted some existing garments to Erin's lithesome form. They would be ready to pick up before the *Delta Moon* headed north again. The rest of her wardrobe had been ordered, one pale green ball gown making Erin look forward to the next time they returned to New Orleans.

Her fidgety manner, however was not the only

cause of her restlessness. Mrs. Brady raved on and on, without losing the pins pressed between her lips, about how much Erin resembled one of her past clients. At the mention of Giselle Asante, Erin had grown inordinately still. She'd known her mother came from a prominent New Orleans family that had cast her out for marrying Jacques Devareau. Was it possible the Asantes of Royal Street were that family?

Erin meandered along behind her two companions, but hardly noticed the fancy displays in the storefront windows of the fashionable buildings that boasted shops downstairs and handsome townhouses above. However, the smells of the food each of the hawkers proclaimed to be the finest set her stomach growling. Soon it was assuaged by a delicious fruit pie that had her licking her fingers and lips when it was gone to remove the sticky and delicious residue.

Thus restored, Erin decided it was time to go on about the private business she'd planned to take care of. The problem was, she could think of no plausible way to rid herself of the escorts Jackson Tyler had assigned to her other than to sneak off when they weren't looking. The fact that the city had so much to fascinate even those who had seen it before made the task simple. While they fawned over a handsome gentleman who was trying to decide which candies to purchase for a lady friend, Erin slipped around the corner of St. Phillip and melted into the crowd.

Balconies hanging with flowers and wrought-iron gates marking the entrances to the courtyards her mother told her about slowed her progress down Royal Street. A passerby obligingly directed Erin to the home of the Asantes family and suddenly the other grand and gracious buildings along the street were of no consequence.

One of those light showers that made the flowers smile, as her mother used to say, began to fall as she stood across the street in the shelter of a wide-

48

spreading tree and studied the three-story brown-stone house in awe. It was every bit as big as those up on the Natchez bluff. The very top floor boasted an octagonal cupola, like a giant crown proclaiming its majesty. A black woman could be seen pulling the louvered shutters on a second-story window next to the covered balcony in preparation for the darker clouds gathering over the river.

Three doors up and three down! It would be too good to be true to have real folks living in a place like that. Why, she might even have a grandmother like Cready! It was true her mother left her family behind because they hated her father, but Erin had no quarrel with them. Besides, what could it hurt just to drop by and say hello? She sobered for a moment. And maybe they didn't know of her mother's death.

She looked both ways on the street that was rapidly clearing of all but carriage traffic and ran across to the steps leading up to the ornate iron-laced porch. After pausing long enough to fix the wayward bow in her hair and smooth out the raven locks curling in the dampness with her fingers, she seized the brass door knocker and rapped loudly.

The third rap had hardly made contact when the door swung open and a tall slender black man with graying hair looked down at her expectantly. With features schooled to indifference, it was only his eyes that revealed the slightest curiosity at the bedraggled sight Erin presented.

"Yes?"

Erin stuck out her hand the way her mother had taught her. "Howdy, My name's Erin Devareau and I'm callin' to see if this is the house my mother was raised in. Her name was Giselle Devareau."

"My word, child! You just step inside and wait right here whilst I get Miss Lydia."

Erin stood obediently in the foyer, her heart about to burst from its chest. She ran her fingers across the

49

plush velvet cushion of one of the queerest sofas she'd ever seen. It was round! Directly over it was a chandelier hanging with crystal droplets that tinkled gaily with the draft caused by the opening and closing of the front door. To the left and right were twin sets of doors leading no doubt into a parlor or office. One of them was cracked open, drawing the girl to steal a quick glance.

It was an office with rich leather furniture and gold tasseled draperies over the windows flanking its mahogany desk. She knew it! This had to be her mother's family, for Erin recalled her grandfather had been a doctor and had his office in the front of the house. Oh, she knew there was kinfolk in New Orleans but never guessed it would be so easy to find them!

"Here she is, Miss Lydia."

Erin whirled at the sound of the servant's voice to see a stately woman sweep into the wide foyer with a rustle of skirts and petticoats. Her black hair was swept back and caught in a net at the base of her neck. Her features were small and well proportioned, like those of the china dolls Erin had just seen in the storefront windows earlier, and just as cold. Erin had never seen ice green, but the color of the eyes staring down at her had to be ice blue, cold as the most wintry of January days.

"Just what exactly do you expect to gain by coming to this house with such an outrageous lie?" the woman demanded in a voice equally frigid. "A handout perhaps?"

A mixture of embarrassment and indignation burned at the base of Erin's neck and worked its way across her face. "Ma'am, I'm just tryin' to find out if I got folks here or not . . . and I ain't told no lie at all. My mama was Giselle Devareau."

"And if you did, God forbid, have *folks*," the woman derided, "here, I suppose you'd expect them to take you in and make something decent out of you?"

Erin's fists clenched at her side as she fought to maintain her manners. "No, ma'am. I'm farin' well enough on my own. I just thought I'd say howdy and maybe take a gander at the place. Mama told me a lot about her childhood home."

"Daniel, show this urchin out . . . the back door," her reluctant hostess added imperiously, before turning back to Erin. "And you! Don't you ever show yourself again on our doorstep." Her lips curled in a semblance of a smile. "The very idea that you might in any way be related to this family is absurd."

A host of words came to Erin's mind to express the same sentiment, but with them came the unbidden taste of soap. Thus reminded, she nodded in compliance. "Guess it don't sit too well with me either, ma'am." She extended her hand politely. "Sorry to trouble you."

As if fearful that Erin would seize one of her neatly manicured hands against her will, the woman withdrew them to her breast. "Daniel, get her *out!*"

"Yes, ma'am. This way, miss."

The servant stepped aside to show Erin through the house to the back entrance when an elderly woman appeared in the doorway, leaning heavily on a cane. A light shawl hung over bent shoulders, its fringed tips swinging with each deliberate step. "You might as well go get my invalid's chair, boy," she addressed the negro. "I've had to get myself in from the rain." She gave Erin's hostess a sharp glance. "Put out in the yard every day like a damned dog!"

"Mother, the doctor said that fresh air . . ."

A green razor-edged gaze dismissed her daughter as abruptly as the disgusted wave of the elderly woman's free hand before shifting to Erin. As if not believing what she saw, the woman bent closer, eyes narrowing. A chin, tilted upward toward her nose for lack of teeth started to quiver threateningly.

"Giselle?" she echoed uncertainly.

The younger woman was across the room before Erin could deny the woman's assumption. "That is not Giselle, Mother! Your eyes are playing tricks on you again. That's just another little beggar seeking handouts."

The older woman threw aside the arm that started to herd her toward the steps, away from Erin. "I know my own daughter when I see her!"

Determinedly, the daughter seized the wizened face between her hands and shook it firmly. "Mother, Giselle died during the war! You remember Papa reading at the funeral and all those people and flowers?"

Something inside Erin cringed at the pain that suddenly glazed the old woman's eyes. "I loved my daughter."

Cradling her in her arms, the woman called Lydia ushered her into the room across from the office. "Of course, you did, Mama. We all did." Once inside the door, she stuck her head back through and hissed, "Daniel, get rid of that little twit before she causes any more trouble to this family!"

The servant nodded, lips fixed in thin disapproval. "Yes, ma'am. This way, child."


A steady drizzle of rain pattered on the roof of his private coach as Jackson Tyler climbed inside, out of the inclement weather. "Driver, Rampart Street!" he called out, starting to close the door behind him so that the driver could proceed to his requested destination.

The door caught as a tart from the bawdy house he'd just retreated from peeped inside. "Here you go,

52

luv. Now Lottie can take the chill outta those bones on a nasty night like this. S'good a looker as yourself can have it half price," she added, running her fingers suggestively over the ample cleavage exposed by the damp clinging dress.

"Not tonight, madame," Jackson acknowledged, trying to keep his rising anger out of his voice. "I've a previous engagement."

For which he was already two hours late, he fumed, closing the door securely and tapping the inside of the vehicle to signal the coachman to proceed. His neighbors and sister's future in-laws were visiting New Orleans on a shopping expedition for their ward and had rooms at the St. Louis where he was supposed to have met them for supper two hours ago. Of course, he'd sent word that unanticipated business had delayed him and for them to go on without him, but he'd still hoped that he could find his own wayward ward, deposit her at the boat, and salvage some part of his evening with the Allens, particularly Gina Marie.

And he might, he thought, settling back against the seat. After Mariette and Anita came back to the boat with their woeful tale of how they'd lost Erin in the marketplace, he'd been so furious, for he was certain it was Erin who had lost them, that he couldn't think straight. Immediately he sent word to the Allens of the possible delay and set off for the Royal Street residence the girls had told him Erin seemed so interested in.

His father and Dr. Paul Asante had studied abroad together as young men, although Jackson was not familiar with the family or the younger physician that had married the family's oldest daughter and currently lived in the grand home on Royal Street. If Giselle Asante had been Giselle Devareau, a fact that would not surprise him considering the gentile woman he remembered, then his troubles might well

53

be over. A young girl's place was with her family, not with the likes of him.

The moment he revealed his purpose for visiting the Royal Street residence, his initially elegant and warm reception became wary and distinctly chilled. Yes, a street urchin had come there with the audacity to claim to be related to the late daughter of Dr. and Mrs. Paul Asante and sister of Lydia Asante Lafon, but the impertinent little ruffian had been promptly sent on her way. Although the adjectives used to describe his charge had crossed his mind on more than one occasion, Jackson could not help the indignation that surged into his voice as he left his tea and cake untouched.

"You see, Mrs. Lafon, regardless of whether or not that girl is related to you, she is alone and motherless in a strange city. I only pray someone with a more charitable heart will look out for her until I can find her. Good evening."

They had hurt Erin. Elly Waters told him that when he visited the return address on Giselle Devareau's final letter, a tenement in back of the bawdy house now fading from view in the back window of the coach speeding for Rampart Street. Erin arrived on the verge of tears that never came— not during the period of questions as to why they hadn't sent for her, not even during the morbid description of her mother's death.

"I told her her mama wasn't no whore like most of us, that she'd been too smart for that. That was why Coleman Horsey hired her to run his place for him and never insisted she pleasure anybody but him. He kept threatenin' her that he was gonna tell her family where and what she was if she didn't . . . blackmail of the dirtiest kind!" the woman derided in contempt. "That lady never know'd no man but Erin's daddy and Horsey and it was Horsey that give her the bad disease." The woman shrugged in a helpless gesture. "Poor little thing run outta here a swearin' and cussin' about killin' Coleman Horsey just as soon as she said goodbye to her mama. I offered to go with her, but . . ."

The slowing of the coach announced their proximity to the cemetery. Jackson drew his cloak around his broad shoulders and pulled his hat down securely on his head. This was the last place he knew to look. If Erin wasn't here, he had no idea where to go. He shuddered as he looked out across the rows of tombs and crypts . . . a veritable city of the dead. He wasn't a superstitious man, but the idea of going in there was unnerving to say the least.

"I'll go along with ye, sor, if ye don't mind," the coachman offered, jumping down from his high perch with ease. "I don't take to meanderin' about alone in this place. I'll bet the wee lass is frightened out of her mind."

The Irishman had been driving for the Delta "O" line since its beginnings. More than one night, he'd taken an inebriated Jackson and John to the townhouse above the business office. If there should be someone hiding among the tombs with the idea of lifting a purse or pocket watch, Mike was a good one to have around.

A hint of a smile lighted on Jackson's lips. "Glad to have you along, Mike."

His thumb on the spring catch that unleashed the sharp blade in the tip of his cane, he led the way past the first wall of crypts. Elly Waters had given him a general set of directions, but even with those they might miss Erin in the ghostly maze of crypts and mausoleums. They turned right and walked toward a large domelike monument belonging to one of the city's wealthier families. Giselle Devareau was entombed in a block of mausoleums south of there.

55

The light casting shadows in the ominously silent setting, the two men walked past the imported Italian marble structure and took a southern pass. In the distant glow of the lantern, a small figure sat huddled at the base of one of the tombs. At first, Jackson overlooked it, for it was motionless, but upon closer inspection, he could not mistake the pitifully soaked green of Erin's hand-me-down dress. The girl was so absorbed in her grief that she did not notice the light from Mike's lantern or become aware of Jackson's presence until he laid his hands on her shoulders.

Her strangled scream startled Jackson as much as he had her. The flowers she'd held in her arms scattered as she jumped to her feet and backed against the cold crypt bearing her mother's name at the top of a list of other departed souls. Her eyes were red and swollen and her face streaked with warm tears and cold rain. Her hands, clutched to a youthful bosom well defined by her soaked clothing, trembled as much as her forced, "B . . . bejesus, Tyler, you've scared me outta ten years growth!"

Her pitiful attempt at bravado was obvious, yet combined with the start she'd given him, the irritation that had ebbed with his sympathy was renewed instantly. "You won't miss it, you worrisome little twit, because pneumonia will take you first, if I don't finish you off myself!" With sharp jerking motions, he shrugged off his cloak and wrapped her in it. "You are more trouble than you're worth!" The small figure swathed in the folds of his cloak stiffened as if he'd slapped her and sought his face in the light with eyes so full of pain that he instantly regretted his words. "Come on, Erin," he encouraged in a gentler manner. "I need to get you in some dry clothes and give you something to warm your insides."

Instead of going into the open arms waiting to

shelter her protectively from the downpour that had ensued, she turned and squatted to gather up the flowers she'd dropped. When the bouquet was restored, she placed it in front of the four-vault-high crypt and whispered her goodbyes under her breath. Without looking at the man waiting patiently for her, she pulled the cloak closer around her shoulders and started walking toward the coachman.

"To the ship, sir?" Mike inquired as the small party reached the waiting coach.

"The townhouse," Jackson replied, opening the door so that Erin could climb inside.

Withdrawing to the farthest corner, Erin shrunk inside the warm folds of material and tried to control the halting breaths and seemingly endless supply of tears welling in her eyes. Jackson took the seat opposite her and proceeded to brush the water from his expensively tailored suit and hat. She observed the process, well aware that if not for her, he'd be dry and most likely on his way to a fancy affair, judging by his attire.

She wished her mother had just left her be. The MacCreadys may have been dirt-poor and uneducated but at least they wanted her. "I don't mean to be," she said quietly.

An inquisitive brow shot up. "I beg your pardon?"

"More trouble than I'm worth."

Jackson groaned inwardly. "Look, Erin, I . . ."

"I didn't ask for you to come after me." With a loud sniff, Erin turned to look out the window at the passing buildings, many dark until the following business day. She was cold now. She hadn't realized it when she was at the cemetery. There had been too much on her mind then . . . too much anguish. She squeezed her eyes tightly and swallowed the sob that threatened her throat.

"Here, kid."

Erin opened her eyes to see a monogrammed linen

handkerchief extended to her. "I'm not crying!" she stated emphatically, not wanting him to think her a sissy as well as a troublesome burden. Cready had broken her a long time ago from showing her feelings, at least in front of anyone.

"I didn't think you were," Jackson answered smoothly. "This weather is making your nose run and I thought you might need this."

Warily, Erin accepted the offering. "Thanks."

"Not that anyone could blame you if you did cry. I know I did when my father passed away."

"You?" Erin was incredulous that a man like Black Jack Tyler would admit to any such thing. She shivered again and pulled her wrap closer.

"I loved him so much that it really didn't matter to me who saw my tears. They were simply another way of showing my love and my despair at his loss." Jackson noted the shivers of cold shaking his companion and the muddy shoes drawing up into his cloak. "It's damnably cold with that rain outside," he observed, folding his arms across his chest with a shudder. "I don't suppose you'd mind sharing that cloak?"

Erin's pale features turned a fair shade of pink over having hogged the wrap when it was Tyler's to start with. "It's yours," she retorted simply, straightening out her legs so that he might sit next to her.

After taking off his wet jacket, Jackson did exactly that.

"I'm going to kill him, you know."

"Who?" Jackson asked, startled by the fierceness that claimed her voice.

"Coleman Horsey. He killed my mother."

"Do you think your mother would approve of that? After all, she went to great pains to see that you would have a good future. I hardly think becoming a murderer was in her plans."

Erin frowned thoughtfully in the dim light cast in

from the lantern hanging on the coach, but stiffened as he placed an arm over her shoulders. Upon seeing that he was only closing the voluminous wrap around them, she relaxed once more, the warmth his body offered too enticing to ignore. His free hand coming to rest on her back as she leaned into him, Jackson settled back and watched the flickering lanterns of the St. Louis Hotel pass by, reminding him of the supper he was missing.

A smile tugged at the corner of his lips. He could well imagine Gina Marie's expression if the lovely belle of Fairbanks could see him cradling this wet bedraggled little urchin. The smile faded. This ward business was becoming more and more complicated by the day.

## Chapter Four

The sun rose to kiss the crescent city after forsaking it to the rain clouds the day before. Erin awakened, snug in an overstuffed bed to the smell of fresh croissants baking in the kitchen of the couple who staffed Jackson Tyler's apartment over the Delta "O" office on Decatur Street. The hot bath in the elegant hand-painted porcelain tub the night before and the spiked toddy Libby Green had given her had been just the right prescription for the chill she'd taken.

But the most wonderful recollection of all was the way Jackson Tyler had stared at her when she emerged to say good night, dressed in a peignoir set he had purchased originally for his sister. It had been a strange look that made her feel weak in the knees and ready to jump for joy at the same time. Her face coloring with the reaction taking place just thinking about it, Erin shoved the light blanket aside and set about dressing for the day.

If she had thought the streets busy her first day in New Orleans, they were literally working with people, carriages, and wagons the second. Jackson was downstairs in the office by the time she breakfasted on Libby's fresh croissants smothered in butter and jam. The housekeeper had fussed over her soiled and wrinkled dress until Erin relented to let her iron it just to eat in peace.

When she left the office of the Delta "O" Line, she'd given Tyler her word that she would not go anywhere but the market place and Jackson Square. As the morning progressed, though, Erin began to think of the old woman sitting out in the courtyard behind the great brownstone house. The longer she thought about her, the more reasons she could think of for justifying a little walk up to Royal Street and back. It wasn't as if she'd get lost and it certainly was not one of the seedy neighborhoods Tyler had warned her about. She would just tell him she was sorry later . . . if he found out.

The courtyards between Royal and Chartres Streets were just as her mother had described. Fortunately for Erin, one of the gates had been left open permitting her access to the rear of the homes where flowers and shrubs bloomed in gay profusion. Using the dome cupola as a homing point, Erin soon found the courtyard she sought, but the shrubbery had grown so tall and thickly around it that she was hard pressed to see over it, let alone pass through it. Its one gate had no latch on the outside, a factor Erin found to be as disenchanting as the fact that the old woman was not put outside as she'd indicated the day before.

A curse rose to the tip of her tongue but she squelched it consciously in keeping with the new leaf she'd turned over in her life. Her mother had told her once, it wasn't the wrappings, but what was inside that made a person. Since Tyler was working on the wrappings, it seemed the least she could do to work on her insides. Shoulders sagging, she started to walk away when she heard the back door open and the sound of voices.

Erin pressed against the hedge, trying to see through its leafy cover. She managed to move aside a small section of the massive boxwood in time to see the black servant Daniel wheeling the lady she thought to be her grandmother down a gently sloping ramp. Her breath would hardly come when he placed the elderly woman not more than a hedge width from her for fear of giving herself away, but the servant was not aware of anyone but the old woman he sought to make comfortable. It was obvious from the pains he took that he was fond of his mistress.

"Now you just ring this bell if you need me," he told her, taking a small silver bell from his jacket pocket and placing it on a wrought-iron table within her reach. "You know Daniel will take care of you."

"I know, Daniel," the old woman acknowledged, her voice devoid of the sharp edge it carried yesterday. If anything, it was melancholy. "You're the only one who seems to give a hoot whether I live or die."

"Now, Miss Marie," Daniel chided gently, "You knows Miss Lydia and Dr. Lafon think the world of you."

Marie! Erin thought excitedly. So that was her grandmother's name. Grandma Marie. She rolled the name over in her mind.

"Until I sign my family's bank accounts over to them for safe keeping, you mean!" Marie Asante declared indignantly. "They already have an inheritance from their father to keep them in the lap of luxury until kingdom come. Don't think I don't see Lydia's eyes, the way they light up when she tells me how I should let her Paul manage my business for me. Humph!" she snorted, rolling the edge of the light lap robe Daniel tucked around her legs in her gnarled fingers. "I wouldn't have any trouble if he'd stop giving me that blasted medicine. I'm going to stop taking it!" she threatened rebelliously. "I'd rather pace the floor all night long than spend my day in a daze."

"Yes, ma'am," Daniel ackowledged in resignation. "Now you call me if you need me."

Was Daniel so glum because her grandmother was

62

right or was he just humoring an old woman, Erin wondered, her curiosity piqued by the scenario portrayed before her. It wouldn't surprise her if the daughter was trying to cheat the old woman out of her money. Lydia Asante appeared to Erin to have an enormous ego that fed on money and the power and prestige it afforded.

A strangled noise distracted her from her reverie. The woody branches of the boxwood scraping her arm, she peered through it to see the old woman dabbing at her eyes with an embroidered hankie. "Put out like a dog every day . . . nobody to talk to but my birds, and that damned cat of Lydia's scares them away . . ."

"I'll talk to you, grandma."

Erin's words came straight from her heart. When she heard them, they startled her, but not as much as they did her grandmother. The old woman inhaled so sharply and clutched at her chest so demonstratively that Erin thought she was having a seizure like one of the kids that used to hang out in Under the Hill. She'd been hurt and ashamed when the little girl died, for she'd thought the child faked them at times just to get attention.

A cold and terrible panic running through her that the grandmother she'd just found might leave her just as her mother had, Erin jumped up and caught a low-hanging branch growing over the boxwood and shimmied across the top with no trouble at all. When she dropped to the ground on the other side, the old woman stared at her as if she were a ghost.

Tears stung her eyes as she fell to her knees at the old woman's feet. "Please don't die, Grandma! I don't think I could stand to lose you, too!" She hadn't meant to cry. She only wanted to talk to her grandmother. But her eyes wouldn't stop and her chest constricted so tightly that there was no place for her anguish to go but out with shuddering sobs.

"Hush, child!" the old woman coaxed gently, her palsied hand reaching out to stroke the thick dark curls of the girl at her feet. "I'm not going to die until you tell me where you've been all these years."

It was a while before Erin could speak. She wanted to. She wanted to tell her grandmother so many things, but her sudden attack of emotion would not permit it. When she did make an attempt her voice was as ragged as her breath and she wished she had Tyler's handkerchief, for her nose wouldn't stop running. To her relief, her grandmother offered her own. Like the soap she'd used the night before, it smelled of lavender. Erin decided right away that the next pay she got, lavender soap was the first thing she'd buy.

"I've been living in Natchez, Grandma." Erin eliminated exactly where, in case her grandmother had heard of Under the Hill.

The old woman contemplated her, reaching out to touch her face. "Why didn't you come home? Papa finally forgave you for marrying Jacques Devareau, you know." Her eyes watered with a twinkling fondness as she went on. "I knew he would. You were his favorite."

Oh God, it wasn't fair, a part of Erin cried out in anguish. She and her mother could have come home. Her mother could have been reunited with the ones who loved her, although somehow Erin could not picture Lydia as one of them.

"He prayed for forgiveness on his deathbed that his litte Giselle would come home."

Through all the confusing emotions tearing at her, Erin realized that her grandmother still thought she was Giselle.

"No, Grandma, I'm not Giselle," she told the woman softly. "I'm Giselle's daughter . . . Erin."

Green eyes like her own narrowed. "Now don't you go telling me that my eyes are playing tricks on

64

me. I know my own daughter when I see her."

Erin smiled patiently. "I look just like Mama, so everybody says." Seeing the old woman was still unconvinced, she pulled her dress off one shoulder. "See, I don't have a birthmark on my shoulder like Mama did."

"Let me see the other shoulder."

Obligingly, Erin shifted her dress to the opposite side. "See?"

"Stand up." When Erin had obeyed, Marie Asante made a circling motion with her hand. "Go ahead, turn around." At her satisfied grunt, the girl faced her expectantly. "What did you say your name was?"

"Erin, Grandma." Dropping her eyes, Erin groaned inwardly. She should have waited until one of her dresses was done. She'd have made a better impression. "I'm so pleased to meet you."

"Where's your mother?"

The pain that had subsided welled again, but Erin managed to answer. "She passed on last month . . . pneumonia," she embellished, seeing no need to explain details she was certain Marie Asante would find abhorrent. Her mother hadn't wanted her family to know of her fate and Erin was not about to betray her now. "We lived in a little cottage at the edge of town and Mama gave piano lessons."

Marie Asante digested Erin's words, pain glazing her expression. Erin let her deal with the news in her own time, experiencing much the same anguish over what was lost and what might have been. When her grandmother sniffed loudly, Erin handed back the hankie, but instead of taking it, the older woman fixed her gaze on her. "Do you play?"

"Yes, ma'am." Actually she'd worked out a few saloon favorites on the piano in the White Palace, selections her grandmother had likely never heard.

"I'd like to hear you. Let's go inside . . ."

Erin saw her reach for the bell and leapt to stay her

65

hand. The woman looked up at her granddaughter in surprise. "No offense, Grandma, but I don't think I'd like to go in there. Maybe if you came to see me on the *Delta Moon* . . ."

"The what?"

"The *Delta Moon*. That's where I live now." She didn't finish the thought with *now that Mama's gone*. She and her grandmother were both trying to deal with that. "I'm a maid now, but one of these days I'm going to be a captain of a riverboat."

"Who says?"

Erin drew to her full height, determined not to let the fact that her grandmother obviously disapproved of her plans affect her. "Jackson Beauregard Tyler . . . my guardian."

"Now why would Giselle leave her only daughter in the hands of a riverboat gambler?" Marie Asante thought aloud. She shook her head in disapproval. "I want you to fetch your things and move in here."

"Oh no!" A hot pink flushed Erin's cheeks at the aristocratic rise of her grandmother's brow. "This is a fine place, Grandma, but I just don't think I could stomach livin' here."

"Didn't your mother teach you to pronounce your words in their entirety?"

"Living here," Erin repeated, her chin stubbornly set. "I just came to visit, Grandma, but to tell you the truth, after yesterday, I don't think I could get along with Miss Lydia . . . and living on Tyler's riverboat is a lot more fun." As her grandmother released her hold on the bell, Erin let out a sigh of relief.

"I don't doubt but what you say is true," Marie chuckled. It was the first time Erin had seen her grandmother smile and the expression did wonders to her wrinkled face. There was actually a family resemblance. "I can hardly stomach living here myself these days."

"You could come live with me, Grandma." Erin's

face seemed to light up as the impulsive idea took root. "I can clean cabins in the morning and serve supper at night to pay for your board . . . and you can share my room. I have a big bed." Jackson would never know . . . until she could prove she could earn enough to pay for room and board for two.

Marie dismissed the idea with a feeble wave. "They'd never allow it."

"Who?" the girl asked, her face falling.

"My daughter and that husband of hers."

"You're an adult, aren't you? Just pick up and go."

A mischievous twinkle leapt to her grandmother's eye. "I ought to just do that. Why, I haven't traveled on a packet in years! Paul and I used to love to take an excursion every spring to Memphis and back . . . and I wouldn't mind meeting this Jackson Beauregard Tyler."

Encouraged, Erin took the idea further. "You could come and stay with us for a few weeks and if you don't like it, this place sure isn't about to go anywhere."

"Not as long as I hold the deed anyway," the old woman grunted. "By gosh, I won't even tell them! When does the ship leave?"

"Late tomorrow afternoon." Excitement bubbled in Erin's voice. "Oh, Grandma, I would be so pleased if you did come."

Marie Asante nodded her gray head. "So would I, Erin." She motioned the girl closer. "Now, my daughter and her husband will not hear of this. They think my health is too frail to do more than sit in a courtyard and watch their damned cat chase my birds, so here's what we'll do."

The plan was a simple one. Her grandmother would pack a few of her things in a carpetbag and toss it out the window of her bedroom. Erin could pick it up when she came to take her to the ship. As far as her family and servants knew, Marie Asante was just going to the courtyard for another session in the sun, but as soon as everyone was inside, Erin would wheel her grandmother through the back gate and they would make for the ship with all haste.

Erin sealed the agreement with an extra bit hug and kiss and repeated the plan to her grandmother's satisfaction before taking the exit to the alley leading through the other courtyards. It was too good to be true. Her very own grandmother was coming to live on the *Delta Moon* with her!

# Chapter Five

Erin fought with the invalid's chair, trying to get it up on the banquette. "Don't worry, Grandma, I'll get you up here."

"I know you will, *ma petite.* If you could get this thing through that back alley, you can certainly handle this," Marie Asante assured her.

The even sidewalks had been relatively easy for Erin, but their first leg of the journey nearly had her in tears for fear of spilling the elderly woman out in the dirt alley. But she persevered, having to stop only once for her grandmother to get up so that she could disengage the chair from the muddy bed it had sunken into. The woman's grip on her arm had been surprisingly strong, renewing Erin's strength, and her grateful smile gave Erin the heart to keep on.

It would have been shorter to go straight to the boat, but her grandmother insisted on stopping at the exchange at the St. Louis Hotel and spent the longest two hours Erin had ever seen. "There we go," Erin grunted, bearing down on the handles to proceed ahead.

"I couldn't sleep last night," Marie spoke over her shoulder as Erin took a second to wipe her brow at the door of the massive hotel. "And it wasn't because I fed my medicine to the plant in the window either. I was just too excited!"

"Me too."

The afternoon hadn't been easy either. When she got back to the Delta "O" office, Jackson was in a foul humor after some sort of disagreement with Elena Cadiz which resulted in the woman quitting. Worse, he'd announced that he'd found a tutor for Erin and expected her to start her lesson the following morning—in direct conflict with Erin's secret plans. If not for John Davenport's timely intervention, the entire scheme might have fallen apart. As it was, John, who turned out to be Jackson's partner in the Delta "O" Line, shamed Jackson into letting her enjoy her first visit to New Orleans before putting her to work at her lessons.

Then the night had come. She'd tossed and turned with excitement, working the plan out over and over in her mind. When Erin did fall asleep, she'd had the most wonderful dream of lying cradled in Tyler's arms. She guessed she'd never forget how warm and safe they felt there in the coach.

"Good day, Mrs. Asante! It's good to see you up and about!" Erin smiled at the gentleman holding open the large brass adorned door of the exchange for them to enter.

"Good to be up and about, Mr. Davis," her grandmother replied brightly. "I don't suppose you're in too big a hurry to help me with some of my business, are you?"

"I am always at my customer's disposal, particularly yours, madame. Here," he said, moving Erin gently aside. "I'll take you personally to my office."

Erin stood, feet glued to the marble floor, uncertain what to do. Her grandmother had told her that the St. Louis contained a bank, a hotel, and several of the finer shops, but she'd had a hard time imagining all of those things in one place until that moment. Its massive columns supported a gigantic dome under which uniformed boys scurried with luggage carts and elegantly dressed men and women moved at a leisurely pace, stopping now and again to gaze through the windows of the shops.

"I just don't know why I bother to fool with him at all," a familiar voice drifted down from the massive set of stairs winding to a second floor around a crystal chandelier that would literally fill Erin's new cabin.

Erin looked up to see a beautiful golden-haired woman flanked by an older couple. That had to be the one who had come to Jackson's apartment last night! She'd know that sugary drawl anywhere. Her suspicion was confirmed instantly.

"But Jackson *is* rich and he *is* handsome," she drawled slyly. Brown eyes scanned the spacious foyer for any admiring eyes there to witness her descent when they fell on the shabbily attired girl standing by the door. "Will you look what the doorman has let in this hotel!"

The words came out in a stage whisper that drew more attention to Erin from other patrons. In spite of the panic that ensued, Erin tilted her chin proudly and proceeded to walk as if she belonged in the elite environment toward the corridor where the banker and her grandmother had disappeared. Sure she'd be glad when that Mrs. Brady delivered her new clothes!

Erin occupied her time by wandering through the shops in the hotel, moving on when a suspicious clerk began to follow her. She was completely lost when Mr. Davis found her in front of a tobacco shop on the lower level of the hotel. He returned her promptly to her grandmother and with a great deal of relief, Erin started once again toward the wharf where the *Delta Moon* was docked.

"Now I got it worked out, Grandma, that you can stay in my cabin and I'll sleep on the floor. I think it'd be best that Tyler doesn't know what we're up to until we get underway."

"Are you afraid of this Tyler?"

"No, I just don't think he'll be pleased, me taking on a stowaway."

Marie Asante burst into laughter, leaving Erin to wonder if she was having fun with her or pleased to be a stowaway. "All right, I'll keep my identity a secret. That way, Lydia will have more difficulty finding me. How does Mrs. Rosie O'Rourke sound?"

Erin grinned at her grandmother's mischievous inclination. "I don't think he'll care who you are, you'll still be a stowaway."

"Stowaway my foot! I'll book passage in one of their best rooms!"

"What?" Erin couldn't believe her ears.

"What do you think I needed to go to the bank for, girl? That money isn't doing me a whit of good collecting dust in Davis's bank. I'm going to travel in style . . . and so are you. I won't hear of you working as a servant."

Erin rolled her eyes heavenward. "Grandma, if you say I'm your granddaughter, you'll give away your identity. Besides, I won't be working that much, except in the morning. Tyler hired me a tutor for the afternoons."

"Did he now?" the old woman echoed reflectively. "Well, I just can't wait to meet this young man. How old is he?"

Erin thought a moment. "At least thirty," she said in a tone that brought a chuckle to her grandmother's lips. "And set in his ways."

"And how's that?" Marie Asante asked, intrigued by her granddaughter's assessment of the guardian her daughter chose for her.

"Well, he's just got his ideas about the way a girl should walk and talk and there just ain't . . . isn't any way to argue with him without him washing your mouth out with soap." She tilted the chair toward her, letting the huge back wheels take the brunt of the step from the banquette to the shipyard. "But he's not as bad as I first thought," she added, deciding to withhold from her grandmother the fact that he was a pervert where women were concerned. "And he's rich and handsome."

"Married?"

"Not that I know of." If he was, his wife should kill him, Erin decided smugly. That's what she'd do if he was running out with other women and married to her. Or maybe just shoot a certain part of his anatomy off like Big Rose did her man.

When they reached the gangway, Marie Asante surprised Erin by beckoning to one of the roust-abouts. Erin could hardly believe her ears as she heard her grandmother tell how Erin had been good enough to direct her to the wharf and offered the man two weeks' wages to help her aboard and then run to the steamer's office to book her fare.

"Now you just run along, dear . . . what did you say your name was?"

"Erin," Erin supplied quickly.

"This handsome fellow and his friends are going to haul me up to the boiler deck and fix me up out of the sun until he can get back with my ticket." To Erin's further shock, her grandmother fished out a silver dollar from the purse she'd packed in her carpetbag and folded it in her hand. "This is for your trouble."

"Uh, thank you, Mrs. O'Rourke!"

"Rosie to you, Erin. See you around!"

The roustabout and one of his friends carried "Rosie O'Rourke" to the boiler deck without even raising a sweat. Erin followed at a distance, amused at how well her grandmother was getting into her act. Why, she was actually flirting with the youngest one, a boy that couldn't be more than a year or so older than Erin herself.

Immensely pleased with the way things were

working out, Erin meandered back to her cabin. The moment she opened the door, she knew Mrs. Brady had been there. On the bunk were three large bundles wrapped in brown paper and several smaller ones. With an excitement kindred to Christmas, Erin attacked her presents one by one until the entire cabin, which was little more than a bed, a small table, and a closet, was covered. Mrs. Brady had even thought of extra ribbons for her hair to match each of her dresses!

Wanting to try it all, Erin stripped off her shabby dress and started putting on the "frillies" the seamstress had selected for her. Compared to the rough muslin drawers she was used to, the smooth caressing silk made her feel positively wicked. The corset was another story. Erin struggled into it without completely unfastening the laces and then worked until her arms ached trying to make some order of it in the back. Anxious to see what the ensemble looked like before she donned her petticoats, she climbed up on her bunk and crouched under the low ceiling, trying to get a semblance of a view in a small mirror hanging over the bunk.

Recalling that her other room had had a full-length mirror on the inside of the locker door, Erin pulled open the wooden door at the foot of her bed. To her surprise, instead of a locker, there was another door. Curiosity getting the best of her, she tried the handle and it swung open, revealing an all too familiar stateroom. That damned Tyler had put her in his closet!

She ought to have been indignant, but Erin was too happy to let the fact that her new room was too small to hold her things dampen her spirits. In a few short trips, she had all her belongings spread on his bed and his closet door open where a full-length mirror held her image from head to toe. Her underclothes were almost too pretty to cover with a dress, she thought, spinning so that her crinolines flared out from her tiny waist.

Suddenly a loud whistle shrieked, announcing the departure of the *Delta Moon* and the ship jolted out from under Erin's feet. With a yelp, she went down in a heap of silk and lace, her new dress in hand, as the door to the stateroom opened.

"Tyler!" she gasped, gathering her dress to her bodice as the tall gambler came to a halt, the packages in his arms nearly spilling.

"Erin!"

"I was just tryin' on my new clothes and I couldn't see in my mirror so . . . ." Erin tried to get up, but was encumbered by the whalebone crinoline that flew up over her back as she climbed to her feet.

"Oh, is she in here, Jackson? I just can't wait to see . . . her," Gina Marie Allen trailed off upon seeing the crimson-faced girl clutching a dress to her bosom. *"This* is your *little* ward?" The *L* in little rolled off the young woman's tongue in contempt. "The one you spent the night with last night instead of keeping your engagement at the St. Louis with me and then had the gall to ask me to help you purchase necessaries for?"

"Erin, I think you'd better go to your own room," Jackson told her grimly.

Hurriedly, Erin gathered up all she could in her arms and tried to get back through the door, but her crinolines would not have it. An expletive of the foulest nature came to her mind, but she struggled with the petticoats in miserable silence until Jackson came to her rescue and collapsed the undergarments enough to squeeze through.

"The door was open," she offered apologetically as he tossed in a pair of drawers that had fallen from her arm.

"It isn't now," he answered in a clipped voice. "And remember what I said about knocking."

Erin winced as the bolt slid shut from the other side. Not to be outdone, she grabbed the door to her own room and started to do the same when the woman's raised voice caught her attention.

"How convenient for you, Jackson!"

"For heaven's sake, Gina, she's only eighteen!"

"Only eighteen!" the woman ranted, reaching a higher pitch than before. "Darling, I am only twenty by two months! As I recall you have been courting me since my coming-out party when I turned *sixteen!* The way you were talking, I thought I was helping to outfit a twelve-year-old!"

"And you were a tremendous help, Gina. I'm certain Erin will be grateful."

"In a pig's eye!" Erin mumbled under her breath . . . although, she was curious as to what sort of necessaries they had purchased for her.

"And I know I am," she heard Jackson say, his voice dropping to a velvet low that sent shivers up her spine.

"How grateful, Jackson honey?"

"This grateful."

As the room fell silent she leaned closer and pressed her ear to the door. A soft moan that reminded her of a cat's purr echoed lowly and Erin backed away in disgust. He must be a hell of a kisser to make her purr like that when she was spitting mad only moments before. She'd have just told the snooty bitch it was none of her damned business what he bought or who he bought it for, that's what she'd say. A wicked gleam lighting in emerald eyes, Erin proceeded with her intial intent and slammed the door. Grinning at the squeal that erupted on the other side, she slammed the bolt into place and proceeded to finish dressing.

The crescent city had faded out of sight by the time Erin had put away all her things and went to Mariette and Anita's room to show them her new dress. She also wanted to be certain that all her undergarments were on correctly, for the corset that pushed her breasts up so that just a hint of them showed above the square cut of her neckline was biting into her flesh in more places than she could count. Shifting one of the whalebone stays to one side, she knocked and stepped inside.

Erin thought her head would swell to the point of bursting, the way her two new friends fussed over her. Anita pulled up her hair into a neat little gather of raven locks and adorned it with a ribbon to match her new turquoise dress. Erin could only hope that Jackson Tyler would be as enthusiastic, since he'd paid for the garment. Besides, she sort of liked that giddy feeling that rippled through her when he looked at her with that warm sterling gaze of his, like he could see the ribbons on her corset.

She was giving herself one final examination in the mirror on the back of the cabin door when she heard the dinner bell ringing and remembered her grandmother. God in heaven, she'd left her on the boiler deck and forgotten her in all the excitement.

Erin's fear for Marie Asante's welfare was in vain. She met her grandmother being wheeled down to the dining salon by one of the white-jacketed stewards whose apparent task was to remain at the woman's disposal. The woman was tittering over something the young man had said, but her laughter faded at the sight of Erin rushing up to her, face flushed.

"Erin, I want you to meet Edward Ryan, my transport when I have need of him. Edward, this is my good friend, Erin Devareau."

"Erin?" the young man repeated quizzically.

Erin met the appreciative gaze of the young man she'd worked with in the kitchen and nodded in embarrassment. "It's really me, Edward."

This time it was Edward's turn to blush, which he did all the way to the tips of his ears. "Well, you look pretty as a speckled pup under a red wagon!"

"I can take . . . Rosie," she caught herself quickly, "to the dining room if you need to get back to the kit—"

"The young man gave you a compliment, Erin! A proper young lady would thank him for it," her grandmother interrupted, pressing her cane against Erin's skirts.

"Thank you, Edward."

"Will you be joining us for dinner, Erin?"

"Oh no, I usually eat with the staff in the kitchen or down below with the men."

Marie Asante frowned in disapproval. "If you're this Jackson Tyler's ward, why do you not have a place at the captain's table?"

"Because I *work* for Tyler, Rosie," Erin said evenly, her eyes flashing a warning. She bent over and gave the woman a kiss. "Now you go enjoy your supper and perhaps later I can join you on deck for a little chat. The river's just lovely at night with all those lights along the bank and moon skipping over it."

Erin knew her grandmother was displeased, but she would just have to get used to the way things were. She might have a new dress, but that didn't mean she had earned the right to sit at the captain's table. Upon watching to make sure Edward had conducted the older woman safely inside the double mahogany and brass doors of the salon, Erin took to the steps leading down to the main deck where Mariette and Anita were holding court with the crew.

Like Edward, her newly made friends were shocked into silence when she entered the mess hall. Mariette and Anita, thoroughly enjoying the astonishment, broke the stunned silence by smugly telling the men that they'd told them so. Two of the stewards jumped up to offer her a seat, nearly knocking her over in the process and it was a toss-up as to which of the three of them had the reddest face. Erin had no idea dressing pretty could cause so much commotion and embarrassment.

She had just filled her plate with the ham and potatoes heaped on large platters in the middle of the table when Edward appeared at her elbow.

"The Captain and Mr. Tyler are requesting your presence upstairs, Miss Erin."

Grandma! Erin thought. What had her grandmother said to cause such upheaval in her life? Erin's stomach knotted as she climbed the steps on Edward's arm, feeling a total fool. As if she couldn't make it up the steps by herself! What was she going to do? she wondered miserably. She didn't even know which fork or spoon to use for what. There hadn't been as many eating utensils in their entire house as there was at one place setting in the main salon.

Although her cheeks flamed as if they'd been kissed by the sun, the rest of Erin's face was chalk white when Edward escorted her past the giant silver water cooler in the center of the room to the head table where Captain Miers and the owners of the Delta "O" Line were seated. To Erin's horror, all the gentlemen rose until the introductions were made and she was neatly tucked between John Davenport and her new tutor—Roderick Sturgis, a stern sort of gentleman with bifocals who took no pains to hide the fact that he was staring at her over them.

"Jackson was just telling us how he came to be your guardian, Miss Devareau," Gina Marie Allen, as Erin discovered was the full name of the femme fatale who had been in Jackson's room earlier, drawled with a speculative look.

While the woman was from a decidedly upper-class family, she chased Jackson Tyler with the same ardor and determination as Elena Cadiz. It seemed that that sort of desperate behavior was not isolated to the *other sort* of women, Erin observed thoughtfully.

"I was saying that your mother and I were close friends," Jackson explained tactfully.

"But that name just doesn't ring a bell," Gina puzzled with exaggerated innocence, "and I thought I knew everybody in Natchez!"

"We lived on the edge of town in one of those little cottages with roses growing along the hedgerow," Erin supplied with more calm than she felt. She didn't care what the others thought, but she didn't want her grandmother to know what her mother had to do to make a living after her father was killed in the war. "Mama gave piano lessons and did mending for folks . . . er . . . people in the town."

"What I meant," Gina reiterated, "was that I knew most of the prominent citizens."

"Then you wouldn't have known Mama or me. We didn't associate with people like yourself."

"Just how did you come to know this woman well enough for her to leave her only child in your care, Jackson?" Myra Allen, Gina's aunt, asked, relieving the brief moment of silence as slicing blue eyes clashed with obstinate green across the table.

"My mother went to school with Mrs. Tyler during better times," Erin spoke up smoothly. "My family's fortune as well as my father was forfeited to the war effort. Mama was left with me to raise as best she could with what was left."

"You poor dear. It's a wonder Auralee Tyler hasn't taken you in."

"Mother has so much on her mind with Jennifer's wedding plans that we decided it was best if she didn't find out until later."

"That is rather convenient, I suppose," Gina sighed to no one in particular. "I'm sure Auralee Tyler is in a tizzy. She's such a gracious hostess!"

"By George, I think if two people would come to

mutual agreement, Auralee and my Myra could put their heads and purses together and have two weddings at one time," Thomas Allen injected with a meaningful look directed at Jackson.

"Now, Thomas, young love can't be rushed," Myra Allen chided her husband.

"That's a lovely sentiment, Mrs. Allen, but I for one agree with your husband." Erin's gaze flew to the mischievous green eyes at the end of the table where Marie Asante sat like a queen opposite the captain. "Especially when it's obvious Mr. Tyler and Miss Devareau are so well suited to each other."

Erin fixed her eyes on her soup miserably as Myra Allen corrected the woman. "No, Mrs. O'Rourke, you have it mixed up, dear. We were speaking of our Gina and Mr. Tyler here."

Her grandmother's laughter brought Erin's head up in apprehension. "Oh, for heaven's sake," she chuckled, shaking her head as she picked up her wine glass for a toast to Jackson. "Well, here's to you, you lucky devil, and . . ." she paused until she had everyone's undivided attention, "to the *Delta Moon!* May the remaining days of its round-trip run to Memphis be as pleasant as this first!"

"Here, here!" John Davenport agreed, taking up his own glass and finishing its contents.

Erin was never so glad to see a meal end. If Gina Allen wasn't practically swooning over Jackson, she was casting barbed looks across the table to where Erin sat talking with her tutor, who, after putting away his meal and part of Erin's, offered to take her for a walk out on the deck to discuss his plans for her course of study. Erin's heart sank, for, not only had the man practically taken over her chair, pressing his leg against her own, but she'd wanted to spend the evening with her grandmother. Reluctantly, she rose to accompany the man when the older woman intervened.

Leave it to Grandma, Erin thought in delight, as Rosie O'Rourke assumed command of the situation and asked to come along, proclaiming her interest in what young ladies studied in modern times. So it was that, when they left, it was with her grandmother in tow. Erin was so relieved that she failed to see the way Jackson hovered near the door and watched as they retreated to the forward deck. At that moment, all that mattered was that her plan was working marvelously, thanks to her ever-surprising grandmother.

# Chapter Six

Last night had been wonderful, Erin thought dreamily, distracted by the passing shoreline that paraded across the portal. She and her grandmother talked until the wee hours of the morning about everything imaginable. They'd laughed together over some of the family stories and cried over the tragedy of her mother's absence from her childhood home.

While Marie Asante had not approved of Giselle marrying Jacques Devareau, it had been her husband that issued the ultimatum that if his daughter left, she would never be allowed back. After Giselle left, the doctor announced that she had died during the war and held services in her memory. Only the immediate family knew any different.

"I was a meek little wife in those days," Marie told Erin. "I let him drive my lovely daughter out of my life forever . . . until now," she added, taking Erin's hand to her cheek. "How much alike you are to the fiery little angel who used to have Paul wrapped around her little finger." The light touch of a hand on her knee caused Erin to start, snapping her out of her reverie.

"Miss Devareau, while I could sit and admire that wistful expression of yours all afternoon, I would suggest you return your attention to Shakespeare."

"Who?" Erin asked, shifting in her seat so that the familiar hand dropped away.

Paying attention to Roderick Sturgis was not nearly as hard as keeping out of his reach. Since the beginning of her afternoon sequestered with him in Tyler's cabin, which was furnished with the only desk on the ship aside from the captain's, he'd found every reason in the world to touch her shoulder or place a hand on her knee. And she hated it when he leaned over her shoulder as she read. His breath was hot as it was foul.

"William Shakespeare, Miss Devareau!" the man exclaimed in frustration.

Erin stifled a yawn. It wasn't that the book wasn't good. In fact, she had gotten more than a good chuckle from it since she started reading an hour ago. But she was tired from staying up most of the night and then rising early to help Hannah with the cabins.

"I tell you what, Sturgis . . ."

"Mr. Sturgis, young woman!"

"Mr. Sturgis," Erin conceded. The man was so stiff, she wondered that he could sit!

"Although you could call me Roderick in private," he suggested, placing his hand once again on her shoulder. "And I could call you Erin."

Erin bristled with irritation. "Blast it, Mr. Sturgis, make up your mind one way or the other! But what I call you in here goes for out there, too," she averred, jerking her thumb toward the door. "And to tell you the truth, I'm plain tuckered and this Kate here is making me down right cantankerous!"

"You are not tuckered, Miss Devareau, you are tired, fatigued, exhausted . . ." Sturgis gave her a patronizing smile. "Young ladies do need their proper rest, something which you did not get last night."

The fact that he'd noticed the time of her retirement slipping past her, Erin wanted to tell him that if he hadn't stayed out on deck so long, her talk with her grandmother might have started that much sooner, but she held her tongue. "No, Rosie and I just stayed up talking girl talk and the time flew." Unaware that her lower lip had poked out, effectively showing her pique, she rolled her eyes up at him. "I promise I'll see if Petrucchio wins his bet or not before tomorrow afternoon, if you'll just let me take a nap."

Roderick Sturgis wavered in his superior stance before resigning with a heavy sigh. "Very well, Miss Devareau, I shall let you by this time, but tomorrow I shall be relentless for a full three hours. In the meantime, read the rest of this act tonight and . . . and compose a letter to Petrucchio telling him what changes you would make in his behavior to win Kate. That will give me an idea of what we need to work on in composition and grammar."

Although the assignment sounded foolish, Erin's face brightened at the early dismissal. She rose from her seat and tucked her book under her arm. "Well, I guess I'll see you at dinner then." She waited for the man to make a move to leave, but instead, he stood before her expectantly. "Thank you," she ventured, uncertain as to exactly what he was waiting for. And what the devil was he looking at? Unaccountably nervous, she marched to the door and put her hand on the knob, but as she did, his closed over it.

"You remind me of Kate, you know, Miss Devareau. I've witnessed a fiery spirit in those verdant eyes that demands to know the mastery of manly love."

Incredulous, Erin caught her breath as she was abruptly seized by the waist and pulled against him. "What the bloody hell do you think you're doing?"

"Don't you feel it, Miss Devareau?" her tutor

breathed heavily against her lips. "Don't you know a longing within your sweet loins that can not be denied?"

"No, and if you don't let me go this minute, I'm going to skewer your sweet longings on Tyler's letter opener and feed them to the fish, you . . ." Erin finished with a string of names that nearly choked the gentleman pressing against her and sent him back in a bounding retreat.

"My word, such . . . such filth!" he expelled in repudiation. "I will not tolerate such rebellion!"

"Well if you don't keep your hands to yourself, you better get used to it!" Erin challenged, picking up the letter opener and balancing it in her hand. "And this!" she added, taking a jab at the blustering spectacled man. Sturgis hopped backward. "Go on, git!" A second jab nearly catching the loop of his watch chain, Roderick Sturgis covered his chest with his papers and backed to the door as Erin circled him, eyes blazing. As his hand fumbled on the knob, she raised the silver blade to her forehead in a mock salute and curtsied with her free hand. "Until tomorrow, Sturgis."

The moment the door closed, Erin slammed the letter opener down on Tyler's desk and stared at it. Its polished edges would barely cut butter and the fancy engravings hardly gave it a lethal appearance, but it had scared the living daylights out of Roderick Sturgis! A mischievous glint lightened in her eyes and her mouth turned up in a smile. She'd bet that four-eyed weasel would think twice before grabbing her again. Longings her foot!

The bout with her tutor having shaken the sleepiness that had ended her studies in the first place, Erin picked up the book she'd been reading and, walking over to the wide berth under the open portal, flipped through it until she found her place. The very idea that Sturgis thought her Kate was as absurd as him imagining himself a Petrucchio!

The cool air sweeping in through the window toyed with Erin's hair which Anita had delightedly tied up with an apricot ribbon to match the second of the dresses Mrs. Brady had made her. From time to time, Erin shifted on the wide bed and refluffed the pillows at her back to help her remain upright. But in spite of her efforts, the hum of the engines and the vibration of the deck slowly faded to a dull drone and soon it became difficult to focus on the words of the book sliding down on her lap.

When Jackson Tyler stepped into his cabin, he was startled to see the sleeping girl on his bed. For a moment, the sight of her angelic face in repose and the ruffles that had hiked up to reveal the lace of her petticoats and delicately stockinged calves made him forget his anger with his new charge over the outrageous behavior during her lessons that had been reported to him. He contemplated the wine-red lips quirked in a dreamy smile, wondering that something that held such sweet promise could scald a man's ears to a fare-thee-well. Or that such delicately boned hands, in spite of their stubby bitten nails, could wield a letter opener with such ferocity that Roderick Sturgis was reduced to stammering in his attempt to disclose the girl's horrible behavior.

Jackson shook himself. Damnation, she had promised to study, and no matter how innocent she looked, he knew from firsthand experience she was a hellion. He'd warned Sturgis of that ahead of time, so the fact that the girl rebelled against finishing her studies and drove him to use bodily force to control her shouldn't have come as any shock to the man. That was one of the reasons Jackson hired Sturgis over the tight-lipped old maid who found it necessary to correct his speech during the interview. But then, he supposed the mild-mannered professor of arts was unaccustomed to dealing with young ladies of Erin's mettle. Jackson had never struck a woman in his life, but by thunder, Erin Devareau would knuckle under if he had to beat her daily and use every bar of soap on the vessel!

But the hand that reached out to jerk her into wakefulness checked itself as the girl on the bed slid even further down and turned on her side to face him with a soft sigh and an unwittingly sultry purse of her lips that quickened his pulses almost as much as the sight of her uncorseted breasts mounded at the ruffled edge of her neckline. Like a wild rose begging to be plucked and full of dangerous thorns.

Stung by the shameful direction of his thoughts and the hot animal reaction that leapt to life within his trousers, Jackson swore beneath his breath and yanked the unsuspecting girl into wakefulness with a rough shake.

Green eyes flew wide open in startled confusion and Erin started to struggle until she recognized her assailant. "Tyler!"

"I have just received a full report on your abhorrent behavior concerning Mr. Sturgis and I want you to know that I will not stand for it, Erin!" Shocked that Roderick Sturgis would dare tell Jackson Tyler about what had happened between them, Erin simply stared up into the hot steel of the gaze boring through her. "Well, haven't you anything to say for yourself?"

Erin's head snapped back sharply with the rough shake of her shoulders. What the hell was he mad at her for? She wasn't the one who started it! "He deserved every bit of it and I ain't takin' back a thing I said!"

"When are you going to learn, Erin? Do I have to use every bar of soap on the ship?" Jackson boomed in frustration. His arm slipping around her waist, he upended her before she could pull away.

Arms and legs flailing helplessly in midair, Erin

hung in the sling of his arm, screaming to the top of her voice. "He called me Kate! He grabbed me and pushed me against the door and . . . arrgh!" Erin shuddered as a bar of soap was thrust into her mouth without mercy.

"To keep you from leaving your studies prematurely," Jackson grunted, "for which he received a barrage of swearing that would shame a roustabout on Silver Street!"

"That's . . ." Erin spat the pieces of soap out on the floor, "a lie!"

"I am going to do this every day, Erin, and every night, if I have to, but so help me you are going to be a lady, do you understand!"

Shrieking with the loud slap that landed across her bustled buttocks, Erin caught on the edge of the washstand as Jackson let her go and pulled herself to her feet. Nostrils flaring with unrequited outrage, she glared up at her antagonist when, in the corner of her eye, she caught a glimpse of the china white pitcher that had replaced the hand-painted one she'd broken earlier.

"Oh no you don't!" Jackson vowed. He grabbed up the set, bowl and all, and raised it over his head.

Angered beyond the point of reason, Erin dropped her gaze below the silver buckle of his belt and drew back her foot with a menacing growl. Jackson's right hand dropped to block the blow and the pitcher spilled from the bowl, crashing beside them and exploding into shards that flew across the room.

"I hate you!" Erin shrilled, kicking at the shattered pottery spitefully. "You're just as bad as he is! You *are!*"

With all her strength she caught the disgruntled man square in the midriff with her fists, grazing her left on the fancy *T* engraved on his buckle. Pain raced from the bleeding knuckle to her fury-dazed mind and she drew the back of her hand to her mouth instinctively. Crocodile tears spilled over her cheeks as she wailed accusingly, "Y . . . you won't believe me . . . ee . . . !"

The sight of her tears diffused Jackson's temper before it could reach its peak with an unexpected onslaught of guilt. It was the first tears he'd actually seen out of her. All that the girl had been through and it had been him that made her cry. Confounded beyond his comprehension, he took a deep breath and exhaled it slowly to impede the thunder of the blood racing in his temples.

"Erin . . ."

"Don't t . . . touch me!"

Panicked by her overwhelming desire to go into the arms that had just assailed her, Erin turned and fled the room. It was bad enough that he'd seen her cry, but she'd be damned if she'd do it in his embrace!

"Erin!" The door slammed in his face as he reached it and the bolt slid into place so that, when he turned the knob, it would not permit him entrance. "Erin!" He banged on the door, but the solid brass hardware mounted on strong mahogany would not give. "Erin, if you don't open this door, so help me, I'll keep you locked up until morning without supper!"

He pressed his ear to the door, but all he could hear were little hiccuping sounds, smothered by a blanket or her pillow, he guessed. A groan of frustration hung in his throat. It felt like his insides were being twisted by each one. Like a sudden bolt of lightning, it came to him that a master key to all the staterooms was in his desk. Jackson rushed over the broken pitcher to fetch it. Leaving the bowl sitting on the edge, he quickly stepped into the hall. However, as he slipped the key into the lock of the small room adjoining his, he heard its secondary bolt slide into place.

This time guilt could not deter the rage that boiled

90

to a breaking point. "All right then, stay there! Maybe by morning you'll change your tune!" For a moment he contemplated kicking in the door, but the sound of the door opening across the corridor stopped him.

"Jackson, is everything all right, darling?"

Jackson didn't speak to Gina Allen at first. He was so furious with his helplessness to control his ward that he couldn't. "Everything is just fine!" he minced out sharply.

Recognizing a mood that was best left unquestioned, Gina merely smiled and waved her jeweled fingers at him. "Then I'll just go back to my little nap. Tah, tah, love!"

Damn her stubborn hide! Jackson fumed, Gina already forgotten as he sank into the chair behind his desk in the privacy of his quarters. He'd seen jackasses easier to reason with! His temper flaring again, he knocked the bowl off his desk with his hand and sent it crashing to the floor. He'd starve her out, if he had to, but he would gain the upper hand!

With one last glance at the door that vexed him as much as the girl behind it, Jackson jumped up from the chair and stalked to his own access to the corridor. A couple of rounds around the texas and a good stiff bourbon and he might be fit company for the formal supper hour approaching. Just as long as he didn't have to deal with Erin Devareau!

In the dimly lit cabin, Erin waited until she heard the dinner bell ring and the shuffle of passengers to the dining room before she lifted her head from the pillow she'd soaked with her tears and got up. She didn't want any supper anyway! Her head hurt from all that crying, she thought grudgingly. Besides, she doubted she could stomach sitting at the same table with Jackson Tyler. She wished he had hit her. It would have been easier than dealing with the emotional blow he had dealt her . . . the fact that he believed Roderick Sturgis over her.

It wasn't fair! She wanted to be a lady. It felt wonderful the way Tyler had looked at her from time to time across the table last night. She'd been unnerved, but he'd made her feel at ease. And it was like they'd shared a little secret when they'd talked about her mother and the house with the roses.

What would he tell her grandmother, Erin wondered suddenly. Oh, Erin, this is a fine set of circumstances you're in! She hopped up and walked to the door. The bolt clicked as she slid it back to open the passage to the larger stateroom.

One look at the broken pottery scattered from one side of the cabin to the other and Erin groaned. She wouldn't have been so angry if he'd only listened to her. She stooped down and began to clean up the mess methodically. At least Hannah wouldn't have it to contend with, she thought when the leather-monogrammed wastebasket under the desk was full. And if it took putting up with her tutor every afternoon to be a lady, Erin supposed she could try to ignore Sturgis's hot breath and busy hands.

But she didn't want Tyler to think it was his bullish behavior that made her give in to his wishes. That in mind, Erin pulled up the chair to the desk and proceeded to write the first of two letters, one to Jackson Tyler and the one she had to do for her composition and grammar. The one to her guardian, she placed in the center of the polished wooden desktop so that he could not miss it. The other, she folded and placed on top of her book in the corner.

She knew that she was supposed to have finished the act she was reading, but by the time she had penned the letters, her head was hurting so badly that it was difficult to read the fine print of the book. First thing in the morning, she'd breeze right through it, she promised herself as she trekked back to her own room.

It was hot in the tiny enclosure and by the time she'd bathed and climbed into bed, a thin film of perspiration caused her cotton chemise to cling to her skin. Although there were louvers in the bottom of her door for ventilation, she felt as if she were going to smother, so she kicked the sheet off her feet and tried to be still. That's what her mother had always told her to do when she complained of the hot humid Mississippi nights. And then she would say something funny and the two of them would giggle like schoolgirls.

Erin seized her lip with her teeth, caught unawares by the nostalgic memory that, until now, she hadn't even realized was one. She hated this grief that sneaked up on her and caught her unexpectedly. She closed her eyes and exhaled shakily. Bejesus, would her eyes never dry up for good?

It was nearly sunup when Jackson returned to his stateroom. He had finished the better part of a bottle of bourbon and lost fifty dollars to John Davenport at the blackjack table, which hadn't helped to improve his humor any more than the censoring manner in which his partner had acted all night. But for Thomas Allen's presence and that of a salesman from Pittsburgh, he'd have told the man to keep his opinions to himself, even if John hadn't actually said anything. He supposed he should have been grateful that Rosie O'Rourke wasn't there as well, for her attitude toward him was no less condemning.

Erin had certainly made an impression on the old woman, he mused, slipping off his jacket and vest and dropping them on the chair of his desk. As he did, a slip of paper traveled to its edge. Reacting instinctively, Jackson caught it and started to put it back when it dawned on him that the remains of the bowl and pitcher had been cleared. Funny, Hannah didn't usually come to his room except in the morning at his specific request . . . and he hadn't mentioned anything about the mess to anyone. In fact, he'd tried to forget about it *and* Erin Devareau for a little while.

It was then that he saw his name neatly penned on the paper in his hand. Bemused, he opened it to see whom it was from and grunted in surprise when he saw the name of his ward in an astonishingly legible and feminine script. By all the saints, what other surprises lurked behind those haunting green eyes that had plagued him to the point that he had been unable to keep his mind on his game!

"Dear Tyler," it read. He'd have to break her of calling people by their last name like a roustabout with his cronies, Jackson mused, a mild humor at the address still managing to put a smile on his face.

"Don't think I am writing this missive because you saw fit to believe me a liar and physically abuse me with soap and your hard-hitting hand. I am not sorry for what I said or did to Mr. Sturgis.

"What I am sorry for is not showing my appreciation for the way you have obliged my mother's last wishes and given me a chance to better myself. I know you don't like me. I don't fit in well with your kind of people, even with the pretty dresses you gave me. My mother taught me how to act and speak properly, but I guess spending so much time with Cready and the people at Under the Hill has caused me to pick up some bad habits that I have to think about very hard in order to break.

"I suppose what I am saying is that I promise to do my best to lose them and act more like Mama wanted me to. I think that's what you're after anyway and it's the only way, besides working with Hannah, that I know to pay you back. In the meantime, I will try to work with Mr. Sturgis. Sincerely, Erin Devareau. P.S. Are those packages under the desk the necessaries you bought me?''

Jackson laughed out loud. It was getting harder and harder to stay angry with the precocious girl in the next room. Right now he wanted to scoop her up and give her the presents he had had Gina help pick out for her. Instead he perched on the edge of the desk and, curiosity getting the best of him, retrieved a second paper folded on top of one of the works of Shakespeare. It was another letter, but unlike the first, it was addressed to Petrucchio.

So that's what she was studying. Suddenly her accusation of her tutor calling her Kate made sense. Well, there was a similarity, he agreed readily enough, going on to scan the equally neatly penned lines.

Dear Petrucchio,

I think you are too hard on Kate. She uses her temper to hide the fact that she is lonely and unloved. All her father and sister can think about is their own happiness, not hers. I know what it feels like to be kicked out of your own family home and it hurts a lot; and when you're hurt, you get angry.

Taking her food away is stupid. She's too afraid of what you'll do next to be hungry and if she does get hungry, she'll only feel meaner. Kindness and love are the answers to your problems. You have to earn her trust and you won't do that by making bets on a person's heart and bullying her around.

As for your own bad temper, maybe a night with one of Maddie Haddie's girls could take some of the starch out of your britches and improve it. At least that's what my Aunt Lil says.

Best regards,
Erin Devareau

Jackson carefully refolded the letter and put it back on the book, a thoughtful expression dominating his finely chiseled features. Inadvertently his eyes shifted to the door separating him from his increasingly complex ward. Without even consciously making a decision, he crossed to it and tried the handle. When it gave, he hesitated uncertainly. Woman or child? he wondered, struggling with propriety.

Drawn into the room without settling the question, Jackson focused his eyes in the dark on the girl curled in a ball on her side. How could one peculiar creature endear itself to so many in such a short time? Davenport was acting like an enraged father toward him and that eccentric old woman was nearly apoplectic when the girl didn't come to dinner. Then there was the crew. The girls adored her, taking to her like little mother hens, and Hannah had nothing but praise for her work. Even the men in the pilot house asked for her if she didn't show up there at least once during the day.

It seemed that he was the only one for whom she saved her less than savory side for. Was he too harsh? A scowl darkened his brow. Thunderation, it wasn't too much to expect honesty and gentile speech from those lips, he thought, unaware at first that he'd been considering them at all as he rose to his own defense. They could produce the most perfect, all too kissable pout.

A curse surfaced among his thoughts as he caught the direction of his thoughts and steered them away purposefully. God in heaven, she was only eighteen! And he was her guardian, not her appointed seducer!

Unaccustomed to such self-reproach, Jackson re-treated to his roomier quarters without a backward glance.

Maybe Petrucchio wasn't the only one in need of a night at Maddie Haddie's, he mused, trying to ignore a more primitive reaction that plagued him even more than his conscience. In a naive sort of way, he had to admit that Erin did have a rather basic understanding of human nature. He stripped off the remainder of his clothing and fell across his neatly turned-back bed, only to rise up on his elbow in surprise. Now who the hell had been . . .

Instantly the image of the girl in the next room came to his mind, as clearly as though he still stood at the foot of her bunk. Although he had not been conscious of it at the time, he had not failed to notice the way the thin cotton of her chemise clung damply to firm and ripe breasts and pulled tightly across her waist, emphasizing feminine curves that begged to be traced with adoring hands. Jackson closed his eyes and swallowed dryly, attempting to banish, not just the image, but all thought of Erin Devareau. It was becoming increasingly clear that he was not as immune to the waif as he would prefer.

# Chapter Seven

The loud shriek of the steam whistle announced the departure of the steamboat from the Delta "O" dock, giving more than one of the ladies strolling along the promenade a start. Erin, accustomed to comings and goings of the vessel, grinned as she finished with her hair and replaced the silver brush in the small chest next to her bed. She would never tire of that sound. Someday, with luck, she'd be the one to give the order to sound the whistle. The scuffle of feet in the corridor reminding her of the hour, Erin pinched her cheeks and hurried out of her cabin, leaving the door to slam behind her.

Many of the passengers who had boarded in New Orleans were already in the dining room when Erin arrived. One of the stewards had seated Marie Asante in her customary chair and was engaged in a flirtatious conversation with the woman as John Davenport held out Erin's chair. With a rustle of taffeta, Gina Allen made a grand entrance on Jackson Tyler's arm and took her place of royalty at the head of the table with her king.

Erin observed the way those silver eyes that held mostly contempt for her lit in amusement at something the young woman said and unconsciously sighed.

"He's actually bored," a sympathetic voice whispered in her ear. Erin cut a sideways glance at John Davenport, unaware that he'd read a thought she hadn't even acknowledged. Yes, it did bother her the way Gina Allen fawned over Jackson and the fact that it seemed to please him immensely. "Look at the way he's toying with the silverware."

Did he do the same thing the night they'd dined together in his apartment, Erin mused, shaking the question from her mind as soon as she realized she was considering it. It didn't matter two hoots to her whether she bored him or not. She merely intended to please him as best she could in repayment for his taking her in.

She managed a conspiratory grin and concentrated on her meal. She really liked John Davenport. During the past few days aboard the *Delta Moon*, she, her grandmother, and her guardian's partner had become a trio frequently found together laughing and enjoying each other's company. He delighted Rosie by taking them to the casino, a place off limits to her as a younger woman accompanying her husband, and taught them some gambling tricks, much to Jackson's irritation. While she might be having trouble with her guardian, the rest of riverboat life was suiting her well enough not to let the likes of Gina Allen spoil her good time.

As usual the talk turned to cotton and Jackson stopped playing with the silver. The next time the *Delta Moon* made her way downriver she would be loaded with the first cotton crop. There would be no room for strolling the decks, for every inch of cargo space would be filled. Nor would there be a scenic view. Portholes, for the most part, would be covered with the southern gold. From New Orleans the cotton would head north to the textile factories and the boat would return downriver with drygoods, barrels of meat, salt, apples, cornmeal . . . staples of every home. The trips would continue until the cotton fields were exhausted and then the excursion season would be upon them.

Erin listened with awe as Marie Asante, joined by the Allens and others at the table, recounted some of the trips she and her husband had made upriver. It was as if the social season moved onto the river with a brief stopover in New Orleans for the Mardi Gras. She had thought the small band that played nightly in the grand salon had been impressive, but the splendid descriptions that the passengers embellished made her initial riverboat travel seem drab.

And New Orleans must be the most exciting city in the world at Mardi Gras! Everyone, save her, had been there during the spectacular celebration and each had at least one story to tell. Clinging to every word, her eyes aglow with the glorious visions Gina Allen painted of last year's parade, Erin was mesmerized.

"Of course, I had to have new jewels to match my gown, so Uncle bought me an exquisite sapphire broach and matching ear dangles to set it off. You remember, Jackson? You said my eyes shamed them. I've never forgotten that," she cajoled coyly, slipping bejeweled fingers over Jackson's arm.

"How romantic," Myra Allen sighed.

"The one you're missing, Miss Allen?" Roderick Sturgis spoke up, breaking a long period of silence at Erin's elbow.

As if reminded, Gina Allen squealed. "Indeed, sir! Mr. Sturgis was good enough to help me search our coach when I discovered it missing from my dress." Frowning, she went on. "I couldn't find it in my room either. Jackson, you must ask the maids if they've found it . . . if that would do any good," she derisively added as an afterthought.

Erin bristled at the insult. Although Gina did not actually say the maids would keep such a find, she

100

certainly insinuated as much. "Hannah and her girls would certainly have reported finding your jewelry if they had done so, Miss Allen. They are very conscientious."

Shocked at the indignation infecting Erin's cheeks and voice, Gina clasped a delicate hand to her chest. "My dear girl, I was merely suggesting . . ."

"More likely you didn't fasten the clasp well and it fell off," Erin went on. "Sometimes . . ." The pressure of a boot on her foot made Erin shoot a startled look at John Davenport where she was able to make out a barely perceptible shake of his head. She let out her breath in exasperation and shrugged. "Why, sometimes we females just get plain ole' careless!" she finished sweetly with a roll of innocent eyes at her mentor.

The tug at the corner of John Davenport's lips was all Erin needed. She'd recovered from her temperamental outburst just like a real lady. Unwittingly, her gaze traveled to the head of the table for additional approval when it clashed with a warning steel one. Now what? She'd backed down, hadn't she? Defiance leaping to the forefront, she turned back to John.

"You know, I remember one time, I lost my mama's locket, the one with my daddy's and my pictures in it. Well, I just knew someone had taken it!" Erin averred, determined to go on in spite of John's grimace. "I suspected everyone who'd been around me that day, all those innocent folks ... . people," she corrected with a darting glance at her tutor, recalling her lecture of the preceding day. Young ladies did not use the word *folks*. "Well, wouldn't you know it! That night when I was preparing to retire to bed, there it was, smack-dab in the middle of my drawers."

"My word!" Myra Allen whispered faintly, her rouged cheeks going pale.

101

"I guess it had slid down my bosom and got hung up . . ."

A loud laugh interrupted Erin, drawing her gaze across the table where Marie Asante's brimmed with humor. "Erin, dear," she managed, "while there is most likely no woman at this table that has not lost a bauble in some similar way, I fear it is the sort of confession we save for feminine ears only."

Erin's face challenged the deep red of the burgundy served with the flaming beef dish that had been the main course as she shrank into submission under her grandmother's gentle reminder. Her gaze flitted around the table, discovering every eye upon her. Summoning her nerve, in spite of her urge to get up and run, she addressed them.

"Forgive me," she said quietly. "I didn't mean to embarrass the menfolk." Although it was beyond her that any male at the table didn't know the type of garments that lurked under the voluminous fashions ladies wore, especially if they'd ever spent a late night in a saloon. She'd seen more than one night end in Natchez Under the Hill with some of the girls parading about in their corsets and stockings . . . some in even less!

To her surprise, Roderick Sturgis seized her hand and lifted it to his lips gallantly. "Such a gracious apology can not help but be accepted, Miss Erin."

"Jackson, I vow I feel faint. I am hardly accustomed to such indelicacy. Would you mind escorting me for a walk around the deck to clear my head?" Gina Allen mopped her brow with the handkerchief Jackson valiantly provided.

For a moment, Erin thought Jackson would refuse, for his irate attention was fixed on her. But after a piercing look that told her her apology had not been accepted by all at the table, he leapt to his feet and ushered the blond-haired woman through

the double mahogany doors leading to the promenade.

Dinner over, the men retired to the gambling
parlor, save John Davenport who insisted on accompanying Erin and her grandmother back to her
grandmother's room. When Erin attempted to apologize again for her melodramatic imitation of Gina
Allen, the gambler brushed the incident aside.

"The woman got exactly what she deserved," he
told her candidly.

"And our Erin is not as practiced in the feline
arena as this Allen girl," Marie Asante observed
matter-of-factly. She reached out and squeezed Erin's
hand. "But we shall work on that, shan't we, my girl?
After all, that pompous schoolmaster of yours doesn't
know everything a young woman should know . . .
and believe me, women like Gina Allen can be
handled effectively and in a ladylike manner."

The evening passed quickly, as did all the times
Erin spent in Marie Asante's company. Like trea-
sures, she tucked away the anecdotes and pieces of
advice the older woman passed on to her in a mind
starved for such things. Even Cready had had a
grandmother to take care of him and tell him stories
when he was little. How Erin had envied him,
although she'd never admitted it to her mother. She
wouldn't have made Giselle feel inadequate for the
world. Her mother had worried enough that she
didn't have a father's strong influence.

The musicians had once again put aside their
instruments when Erin left her grandmother for the
night. As much as they both were enjoying each
other's company, the older woman had finally
pleaded exhaustion, bringing an end to the evening.
Erin promised to send a girl up from the kitchen with
her grandmother's customary cup of tea before
retirement.

"Oh, and do return this spoon to the kitchen for

me, dear," Marie asked, picking up the item from the dressing table. "I forgot to put it back on my tray this morning when I had breakfast in my room."

Erin took the spoon and slipped it into her pocket. "Of course, Grandma." Bending over, she gave the old woman an affectionate peck on the cheek. "G'night, Rosie."

Marie's eyes twinkled. "G'night, child," she mocked fondly.

Erin had just reached the companionway enclosing the steps leading to the deck below when a voice halted her in midstep.

"And just where do you think you're going, young lady?"

Erin turned and grinned as John Davenport caught up with her. "To the kitchen to see to Rosie's tea."

"I'm on my way there. If you'd like, I can have it sent up," John offered generously. "Besides, the men on the bridge were asking for you."

Erin's face brightened. "Really?"

"To quote one of them, 'They just don't know things are right until Miss Erin checks in and tells them so.'"

"Well," Erin began sheepishly, "I wouldn't want to keep them in suspense. G'night, John."

"Good night, princess."

Erin loved visiting the bridge. Each time she did, she left with a treat, this time leftover cake from the grand salon's dessert menu, and another tidbit of knowledge that intrigued her. As she meandered along the deck, she continued to stare at the crescent moon, tilted down, like a tipped cup. It would not hold water, she'd been told, which meant that rain was in the making for tomorrow's weather. They'd called it a wet moon.

Preoccupied with the upcoming weather and the perturbing possibilities it presented for a low-lying riverfront community like Natchez Under the Hill, their next stop, she hardly noticed the couple embraced in the companionway until she was upon them. Her startled gasp gave her away first, making it impossible to retreat unseen.

"Erin," Jackson Tyler acknowledged tightly as he drew away from Gina Allen.

"I was just going to bed . . . to retire," she corrected quickly. There were so many expressions young ladies were not supposed to use, that it was a wonder they could express themselves at all, she thought in frustration. "Good night."

Avoiding the superior gaze cast her way by the fair-haired woman hovering close at Jackson's side, Erin stepped through the door. No doubt they were breathing heavy again before she even slipped the bolt shut, she mused in disgust. Her mother had once told her ladies didn't kiss men like that unless they were married to them. Yet Gina Allen was supposed to be a lady. With a shrug, Erin dismissed them both and hurriedly prepared for bed.

When Jackson's door closed, it crossed her mind that he'd not entered the cabin alone. So it came as a surprise when she heard his knock on the door adjoining her room. Gathering the light sheet to her chest, she sat up and bade him enter, a frown creasing her smooth brow. Well, this was it. Here would come the lecture about discussing drawers in mixed company.

Jackson stepped inside and allowed his eyes to adjust to the lamplight filtering in from his suite, until the girl sitting on the bed came into clear focus. How could she appear so innocent, he wondered again, meeting her curious gaze evenly. Damn her, if he hadn't taken the broach from under her mattress and convinced Gina that he'd found it in the hall . . . Was there no end to the trouble that seemed to follow Erin Devareau?

"I have saved your lovely hide tonight, Erin, but I will not do it again," he averred strongly. He captured the delicate taper of her chin in the cup of his hand. "It is one thing to pilfer silver from me, but stealing from my passengers is unthinkable . . . do you understand?"

Erin shook her head in bewilderment. Was he drinking, she wondered. "I don't know what you're talking about."

Jackson's lips thinned. Obviously, she hadn't missed the broach. "Gina's broach, Erin. I took it from under your mattress and returned it to her. Fortunately for you, she thinks she misplaced it."

"What?" Erin was incredulous. "Why I . . ." she sputtered. "I never took her broach and I sure as hell have not been pilfering your damned silver!"

Before she knew what he was about, Jackson snatched her off the bed and deposited her in a heap at his feet. "It doesn't surprise me that lying remains one of your many vices," he grunted, seizing the dress she'd laid on the foot of the bed and slinging it at her, "but you should at least learn when it is . . ."

The sudden ring of the spoon she was supposed to have taken back to the kitchen for her grandmother caused him to break off abruptly. Erin groaned inwardly, well aware of what he was thinking as he reached down and picked it up. No thundercloud she'd ever seen was as ominous as his face.

"Adding to the collection, are we? What is this, your warped version of a hope chest?" With that, he yanked the mattress off the bed and sent the silverware hidden under it scattering.

Speechless, Erin picked up a fork that landed in her lap. "How did these get here?" she wondered incredulously, unaware that she'd voiced her thoughts until Jackson sneered.

"How indeed!"

Erin flushed angrily. "Why would I want to steal

106

your bloody silver? Bejesus, if I did, I sure as the devil wouldn't hide it in such an obvious place where a maid could . . ." Color left her cheeks as she returned her shaken gaze to him. "Does Hannah think I stole this?"

Her chest twisted painfully at Jackson's nod and she sank against her heels. It was bad enough that Jackson thought her a thief, but Hannah . . . Erin knew a setup when she saw one and she had been set up royally. But who . . . and why? She swallowed the blade of despair that rose in her throat.

"But she thinks you only did it because you still feel threatened about your future . . . out of habit, so to speak."

Turning her head away from the light that betrayed her wounded feelings, Erin blinked madly to rid her eyes of the tears that welled there. Don't cry. Not now. Not in front of him. She inhaled deeply and spoke through clenched teeth. "And what do you think, Tyler?"

To her astonishment, a heavy sigh escaped behind her, instead of the angry outburst she anticipated. "I don't know, Erin. I don't know why you feel that you have to do something like this, now that you are my ward. My God, girl, I've tried to provide everything a young woman needs!"

"I didn't do it." She raised her gaze to the assessing silver one, but saw no sign of the belief she so wanted to be there.

"Damn it, Erin, if you'll just tell the truth, for once in your despicable life . . ."

The words only added insult to injury. Erin sprang to her feet like a cat and lashed out against his cheek with a resounding slap. "Damn you," she swore brokenly. "If I am so despicable, then put me off in Natchez and you'll never see me again! I don't need you and I don't need your damned silver!"

The stinging of his cheek urged revenge against

this hellcat, but the unbridled passion swimming in her eyes reached beyond with an equally primitive provocation. He seized her arms roughly and heard himself retort in kind. "Don't think that would not be tempting!" But letting Erin Devareau out of his clutches was the farthest thing from his mind at the moment. He'd never seen fury in such tantalizing form before. It would put even Gina's infamous tantrums to shame!

For the longest moment, silver battled with emerald. The thin strap of her nightdress slid off one shoulder with the rough shake he had given her, threatening to slip over the peak of a ripe breast that held it precariously in place. Beneath his hands, the satin of her flesh registered its warmth and began to spread through him, serving to fan more, this ageless fever was gaining momentum.

In the dim lighting, Erin was distracted by the strange fire that leapt into her tormentor's gaze, making his anger seem small in comparison. Something was changing between them, even as she watched. Inadvertently, she moistened her suddenly dry lips in anticipation. Of what, she wasn't certain. She only knew that some other force had entered the scene, a strongly infectious one that sent her pulses racing unaccountably.

The hands on her shoulders tightened, drawing her close until the silver gaze devoured her every thought, leaving her helpless to resist the lips that closed over hers possessively. Suddenly the suppleness of her body was molded against his lean and powerful one, held there by arms that banded around her. Her heart felt as if it would burst from her chest to get at the one thunderously beckoning to it from beyond the muscled flesh that separated them and her head began to swim with the heady force of the tongue plundering her mouth. Just when she thought she'd lose consciousness from the bombardment of sensations registering from all quarters of her body, he granted her reprieve.

The break in the consuming contact brought a rush of reason cutting through the heady reaction and restoring a semblance of strength to her knees. With it came a panic that made her shove against the chest that had so disconcertingly tantalized the softness of her breasts with its sheer masculinity.

"I vow, I feel faint!" she managed, grasping at an excuse to get away from this bizarre punishment. Her hand flying, palm up, to her forehead, Erin dropped back against her pillow, her face turned away to hide her confusion. It was a punishment, wasn't it? He was angry, wasn't he? At least with the bloody soap, she'd known!

It was an obvious ploy, but it worked. Jackson found himself struggling with a confounding mixture of amusement and desire. *Under other circumstances,* he mused, his eyes raking over the feminine form so provocatively displayed by the thin twisted nightdress. He checked his train of thought abruptly. God in heaven, what was this incorrigible, yet bewitching creature doing to him?

"I really do," Erin repeated with an edge of desperation, peering out from under her upturned palm to see if he was going to go. Actually, her threat was not far from the truth. She'd never dreamed a kiss could knock the knees out from under her like that! No wonder Gina Allen was clinging to him like molasses on a hotcake.

Or was she being punished? No. The woman was far too smug and satisfied to be feeling what she was feeling, Erin decided uncertainly.

Jackson drew himself up to his full height, unable to give vent to his humor due to his own quandary of potent emotion. "Very well, Erin. We'll continue this discussion another time, but I will not leave until you promise me that you will not steal another thing.''

Erin nodded, desperate to be alone to sort out what had just happened. "All right, I promise.'' She wanted to add, "but I didn't do it,'' except that further argument might prolong her guardian's stay, and at the moment that was the last thing she wanted.

# Chapter Eight

Erin smoothed out the skirt of her blue dress nervously as the gangplank was lowered near the wharfboat—the same one that, a few weeks ago, she had abandoned to take to the water in order to escape Black Jack Tyler's ire. Had it only been a couple of weeks? She scanned the familiar docks and main street shooting up to the bluff city of mansions and finer establishments. It looked . . . different.

"There ye go, Miss Erin," one of the deckhands called out obligingly when the gangway was secure. "Now you be careful. This ain't a place for a lady to be wanderin' about alone."

Erin smiled at the crewman's assessment of her. A lady! Perhaps Tyler's obstinance and Sturgis's lessons were making a difference in her. She hurried ashore, scanning the sudden scurry of roustabouts and locals selling their wares for Cready. She could just see his face when he saw her all gussied up in a dress. Like as not, he'd swallow that tongue he was always sticking out at her.

The more familiar faces she passed, faces belonging to people whom she'd grown up around, the more convinced she was that she had indeed changed. Why, no one knew her! Not even old Annie, the black woman who often spared one of her fresh baked pralines for her. This time Erin had paid with coin, but instead of identifying herself, she went on silently.

Perhaps it was just as well no one did know her, considering what she had in mind. If anyone could pull off making her grandmother think that she and her mother had lived the relatively normal, if meager, life she had described to the woman, Cready and his folks could. She just had to speak to them first, prepare them for possible questions.

Maybe Molly MacCready could even stir up a tasty stew for supper. Some plain cooking would be welcome after all those wine-soaked French dishes served in the main dining salon and maybe settle her grandmother's stomach, since the woman had been complaining of a grippe when Erin had checked in on her that morning before going about her chores.

Erin jingled the coins in her purse, only enough to reassure herself that she had enough to buy the beef from the butcher and not attract the attention of anyone desperate enough to snatch a lady's bag. Again her lips twitched. Yes! Just as soon as she found Cready, they'd go get the beef, lean chunks as well as the necks they usually had to bargain for, and surprise Miss Molly. She'd help clean up the shack a bit and then go back to the ship to propose a dinner at the house of the family who helped Giselle raise her.

With a spring in her walk, Erin gingerly crossed the narrow boardwalk that ran in front of the saloon and stepped up into the building under a sign boasting FIVE FEATHERS WHISKEY. Since it was early in the day, there were only a few customers in the establishment and one or two of Horsey's girls looking somewhat worse for the night before gathered around a table strewn with cards. Behind the bar, Mac MacCready took inventory of the cigars stored in a glass jar with a wooden lid he kept behind the counter.

"Mac?" Everyone called Mac MacCready "Mac" and Erin was no exception.

"Damn it, gal, can't ye see I'm in the midst of my countin'?" Bushy black eyebrows lifted and then narrowed suspiciously as the bartender raised his gaze to that of the young lady reflected in the beveled glass mirror behind the bar.

A giggle escaped Erin and, in spite of her resolve to let him guess who she was, she admitted, "It's me, Erin!"

"Well so it is!" the man exclaimed, turning to examine her directly, not trusting the mirror. "And big as billy be damned in that fine dress! The spittin' image of your dear mother, God rest her soul." Although Erin had never known Mac MacCready to set foot in a church, he crossed himself like the holiest of parishioners and then raised his voice. "Cready! Cready, ye half-wit, come see who's here to visit us!" To make certain the boy in the back room knew he was being paged, the barkeeper struck the polished bar with a powerful fist and bellowed in a voice that shook the clean glasses neatly stacked on a shelf behind him. "Cready!"

Erin wondered who was washing the glasses, now that she was no longer employed at the saloon, but her answer became apparent the moment her childhood companion appeared in the doorway, his rolled-up sleeves and apron soaked.

"For the love of Mike, Pop, me'n the dead at Saint Paul's on the bluff heard ye the first—" Cready broke off and stared through his mop of dingy brown hair at Erin. "Wart?"

For once Erin did not mind acknowledging the name that, a few short weeks ago would have led to the two of them scrapping on the floor. "In the flesh!"

Cready scowled. "Looks like that Tyler didn't go too hard on ya after all."

113

"He's not so bad as I'd heard," she confessed. "Although he can be stubborn."

"Like someone else we know, eh, Pop?"

Erin joined in the shared amusement and slid up on a bar stool, very much at home. "I have so much to tell you!" she exclaimed, her green eyes dancing with excitement. "Got sarsaparilla?" Proudly, she produced enough coin to pay for three. "All around, of course."

Although it was one of her favorite drinks, Erin hardly touched hers as she unfolded the tale of what had happened to her since she last saw her friends. She told of finding her grandmother and, in hushed tones, how the two of them had kept up a charade so that her horrid aunt and uncle couldn't make the old woman go back home. She described her life on the steamboat as being just short of heaven and even gave Sturgis a decent representation. Careful not to alienate her former *family*, she portrayed Jackson as a strict, but fair guardian, for, in truth, she was not certain that she could put into words feelings that ranged from wonderful and warm to the very opposite about the man.

"He's fair enough, I suppose," she ventured slowly, when asked how she liked her guardian. "He's been more than generous to me," she added, lifting the hem of her skirt to show off her fine stockings and delicately crafted slippers.

"And he will be, my dear, until he tires of your freshness, your novelty, so to speak."

Erin's smile faded at the sound of Coleman Horsey's deep southern drawl. When she was little, she used to think he almost purred like the kittens she often played with in the alley behind the stores and establishments along the lower end of Silver Street. What was he doing in the saloon this early in the day, she wondered grudgingly. He'd never meet her mother to go over business until after the noon hour,

114

lest he have to rise from the bed of one of his trollops before his night's sleep was out.

She turned with a cool appraisal. He hadn't been up long. The nick on his cheek from a recent shave had only just clotted and he smelled of the toilet water he used almost as heavily as his girls used their cheap perfume. His toupee, a good shade darker than the thinning gold hair fringing it, was parted as it had been for as long as she could remember and the mole above the right handlebar of his mustache rose as he grinned at her.

It was the same yellow smile he always had for her, patronizing. Before it had been to placate her mother, who threatened to have him killed if he ever touched one hair of Erin's head. Erin would never forget it. It was one of the few times she'd seen Giselle Devareau stand up to the man.

Erin had just scrubbed the floor of the shack that she and her mother worked to keep as clean and cozy as their circumstances would allow and he had tracked in mud. She had held her tongue then, only daring to antagonize her mother's employer with condemning looks. But when his cigar carelessly rolled onto the table and burned a hole in the lace doily she and her mother had just finished, she could stand it no more.

Upon calling him exactly what she thought him, a vulgar term she'd learned from working in the back of the saloon, she had been sent sprawling across the room with an unrestrained backhand. Then Giselle was upon the man like a vengeful fury, taking him completely by surprise. Erin had first thought he was going to kill them both, but instead, he ordered her to Molly MacCready's so that he could speak to her mother alone. She would never have gone, but for her mother's strained insistence.

"Unlike you, Horsey, Tyler is a gentleman." Erin intended to insult him, but his grin widened instead of waning.

"You've inherited your mother's quick tongue as well as her beauty, Erin." He approached her and, before she knew what he was about, lifted her hand to his lips. "Let us hope, you've her wit as well. I've a proposition for you."

Erin snatched her hand back and wiped it against her skirt in obvious distaste as she slid off the stool. "I'm smart enough to know scum when I see it," she declared, meeting his jaundiced gaze squarely and then dismissing him with a proud turn of her head. "I'm going to Mol . . ."

The sudden bite of fingers in the flesh of her arm made her gasp sharply. She swung about, fist drawn, when her gaze clashed unexpectedly with steel gray, sparking with outrage. Her intended curse for Horsey fell away to a startled, "Tyler!"

"Don't you ever leave the ship again without my leave, young lady, and never . . . NEVER set foot again in this place. By God, I ought to turn you over to Horsey, for all the trouble you've been!"

"You just may have to do that, Tyler, whether you want to or not." Erin's struggle stopped instantly, her attention riveted to Coleman Horsey as he reached into his pocket and withdrew a document. "This is what I intended to discuss with you, Erin. Your mother's last will and testament." He unfolded the parchment and held it so that both Erin and Jackson could see it. "It basically says all her belongings are left to me as well as the guardianship of Erin until she reaches the age of twenty-one."

"No!" Erin whispered, suddenly seeking the protection of the man whom, only moments before, she had struggled to escape. "Mama would never do that! She hated you and I hate you!"

"See for yourself, Erin. It's your mother's hand-writing and witnessed by Lil."

Jackson grabbed the paper and scanned it quickly.

He had wondered what in the name of heaven would happen next as he'd begun his search along the docks for his errant charge, for the morning had been straight from a nightmare. It seemed the police were looking for Erin in connection with the disappearance of her grandmother. It didn't take much deduction to guess that Rosie O'Rourke was the missing Marie Asantel. Jackson could have kicked himself for not noticing the resemblance sooner. However, he wanted to confront the two conspirators together, hopefully before the woman's daughter and her husband arrived from their hotel on the bluff. Hence, he'd left John stalling the authorities until he could find his missing charge. And now this!

"As for you, sir, if you will kindly leave the girl and these premises peacefully, I shall not press charges against you for abduction."

"Abduction!" Jackson exclaimed, the current dilemma commandeering his full attention.

"More than one witness saw you dragging this child off to your ship a few weeks ago against her will."

Erin swayed against Jackson as the impact of what the man she'd once sworn to kill was saying struck her full force. Her face, pale as the delicate lace adorning her neckline, turned up to him as if seeking for some reassurance that this could not be. The quicksilver gaze, however, was not for her, but coolly assessing the two men who rose from the table at the snap of Horsey's fingers.

In spite of the impending danger, the irony of the situation struck Jackson. Years ago, in this very saloon, Giselle Devareau had taken a great risk to save his life. Now it was threatened again . . . if he chose to honor her dying request. The difference, he mused, was that now, he was no longer the green youth out of his element. The pearl-handled pistol that was as much a part of his costume as his trousers seemed to appear from nowhere, the click of its hammer stopping Horsey's thugs in their tracks. A cold smile settled on Jackson's lips, speaking of a deadly assurance that was as unsettling as the weapon itself. There were times his less than savory reputation, born of reckless youth and a source of great distress to his mother, came in handy.

"You know that gun can't shoot us all," Horsey remarked, apparently nonplused.

"No, but I'll wager at least two of you will have need of the coroner's services before I give it up. Erin," Jackson snapped to the girl at his side. "Run back to the boat and don't stop until you get there."

Instead of compliance, the crash of a bottle on the edge of the bar defied his order, drawing a darting glance to where Erin held its jagged remains poised in readiness in her hand. Gone was the momentary fear that had managed to stir a protective side of his nature that Jackson did not often recognize and in its place was sheer spitfire. He swore under his breath. "Get out of here!"

Erin shook her head, her heart wedged against the back of her throat. "We're in this together, Tyler. I go when you do."

Horsey's laughter echoed in the thick silence. "Go back to your game, gentlemen," he instructed, his gaze shifting to where Erin hefted the broken bottle neck in her hand threateningly. "It's just a matter of time, my dear, before you return to where you belong. Even now, I think Mr. Tyler is seeing the impossibility of his predicament with you. In the meantime," he smirked, bending over to pick up the document lying at Jackson's feet, "I will proceed through legal channels with this little ace in the hole." He contemplated Erin's free hand, as if considering another show of gallantry, but the sight of the broken bottle remnant in her other hand discouraged him. "Good day, my surprisingly lovely Erin."

118

"I'm not *your* Erin," Erin protested grudgingly. "Or anyone's for that matter," she added emphatically as Jackson, the danger of confrontation having passed for the moment, pried her weapon from her fingers and tossed it aside.

"Don't test me, Erin," he warned, taking her by the arm and ushering her toward the door.

The same cold impassionate tone that had backed down Horsey's henchmen prevented her from objecting. Instead, she called a hurried farewell to the MacCreadys over her shoulder and stumbled out into the street. Besides, Tyler was the lesser of the two evils at the moment. A frown creased her brow as she attempted to keep up with Jackson's impatient stride. Just what was Horsey up to? The two of them couldn't say "spit" without arguing, so surely he didn't expect her to kowtow to him like her mother did. So what did he want?

"You just seem to be in demand today," Jackson replied sarcastically at her elbow, answering the thoughts she'd inadvertently voiced aloud. Although he wondered the same thing. What did Horsey want of Erin besides the obvious . . . and how did he know the nature of the letter Giselle Devareau had sent to him? The MacCreadys, perhaps? "How much do you trust your friends . . . the MacCreadys?" he asked grimly.

Taken back by the unexpected question, Erin shrugged. "Well enough. Why?"

"They didn't come to your rescue back there," Jackson reminded her. "And the young one certainly didn't mind turning you in to save his own skin a couple of weeks ago."

"They have to live under Horsey's thumb," Erin answered defensively. "He can make it mighty miserable for them . . . and Cready was scared out of his wits that night. You said you were going to kill him!" she pointed out dryly. "Of course, now that I know you, I know you were just bluffing."

Erin regretted the words the moment they were out. The cold silver gaze that had backed down two of the meanest men at Under the Hill settled on her, knifing through her innermost thoughts. "Is that so?" There was nothing in Jackson's manner or tone to support her opinion. Erin looked away, her face coloring profusely. Perhaps she'd been premature in her assessment.

The remainder of the short walk to the gangway was spent in silence until Erin came to an abrupt halt, nearly causing her escort to run her over. "I forgot, Tyler! I have to get Rosie some blackberry brandy!"

"You mean your *grandmother?*" At Erin's blank astonishment, he went on. "The reason I discovered you missing this morning, Erin, is because the police visited my office. It seems you've been accused of abducting Marie Asante from her home."

Rallying quickly, Erin protested. "That's not true! Grandma wanted to come with me! They treated her like some old dog penned up to die." A plaintive hand reached for Jackson's arm, betraying her heartfelt fear, not of the authorities, but of losing what she had only just found. "She's my only family left! I had a right to get to know her as her granddaughter." Erin searched futilely for some show of understanding on the handsomely chiseled features considering her—the poker face that accounted for Black Jack Tyler's reputation as a costly opponent at the tables.

"Why the charade?"

One scoundrel certainly could understand the motivation of another! Erin forced an impish grin. "That was Grandma's idea. It was all a part of our adventure. We've had the most fun. She's absolutely wonderful, don't you think?"

Jackson rolled his eyes heavenward, abstaining

from comment as he motioned Erin into the corridor leading to the office where he'd left John Davenport with the authorities. It appeared Erin's penchant for mischief was hereditary!

The office was empty, which meant that, most likely, the Lafons had arrived and that Rosie O'Rourke, or actually, Marie Asante, no doubt was answering for her part in his ward's latest escapade. As they emerged from the stairwell leading to the boiler deck, Jackson took a deep breath and pressed his hand against the small of his reluctant charge's back, crushing the wide feminine bow cinching a petite waist and propelling her forward. The sooner this was over with the Lafons, the better.

Yet, before he could summon a tactful greeting, a woman with a tear-streaked face he recognized as Lydia Lafon, pulled out of her husband's embrace and flew at Erin viciously.

"You selfish little opportunist! You spirited my mother off in her feeble state of health and now you have killed her just as certainly as if you'd thrust a knife deep into her heart!"

"Lydia!" Dr. Lafon protested, dragging the woman away from a stunned and paling Erin.

"What is going on here?" Jackson demanded, turning to the officer standing near the open cabin door.

"We found Mrs. Asante dead in her cabin, apparently of a heart attack," the man informed him grimly. "I don't suppose this would have anything to do with the abrupt disappearance of your charge?"

"She went shopping . . ."

"You're lying!"

Jackson turned in disbelief at the vehement disclaimer to where Erin pointed an accusing finger at Lydia Lafon. "Grandma wanted to go with me! And she's not dead! She's not!"

Panic setting in at the wild accusations being made

at her, Erin shoved past the officer standing in the door of her grandmother's cabin and fled to the bedside of the still blanket-covered figure. They were wrong, she thought fervently, snatching away the coverlet to reveal the familiar face she'd come to adore in the last few weeks. She was just sleeping soundly. Sometimes she had to shake her grandmother two or three times to wake her up.

"Grandma! Wake up!" she whispered brokenly, trying to ignore the deathly pallor of Marie Asante's usually rosy cheeks.

Instead of the soft warmth she'd come to associate with her grandmother, a lifeless cold met her touch, a cold that brought home the finality of the repose on the woman's gentle face. How had this happened? a voice cried out in protest as grim reality numbed Erin's tortured thoughts.

"It was her heart," she heard a matter-of-fact voice declare in the background. "She left without her medicine and her condition was such that she could not cope with the excitement of this travel."

"You and I both know that girl killed her, Paul!" Lydia Lafon spoke up vengefully. Her voice became louder as she entered the cabin. "You killed my mother, you thoughtless little swine! You're just like your mother was, selfish and a slut. Did you really think you could usurp my inheritance by sidling up to an old woman who did not possess all her mental faculties?"

Stung, Erin spun away from the bed to retaliate, but suddenly stopped. The emerald fury in her eyes died long enough for her to gently replace the coverlet, as if trying to protect her grandmother from hearing the horrible lies spawned from her remaining daughter's mouth. When she turned back, the fire had been mastered by ice and her trembling chin was steeled in proud defiance.

Jackson could not help but wonder at the restraint

122

with which she approached the shrieking woman, but stood ready to intercept her should she turn into the hellcat he'd known her to be. If she did, he couldn't blame her. Not the way Lydia Lafon was carrying on.

"*My grandmother*, Mrs. Lafon—you will forgive me if I refrain from calling you Aunt Lydia, won't you, since neither of us are inclined to be fond of one another," she injected haughtily. "My grandmother possessed more of her mental faculties than you gave her credit for. Had you spent more time with her instead of with your high society friends, had you actually sat down and talked with her, instead of putting her out in the garden every day like a house pet, had you taken her on outings, instead of keeping her locked up like a simple invalid, you would have known her for what she really was . . . a wonderful lady with a delightful wit and an infectious zest for life."

Erin's regal manner and impeccable eloquence astounded Lydia Lafon, reducing her objections to a flustered, "How . . . how dare you!"

But Erin did. She met her aunt's indignation with green ice, hard and yet, breathtakingly lovely and full of passion. Man and woman alike were spellbound by the transformation. No longer was she the street waif, intimidated by her highborn relative who took for granted a treasure Erin would have given up a world of fortunes for. "You've had her all your life and treated her like a leftover from your past, something you no longer needed. Well, I was starved for that leftover, lady, and she was starved for my love. Usurp your inheritance? Hah! I wouldn't dream of it! Not if it makes me like you."

"I want her arrested!" Lydia screamed hysterically. "I insist!"

"On what grounds?" Jackson spoke up, slipping a supportive arm about Erin's waist. "I didn't think people could get arrested for telling the truth?"

Erin watched the feathered breast pin heave above the indignant swell of her adversary's chest. "Paul, will you let them address me like that? They're obviously collaborating together to get Mother's . . ."

"Enough, Lydia!" Dr. Paul Lafon's voice thundered, giving Erin a start and silencing his wife instantly. She stared at the shorter of the two, reassessing her opinion of the man who had struck her as being henpecked at first. "It is apparent to me that this young lady, in spite of her brash behavior, meant no harm to your mother. She couldn't have known her grandmother needed her medication."

"But Paul . . ."

"She did not know of your mother's heart condition, Lydia. Surely, even you must acknowledge that!" He turned away from his speechless wife and gave Erin a sympathetic look. "My apologies, Miss Devareau, for my wife's hysterics. In spite of what you might think, she did love her mother and did the best for the woman that she knew how. She feared too much activity would excite your grandmother's ailing heart."

Erin tried to shut out the sudden wail that collapsed the grieving woman into a heap of fashionably gathered skirts on the deck. She could handle the hostility. The resulting anger fortified her against a like grief that threatened to take her over as well. This sympathy from unexpected quarters, however, managed to disarm her. Shoulders that had been squared fell and a single tear thawed to escape the reserve she had managed to hold back. It was wrong, she thought miserably. It was all wrong.

"But it was her stomach that ailed her, not her chest," she protested shakily. She turned to Jackson Tyler. "She sent me for blackberry brandy to settle it. How could she die from the grippe?"

"The grippe?" Dr. Lafon repeated in bewilderment.

124

"She was up all night with the stomach grippe," Erin informed him, her hand moving low over her abdomen in demonstration. "Up until then, it's been all any of us could do to keep up with her, right John?"

John Davenport, who had slipped into the background nodded. "She certainly appeared hail and hearty to all of us . . . even joked when I took her her tea last night."

"*You* went to my mother's room and she an invalid and alone?" Lydia Lafon gasped, nearly fainting again as one of the policemen helped her to her feet. Her face reddened with apoplexy as she added derisively, "A *gambler?* What manner of life did these people reduce my mother to?"

"Sheriff, if you don't mind, I should like to examine my mother-in-law further," Paul Lafon spoke up, ignoring his wife's renewed outrage.

The law officer shrugged with a decidedly relieved expression. "Suits me, sir. If you don't need me any more, me n' my men'll mosey on back to town, since there wasn't no kidnapin' after all. Want me to send for the coroner?"

"That would be appreciated." Dr. Lafon picked up a black bag near the cabin door that until now Erin had not noticed, and turned to eye his loudly sniffling wife. "And perhaps, sir, you would see Mrs. Lafon back to the hotel. I don't think this is the place for her at the moment."

"B . . . but Paul . . ."

"I insist, Lydia. You're overwrought and need your rest."

Erin was certain that the only reason Lydia Lafon left without further protest was that the alternative of remaining in her company was less attractive. Without sparing her departing aunt a second glance, she started for her grandmother's bed after the doctor, only to be restrained by a firm hand.

"I think you've had enough distress without this, Erin," Jackson told her gently, planting himself between the girl and ushering her through the door of the enclosure.

"But I have to know, Tyler," Erin pleaded. "I just couldn't bear it if I caused Grandma to die."

"I promise, I'll tell you as soon as I find out. In the meantime, why don't you let John take you to your cabin."

"Good idea, kid." Davenport slid off the rail and put his arm over Erin's shoulder.

"You'll tell me the truth?" Erin asked of Jackson, her eyes full of an anguish he could feel.

The truth was, Jackson would rather take Erin to the cabin himself. He wanted to hold her and tell her she wasn't to blame for Marie Asante's death. He wanted to ease her misery with a compulsion he was at a loss to understand. But he didn't trust Paul Lafon. Instinct warned him something was wrong.

"I promise, Erin." He leaned over and gave her a reassuring peck on the cheek before following the doctor into the cabin.

Fingers going of their own accord to the place where Jackson's lips had touched, Erin allowed Davenport to usher her up to the texas deck. It wasn't until she sank on her cot, that she realized how drained the discovery of her grandmother's death and the stormy confrontation with Lydia Lafon had left her. Her hand shook as she accepted the glass of fine Kentucky bourbon Jackson kept in his liquor cabinet that John poured for her.

It burned all the way down, making her wonder how men could swill it like fresh pumped water on a hot day. At least she had an excuse for the disciplined tears that broke rank and trekked silently down her cheeks.

John Davenport watched her struggle bravely with her emotion, reminded painfully of another time and

126

another pair of green eyes that to this day haunted his memory. He'd been a coward then and, he supposed, now was no different. If the *Delta Moon* was delayed in departure, he'd make certain he was on the first steamer bound for New Orleans tomorrow. He'd been a fool to take the risk of coming to Natchez in the first place, but he'd been intrigued by Erin Devareau. He would not remain the fool.

# Chapter Nine

The steam whistle of a departing vessel broke through the morning hubbub on the docks and drew Erin out of the light sleep that had claimed her. Maybe it was all a bad dream and when she dressed and checked in on her grandmother, she'd find her in her cabin teasing Edward over a cup of hot tea. But it wasn't, she realized, catching sight of the door to Jackson's adjoining room ajar. She crawled to the edge of her bunk to see the slipper she'd wedged in it. No doubt Tyler thought she was just being childish, but somehow it had made her feel better to know she was not completely alone. He'd humored her anyway.

Erin twisted the satin drawstring on her drawers and listened until she could hear a steady breathing sound coming from the other room. He'd told her that Dr. Lafon had taken what was left of her grandmother's tea to an apothecary. Considering what Erin had told them of her stomach misery, he'd proposed that she might have been poisoned. Only old Mathers had gone visiting his niece in the country, so they'd had to leave the cup with the authorities until his return sometime today. But it was as unlikely that anyone would want her grandmother dead as it was that Erin had intention-

128

ally brought her to harm.

The uncertainty that had plagued her all night washed over her once more. Had the travel hurt her grandmother? Had that medicine she complained about been vital? Erin closed her eyes tightly, as if to shut out the doubts. She would have asked her grandmother more about her illness if the woman had acted sick, but her only complaint was tiring out quicker than she chose to . . . and the stomach misery of course.

Unbidden, a sob rose to the back of her throat. Desperately, Erin reached for her pillow to catch it before the man in the next room heard her. It wouldn't do for him to see her cry. As she did so, the whiskey bottle John Davenport had fetched to settle her nerves rolled off the mattress and onto the crumpled dress Erin had tossed on the floor. The two glasses she'd finished hadn't done a thing but make her sleepy. They hadn't made her forget as he'd boasted they would. But it had made her stop thinking about it for a little while. She lifted the bottle, examining the remainder. Perhaps more was the answer.

Although it didn't burn quite as much this time, it hadn't improved in taste any since last night. Consequently, there was little to do except take a deep breath and down the blasted mess. Erin did so quickly. Her mother had told her on more than one occasion how good she was at taking medicine. Nevertheless, she did require something to chase it. Without taking time to use the glass on her bedside table, Erin seized the water pitcher and gulped down the water until most of the taste was out of her mouth.

Bejesus! she thought, falling back on her pillow, her camisole soaked from the frantic dribble. If she had to drink that rotgut every day, she'd never be a proper drunk, that was sure. She wiped her mouth on the back of her arm and squared her jaw resolutely as

129

Lydia Lafon's cruel accusations filtered in through the aftershock of her offended senses. If whiskey could make a man forget a wife of several years, why in the bloody blazes couldn't she just forget her anguish for a little while?

She studied the empty bottle. More? Her nose wrinkled and she shuddered at the idea. Why couldn't it be wine. It was the wine served on the boat that was more to her liking. Now *that* she could drink down with the best of them, she thought logically. And if she wasn't mistaken, Jackson Tyler kept a private stock in the cabinet under his bunk. Madeira, if she recalled the label correctly. Sturgis had said it was an expensive import, named after a group of islands off the African coast, but all Erin wanted to know was how to say it. She knew what it was—a high-class wine for his high-class women. Jackson Beauregard Tyler would have no less. Her nose wrinkled again as she thought of Gina Allen. Well, she was just as good as that feather-headed blonde . . . or would be someday, if she studied hard and concentrated on it.

Thus resolved, Erin bolted upright, but the room swayed unsteadily and she sank to her knees. "Bejesus!" she whispered in surprise, not realizing just how long she'd delayed in making her move or how quickly the strong bourbon could react in an empty stomach. She'd heard men at the bar laugh about the liquor going to a man's head, but it was her legs that were giving her the trouble. More carefully this time, Erin climbed to her feet again and waited warily to see if the room was inclined to further shenanigans. When nothing happened, she proceeded quietly into the other room.

The clothes Jackson had piled on his desk chair slid to the floor as Erin passed by stiffly, concentrating to be certain her legs would not fail her again. Instead of the cabinet beneath the bunk catching her

130

attention, however, it was the sight of the sleeping man on the bed. She'd seen sleeping men before, she could not deny it. But it struck her plainly that Jackson Tyler could not be compared to the derelicts that frequented the streets and alleys near Under the Hill. For one thing, all he wore was a strip of sheet covering *what counts*, as the girls over at the saloon would say. Erin smothered a wicked snicker behind her hand as he rolled over on his back and settled once more.

Firm, well formed legs were sprawled, one crooked around the sheet, the other peeking out from under it. His chest, lightly furred with the same dark hair as his legs, rose and fell gently. Yet its muscled ridges left no doubt as to its underlying strength. Distracted, Erin resisted the urge to explore it with curious fingers and focused on the cabinet door beneath the bed.

The brass latch was tight, requiring more than the light lift Erin gave it and forcing her to squat unsteadily for better leverage. When it did give, the door flew open and she went down with a soft thud on her derriere. "Bejesus!"

But instead of the decanters she expected lining the inside of the cabinet, an iron door forbade further entry. Bewildered, she reached for the shiny knob in the center and glanced at the other door. Odd, she mused. She thought the only safe on the ship was at the purser's office. She had to give it to Tyler; he was first rate, all the way.

There was a man in Natchez that bragged he could open a safe, just by listening for the clicks in the combination. Had a golden ear, he said. More out of curiosity than anything, Erin placed her ear to the door and turned the dial slowly. Surely enough, there was sound! She frowned. Not a click, but more of a creak . . .

"Got you!"

"Bejesus!" Erin shrieked, arms and legs flailing as she was lifted free of the floor by the drawstring of her bloomers and hauled onto the bunk. "Dad blast it you possum playin' polecat, let me go! All I wanted was something to drink!"

"The drink," Jackson grunted, catching a knee in the abdomen as he dragged her over him and cornered her between him and the wall, "is in the other cabinet, you little thief!"

"I *know* that now!" Erin shot back indignantly as she backed against the cool polished paneling from the warm body closing in on her. Belatedly, his accusation came home, driving the ire from her gaze with a dejected moan. "I know you're not going to believe me, but I was just listening for the click. Hells bells, I've never had the like of trouble since I got hung up with you!"

The very fact that he could easily say the same thing left Jackson incredulous to say the least. "Trouble!" he roared, tugging her under him as she squirmed to get away. "By thunder, I didn't know the meaning of the word until I met you! I never knew one bedraggled little street urchin could disrupt so completely the lives of everyone she came in contact with. What are you going to do next, Erin? What?" The struggles of the girl pinned beneath him suddenly ceased, making him aware of how roughly he'd shaken her.

Bejesus! he thought in exasperation, more oblivious to the infiltration of Erin's favorite expletive in his thoughts than he was to the fact that she had managed to get under his skin so very thoroughly. He inhaled the clean smell of the soap she'd washed with, faintly and pleasantly scented, not like the cheap perfumed bars his casino girls used or the expensive oils Gina soaked for hours in. Soap and whiskey. God in heaven, had she taken up drinking as well? Although, he decided, his irritation fading quickly, she'd come a long way from the muddy waif he'd brought aboard a few weeks ago. A long way, he mused, staring at the delicate profile turned away from him and the sooty thick lashes blinking like a woman's fan fluttering on a hot day.

"N . . . nothing."

Jackson shook himself mentally. "What?"

Green eyes, magnified with an anguished glaze turned toward him. "I won't do anything else wrong, I promise. Just don't let them take me away." A sliver of the glassy surface seeped out the corner of one eye and hovered there uncertainly, catching Jackson's attention.

He'd just discovered her with her hands on the combination of his private safe, emboldened by the whiskey no doubt. He knew she took Gina's brooch and silverware from the kitchen, although the why of it still eluded him. His partner was likely to be accused of murder because she and that half-senile old woman had set out for an adventure bigger than both of them and all he wanted to do at the moment was kiss away her fears. He started with the tear.

"I'm not crying!" the girl protested, turning her face toward the rumpled pillow once more.

Jackson caught her chin. "No one said you were, kid."

"And I'm not a kid."

That could be no more apparent to him. The thin material of her bloomers and camisole did little to separate him from the feel of her soft and feminine curves.

"Are you going to kiss me on the mouth?"

"It's crossed my mind," Jackson admitted, disconcerted by her directness.

Erin's pulse leapt at the thought, recalling vividly the last time those lips had wreaked havoc with her senses. Fact was, she wasn't at all sure her head was clear enough at the moment to deal with that.

"Would you mind just holding me first, Tyler?" And maybe the room would be still, she thought, giving in readily to the arms that released her wrists and enfolded her.

The room did still and Erin felt warm, wonderfully warm . . . and, oddly enough, safe. She entwined her legs around one of his and tucked her head under his rough-shaven chin. "I never got this close to a naked man," she observed candidly.

Jackson swallowed dryly. "Seen a lot of them, have you?" he prompted, his curiosity piqued by her lack of discomfort.

"Enough, I suppose. Though the ones I've seen looked better with their clothes on." Erin worked up enough nerve to run her fingers through the dark crisps of hair beneath her chin. "It doesn't seem to matter with you."

A chuckle shook her. "Thank you . . . I think," he added wryly.

After a moment of silence, she spoke again. "I appreciate you taking up for me today. I'd take you and your soap any day to Mama's sister."

"Erin . . ." Jackson caught the fingers that were testing his restraint beyond its endurance. She couldn't know what she was doing to him. "Maybe you had better get back to your cabin."

He felt her recoil in reaction to his words and regretted them instantly. Rolling aside, he allowed her to crawl to her knees and took advantage of the opportunity to hide the most obvious of her effects on him with the sheet. To his surprise, anger instead of hurt flashed at him.

"I wish you'd make up your mind whether you like me or not!"

"I *do* like you, Erin," Jackson reasoned, wondering at her mercurial nature. "Though God only knows why!"

Somehow reassured, Erin surveyed her guardian

thoughtfully. "Maybe we're just two of a kind."

"How do you figure that?" It never ceased to amaze him how quickly she recovered. Life with Erin would be an emotional tug of war at best.

"Well, you can be a scoundrel or gentleman and I can be a rascal or a lady, depending on the circumstances."

A sharp knock on the door checked Jackson's retort. "What is it?" he barked, sliding off the bunk and securing the sheet about his waist. This was just what he needed, someone finding his ward in his bed half dressed and he naked. "Ladies don't get caught half naked in a man's bedroom!" he reminded Erin under his breath. "Now get out of here!"

"Mr. Tyler, we gots de sheriff downstairs lookin' to see you an' Mr. Davenport."

Jackson snatched up his trousers, regrouping his thoughts. "Then get them some coffee and have Mr. Davenport meet me in the casino."

Erin crawled off the bunk carefully, presenting a fetching view that was not wasted on her companion. "And gentlemen don't get spike hard with gentile thoughts," she quipped saucily, carrying on without regard to the interruption.

Jackson's face burned with the scarlet color that flushed it. Choking on the curse that exploded in his mind, he snatched off the sheet and threw it at her, abandoning all attempt to protect her from something she was irritatingly familiar with after all.

"But Mr. Tyler," Hannah wailed outside the door, her voice taking on a hysterical note.

"What, damn it?"

Erin would have dodged the sheet that came hurling at her, but at that moment the room shifted dramatically.

"Mr. Davenport, he's done gone, bags an' all."

Jackson's fingers halted on the fastens of his trousers. "Check the kitchen!"

135

"Tyler!" Erin gasped, groping for the side of the bunk in desperation.

Jackson pivoted at the panic in the girl's voice. Gone was all trace of the humor she'd enjoyed a moment before. Her eyes were over wide and her face white as the underwear clinging to her shapely form. Suddenly her hands flew to her temples and she cried out as her knees buckled under her. "I vow, I feel faiin . . ."

In one stride, Jackson caught her and scooped her limp form up in his arms.

"But Mr. Tyler, his bags . . . !" Hannah insisted.

Jackson rolled his eyes heavenward as he laid his unconscious charge on his bed. Bejesus!

# Chapter Ten

Erin set about dressing for her grandmother's funeral service without the help of Yvette. The upstairs maid of the Lafon household on Royal Street was never around when Erin needed her. She struggled into her corset and the full array of petticoats, determined to look her best. She had to make a favorable impression on the gentry that would be attending the service, with or without Jackson Tyler.

Jackson promised he'd be there, she thought, working at the fastens in the back of her dress awkwardly. Surely he wouldn't begrudge her the fact that she'd wanted to accept Lydia Lafon's invitation to stay at the house during the mourning period preceding her grandmother's burial. After all, it was a chance to get to see her mother's childhood home. She even had Giselle's old bedroom.

That things hadn't gone the way Erin had expected had been a disappointment. Instead of introducing her to the friends of her mother's family who came to offer their condolences almost from sunup until sundown, Erin was confined to her room, hidden as though the family considered her some dark scandalous secret. The French maid was her watchdog, assigned more to spy on her than assist her. Aside from old Daniel, everyone treated her as if she carried some dread disease.

Daniel, however, made up for them. In the short visits to her room to serve her meals and snacks, the older gentleman plied her with stories of young Giselle Devareau, remarking each time how much like her mother Erin was. Giselle was the more precocious of the two sisters, always up to mischief and always possessing a mind of her own. The servant speculated that the irreconcilable riff between her and her father, who adored his eldest daughter, stemmed from their like personalities. If her mother had been a son, things would have been different, he'd told Erin.

At the ring of the front doorbell, Erin rushed to the window to view a handily placed mirror Lydia Lafon had mounted on the side of the house in order to see who was standing at the door in case she chose to be indisposed to that particular guest. She'd hoped it was Jackson, come to rescue her from the isolated tower of her room, but, to Erin's astonishment, it was not her guardian that stood there, but Elena Cadiz! Thinking her eyes were deceiving her, she rushed to the side window to watch as the Hispanic girl walked around the house to the servant's entrance in the rear. Now what would Elena be doing here? Her brow knitted in confusion, Erin went back to the task of fastening her gown.

Predictably, Yvette came in just as Erin finished putting her hair up, securing it with a comb to which was sewn an ivory satin cluster of roses set amid a bed of deep green velvet ribbons. "Miss Erin, Mrs. Lafon ees leaving with her husband een the family carriage early for the photographer as soon as her new hairdresser is finished with her. She's . . ." The upstairs maid broke off at the sight of the girl, fully bedecked in the palest green silk. Erin glanced down at her dress uncertainly. "Is something wrong?"

She chose the ball gown over her other dresses because it was the most beautiful garment she'd ever seen and she wanted to make only the best impression. Of course, black was more suitable for the occasion, but Erin didn't even possess a ribbon of that color. Worse, she'd misplaced her necklace on the *Delta Moon*, so that she had nothing to wear about her neck. Her hand went to the base of her throat self-consciously as, once again, she wracked her brain trying to think when she had taken it off. Perhaps the clasp had broken as Jackson suggested when he found her tearing through her cabin in a panic.

He had been comforting, the soft brush of his lips across her forehead distracting her from her search momentarily, but he didn't understand. The locket had been all that was tangible of her identity. She felt as if she were stranded between two worlds, no longer belonging to either.

"Oh no, mam'selle. It ees just lovely!"

Dismissing the missing locket for the time being, Erin narrowed her gaze suspiciously as she saw the woman look away. She didn't trust Yvette any more than she did her aunt. According to Daniel, her real name was Maybelle Dodd and she was no more French than he was. Her compliment was shallow at best, Erin mused warily. Was there something else wrong? Something she did not see? *"Merci, Yvette." And that wart on your nose looks like a rose,* Erin went on in fluent French, giving in to a sudden spiteful urge to vent her frustration.

*"Bien,* mam'selle," the maid replied uncertainly. "But what I was to tell you ees that madame has hired a hack to take you to the church. Eet will be here shortly."

Erin was tempted to try the maid further, but for an

equally sudden pang of guilt that took the fun out of it. The woman didn't even realize she was being put on. "I'm ready any time," she answered with a dejected sigh, her thoughts returning to her guardian. She so hoped Tyler would come soon.

The sound of a carriage outside revealed that the Lafons were on their way to the church, so Erin fetched her purse in readiness for her own to follow. The minutes, however, dragged into an hour, during which Erin became increasingly restless. She moved from the window seat to the bed, ever careful not to wrinkle her gown, and tried to pass the time with the photographs. When the clock in the large hall outside her room struck the hour again, however, she scowled with impatience. Where on earth was Jackson Tyler and, even if he didn't have the decency to honor his promise to stand by her at the funeral, where was this promised ride?

One would almost think they didn't want her to attend . . . Color flamed in Erin's cheeks before the thought came to completion. In a landslide of silky material, she slid off the high canopied bed and ran to the window.

The cool damp air left by morning rain clouds that still held the sun at bay rushed in as she opened the casement windows and leaned out to look down the street. The last tones of the church bells came to an end, officially declaring the hall clock too fast. Traffic, which had flowed freely along the street most of the morning was delayed, making it impossible for Erin to see what the holdup was further along.

But she could guess. Damn them! she swore silently. They were having the funeral without her! A little longer and they might have succeeded in getting by without even acknowledging that they'd had a guest, let alone that Giselle Devareau's daughter existed. Keeping her under their roof had

140

not been out of any semblance of remorse after all. She had played right into their hands!

"Mam'selle!" Yvette exclaimed, shoving Lydia Lafon's copy of *Harper's Bazaar* behind her as she leapt from her lookout near the stairwell. "But zee hack has not yet come!"

Erin halted as the girl jumped in front of her. "And it isn't going to, is it?" she accused hotly. "Now step aside, *Maybelle!*"

Shaken more by the threatening look on Erin's face than by the familiar address, the maid floundered. "But madame said . . ."

Erin grabbed the front of her apron bib and started to throw her aside bodily when she screamed. "If you go to that funeral, I'll lose my job . . . I got a baby to feed!" Gone was the French accent and all the airs the maid had lauded over Erin since they'd met as the girl dropped to her knees wailing.

Momentarily at a loss, Erin glanced down the steps to see a group of black servants gathering at the foot, but the only one she recognized was Daniel. The same, however could not be said of a stout graying woman who screeched loudly, "Lawdy, it's Miss Giselle's ghost come to take her Mama home!" Erin's eyes widened as the woman slumped to the floor and began to chant. One by one the others began to join in the mounting hysteria.

"It ain't Miss Giselle, it's her daughter. I tole you dat!" Daniel shouted in a vain attempt to stop them.

Erin had been with Annie once to a river baptism and enjoyed the spectacle, even taken a dip herself to the background of the melodic spiritual music. But this was different. For one panic-stricken moment, she was tempted to run back into her room and lock the door. Old Annie had told her more than she wanted to know about the voodoo practice among the Louisiana blacks and the last thing she wanted was to tangle with some of them.

Although, in their black dresses and white aprons, they looked no different from the servants Erin had seen shopping for their employers at the marketplace in Natchez. "Dey's voodoo niggers in N'awlins," Annie had told her, her voice rising in such a way as to give rise to the hairs that grew at the nape of necks of the youngsters she entertained. "Got queens, dey do! De devil's own childrens."

The way they were all kneeling about the one in the center left Erin a bit unnerved. It was Daniel's indignant voice that managed to restore her reason. "Now you all gits back to de kitchen. Dis gal needs to say goodbye to her grandmother."

"Pleez . . . don't go," Yvette pleaded as Erin gathered her skirts to step around her. "I got to have a job or my landlady won't keep Jasper and we'll be out on the streets. He ain't got a daddy to take care of us."

Again Erin hesitated. While she might not feel sorry for the maid, she could easily relate to what it was like not to have a father to care for her. But she had to go. She just had to set things to right for her mother. Her mind raced quickly. "Do you like working here?"

Maybelle sniffed, wiping her nose on the ruffled sleeve of her dress. "Sometimes what you like to do and what you have to do aren't the same. I only want to take care of my baby. A woman'll do what she has to for that."

Erin glanced at the clock anxiously, her memory stung by the woman's anguished plight. Suddenly she reached down and helped the maid to her feet. "Look, if you want a better job, you go get Jasper and take him to the Delta "O" office on Decatur Street. Tell them I sent you and I'll explain when I get there."

"You mean, *you'll* find me a job?"

"Yes!" Erin replied hastily. "I know the owners."

It was the least Jackson Tyler could do. After all, he'd promised to come. Fingers crossed that she could carry through with her own promise, Erin flew down the steps two at a time, driving the servants back against the wall as she hurried past them.

"God bless you, Miss Erin!" Daniel called after her as she started down the busy street.

Erin was blind to the attention she drew as she fled down the streets, skirts billowing in the slight breeze. Nor did she notice the discomfort of the damp air that raised gooseflesh on her bare back or the puddles that soaked the hems of her crinolines. Her only thought was to reach Lydia Lafon at her most vulnerable moment—in front of the elite society the woman worshipped.

The ceremony was over when Erin breathlessly reached the giant trees shading the front of the cathedral grounds. The last of the mourners offered their condolences to the Lafons on the wide stone steps as the elaborately carved wooden casket carrying Marie Asante was placed inside the crepe-draped hearse. The sight of it slowed Erin's pace to a walk, a purposeful walk during which she took the time to compose herself. After all, while she did seek a form of vengeance, she intended to do so on equal grounds with her aunt . . . as a lady.

Chin tilted proudly, Erin walked up the steps among the black-clad group that fell aside to let her pass. Hushed whispers of surprise echoed all around her, but her eyes were on the black-veiled woman engaged in conversation with the robed priest.

"It can't be Giselle! She's so young!"

"I can't believe my eyes!"

"Well, she's certainly no ghost! My word, what a beauty!"

143

"But her clothes! Why, she's dressed as if going to a ball, not a funeral. Such disrespect for the dead!"

Erin flinched at the biting comment, but continued up the steps until she stood squarely before Dr. Paul Lafon and his wife. Although she now had their undivided attention, neither of them so much as uttered a word, as if her appearance had robbed them of speech.

"Aunt Lydia," Erin began in a tone much bolder than she felt with so many critical eyes upon her. "I pray you will forgive me for being late. My carriage was detained in the traffic, so I hurried on foot, sooner than miss Grandmother's funeral."

"Good heavens, Lydia, you never mentioned that your sister had a child. How like Giselle she is!" a matronly woman exclaimed at her aunt's elbow.

"I fear my mother's family did not know of my existence until Grandmother Asante and I met by chance on the *Delta Moon*," Erin responded sweetly in her aunt's defense. "It's just a shame that such a tragic circumstance has brought us together after so many years." Erin spun about gracefully, her cheeks flushed a radiant pink as she addressed those around her. "I also must beg indulgence over my attire. I was hardly prepared for such an occasion, traveling as I was, but I thought," she paused for a dramatic interlude, "that it would be better to pay my last respects in what I had, rather than not appear at all."

"How like . . . your mother," Lydia Lafon responded coolly, her face hidden beneath the black netting of her hat. "So . . . spontaneous."

Erin managed a sad smile. "I only wish we had more time to get to know one another, but my guardian insists that we leave for Natchez when the *Delta Moon* departs tomorrow. However, if you wouldn't mind, I'd like to ride with you to the family crypt."

144

"Of course," her aunt acknowledged, her voice barely audible, as if she were on the verge of a swoon.

Erin took a place in the family carriage beside the inquisitive matron, who was introduced as Paul Lafon's mother, Heddy. The couple seated across from them contented themselves to stare at Erin as if she might carry the plague, so, aside from her barrage of questions, which Erin parried with ease, the journey a few blocks away to St. Louis Cemetery passed in strained silence.

When they followed the casket to the massive marble tomb that dominated the skyline of the citylike graveyard, Erin didn't have to act saddened. The sight of her grandmother's coffin being carried ahead drove home the reality of a loss that had, until that moment still seemed unreal. Her anguish twisted in her chest, opening another wound not so old and just as painful. But, as her gaze traveled the narrow path leading to the small innocuous cell where her mother rested, she summoned her resolve.

"Aunt Lydia," she spoke up as soon as the priest finished his final prayer and the group began to disperse at the edges. "While I know we've only just met, I have something to ask of you."

Lydia Lafon's gloved fingers tightened on her husband's sleeve. "I knew it!" she whispered under her breath. "I knew sooner or later she would . . ."

"Lydia!" Paul Lafon's sharp command cut her off abruptly.

Making sure that those within earshot could understand her, Erin spoke again. "You know that Mother died at my birth and the dear family that took me in had no idea who she was, her being new in Natchez. Then Father never returned from the war, so . . ."

"What is it that you want, Erin? Your aunt and I will be only too happy to oblige."

145

The undisputed center of attention, Erin smiled sadly. "I've one request before I leave. Because Mother's name was Devareau rather than Asante at the time of her death, and because it was only known that she was from New Orleans, the Tylers had her remains placed in a crypt nearby. I would like to see her moved to rest beside her mother."

Only the sound of some children playing on the other side of the stone wall in the distance broke the stillness. It was as if the entire entourage awaited the inevitable reply. Paul Lafon's expression was inscrutable, but had Erin been able to see beneath the veil that hid her aunt's face, she would have seen relief, not the dismay she anticipated.

"Oh!" the senior Mrs. Lafon sniffed loudly. "My dear, I knew your sister's life had been tragic, but this dear child . . ." Erin winced as she was caught in a perfumed hug. "How many times I have heard your mother lament that she had no grandchild!"

"Mother, I hardly think this is the place!" Paul Lafon warned the older woman under his breath.

The older woman's hand flew to her mouth as she realized her error. "Oh, dear, I didn't mean . . . what I meant to say is, I am sure Marie was delighted to have met you." A quizzical frown suddenly creased an already wrinkled brow. "But how did you two discover each other?"

"I'm told I look like my mother. While I did not know Mother's maiden name, Grandmother knew her married one."

"But rumor had it that a servant girl made off with Mrs. Asante," someone else brought up.

"She did have a girl in her employ," Erin replied calmly. "They were quite a pair of conspirators when they told me how they'd sneaked off to see the river one more time. I'm sure Aunt Lydia was beside herself."

"Oh, I was," Lydia Lafon concurred quickly. "But, from what I can gather, Mother's last days were spent in luxury, treated like a queen on a floating palace and united with her newfound granddaughter for the first time."

A warning squeeze was placed on Erin's arm under the guise of affection, reminding the girl of the conversation she'd had with her aunt the first night in the Royal Street residence. The circumstances surrounding Marie Asante's suspicious death were to be kept among the family to avoid scandal.

Erin had thought then that her aunt didn't know the beginning of the meaning of scandal, something Erin would swiftly alter if she would not have Giselle Devareau moved from the paupers' section of the cemetery to the Asantes' Italian marble crypt where she belonged.

"It was a lovely journey," she remarked wistfully, before steering the subject back to her intended purpose and away from a subject she was certain neither the Lafons, nor she wished to discuss. "But, about Mama . . ."

"Are you certain that is *all* you wish?" Paul Lafon insisted somewhat dubiously.

Erin leveled an even gaze at him. "All I wish is for Mama to be where she belongs."

"That, my dear child, is the very least we can do," the doctor asserted generously. "My wife couldn't rest knowing such an injustice existed, regardless of how inadvertent it was. Consider it done."

The simple request seemed incredulous to Heddie Lafon as it did to those that made the ripple of astonishment around them. "But dear, surely you must be interested in any of your mother's . . ." The woman broke off suddenly, interrupted by a fashionably dressed gentleman who emerged from the cluster around them carrying a silver-tipped cane.

147

"Mrs. Lafon, I can appreciate what you are saying, but Erin has a life of her own, developed apart from the Asante family." Brandishing a charming smile, he lifted her gloved hand to his lips. "Permit me to introduce myself. I am Jackson Beauregard Tyler of . . ."

"Those *Natchez* Tylers!" Heddie Lafon exclaimed meaningfully, saving the gentleman who slipped a supportive arm under Erin's elbow the necessity of going on further. "My dear, do not tell me that *this* is your guardian?"

Erin nodded, the relief Jackson's reassuring presence afforded nearly buckling her knees. She had done it. She'd gotten them to admit her mother's existence and agree before their friends to comply with her wishes. Yet, now that she'd achieved her purpose, she felt somewhat drained.

"You can see why my niece is enormously content with her life as it is, Mother Lafon," Lydia Lafon injected, her nerves beginning to fray. "Now, before that cloud starts misting on us, I suggest we resume this reunion back at the house."

"Erin, I regret to snatch you away from your family, but something has come up and I must get back to my office," Jackson announced, leaving little room for objection. Not that he would have heard any from the girl looking up at him with shining eyes. With a surreptitious wink, he turned to shake Paul Lafon's hand. "I'm sure that we'll be seeing more of each other in the future, now that Erin knows she has family here in the city."

"Do that, sir. Shall I send your ward's things to the ship?"

"I'd appreciate that, sir. My sympathies again, madame," Jackson addressed Lydia Lafon with a short nod.

The cloak her guardian slipped over Erin's

shoulders was not nearly as welcome as the arm he offered to lead her back to the shiny black coach with DELTA "O" painted on the door in the same gold as the decorative pinstriping. She should have been angry at him for nearly missing the gathering altogether. Even though they'd both been led to think the service later in the day, he had promised to come early. Yet, she was so glad to have an ally that, when the coachman closed the door of the vehicle, its half-drawn canvas curtain flapping to a standstill, she threw her arms around his neck and planted a loud kiss on his lips.

Taken aback, Jackson basked in the warmth of the smile bestowed upon him and permitted her to then settle against his chest as she sought the additional warmth of his arm. "What was that for?"

"For coming to my rescue."

"It didn't seem to me that you needed rescue. That was quite a performance!"

Erin pulled away, eyes brightening. "Do you think so? Do you think they'll put Mama with Grandma?"

"I don't see where you left them much choice."

"And do I look like a lady?" Suddenly self-conscious, Erin smoothed out the wrinkles in her gown. The tufted leather seat creaked beneath her as she moved to show the dress to its greatest advantage, given the limited space in the carriage.

"You look ravishing, Erin."

Her face fell. There was something wrong. Jackson's face was expressionless, lacking the same conviction his tone did. Was it the choice of her gown? "I know I should have worn black, but this was the best I had."

Jackson put a finger to her lips, silencing her and swallowed the blade of emotion wedged in his throat. Damnation! He hadn't expected it to be this hard, he thought, watching trouble light on the expectant

149

face turned up to him. He wondered just how much more his ward could take right now. True, she'd pulled a magnificent triumph back there, but it had taken its toll. Her hands were shaking in the aftermath and the hug she'd given him had told him more than her brave front.

"John's dead, Erin. That's why I was late. I had to identify his body." He reached into his pocket and drew out a small chain. "This was among his possessions." Swinging on the end of it was a small locket—the one that had been given to her by her mother.

# Chapter Eleven

John Davenport's body had been found lying in a back alley behind a brothel on Gallatin Street near the French Market. His face had been beaten beyond recognition, not uncommon for a robbery victim who put up a fight, which John no doubt had done according to the police. His wallet, the rings that sparkled with warning to unseasoned gamblers at his table, and anything else of value that the thieves might have discovered were all missing. It was only by his clothing, the familiar fashionable russet suit and monogrammed tie that made identity possible for Jackson Tyler. And it was in a pocket concealed in the liner of his partner's jacket that the police had found the locket missed by the murderers.

It seemed his partner had checked in the office upon arrival on the *Delta Star* and cheerily left for a night on the town. What puzzled Jackson was what John, who frequented only the best of the gambling parlors the quarter had to offer, was doing in that section of town. Neither that, nor any other of the confounding pieces of the puzzle concerning Marie Asante's death fit. The further discovery of a note left at the Delta "O" office only served to confuse the issue more.

Dear friend,

There is little time to explain my hasty departure except to say that I had nothing to do with Rosie O'Rourke's death. I am, however, convinced that it has something to do with a danger to Erin. I intend to investigate a few suspicions from this end, but, should something happen to me, I want you to give whatever interests I have after my debts to your ward. She's positively charming and deserves more. More importantly, protect her at all costs. Trust *no one* with her interests other than yourself.

John.

Jackson didn't show it to the sheriff. As far as the authorities were concerned the case was closed. His partner had poisoned the old woman, taken her money, and fled to New Orleans to meet a fitting death. Sheriff Dixon, who had enjoyed himself immensely on the river journey thus far, had left Jackson to accompany his wife on a shopping expedition while Jackson proceeded with all haste to find Erin. The *no one* in John's last letter meant the Lafons, as far as he was concerned.

"You're not eating," he reminded the quiet girl seated across from him.

He should have known Erin would cope, at least emotionally. Aside from her very real and equally brief distress over the loss of her necklace, he'd seen her brave emotional storms that would reduce the most mature women to a state of hysteria. But then, considering her background, she would have had to be strong to have survived life Under the Hill without becoming a victim of it.

Erin finished the last of her wine and allowed the steward, who appeared almost before she could return the empty glass to the linen-covered table-cloth, to refill it. "I had some cakes and chocolates before I went to . . . to the cathedral," she offered apologetically.

Jackson had been so considerate of her. He'd insisted on taking her to one of the most elite restaurants in the city and ordered a sumptuous fare to which she'd done little credit. It was just that, at the moment, she simply couldn't eat. The confrontation with the Lafons had left her shaken, although satisfied, and now the shock of the news about John . . .

She couldn't believe the man who had befriended her had been her grandmother's murderer, which was a moot point, for now no one would ever know. He had plenty of money according to Mariette and others on the ship, although none of them knew anything of his past. And why would he have wanted her necklace? All she knew was that he had been well liked by everyone who knew and worked with him and that she was no exception.

"I don't believe John poisoned Grandma," Erin blurted out suddenly. For the first time since he'd broken the news of John's death to her, she saw a flicker of a smile on Jackson's drawn face and realized that perhaps she was not the only one in need of comfort. "He was a good friend, wasn't he?" she stated rather than asked.

"Something akin to a brother."

"Had you known him long?"

"A handful of years, I suppose." Jackson sighed wistfully. "Ah, but what times we shared. I learned a lot from him."

"Me too." Erin saw instant disapproval light in Jackson's gaze and saucily quoted straight from one of John Davenport's favorite sayings, "It takes one to know one."

This time Jackson laughed out loud. It was no wonder John had been charmed by his ward. They were two of a kind. "I think it's time we went back to

153

the apartment. It will be quieter than staying over on the ship tonight, what with the final loading going on."

"But my clothes are being sent to the ship," Erin reminded him.

With a look that made her feel perfectly wicked and in a tone that sent shivers of delight up her spine, Jackson lowered his voice. "We'll think of something."

He summoned the waiter and paid the check, tipping handsomely, before escorting Erin to the coach waiting on the street. Like royalty, he helped her inside and then took a seat beside her, gathering her under a protective arm. The tap of his cane against the roof of the vehicle sent them along their way through the streets that were beginning to thin out of traffic with the coming night.

During the short ride to the Decatur Street residence, Jackson proceeded to tell Erin of the arrangements he'd made with the coroner for the body he'd identified, a morning burial, so that the *Delta Moon* would only be held over a half day from her schedule. John would be interred at the same cemetery as her grandmother and mother, except that his tomb, like her mother's first, would be shared with the remains of persons not related, his having no family crypt.

Sobered from the fleeting warmth they'd shared over dinner, Erin shuddered. It was a practical, but almost heathen practice to allow a corpse occupation of one of the holes in the assorted crypts and mausoleums for one year and then to cremate the remains and toss them in to make room for another. The inability to bury them in the low-lying ground made it a necessity, Jackson explained to her, but it was a maintenance she was loathe to think of and she was heartened to know that now her mother would not suffer such a fate.

Upon arriving in front of the steamship office on Decatur, Jackson ignored the CLOSED sign hanging on the door and opened it with his key to gain access to the apartments above. As Erin stepped past to precede him, she was surprised to see Reds Jones, the ship's engineer making his way up the street toward them, hailing Jackson with his large proportioned hand.

"Beggin' your pardon, sir, but if you got time, I'd warrant a word with you."

"Of course, Reds," Jackson acknowledged as graciously as if he'd addressed one of his social peers, "Come up and share a glass of bourbon with me. I'm certain Erin will excuse us if we take on something a bit stronger than wine."

Her mind already on something else, Erin nodded absently. "Of course, but would you mind if I took a bath in that fancy tub of yours?"

"My house is yours, Erin," Jackson responded magnanimously.

Missing the amused exchange of glances between the men, Erin turned and bounded up the stairs ahead of them, delicate skirts clenched with a vengeance in her hands. At the top she recalled Sturgis's complaint that she had to allow gentlemen to open doors for her and waited patiently until her host caught up to perform his God-given duty in society. Considering her success at the Lafons and at the restaurant, acting ladylike was becoming more natural, she thought, quite pleased with herself as she preceded the men into the large parlor.

There was a fire dancing in the hearth that gave the place a homey feeling, issuing a warm welcome from the damp chill outside. Erin started toward the door she thought led to the bedroom she had previously occupied and then hesitated uncertainly. Jackson, who moved to the liquor cabinet to serve his guest his promised drink noticed her awkwardness immediately.

"Go on in, Erin. I'll have Libby draw your bath."

Thus reinforced, Erin opened the door and started inside when she was startled by a small child who streaked past her and across the room.

"Boy, you get back in here!"

The child, naked and dripping wet, squealed in delight as he circled the sofa with the unsteady steps of one who had not been long walking, let alone running, and crashed into the long legs of a speechless Jackson Tyler. Jackson caught the baby before it fell to the floor and hoisted it into the air, holding it off to avoid being soaked by his wet and squirming prey.

"What the . . . ?"

Before Jackson could finish his incredulous question, a woman garbed in little more than rags burst through the bedroom door, her eyes widening upon seeing the man with her giggling child. "Oh, excuse me, sir! I didn't know you were home and Mrs. Green said . . ."

"Mrs. Green knows about this?"

The woman froze in her tracks at the imperious demand, her gaze fixed on the child. "So does she! She sent me here!" Maybelle Dodd squealed, pointing to Erin. "For the love of God, don't hurt my baby!"

Erin straightened under the expectant silver gaze that swung to her. In the aftermath of the news of John's death, she had totally forgotten Lydia Lafon's ex-French maid. "I need to talk to you, Tyler."

"Indeed, madame, you . . ." Jackson broke off again, this time distracted by the steady and warm flow of liquid streaming down the front of his waistcoat.

"Jasper!" Abandoning any danger this foreboding man might present to her for the sake of her child, Maybelle Dodd dashed across the room and snatched the baby into her arms. "He don't know better, sir!"

In a pitiful effort to make up for her son's faux pas, she attempted to brush the man off with her apron. "When my landlady heard I'd quit my job, she threw us out. We got no place to go!"

"Madame," Jackson seized her arm to stop her flustered ministrations. "That will not be necessary. You may finish dressing the child while I speak to my ward. Reds, if you'll help yourself . . ."

"Go ahead, sir. I got plenty of time," the engineer responded, tongue in cheek.

Jackson pointed to the other door which Erin presumed to be his own room with an authoritative, "If you please, *Miss* Devareau," that left little consideration as to whether she did or did not please.

Quietly Erin rushed into the room ahead of him. It was simply, but richly furnished. A huge sleigh bed dominated the center with accompanying furniture gracing the walls surrounding it. A hunter's print of burgundy against ivory was tailored to the bed and the windows with straight lines instead of the ruffled fullness that had been characteristic of her mother's old room. One could not doubt that its occupant was masculine.

The door clicked behind her and she spun from her quick assessment of her surroundings to explain the reason for Jasper and Maybelle Dodd's presence. "I promised her a job, Tyler. She was hired to keep me from going to Grandmother's funeral and said she'd lose her position at the Lafon's if she didn't stop me . . . and then she started crying about having a baby with no father to raise . . ."

"And you told her to move in here?" Jackson paused in the midst of shrugging off his accosted jacket and stared at her incredulously.

"No, I told her you'd give her a job." He continued to stare. "Well, I *had* to do something!" In an effort to improve his humor, Erin reached for the jacket and helped it the rest of the way off. "It isn't easy for some

157

women, you know. You men have your fun and then leave them to do one of two things." She left the jacket on the foot of the bed and proceeded to unbutton the silver waistcoat that had taken the brunt of Jasper's innocent assault. "She could either end up in a brothel or work her fingers to the bone for people like Lydia Lafon."

"Or me?" he asked, intrigued that Erin didn't seem the least bit awkward at removing his clothing. It was that uncanny mix of worldliness and innocence that made her irresistible.

Erin's fingers halted on the stiff removable collar of his shirt. "You wouldn't throw her and the child out on the street, would you? Maybe she could be my French maid. Ladies are supposed to have maids," she reminded him.

Jackson smiled indulgently. "Not with children. Where did you become so deft with gentlemen's attire?"

"I've undressed a man or two in my life," Erin retorted with an air of authority until she realized what she'd said. "That is," she reiterated, her face coloring profusely, "I've helped Mrs. MacCready put Mac to bed a time or two when he was in his cups."

"Maybe I should consider taking you on as my valet, rather than my ward."

A dancing light in Jackson's eyes telling her she was on safe ground once more, Erin made fast work of the buttons hidden beneath the stiff false front of his shirt and slid the garment off his broad shoulders, trying to ignore the sheer power of attraction the sight of his naked torso worked on her.

"You're not used to holding children, are you?" she asked in an attempt to divert the conversation from uneasy ground. Turning briskly, she set about wrapping up the soiled shirt and waistcoat in a neat roll.

"Don't tell me handling children is yet another of

your endless talents?'' he teased, slipping up behind her so that her crinolines were pressed against the footboard of the bed.

"I've helped Mrs. MacCready with the younguns she takes care of from time to time," Erin managed, her voice suddenly tight. She could sense his warmth, rather than feel it so near to the flesh bared by the low dip of her gown in the back. "At least I know enough not to hold a naked baby boy *facing* me!"

She stared at the neatly made bed, the two pillows plumply fluffed at the head and tucked in by the spread. Yes, she had undressed drunks. Yes, she had seen naked men. She'd even been in Tyler's room on the ship, alone with him. But something was happening, something she could not put a finger on that was making what she usually took in stride, most disconcerting. And never once had thoughts about sharing a bed . . .

"Are you going to give Maybelle a job?"

Jackson found himself shaken from similar ponderings and backed away at the sound of mild panic in Erin's voice to fetch a clean shirt from the chest of drawers. "I'm certain that we can find something for her, although the child is a problem, if she's to be aboard one of the Delta ships."

Relieved, at least for Maybelle and Jasper, Erin halted in her flight toward the door and ventured to squeeze the man who warmed her heart with his generosity from behind. "I knew you would! Thank you, Tyler! I'll go tell her."

"Erin!"

Erin stopped, hand on the porcelain knob, and looked back expectantly. "Yes?"

"The name is Jackson."

"Thank you . . . *Jackson*," she conceded, a shy smile gracing her lips.

His ward was nowhere in sight when Jackson emerged from his room, freshly attired in a clean shirt and trousers. Since he had no reason to go back out for the evening, he chose to leave his coat and other dictates of fashion in his room. Ignoring the grin that still haunted the engineer's lips over his mishap with the youngster, Jackson went straight to the business at hand, namely his private investigation of Marie Lafon and his partner's death.

Reds's brother-in-law had access to the Lafon attorney's files which failed to produce any will aside from that leaving Erin's relatives everything, which baffled Jackson. He was certain that the old woman must have left something to Erin to stir up all the interest in his ward and fire Lydia's sudden affection toward her. What confused the issue further, was that the lawyer was summoned to the bank the day Marie Lafon had made the large withdrawal to fund the trip. A junior clerk had been sent to fetch him according to Reds's sources.

Then there was John's parting warning to protect Erin. But from what and whom? If there was no will, she was no threat to the Lafon's. Something was missing, some vital information that would tie all this in. Once again Jackson sent Reds to his sources, this time to check out everyone who saw Marie Lafon that day at the bank, from the president of the bank to the clerk who ran the errand. They had to have overlooked something.

"You think the girl's in danger?" Reds questioned grimly as he tucked his hat under his arm to leave.

"John did. At any rate, I'm taking no chances. Have Erin's things moved back into the cabin across the hall. It's only fitting and I can still keep an eye on her," Jackson explained hastily, out of some uncharacteristic need to do so. "She'll have all meals with me and be served solely by Hannah. We'll take Hannah into our confidence."

After the engineer left, Jackson took the ledger containing the quotes on work to be done to the *Delta*

*Moon* and tried to concentrate on the numbers. He'd done all he could where Erin was concerned and there was other business to be dealt with. However, the appearance of his ward in Libby's oversized flannel gown and robe—Jackson not trusting himself twice to permit her the fetching peignoir set— and the laughing little cherub she'd added to his increasing responsibilities, made it impossible to make sense of the figures. Instead he found himself smiling quietly at their frolic, intrigued by the woman-child who alternately shifted from playmate to mother figure when Jasper was imperiled by his unsteady walk too close to the furniture.

It was only after the little one had tired and Erin took him to her room to put him to bed, that Jackson finally became absorbed in his work. There was a great cost involved in refurbishing the *Delta Moon* to its original palatial elegance, one that could only be justified by updating the engines. Fortunately she was a side-wheeler and could be easily adapted. Her hull was as solid as the day she'd been put to water and much of the cosmetic work he was having the crew do in their spare time had already given her the look of a new vessel.

Gina Allen had offered her services for the final decorating, having traveled on some of Europe and the East Coast's most luxurious liners. At first, Jackson was inclined to refuse, for, from what he'd seen of Gina, she gave the impression of being frivolous. However, after going on that little shopping expedition with her for Erin, he'd seen her haggle the shop owners of the more expensive stores down to a good and fair price. She was no fool and Jackson had no doubt she could work wonders with the budget he and John had allocated without sacrificing quality or taste.

Naturally, she would receive a commission for her work, no matter how much she protested. As much as he admired Gina for her beauty and brains, he knew enough not to become indebted to her. Business and women did not mix.

The way John had projected it, the *Delta Moon* would pay for her renewal in a few years. Increasing her speed meant increasing her ability to provide a sufficient return. She'd become a first choice for both travelers and vendors. She'd also be more reliable and safer than most of her competitors with her new technology.

A faint scent of perfumed soap preceded an unexpected whistle, startling Jackson from his concentration. "Whew! That's a lot of money!"

"I thought you'd retired with young Jasper," he remarked, somewhat irritated by the start Erin had given him.

"Oh, I couldn't possibly sleep right now. Would you like a drink?" Without waiting for a reply, she walked to the liquor cabinet and filled a fresh glass with bourbon.

Jackson, once again taken back by this new inclination to wait on him, pointed to the door below. "There's something lighter inside, some Madeira and sherry, I think."

Completely at ease, Erin poured herself a sherry and carried the drinks over to the sofa where she perched on the chair arm beside her guardian. "I hear the Neilson brothers do top-notch work. At least that's the talk along the docks." Curious eyes cut over to the sheet now resting in Jackson's lap. "Is that a proposal to do the *Delta Moon* over?"

Intrigued by her interest, Jackson handed over the paper. "See for yourself. I understand from Mr. Jones that you've taken quite an interest in the ship."

Erin scanned the first page. "It's my home now, why shouldn't I?"

Content to watch, Jackson lazed back while Erin took her time reading through the pages of the contract. It surprised him that she didn't simply flip through them and make some comment on the final figure, almost as much as the questions she asked, questions that indicated she was no stranger to the riverboat trade.

"I grew up on the docks," she told him, when he questioned her as to the source of her knowledge. "I've been listening to rounders and riverfolk since I can remember and always wanted to live on one of those boats. That's why I'm so obliged to you, for taking me on like you did." Her gaze sparkled with a sincerity that touched Jackson with a stab of guilt over the restrictions he was about to impose on her. "I want to know everything about the *Delta Moon*, work every job on her, so that when I get to be . . ."

"Erin . . ."

Her dreamy dissertation interrupted, Erin stopped and looked at him curiously.

"For your own safety, at least for the next few weeks, I want you to suspend your wanderings about the ship. You're not to go anywhere without either Hannah, myself, or your tutor."

Erin bristled suddenly, jumping to her feet. "I did not take that bloody silverware!"

Jackson scowled. "I wasn't even thinking about the damned stuff!"

"Then why can't I walk about the ship? Haven't I been a lady?" she demanded of the man who rose to look down at her. She hated being short. It meant being talked down to and she didn't like it at all. As if to gain a bit of advantage, she lifted her chin a shade higher in challenge.

She had been a lady. She hadn't cussed or done anything to bring Tyler embarrassment and now he was locking her up on the ship like the Lafons had locked her up in their home.

"It's for your own safety."

"That's as much as what *they* said," she accused hotly. "They kept me shut up in the room ... wouldn't even let the servants see me! They even tried to get by having Grandma's funeral without my knowing, they were so ashamed of me." Her voice cracked with the pain that had so recently been inflicted. "Well, you won't do that to me, Jackson Tyler, because I won't stand for it. I'll run away first!"

Jackson caught her arm as she whirled away to stomp off to her room. "Erin!"

"What do you want from me, Tyler?" Erin bit her lip, determined not to cry. Why was it always so easy to cry in front of him? "I'm doing the best I can!"

"Of course you are," Jackson heard himself say gently as he pulled her to him. He didn't want to frighten her, but he had to convince her this was right. "And I'm proud of what you're doing. You've turned from a ragged street urchin into a Cinderella. In fact, you're too pretty, Erin. So pretty that I want Hannah or myself to be with you to protect you from unwanted attentions from the men. Remember, that was why you dressed like a boy before."

"I can take care of myself," Erin wavered, cottoning to the idea that Jackson wanted her protected from other men's attentions. Could he be jealous?

"When you are not with your tutor, I want you on my arm ... training as a ... a hostess of the *Delta Moon*." He waited for her reaction.

Slowly Erin raised a beseeching gaze to his. "And you don't believe I'm a thief?"

"I don't make a habit of holding thieves like this," he whispered, drawing her closer, "nor would I dream of kissing one like this."

His lips found hers, coaxing the bottom one fixed between her teeth out of its captivity and into another more sensual one. The sweetness of the sherry was

164

intoxicating, but not nearly as much as the taste of her yielding to him, her defenses crumbling until she was clinging to his broad shoulders for support. Moving his hand down over the nicely rounded bottom that had teased him earlier during her playful romp on the floor, he brought her even closer until his manhood responded eagerly to the press of her flat stomach and hips against him.

"Miss Erin, is Jasper . . . oh!"

With a gasp, Erin tore out of the heady embrace, her face deepening to a scarlet hue. Her heart was thundering and her pulses beating erratically, yet those symptoms were mild compared to those warm stirrings that seemed to leap at Jackson Tyler's slightest command.

"Miss Devareau will be with you momentarily," Jackson answered, breaking the silence with a clipped command that was enforced by the fingers tightening about Erin's arm.

Standing her ground, despite her urge to run from the man and the feelings he instilled in her, Erin lifted a resentful gaze to Jackson as Maybelle hastily disappeared inside the bedroom in compliance. He hadn't given her an answer. He'd sweet-talked his way around it, like so many men Erin had heard about. Perhaps like her father had sweet-talked her mother.

"And just who, you silver-tongued polecat, is going to protect me from you?" she derided shakily. "Now, if you will unhand me, I'll be retiring."

Although Erin had been born and reared in one of the lowliest existences on earth, Jackson felt the sting of her royally delivered words. Properly chastised, he released her. He followed her exit with his gaze, as queenly as any he'd ever witnessed, and when the door clicked shut behind her, picked up the glass she'd filled for him earlier and filled it again.

It was nothing, he told himself. Absolutely

nothing a night at the Absinthe House would not alter . . . or lead to altering, he amended laconically. The sudden wail of a baby in the other room, followed by the patter of feminine feet rushing to its aid sealing his decision, Jackson put down his glass and strode purposefully into his room to dress for the New Orleans night.

# Chapter Twelve

The gambling parlor was smaller, yet no less elegant than the grand salon. After meals in the salon, many of the tables were moved aside for the entertainment of the small band that provided dance music. At the opposite end, cozy groupings were made, conducive to conversation. Amid the scented aftermath of the fare served earlier and beneath the extravagant chandeliers that sent lights dancing off mirrored walls with a grandiose effect, many guests remained until the last notes were played before retiring to their rooms.

In contrast, while some guests swayed to the music and engaged in stimulating discussion, many of the men preferred the decidedly masculine atmosphere of the casino. With the music faint in the background, a more subdued exchange of words could be heard here in the midst of tobacco smoke and the mingled scent of the fine liquors kept in a polished walnut cupboard behind an equally elaborate bar. Stewards stood in crisp white near the tables, which were set in a long single row across the length of the room, ready to accommodate any gentleman with a taste for a drink.

Seated at Jackson's left, Erin was oblivious to the stylish Corinthian columns supporting small arches, under which were doors to staterooms belonging to many of the men seated at the tables. Instead, she concentrated on shuffling the cards with a collected demeanor that was far from what she was feeling.

That her guardian even considered letting her take Anita's place in the casino, let alone consented, had left her giddy with excitement. But the employee was deathly sick with a cold brought on by the chilly change in climate and the ship was booked full of cargo and passengers, which meant a lucrative night in all quarters. When the vessel pulled out of Baton Rouge, she was loaded to the guards that were now skimming the muddy waterline. After pleading and then swearing on her mother's grave that she'd play honestly, that he could even watch her, Jackson gave in.

And watching her was exactly what he was doing, which made playing the game difficult at best. He hadn't approved at all of the dress Anita insisted she wear, for she needed to look like one of the casino girls, not the prim little mouse who had been seated at his elbow at meals and at the tables since they'd left New Orleans. Besides, there hadn't been time to change back into one of Mrs. Brady's dresses.

While the garment wasn't as lovely as the pale green ball gown made just for her, the form-skimming scarlet dress certainly left no doubt that Erin was all woman. She'd spent what seemed like hours in the girls' room getting stuffed here and cinched in there until she wondered if she'd be able to bend enough to sit down at the table.

"Just lift your bustle a little, honey. That ought to take the men's mind off of the game for a minute or two," Mariette had teased.

And the neckline had dipped so provocatively in the front that Erin insisted on stuffing in a black lace-fringed hankie to fill the void of cleavage her smaller breasts could not quite manage. It was bad enough

168

with those pads in her corset that shoved them up to mound nicely under the sequined heart appliqué that encompassed her bodice and tapered down to her narrow waist.

"I think they're shuffled sufficiently, Erin," Jackson prompted her, failing to hide the impatience in his tone.

"Ah, let the lady take her time," one of his patrons insisted, giving her a bold wink. "I could just sit here and watch all night."

"But there are others who wish to play, sir," Jackson countered smoothly. "Erin . . ."

With an embarrassed smile for her staunch defender, Erin began to deal the cards. They were new and had a tendency to be stiff and stick together, unlike well worn ones slickened with use. Still, she handled them as if she had been doing so all her life, which she had for as long as she could remember.

In fact, it was from cards that she learned her numbers. That was far before she was forced to attend the schoolhouse on the bluff. She could even add, at least as high as it took to play blackjack. She had to. If not, Cready and the other boys would cheat her of her buttons, stones, or whatever the ante of the day happened to be. While thimble-rigging was her specialty, the card games played in the saloon were her second.

If any of the men at the table had taken heart that Black Jack Tyler was sitting out to train a new girl, they soon realized they had jumped prematurely. With uncanny instinct Erin knew when to fold her cards and when to hang in until the showdown. It didn't hurt that lady luck was on her side, for she'd dealt the house incredible hands. While her companions got high on the liquor being served so freely, she soared on her success and the occasional satisfied smile that settled on her guardian's lips.

Aside from her mother and, recently, her grandmother, Erin never had cared in particular whether or not she pleased anyone. Of course, she was determined to please Jackson Tyler because he was doing so much for her. However, during the last few days of her enforced companionship with her guardian, she had learned that there was a certain pleasure involved as well. Those approving smiles could send her heart tumbling into somersaults and being the sudden center of so much gentlemanly attention was immensely satisfying.

Since that night at the apartment, Jackson had been nothing but a gentleman and, to say the least, his behavior was flattering. Erin had never been treated like a queen. He opened doors. He ordered for her, choosing dishes she'd might never have tried otherwise. He escorted her on walks along the cotton-encumbered decks during which they exchanged river lore. It was almost like being courted, except that Erin realized the sobering truth of the matter. He still didn't trust her.

Every night she checked her bed and, if she found further stolen items, waited until the wee hours of the morning and sneaked them back into the kitchen. It was ironic that she was having to resort to dishonesty to stay honest, but, more than anything, she wanted Jackson Tyler to give her his trust.

When he finally left her table to go to another, she could have squealed with delight. This was it. This was her chance to move up from housekeeping to working in the casino. Heaven knew, it was certainly more fun. Maybe she could even take John's place someday, although she was not so foolish as to think that would come as quickly as the rest of her good fortune had.

"Now that your watchdog has gone, honey, what do you say we take a stroll along the deck later on? A pretty little thing like you shouldn't go unescorted to her cabin."

Erin met the avaricious gaze of the salesman who'd slipped in beside her in Jackson's vacated chair with a sweet smile. "I'm sorry, sir, but I only play one game at a time." It was that and several other lines she'd heard down at the saloon since she was old enough to walk that kept the men at her table at bay and utterly enchanted.

After the first few hands, Erin was beginning to think that lady luck had left her with Jackson Tyler. Although she was keeping the house losses to a minimum with good playing sense, some of the other men were taking a terrible beating. The newcomer from Memphis would shift his cigar from one side of his mouth to the other and rake in his earnings, affording her a suggestive wink each time.

"I might not be taking your money, honey, but these gentlemen are being most accommodating."

"You do seem to be having a streak of luck," Erin agreed. *And moving like you got an itch*, she thought.

She dealt a few more hands, occasionally flashing a flirtatious smile to the side when she was caught observing her fellow player. It could be that he naturally held his cards in the palm of his hand. It could be that there was an outbreak of the hives on his right leg, the way his hand kept slipping down to assuage it. It could also be that he was slipping cards out of his sleeve. Besides, not many salesmen wore diamond breast pins in the shape of a spade. No doubt, like the others at the table, he thought he could flimflam her. If she could just catch him at it . . .

They played another round, Erin becoming friendlier in a new and intriguing game she'd seen played often enough in hopes that a little distraction might cause him to slip. That it appeared to be working was a startling and heady discovery for her. However, her elation faltered when one of the other men at the table quit, emptying his pockets inside out to show he'd lost all he could. He left, complaining that his wife was going to have his head and Erin felt a surge of guilt for her selfish satisfaction, twinged with sympathy for the loser.

Blast that cheating devil! He had to slip sometime, she mused in exasperation. Erin fought the urge to use fire to fight fire. She could easily deal an ace off the bottom of the deck, but with her luck, it would be the same one he duplicated and he'd accuse her of cheating. Her determination renewed, she gave the man an utterly provocative dip of her lashes as she turned up his third card when there was a sudden viselike grip on her shoulder.

"May I see you, Miss Devareau?" Jackson Tyler asked, so firmly that there was no question at all in his voice. "Mariette will fill in for you."

To Erin's surprise, Mariette stood on her other side. Bewildered, but relieved for the chance to tell Jackson of her suspicions, Erin rose from the table and, with a little wriggle, shifted down the dress that had crept up on her hips, a motion not lost on either her guardian or her table companions.

There was a group of men gathered in front of the double doors, left open to allow fresh air into the casino, so they had to walk past a long stack of battened-down cotton bales to gain some semblance of privacy. It wouldn't do to have the other customers knowing there was a dishonest game in progress. The *Delta Moon* had a reputation to salvage from Horsey's previous ownership, not underscore.

She walked ahead of Jackson with a brisk gait, unaware of the enticing swish of the sequined bow on her bustle that had captured his attention. When she was certain they were out of earshot, she turned abruptly as the same grip that had extracted her from her chair assaulted the bare flesh of her arm again.

"Tyler!"

"Just what kind of game were you playing in there, young lady?"

The exclamations came simultaneously, followed by a startled silence on Erin's part and a demanding one on her guardian's. "Blackjack," she answered simply, bewildered by his obvious annoyance.

"I've seen more ladylike behavior from the most practiced tarts on Gallatin Street! That salesman from Memphis was all but drooling down the front of your bodice, not to mention the others at the table!"

"Oh *that!*" Erin caught on with a guileless snicker. "I certainly hope so." At her guardian's dumbstruck look, she went on. "That scoundrel thought he'd take advantage of a new girl and fleece the customers, but I caught onto his game. I'm not as dumb as most folks think," she added proudly. "I know he's cheating, Tyler, and you run an honest ship!"

That coming from Erin, coupled with the outrageous manner in which she had behaved left Jackson at a rare loss for words. What other surprises did his ward have in store for him?

"Well, let's not stand here lollygagging! Let's go throw the sonova . . . buzzard," Erin stumbled, her cheeks flaring to a shade rivaling her gown. "Let's throw him out of the game before he cleans out the house as well."

If she was so adept at the little game he'd just seen her play, was it possible that she knew more of other things? That he'd been treading on eggshells trying to be a gentleman for naught, when all he could think of night and day was what it would feel like to have Erin naked and clinging to him in his bed? Damnation, if he thought for one minute . . .

Erin shifted uncomfortably under the strange look in the eyes raking over her. This certainly was not the reaction she expected. She thought Tyler would be glad, and maybe a bit surprised, that she'd flushed out a cheat. Nervously, she tugged at the gown that had worked its way up on her hips again and cursed a figure that was more rounded than the straight one Anita had to pad out. When she glanced back up, however, she was riveted to the spot by the fire smoldering in her companion's mercurial gaze.

"Don't try your wiles on me, Erin, or you may find you've met more than your match."

"Wiles?" Erin echoed blankly.

"Don't tell me you don't know that half the men in the casino tonight have been absolutely fascinated with that enticing little wriggle you've mastered so suddenly, not to mention that dress. You've become quite a little showpiece!"

Erin's mouth dropped open with incredulity. A showpiece! He was the one who took her out of her boy's clothes and put her in dresses to start with! Here she was trying to keep him an honest ship and he was chastising her because her dress didn't fit right! "Well, if they had a damned wire cage strapped to their ass, I imagine they'd wriggle, too!" she flared back. "Now are you going to throw that man out of the casino, or do I have to do it myself?"

The verbal slap jolted Jackson from the sudden obsession that had overtaken him, an obsession that he found more irritating than any of his charge's actions. It was compounded by the fact that he'd been so caught up with Erin that he'd overlooked a cheat at his own table, one she'd picked up on instantly! "*You* go to your room!" he ordered irritably. "I'll see to my own business!"

Erin stood her ground. She was right and he was wrong. She didn't care if he beat her black and blue, which at the moment, considering his dark countenance, was not out of the question. "Then stop threatening me and go do it," she managed icily, taking the edge of her challenge with an added, "Meanwhile, I'll change into something less offensive."

"See that you do!" With a look that promised their confrontation was far from over, Jackson pivoted and stalked off, disappearing beyond the bales of cotton and into the cluster of men gathered near the rail in front of the casino entrance.

"*See that you do!*" Erin muttered under her breath, making her way to Anita's cabin with the sting of his injustice still simmering in her blood.

She blurted out the entire story to her friend as she jerked off the scarlet gown and did away with the paraphernalia that accompanied it with obvious distaste. Being a lady was becoming too much! The harder she tried to please Jackson Tyler, the worse he acted toward her and she would be damned if she'd stand for it anymore. He would take her as she was or she would leave. She froze in her efforts, liking the alternative even less.

"I don't know what more he wants of me!" she exclaimed in exasperation as she hauled one of her day dresses down over her hips and let the skirts fall naturally from her waist. "I don't understand that pompous self-righteous polecat!"

"Maybe he's just put out because you showed him up," Anita suggested, her voice nasal from her cold. "Men don't cotton to bein' showed up by womenfolk."

"He should have been grateful, not accusing me of being worse than a tart on Gallatin Street!" Erin didn't know anything about Gallatin Street except that that was where John's body had been found, but she did know what a tart was and she certainly could fill in the rest of Jackson's accusation well enough. The whole of Natchez Under the Hill would make Gallatin Street look like the city on the bluff, she imagined petulantly.

"Jackson said *that?*" Anita coughed in astonishment.

"Damned right, he did!" Erin looked at her reflection in the mirror. Even the dresses he'd bought her showed off her figure, something she'd long tried to hide. They had sure earned her her share of smiles from the men in the crew, as well as passengers. If Jackson Tyler didn't like that, then why the bloody blazes did he put her in them in the first place? Her nostrils flared with renewed fury. "Jackson Tyler hasn't begun to meet his match," she vowed under her breath to the girl in the mirror.

Leaving a bemused Anita to her hot toddy and the turpentine-soaked flannel on her chest, Erin stormed through the corridor toward the cabin Tyler had reinstated her in. But when she reached the door, instead of going into her own cabin, she fished the maid's key out of her pocket and slipped into that of her guardian. With a spiteful glint lighting in the green depths of her eyes, she began to rummage through the orderly closet containing the tailored suits that set off Jackson's masculine figure so well.

It was too early in the evening to retire, she mused as she tugged on a pair of trousers under her dress. The waist was sizes too big, so after making two large pleats on either side, she folded the waistband over to hold them in place. The hems she rolled up carefully on the inside so as to present a decent bottom. Adequately impressed with her progress, Erin did away with her dress and replaced it with one of the neatly pressed and starched shirts folded in the trunk against the wall.

The ascot tie proved the most challenging of the masculine attire. Erin wished Jackson wasn't wearing his string tie, for the ascot tied in the same manner, a wide bow, hardly looked fitting. She examined the end result in the mirror critically. The suit hung on her, in spite of her alterations, but it would make her point and that was all she cared about. Swimming under the masculinely tailored lines, her figure hardly showed at all. A beaver top hat that she'd found in a box in the bottom of the locker sank on either side of her head to her ears, but was a crowning glory that managed to suffuse a humorous, if somewhat devious, twinkle into an otherwise sullen gaze.

Anxious to make her appearance in the casino before she lost her nerve and her trousers, Erin seized the doorknob and yanked open the door. The sight of a man standing in its frame, however, caused her to gasp and freeze in mid-step.

"Sturgis!"

"Miss Devareau?"

Of all the luck! Erin stepped back, partly from astonishment and partly to get beyond the range of the smell of whiskey that burst forth with her name.

"What in the devil are you about?" the tutor stammered, shocked at the change in the young woman whom he'd sought out after Jackson Tyler returned to the casino. Since she'd left the dinner table, he hadn't been able to take his eyes off her. She'd bewitched him before with her saucy manner, but as he'd nursed one drink after another, the sight of her in that revealing gown had played havoc with the baser instincts usually unstirred by the typical complacent female. They only generated contempt in his mind.

"It's none of your business."

He looked at the stubborn set of rosy lips that had set his imagination wondering more than on just those occasions when he happened to be in her presence. Now there was spirit that could make his blood boil. The less satisfying roles of the ardent admirer and that of a compassionate companion having failed to bring her under his control, there was only one other way to reach one like this. Every man knew a rebellious woman simply begged for domination.

The sight of her in men's clothing, however, had

taken him back. "I am certain that Mr. Tyler would not approve of this . . . this charade of yours. It's unbecoming to a lady."

"To hell with being a lady!" Erin declared hotly, too absorbed in her own passion to pay heed to that kindling in Sturgis's gaze. "I'm tired of being a lady!" Stepping up to the man, she tapped him on the chest. "Now out of my way, Sturgis. I'm in no mood for your lectures!"

Catching the man off guard, Erin shoved past him and marched toward the companionway leading onto the deck. As she shoved the polished brass door open, a wiry arm took her by surprise and a hand silenced the startled curse that erupted from her lips. Reacting instinctively, she tried to catch her foot between the closing door and the jamb, only to have it jerked roughly through. A burning pain raked the skin of her ankle through the coarse material of the trousers. To her horror, the garment remained, hung on a loose bolt, as she was dragged back inside the cabin.

Having risen to the role he favored best, Roderick Sturgis forced the struggling girl into the room and closed the door behind him. It was early in the evening. Most of the officers and members of the steamship staff who lived along this corridor would be hours from returning to their cabins. Even if the girl put up a fuss, it was unlikely to be heard—not like it would be during the lessons that had become so trying for him. He'd patiently watched for enough evenings to know this.

"Then since Mr. Tyler is likely to be through with us both before this night is over, I see no reason why we shouldn't make the best of it." A lascivious gaze ran the length of the exposed leg revealed beneath the tail of the starched shirt.

Erin picked herself up from the floor where she'd fallen, her eyes widening as she watched him take the key she'd inadvertently left in the door and lock it before placing it in his vest pocket. The man was acting crazy again, she thought, Jackson's letter opener coming to her mind as the logical solution. She leapt for the desk and yanked open the drawer, her groan of dismay at finding it empty blending with a knowing laugh.

"You'll find it under your mattress . . . with a few other of Tyler's personal belongings."

"You!" Erin gasped, her brow furrowing in confusion. "But why?"

"Take off that shirt, my dear, and I'll tell you."

"Go to hell!" Seizing the book of literary collections that she'd been studying from the edge of the desk, she threw it at the man approaching her and glanced about for another weapon. Her heart, thawing from the initial shock that her tutor had been the one framing her for stealing with the realization of her danger, seemed to beat the very breath from her lungs as she turned and raced for the bunk where other volumes were neatly shelved.

"Never strike your instructor, my dear."

The eerie calm of the chastisement echoing so close behind her made Erin turn her head slightly from her desperate task. Suddenly her ears roared with the explosive impact of her school book against the side of her head. Stunned, she collapsed facedown on the bunk, blinking with pain.

"We're two of a kind, you know, Erin . . . being forced to be what we aren't. We should comfort each other rather than be at odds," Sturgis whispered breathily in her ear.

Erin protested as she was rolled over and tried to swing arms that would not obey her will at him as he hauled her up onto the mattress and straddled her. The sudden movement sent lights flashing across her vision with shades of blackness shutting them out intermittently.

179

"You'll never be what Tyler wants you to be. That's why I put the silver under your bed. I don't want to see you get close to the man when you'll soon have another guardian."

"Noo . . ." Erin mumbled, trying to regain control of her limbs.

"I heard the sheriff tell Tyler that Horsey has better evidence that your mother wanted him as your guardian. Horsey's letter is in her own writing."

Somewhere in the recesses of Erin's mind, she recalled the glimpse she'd had of the document Horsey flashed in front of them at the saloon and a wild panic set in, worse than that caused by the harsh fingers fondling her breasts through the rough starched linen of her shirt.

"If Horsey does get your custody, you can count on me being a regular customer, since I'm damned set on being your first."

The rip of Jackson's shirt as it was torn away to expose her warm flesh to the cool air of the cabin and the heated gaze of her assailant managed to penetrate Erin's daze. As Sturgis slid down to viciously suckle the tip of her upthrust breast, as if his sole intent was to inflict pain, Erin fought the bile that rose in her throat, recalling another scene, one which she'd witnessed long ago. Had that been Roderick Sturgis mounted on one of her aunts like a crazed cowboy and whipping her with a short crop?

"Bastard!" Erin rallied, bringing her knee up with all the force she could muster. The blow, rather than stopping him short threw him forward with a grunt. Before he could push himself up, Erin sank her teeth into his shoulder.

"Jezebel!" he screamed, tearing away so abruptly that she thought she'd lose her teeth with the material of his jacket.

For a moment, she thought she stood a chance of throwing him to the side, but before she could, the ascot she had tied in a bow about her neck earlier was suddenly snatched up, drawing her with it until her face was only inches from the red mottled one of her attacker.

Erin's blood stilled in her veins with the certainty that he was going to kill her. She tried to breathe, but the tightening noose of silk would allow no air in or out, any more than the heavy weight of the body crushing hers. Frantically, she beat on the narrow shoulders of the wiry man until once again her limbs would not obey her. She tried to focus on the light above the bunk against the darkness that began to fill her vision.

The image of the brass lamp had all but faded when the weight was suddenly lifted. A loud crack exploded nearby followed by the crash of a chair overturning, but Erin could not see its source. Nor did she question the physical disappearance of the threat. Instead she listened, fearful of its return before she could regain full consciousness.

"I ought to throw you in the river for this!" Jackson? she wondered at the sound of a male voice hoarse with rage. There was a loud grunt and the sound of flesh and bone clashing. Somewhere in the room a picture fell from the wall and crashed amid more scuffling.

"Me? Look at the seductive little jezebel! She's been tempting me since the very first day with those little looks and smiles." Roderick Sturgis's voice rose to a level near hysteria. "God in heaven, man, surely you've seen it for yourself! Even gentlemen such as we have a limit to our forbearance! I tried to stop her from wearing those men's clothes to the main deck and embarrassing you and she began to tear them off. I . . . I couldn't help myself!"

Jackson nearly choked on his fury, keeping the smaller man pinned against the door with one hand, his other fisted and ready to strike. He'd not been able

181

to get Erin out of his mind. She'd been right about the swindler. The man had admitted it, grateful that Jackson had asked him to step outside for a smoke rather than start a scene in public.

Maybe she'd been acting, mimicking what she'd seen most of her life. God knew she had a talent for it! He'd admitted to himself that her act had nearly been his undoing and that was what had eaten at him. Erin could get under his skin quicker than anything or anyone he'd ever come across.

He was just coming to grips with that when he found a pair of his trousers hanging in the corridor door on his way to seek the girl out and try to make amends. Bemused, he had been about to knock on her door when he'd heard a scuffle in his own quarters.

"She's had us all fooled, when all the while she was just like the whores who raised her. Take what you can get and give just what you have to to get by. She even bit me!"

"Enough or I'll shut you up permanently!" The fist that had been held back, suddenly lashed out, clipping the tutor in the jaw. The clutch Jackson's other hand held on the man's collar gave way under his victim's collapsing weight and Jackson stood back to let him slump to the floor. "You're fired," he muttered through teeth clenched so hard they ached, like the rest of him, for further release. He was literally shaking with the urge to carry out his threat, to take the offensive words he'd just heard and shove them back down Sturgis's throat along with his uneven teeth. He wanted to kill the man for saying those things about Erin . . . the same things he'd intimated to her earlier.

"My God!" Mariette's stunned exclamation from the open door where she unexpectedly appeared shook the confusion from Jackson's normally clinical mind and helped restore some order.

Exhaling deeply, he reached down and hauled a

half conscious Sturgis to his feet. Assuming control of the bizarre situation, he motioned toward the bunk with his head. "See to Erin while I take this sniveling bastard below."

"What happened?" the woman asked, stepping clear of the men to rush to Erin's aid. She covered the girl's nakedness with a blanket and glanced back expectantly at the somber man who stared at the bunk as if trying to fathom the circumstances himself.

"I'm damned if I know." It was a pained admission, fraught with confusion that had been momentarily put aside for sanity.

Yet, it was not as painful as the wound it inflicted. Erin squeezed her eyes tighter and seized her lower lip in her teeth. How could he believe Sturgis! Her nails bit into the flesh of her palm in rebellion to what she'd heard. Bejesus, why couldn't the blackness she'd been battling take over now and stop this hurt? She wasn't aware that she'd whimpered in her agony until she felt Mariette's gentle hands on her shoulders.

"There now, honey. It's going to be all right. Tell Mariette what happened."

Erin didn't want to tell anyone what had happened. No one would believe her, she thought, caught up in a terrible despair. No one cared. No one loved her. The only ones who had were gone. A sob rose in her throat and she valiantly fought to swallow it. She drew the blanket tighter around her shoulders and shuddered. "Go a . . . away!"

"I wouldn't think of it!" the woman objected. "Not until you tell me what this was all about." Her voice softened and Erin felt her brush the hair from her face. "Did that old buzzard hurt you, honey?"

"No." Not like Jackson Tyler had. Why did it have to matter so much to her?

"What are you doing in Jackson's clothes anyway?"

183

Erin shakily heaved a sigh of resignation. It was evident that Mariette was going to keep questioning her until she found out what had happened, so, hesitantly at first, Erin began to tell her how angry she'd been with Jackson. What she thought would come hard, came easy with Mariette's gentle coaxing and the burning whiskey the woman gave her to settle her nerves. The whole story spilled out, including Erin's heartbreak that Jackson Tyler didn't trust her—that he'd believe a lecherous old man over her, even though she'd been the one nearly unconscious from strangling and helpless to defend herself.

"He . . . he's even been stealing silver and putting it under my mattress so Jackson wouldn't want to keep me!" she added with a wail of dismay. "I . . . I've been sneaking around at night trying to put it back."

"Why don't you tell Jackson?" Mariette suggested sympathetically.

"He won't even listen!" Erin sniffed, covering her face with a pillow lightly scented from the after-shave she'd come to like so well.

"That's not true, Erin."

Erin burrowed even deeper into the plump down ticking at the sound of Jackson Tyler's voice. She refused to see the haggard expression on his face or the disheveled appearance that resulted from his ready defense of her.

Pulling off a tie that had come undone in the fray, Jackson tossed it on the desk and helped himself to the whiskey Mariette had left out, his thoughtful gaze never leaving the girl drawn into a ball on the bunk.

Mariette slipped off her perch on the bed and started toward the door. "Unless you want me to stay, I think I'll leave you two to talk."

"I think I can manage," Jackson replied tightly. "*She's all right, just hurt feelings and wounded*

184

*pride,"* the woman mouthed silently for Jackson's benefit only as she passed him to leave, but at the entrance she looked back. "A little patience might go a long way," she advised to no one in particular before closing the door behind her.

Patience, Jackson reflected, studying the figure huddled in the corner of his bunk. He used to think he possessed a great deal of it. He had to in his business. What had he gotten himself into with this girl? God knew, he wanted to believe her. In the corner of his eye, he spotted his dress hat lying on the floor and bent over to pick it up and return it to its proper place. And what had she been up to, wearing his clothes?

As he put the hat back in the locker, trying to assemble exactly what it was he wanted to say, he heard Erin moving and turned to see her slide off the bed, the blanket drawn tightly around her. Her eyes were swollen and red, but it was the ugly marks around her neck, exposed by an open ascot Mariette had loosened, that commanded his attention.

Once again a protective surge swept over him, tearing him between taking Sturgis out of his engineer's custody to personally toss him over the side and taking the disconsolate figure making her way to his door in his arms. He chose the latter.

"Erin . . ." he began compassionately.

"Don't touch me!" Erin shrieked. She tried to pull out of his stronger embrace.

"Erin, we need to talk."

"Why? You don't believe anything I say!" Erin would have stuggled further, but her head ached from where the book had struck it and her throat burned from the fierce constriction. Instead, she leaned into his strength, trying to ignore what she needed so desperately.

"I told you, you're wrong."

"Why?" she asked bitterly. "What's changed?"

185

"It's hard to believe anything wrong of someone you care for." There! He said it. He did care for Erin. She'd managed to endear herself to him, in spite of the wild escapades that kept him on edge from one moment to the next. It suddenly felt as if a heavy load had been lifted from his chest, one Jackson replaced with a much lighter one as he scooped the unsteady girl up in his arms.

"Care for?" Erin echoed, too distracted by the admission to protest as he deposited her on the mattress.

"Roderick Sturgis has no idea how close he came to meeting his maker when I burst in here and saw him hurting you."

"I didn't invite him in, he . . ."

"Shush," Jackson whispered against her lips. "It doesn't matter."

Whether it was her pounding head demanding comfort or the sweet assault on her lips that bade her lean back against the pillows, taking him with her, Erin didn't know. What she did know was that this was what she wanted . . . needed. Yet his disclaimer would not give her peace.

"But it does matter," she breathed shakily against his cheek as his lips made a trail of tiny kisses around to her ear with a devastating effect. Her words drifted off with a tiny moan at the devilish work played by his tongue. "I have to know you trust . . ." Her voice caught in her throat, erupting into a small whimper as gentle fingers ran across the swelling hidden beneath the silken raven tresses they explored. "My head," she explained, wincing as her companion ventured to examine her more closely.

Jackson shook himself sternly to stem the surge of mingled rage and passion that tortured his mind and body. Erin was hardly in any condition for seduction which, if he allowed himself to comfort her much more, would become impossible to resist. He knew the moment Mariette left that he should have insisted she remain. Even in his tattered shirt and blanket, Erin was more desirable than any creature he'd ever seen.

For that very reason, he'd hardly been able to condemn Roderick Sturgis for lusting after her. The man's loss of control was almost understandable. And heaven knew, Erin had provoked Jackson on more than one occasion to the point that he'd wanted to throttle her himself. How could he in clear conscience unconditionally blame a man for something so easy to relate to?

At any rate, he was putting Sturgis off the ship in the morning. He and Reds decided, considering the man's insistence that Erin had led him on and her witnessed behavior in the casino, that that would cause the least scandal and trauma for the girl. Yet, as Jackson saw her lovely features draw tightly at the light touch of his examination, it was very hard not to back down from his decision.

"We ought to put a cold cloth on that lump," he observed clinically before walking over to the agate water pitcher borrowed from one of the crew's cabins to replace the two sets his ward had cost him. He poured water into a matching bowl. After soaking and wringing a towel he made his way back to the silent girl on the bunk.

"I want to go to my own cabin," Erin announced, meeting his gaze evenly as he gently placed the folded cloth against the swelling. She really didn't want to leave. It was uniquely pleasant to see Jackson Tyler, sleeves rolled up and jacket and vest discarded like the doctor that sometimes tended the girls at Horsey's when one of Lil's home remedies for unwanted pregnancies failed, in this new light. She wanted to stay and tender whatever it was that was subtly developing between them. Yet, his evasion of her plea for his trust was too cruel to permit her to enjoy it.

"You've had a blow to the head. Someone needs to watch you."

The impartiality in his tone broke the fleeting delusion she'd fancied instantly. "Then Mariette . . ."

"Is busy at the casino."

"Hannah?"

"In the kitchen."

Erin clamped her jaw tightly. "I'm all right."

"No, you're not," Jackson insisted with a touch of growing frustration. "Your legs are so wobbly, you can hardly walk! Damnation, Erin, must you always be so . . . difficult?"

Erin drew the shapely length of leg that had interrupted Jackson's speech under the blanket and shot back defensively, "If you don't want to be my guardian anymore, just say so! I managed without you for six months while Mama was sick. I can do it again. I don't need you or Horsey!"

A dark eyebrow arched into a scowling brow. "Forget Horsey! I'll see him in hell before he lays a finger on you."

The threat was said with such vehemence that Erin could not doubt Jackson meant every word he'd said. "So will I," she replied, finding at least one thing on which the two of them agreed.

Jackson ignored the obstinate innuendo. So help him, he was trying! There had been enough confrontation between them without rehashing the argument that she forget her intended revenge on Coleman Horsey. What he needed to do was brighten the dismal face turned toward him.

"Besides, I'm getting used to this guardian business, although it's taking more of an adjustment than I had counted on," he added with a bone-melting grin. "The usual parent has a whole lifetime of raising a little girl before dealing with her as a young lady. While that has its decided liabilities, as little Jasper so illustriously illustrated for me," he injected, his wry admission rewarded with a twitch at the corner of a wholly beguiling pout, "I suppose, it also has its benefits. After all, I never claimed to be totally adept at this!" He shrugged, his wide shoulders drawing his shirt taut against a broad chest. "Maybe we both might try a little more patience, like Mariette said. What do you say?"

The normally impenetrable gray eyes kindled with an undeniable sincerity that managed to infect Erin with a glow her pinkening cheeks only hinted of. She wanted more than anything for Jackson to like her, to believe in her. It just seemed that circumstances always pointed against her.

Sturgis's lies could have appeared believable, she supposed. She had flirted with the salesman and maybe Sturgis had seen her. Maybe she'd played with fire and been burned, as she'd often heard Aunt Lil and the girls say when one of them had gotten roughed up a bit.

And Jackson had fought for her, she rationalized as the man replaced one damp rag with a fresh one. He'd punched Sturgis in the face, as if he didn't like the things the man had said and . . . and when he acted like this—so gentle and caring and yet, adorably humorous—who could hold anything against him? She heaved a resigned sigh that caught as he felt once more for the lump to place the cool cloth over it. The sight of the dark fur thickening from a fringe at the base of his collarbone to spread over a muscular expanse revealed by his open shirt was distracting from the tenderness of her wound. She wanted to reach up and explore it, but held back. It was disrupting enough for him to touch her, even impersonally as he was doing now, let alone for her to feel his flesh, warm and vibrantly male beneath her fingers.

She curled them against her palm and closed her

eyes, unaware of the sensual diversion her tongue made as she moistened her suddenly dry lips. In time, she rationalized, forcing her thoughts back on track, if Jackson got to know her better, he wouldn't believe anything bad about her. With Roderick Sturgis and his pranks out of the way, that was more possible than ever. He'd know she wanted to be a lady . . . for him and all whom she loved.

"Maybe you're right," she answered softly, basking in the warm and tender look her answer evoked.

## Chapter Thirteen

"I guess we did too good'a job on you last night from what I hear," Anita sniffed as she tried to discipline one of the curls that would not sweep up into the pert topknot gracing the top of Erin's head. "I'm surprised Jackson's letting you take my place again tonight."

"Me too," Erin answered evasively. Although, she was astonished. When she'd broached the subject tentatively that morning, having awakened in her guardian's bed to find him sleeping head on folded arms over his desk, he'd considered it for a prolonged moment and then agreed.

There were, however, conditions. One was that she must be feeling up to it, to which Erin promptly declared that, aside from a sore spot on the side of her head, she was fine. The other was that he chose the dress and accessories she would wear.

It had struck her as odd that he knew more about what women should wear under their clothes than she did. But then, a man like Tyler, she supposed, would know those sort of things. No doubt he'd taken enough clothes off of women in the past to have earned such knowledge.

The dress he'd chosen was one of the newer ones Mrs. Brady had sent. The neckline was high and adorned with a dark green ribbon that matched the stems and leaves of the flowers on its sheer printed material. The bodice was lined with a camisole the shade of the neutral background of the print, as was the skirt. The sleeves and remainder of the chaste bodice, as well as the gather of ruffles in the back which draped the skirt across Erin's figure most becomingly, were decorated with the same ribbon as the choker collar. Erin thought it made her look like Mrs. Emory, her grade school teacher, except that Mrs. Emory's calico dresses weren't quite as fine.

"You look as highfalutin' as that neighbor of his, Jackson's always sportin' around on his arm."

"But Erin doesn't have to work as hard to be that way," Mariette piped up, affording Erin a surreptitious wink. "I just wish there was more we could tell you about how ladies think and act, but it would be guesswork at best."

"We could'a done a better job than that weasel Sturgis!" Anita derided. "Imagine Jackson lettin' him walk off the boat at Bayou Sara and the law right here on board!"

"Come on, 'Nita, you know he was just tryin' to keep Erin from some mighty embarrassin' questions. 'Sides, how would it look to the sheriff if the man Jackson hired to tutor the kid tried to rape her? It sure wouldn't show Jackson was a good choice as guardian and he's got to prove that or that bastard Horsey . . ." Mariette caught herself upon seeing the green eyes swing to her with undivided attention.

"Horsey really has a chance with that letter?" Erin asked, her color fading beneath the slight brush of rouge Anita had rubbed on her cheeks.

Mariette forced a light laugh. "Not against Jackson Beauregard Tyler of Retreat! Horsey might have the letter, but Jackson has the family, the blue blood, so to speak. It ain't like it's one gambler against another."

"And Jackson ain't gonna give you up. He holds on to what's his," Anita joined in.

"And from the way he keeps an eye on you, honey, he considers you his. I thought he was going to kill Sturgis when I come up on them last night."

"And I'll bet you got some mighty special care," the woman putting the last of the pins in Erin's hair suggested slyly.

Erin felt the blood burn its way to her face under the speculative looks fixed on her. Anita was right. Tyler couldn't have been sweeter or acted more concerned. He'd made her laugh, which didn't help her head, but it helped her spirit. She drifted off to sleep chuckling over his disdainful dissertation on his helplessness with small children.

"I suppose they're tolerable, if they're someone else's," he'd told her, tongue in cheek. "Although I've seen more than my share that I would like to toss over the rail when their parents weren't watching."

Under other circumstances, Erin might have defended the smaller version of the human race, for she loved helping Mrs. MacCready with the children she cared for. However, she had let him ramble on, charmed with this lighter side of his character and not wanting to say or do anything to halt the gentle ministrations he continued as he entertained her. After she'd drifted off to sleep, she could have sworn he'd kissed her, lightly, like the brush of a warm summer breeze across her cheek.

"What is it like to have a man make love to you?" Unwittingly, Erin's question answered the unspoken one that had been dangling in her companions' minds when Hannah had discreetly reported to the girls at the noonday meal in the crew's kitchen that Erin's bed had not been slept in. There were few, if any secrets in the little shipboard community, and now there was one less.

"Well I'll be damned!" Mariette marveled, having

193

been certain that what she'd witnessed brewing between her employer and his ward had finally come to its natural conclusion. The normally congenial Jackson Tyler had been as irritable as a penned-up boar since Erin had come aboard and frankly, the sooner those two were together, the better. That the girl was still untouched after a night in Jackson's cabin left her speechless.

"Don't just stand there grinnin' like a constipated jackass, tell the girl, Mariette!" Anita declared, adding a smug, "I told you so," mouthed silently over Erin's head.

Shaken from her stunned state by her roommate's sarcasm, Mariette jumped up from her perch on the edge of the dressing table and twisted a scented handkerchief in her hands. Doing something was one thing. Describing it was quite another. "It all depends on the man, I suppose," she began cautiously, disconcerted by the curious gaze leveled at her. "It could be the damnedest good time you ever saw or downright disgustin'."

"Bear in mind, kid, Mariette and me are casino girls, not professionals like you . . . your mother oversaw."

"Mama ran the saloon, not the girls," Erin replied tersely.

Anita offered a sympathetic smile. "Of course she did. I didn't mean . . ."

"What 'Nita's tryin' to say is that most of our experience, since Jackson sees us paid so well to keep a decent ship, is that of our own choosin', if you get my drift."

"Heck, sometimes we don't even take a cent."

Mariette snorted, exchanging a knowing look with her roommate. "I've seen a time or two when it was so damned good, I'd have to pay the devil!"

It was beyond Erin's comprehension that this could be true, not after what she'd witnessed with her own eyes. Her shocked face nearly made it impossible for the others to suppress their smiles.

"Look, honey," Mariette spoke up, turning away so as not to appear to be laughing at her serious charge. "I got me this book about what goes on between ladies and gentlemen. It never made much sense to me, but then 'Nita and me aren't the best readers. It's old, of course . . ."

"So is what we're talkin' about!" Anita quipped saucily.

Mariette dug deep into a trunk loaded with ruffles, satins, and other frillies intended to enhance her figure and came out with an unimpressive volume compared to those gilded and leather-bound ones in Jackson's collection. "My aunt gave it to me and Mama would have died if she knew. There's things in here it ain't considered proper for a woman to know, let alone a single gal."

"In other words, keep it hidden. Somebody catchin' you with it might get the wrong idea," Anita advised meaningfully.

"'Sides, you can't even get material like this in the mail nowadays, though damned if I can say why. I know many a woman would be tickled to know how to keep from gettin' with child without givin' up the fun of things. Anyways, keep it to yourself, kid."

Her curiosity intensely piqued, Erin nodded and took the book gratefully. In black and white, there was less likely to be the conflicting views she'd run into in her personal exposure to such things. If only her mother were alive, things would be so different. Giselle Devareau had had a way with words, of making Erin understand things. And this was something that was suddenly important for her to understand.

Taking advantage of the brief space of time before the dinner bell rang on the boiler deck, she quickly retreated to her room to peruse through the *Fruits of*

*Philosophy* before her presence at Jackson's side would be required. Upon reaching her door, she paused to listen at the one across the hall, certain that her guardian, like most of the passengers, would be dressing for the evening. Reassured that Jackson Tyler was thus occupied, she slipped into her own suite and climbed upon her bunk to get comfortable.

It wasn't hard to tell which section of the text was devoted to the subject of her interest. It was stained and yellowed with age and evident use. Skipping the rest until later, she concentrated on the author's recommendations concerning "connexion." The revelation was startling.

Frequency was discouraged as it was said to impair mental faculties of both parties, result in exposure to disease, and, in the case of the male, cause weakness likened to the loss of forty ounces of blood! Furthermore, it rendered couples irritable, unsociable, and melancholy.

Erin frowned, digesting the contents skeptically. She'd been led to believe it was the lack of such things that contributed to a cantankerous disposition. Yet, concerning the disruption to mental faculties, she'd seen men and women who lost their heads over each other. Heaven knew, when Tyler kissed her, she couldn't think worth two bits!

A diet of milk and vegetables was recommended for bachelors and one of meat, turtles, oysters, and red wine for those who preferred a spur to their lovemaking. But what of women, she wondered, turning to the pages ahead dealing with avoiding pregnancy. Her attention riveted to the informative reading, she didn't hear the short knock on her door above the steady drone and vibration of the ship beneath her. Nor was she aware that she was not alone until a shadow blocked the light coming in through the portal.

"That must be some book," Jackson Tyler remarked, leaning over to see what she was reading.

Face flaming to a color that rivaled the sunset on the western bank, Erin slammed the book shut and slid off the bunk. "It is," she answered truthfully, clutching it to her bosom, her hands sure to cover its identity.

"One of mine?"

"On navigation." She slipped it under her pillow and smoothed out the coverlet she'd disturbed to do so. "I'll put it right here so I can continue later when we're through in the casino. Reading helps me sleep sometimes," she went on nervously.

Jackson curiously surveyed his charge. He'd hoped to dash this silly idea of her becoming a river pilot, but not to the point that she would try to hide her aspirations from him.

"I'm absolutely famished!" Erin exclaimed, turning an overbright smile up at him as she locked elbows with him. "And I can't wait to go to the casino. I just love the games."

Her ruse, no matter how transparent, was perfectly charming. Jackson covered the small hand on his arm with his own. "Then let's get on with our evening, mademoiselle."

The returning smile he bestowed upon her nearly made Erin forget her book completely. It washed warm all over her and tightened her loose grip on the arm beneath the rich material of his suit.

Tyler was one of those men who was beautiful, not in a feminine way, but a decidedly masculine one. Although his clothing always fit to perfection, Erin was certain that the most ill-fitting garment would look noble on his well-formed body. He even looked noble without clothes.

"I must commend Mrs. Brady on her handiwork," Jackson told her upon emerging on the lower deck where passengers gradually made their way toward the double doors leading to the main salon. "You're radiant in that dress, Erin." It was not nearly as provocative as the one she'd worn the night before and yet Jackson could not take his eyes off her. Bathed in the brilliant fanfare of light afforded by the sunset, radiant was hardly a fit description of the natural glow Erin exuded. The dress, although pretty, he realized, had nothing at all to do with it.

"I was going to say the same thing about you."

The guileless remark so like the girl on his arm nearly robbed Jackson of his senses. At that moment, all he could think about was sweeping her into the cover of the cotton bales and tasting the sweet lips from which it had come.

"Tyler, there you are! Did you get a chance to look at any of those numbers I gave you?"

Jackson shook himself of the innocent spell cast by his charge and turned to greet the railroad representative from Philadelphia who had occupied the better part of his day. A group of businessmen were looking for investors in a new venture that had greatly spurred his interest. The fact that the man was an old friend made it a pleasant as well as challenging afternoon.

"Indeed, I did, J.P. In fact, I made some notes here." He reached inside his coat pocket and winced. "I seem to have left them in my other jacket. Would you . . ." Upon seeing the appreciative sweep of his associate's gaze directed at Erin, Jackson stiffened and struggled with the instinct to draw the girl possessively under his arm. After all, she was a beauty and as such, bound to draw male admiration. He forced aside his natural inclinations rebelliously. "Permit me to introduce my ward, Miss Erin Devareau. Erin, this is—"

"J.P. Renolds of the railroad commission, at your service." The railroad man, while lacking the gallantry of the southern gentry, took Erin's extended hand in a firm clasp that lingered longer than

198

Jackson cared for. "I am enchanted. Perhaps, if your guardian would care to fetch his notes, I might be granted the honor of escorting you to your seat."

Renolds was not an unattractive man with his golden hair and stylish mustache, nor was his smile defaulted by the sincerity in his gaze. The fact that he shook Erin's hand, like an equal, left an impression that helped overcome her awkward acceptance of such open admiration. She glanced expectantly at Jackson in time to see an angry flash fade to an impenetrable look.

"I'm sure Erin will keep you entertained until I can return," Jackson conceded, handing the hand on his arm over to his associate with polite grace. "We'll try a burgundy tonight," he instructed Erin so as not to hold up the order at the head table with his absence.

Pleased that she, for the time being, would get to order for Jackson for a change, Erin eagerly accepted the arm of her new escort and proceeded into the dining salon. J.P. Renolds finished his introduction of himself as she did so, continuing to tell her over the wine that was promptly served that he was trying to interest Tyler in investing in a railroad company that held a promising future and could reach farther and faster into regions where water could not carry one. Furthermore, the railroad was not subject to the whims of nature like the steamboat trade where a high or low tide affected by rain or lack of it could keep a boat from landing.

Although Erin was fascinated by Steven's presentation, she was more entertained when Jackson rejoined them. It seemed the two were schoolmates from West Point where both had managed to be expelled before the end of their first year. Although each accused the other of being the true culprit in their misadventures, Erin's newly discovered information in Dr. Knowlton's book seemed to explain the reason for their irreverent behavior. Besides the fact that neither of them seemed to know the meaning of the word, *moderation,* how could young bachelors be expected to behave with a diet of rich wines and succulent roasts so readily available to them, if not at the academy, at the taverns they frequented nearby. The pursuit of the feminine sex and fine liquors had but one possible result—it addled their brains and got them kicked out of school.

After the nonetheless delightfully entertaining repast, the men broke away to smoke and Erin made her way straight to the casino to help Mariette set up. Like the night before, there were already some of the more devoted gamblers present, no doubt involved in private games that had started that afternoon. With a glass of wine more to her liking, Erin settled at her own table, her blood racing with the same excitement as the previous evening. Hopefully tonight there would be no cheats, just honest men seeking an evening's amusement with the chance of a little profit.

The salesman who had caused all her trouble had gone ashore that morning with Roderick Sturgis, glad that Jackson had not called the attention of the law to him. Ironically, the chance stopover had brought aboard J.P. Renolds who recognized the *Delta Moon* as one of Jackson Tyler's ships and sought out his friend to solicit his interest in the railroad venture.

Erin smiled and began to deal the cards to the men who had quickly filled her table. It was a more than fair exchange. In fact, she almost wished they were another day from Natchez, for she wanted to hear more about the railroads, particularly the one that crossed the whole of the United States.

Although her concentration was fully on her game, when Jackson Tyler and J.P. Renolds entered the room and took a place at the bar, Erin did not miss them. Nor did Mariette. The woman's eyes followed Renolds and remained with him until his sharp blue gaze collided with them. A grin tugged at Erin's lips as she revealed her hand and raked in her winnings to the polite moans of her fellow players. The two friends must have created quite a stir among those fancy ladies living near West Point, especially in uniforms.

"So what kind of future do you intend for your . . . ward?" Renolds finished, sending a wink to where the raven-haired girl resided over her table like a prima madonna surrounded by iniquity.

Jackson pondered the question that had plagued his mind since his discovery that his charge was a girl. "Once I make a lady of her, marriage to a suitable gentleman, I suppose . . . one who can take good care of her." He'd already told his companion something of Erin's background to explain his guardianship.

"She had me fooled," Renolds commented frankly. "There must be something to that Creole blue blood running true. No matter what the environment, it just comes through."

Jackson had to laugh. He could imagine the expression on J.P.'s face if Erin were to cut loose with the full thrust of her expressive vocabulary. "At least the hot-tempered part of it is true," he concurred wryly.

"And where there is passion of one sort, there lies fire of another," the golden-haired man quoted from another more reckless time when speculation as to a particular young woman's nature had kept them awake after curfew.

"That, my friend, no man will know until she is wedded and bedded by a proper husband . . . at least as long as I am her guardian," he warned through a smile.

Renolds looked back over to where one of the players at the table scrambled to pick up a card that had slipped from the pile Erin shuffled. "Then you, my friend, have my deepest sympathy. If you'll excuse me, I think I will buy that luscious blonde at the other table a drink. Hers is empty."

Leaving Jackson to ponder his parting words, the broker turned and walked over to where Mariette was bantering saucily with the men at her table to find out just how far that interested look she'd given him earlier would go. Athough he would prefer to escort the intriguing Erin Devareau to her room at the night's end, he'd learned a long time ago not to cross Jackson Beauregard Tyler, whether dealing with cards or women.

When the house tables officially closed sometime after midnight, Erin was not the least bit sleepy. She'd done well for the *Delta Moon* and looked forward to tomorrow's pay which she'd earned with her wits rather than the hard work and sweat that provided her earlier compensation. Her savings were already greater than a summer's worth working with Cready, since she wasn't forced to split it and spend the remainder on food and other necessities.

She glanced over to where Mariette was enjoying another glass of champagne, the expensive imported kind, with J.P. Renolds and sighed in disappointment. From the way they were ogling each other, it was doubtful Renolds would return to his cabin alone. She'd been thinking about that railroad investment and wanted to find out how much a share might cost. After all, it never paid to put all one's eggs in one basket.

Her lips thinned as Mariette linked arms with the man and accompanied him, a fresh bottle of champagne in hand toward the double doors leading to the deck. She didn't disapprove of her friend, she told herself sternly. It was not her place to do so.

Besides, it was evident from the bold wink that was suddenly flashed back at Erin as they disappeared through the entrance that this was one of those occasions of choice Mariette had spoken of.

Erin placed a thoughtful finger against her chin, wondering if Renolds could be the sort that her friend would have to pay. The very idea brought an embarrassed rose to her cheeks as it registered fully what she was contemplating.

"You seem quite taken by my old friend," Jackson Tyler speculated at her elbow.

Upon meeting his gaze, Erin smiled nervously. Sometimes she could swear those quicksilver eyes could see right into her innermost thoughts and what was on her mind at the moment was something she would just as soon Jackson Tyler did not discover. "I am," she admitted, "but it seems that Mariette is too. I thought I might discuss some business with him."

The mention of business deflated the building resentment Jackson felt in spite of himself. Of course, he was only concerned that a man like J.P. could sweep an inexperienced girl like Erin off her feet like a predator that was more than a match for its prey. But if business was his ward's only interest in him, perhaps he needn't concern himself overmuch, except to satisfy his curiosity as to its nature.

"I would be glad to speak to him on your behalf if you'd tell me exactly what sort of business you might have with him." Jackson motioned toward the door. "Why don't we take to the hurricane deck for some fresh night air. It's a bit stuffy in here."

Erin complied willingly, for the night of continuous tobacco smoke had made the air thick, in spite of the secondary doors that had been propped open on either end of the room to ventilate it. Accustomed to late hours, she was glad for the opportunity to rise above the clamor of the engines to the top deck and walk off some of her restlessness under the stars.

The bow of the ship cut silently through the muddy waters illuminated by the sweeping floodlights mounted on its bow. Crew members on duty scanned the water for floating debris that could render the *Delta Moon* helpless with a broken paddle wheel or damage the hull, endangering the lives of its passengers and its cargo. The cotton bales on the lower decks made it nearly impossible to see them and only the tip was visible of the large stage used for boarding and disembarking that rode high above the water like a giant battering ram of old.

But it was the stern of the ship that drew Erin to the rail where she could watch the massive paddle wheel churning the muddy water white as it clawed its way upriver. She'd spent hours there since fate had brought her aboard the *Delta Moon*. The steady rhythm was the heartbeat of the ship and endeared to Erin's own heart. She could never give up the river for a pair of steel tracks. However, where she intended to live and where she invested did not have to be one and the same.

"What do you think of Renolds's proposition to invest in the railroad?" she asked, breaking the silent camaraderie that had encompassed both her and the man at her side.

Continually surprised at the things that crossed Erin's mind, Jackson shrugged. "There are a few things I would like to check out, but his theory is sound. The railroads are the future."

"If I had a lot of money, I think I would invest in it. How much do you think a share would cost?"

"That would depend on how the stock was broken down. Renolds is looking for twenty to thirty thousand dollars per investor."

Erin turned away from the rail and raised her gaze to the stars. "Damnation!" she swore softly. Saving one thousand dollars was as likely as being able to reach up and pluck one of the twinkling spectacles from the sky, but twenty thousand!

Jackson smiled sympathetically. "Why don't you leave investments to the men and concentrate on becoming the wife of a man who is capable of doing that for you?"

"Because men up and die and leave women with affairs completely foreign to them. That's what happened to Grandma, but she learned real quick when she found out her lawyer was losing her money." Erin shook her head resolutely. "No, if I have the wits to earn my money, I sure as the devil won't let some man put it at risk. I'd rather do it myself."

"So you're going to give up this idea of captaining a riverboat to become a railroad queen." One thing Jackson could say for Erin, she had spunk and ambition, coupled with an imagination to match.

"No," she answered, her eyes taking on a glow that reflected the stars overhead. "I won't leave the river, not permanently anyway," she added, her mind drifting to the cross-country trip by rail. "I just couldn't. Sometimes I think my heart beats to the same drum as that paddle wheel, like this muddy water was as much a mother to me as Mama was. I'd go plumb crazy if I left it for too long. I want to own a riverboat one day and live on it. I bet there are kings that don't live this good. Maybe I'll leave the captaining to a good man, but I'll want to know as much as he does."

"So he doesn't risk your boat?"

"Exactly. I may put my money in the railroad, but my heart will always be here on the river," she sighed, turning in time to catch a glimpse of humor in her guardian's gaze. Instantly Erin regretted sharing her secret. She'd forgotten Tyler's previous skepticism. "Damn you, Tyler, go ahead and laugh!" she challenged, her face flushing in mingled embarrassment and anger. "But I've already come from

205

carrying wood for the firemen to working in the casino!"

"Because you are my ward, Erin."

Erin rose to her full height, but still had to look up to meet his amused gaze. "I am equal to the job and you know it! I've worked twice as hard as anybody at whatever you've given me to do, worked till I dropped without complaining . . ."

"And won the hearts of every crewman, man and woman, on the ship in the process," Jackson interrupted, silencing her with a gentle finger pressed to her lips. He was tempted to tell her of John's bequest, that she was his full partner in the Delta "O" Line, but held back. Now was not the time. There were too many questions that needed to be answered and, considering her impetuous nature, Erin was better off knowing as little as possible.

The night air was cool as the *Delta Moon* cut its way through it. It caught and played with the tendrils of hair that framed the face Erin turned up to him, a face illuminated by the ship's namesake. When he dropped his voice like that, it seemed to trip like velvet fingers along her spine. "Are you sorry you got stuck with me, Tyler?"

Jackson pulled a somber face and placed a hand on either side of her on the rail. "Now let me see. There was a handsome sum due Mrs. Brady for your clothes . . . and I now have an extra servant at the Decatur Street residence, not to mention Jasper," he added with a laconic grimace. "We won't discuss Roderick Sturgis, for I surely erred in hiring him, but I must consider the loss of two imported bowl and pitcher sets and numerous bars of soap . . ."

Erin could feel the heat of his gaze racing through her like a wildfire, nearly robbing her of breath as it dropped to her slippered feet and slowly, assessingly, worked its way back to her own. "If you keep an a . . . account, I promise to try and pay you ba . . ."

206

Lips gently brushed her own. "There," Jackson whispered. "Paid in full."

While Erin would not accept such forgiveness for the reimbursement she owed Jackson Tyler, she could not bring herself to object to do anything to spoil the moment. What would Mariette do, she wondered, held transfixed by the silver gaze that intensified as it delved into her own. She felt a hand move to the small of her back and inhaled deeply as the scant distance between them closed. There was no escaping, even if she had wanted to.

She met the kiss that completed the molding of their bodies, her arms snaking inside Jackson's coat as if to get closer and seek refuge from the damp spray that hovered in the air over the stern of the ship. His embrace was warm and strong, his fingers masterful as they worked their way down over her buttocks in a massage that erupted in a burst of heat that flushed through her. But it was the hungry sensual assault of his mouth on her own that rendered her knees weak and left her gasping for breath when he drew away only to devour her visually.

"Is this what you want of me, Tyler?" she murmured softly against his chest. She hugged him tightly to give her legs a chance to recoup their strength. As abhorrent as the idea of making love to a man had once been to her, Erin realized that Jackson Tyler had changed all that. There was a part of her now that yearned to know what it would be like with him. She was so wrapped up in her bewildered feelings that she failed to notice Jackson's posture stiffen, nor could she guess the degree of resolve it took for him to draw away from her soft and yielding body.

"No, Erin," he managed hoarsely. "I want you to become a lady and marry someone who will cherish what you are."

*Like you?* Erin thought, checking the query before

it came out and humiliated her. Of course he wasn't speaking of himself. Otherwise he would have said so. "I see," she managed through her confusion and disappointment. It didn't make sense. She knew that look. She knew he wanted her. But what he was saying and what he was doing were two entirely different matters. "I'm just not sure I want to do that anymore . . . especially the marriage part." She moved away from the rail and walked toward the hatch leading to the lower deck. "I think I'll go read a little," she called over her shoulder, her disconsolate expression forcing Jackson to look away. "See you tomorrow, Tyler."

# Chapter Fourteen

"How can you be so sure?"

Erin stopped in mid-step in her pacing path across the expanse of her cabin to stare expectantly at her guest. They had only been in port an hour and the breakfast she'd wolfed down in order to watch the lowering of the stage seemed to turn against her at the news just passed on to her by Cready. Why did Coleman Horsey insist on plaguing her very existence?

Cready picked up the silver-handled hairbrush Jackson had given her and replied laconically, "'Cause I overheard 'em. Horsey's lawyer said Jackson's wasn't written by your ma and a New Orleans whore's word wouldn't carry any weight. Horsey's got one written in your ma's own hand, plus the girls are swearing that's what they always heard her say . . . that he was the father you never had."

Erin clenched her teeth. "The lying bunch of . . . bitches," she finished stiltedly. Being around Tyler had done wonders for her vocabulary. She was having to think to cuss properly. "What do you think he's after?"

Her question brought Cready's attention to her, brown eyes sweeping meaningfully over her corseted figure. "You ain't as hard to look at as you used to be." He grinned at the color his crude compliment brought to her cheeks. "And your temper seems improved a bit."

"He knows better!" Erin protested hotly, ignoring the friendly jibe. "There's got to be something else."

Cready put the hairbrush down and perched on the edge of the dressing table. "They was talkin' about a will, but that would be your mama's, most likely. He already came to our house and took the papers your ma gave mine to keep."

"He what!"

Blood pumped furiously through the dilated veins in Erin's slender throat as she choked on the news. The gall of the man! Suddenly, the disciplined damn of expletives broke free as she stormed back and forth in the small space in the cabin. Fully aware of her tendency to kick things, Cready stayed clear of her, watching her in a combination of sympathy for her plight, awe at the beauty that had been hidden underneath his old clothes for so long, and pure admiration for her way with words.

"Those were *mine!*" she gasped, her color having grown to a mottled shade of red. "I only left them because I wasn't sure how livin' on Tyler's boat was gonna work out! Bejesus!"

Braving the swing of the arms that flew out at her side in frustration, Cready stepped up and clamped rough hands on her shoulders in an attempt to restore some calm to the girl before she got in one of her tirades and wreaked the place. "What you need to do is calm down and think of a plan to get that paper out of Horsey's hand," he reminded her. "I'd hate to see you give up all this 'cause you was too hotheaded to do anything but rant and rave. That's what them fancy women would do, not you, Wart."

Erin's head snapped up at the use of the name he continually tormented her with, her eyes shimmering with emerald fury. But there was no mockery on Cready's face. Instead there was genuine concern and something else, an affection similar to that which she had seen when he played with his dog. On Cready, that was considerable.

"Have you got any ideas?" Her shoulders fell with the deflation of her despair. Lose all this? No, she couldn't let that happen. Even more so, she couldn't let Horsey take her away from Jackson. An appalled shudder ran through her, forcing that possibility out of her mind.

The chintz material soft and feminine beneath his callused hands, Cready followed his instinct to draw Erin closer and cleared his throat. "I been thinkin' that we need to steal it."

"How?"

"Well, I'd 'a done it sooner, but I'm too big to fit through that little window in the room where that big bathtub is that Horsey and his gals waller in. We can reach it from the porch roof in the back."

"And he keeps his strongbox in that washstand in the corner!" Erin whispered, catching on to the idea. She hugged him in delight. "Oh, Cready, I know we can do it! He'll be in the saloon tonight for sure. I can meet you out back right after dark."

"You sure smell good, Wart."

Startled by the husky compliment and the realization that she was nearly in Cready's embrace, Erin shoved him away abruptly. "What the hell do you mean by that, Michael Augustus MacCready!"

Cready frowned, somewhat bewildered himself. It wasn't that he was an innocent anymore. The girls at the saloon had seen to that when he was only fourteen. And he'd beat the devil out of one of his friends for even suggesting he'd have anything aside from a business relationship with Erin Devareau.

"Hells bells, Erin, you've changed!"

Erin straightened warily, her head cocked at a pert

211

angle as she considered the way her old friend was acting. Suddenly her eyes widened with the dawning recognition of yet another familiar look. It wasn't anger, as his voice had indicated. It was the same kind of flame that kindled whenever Jackson Tyler was about to kiss her. The discovery left her intrigued. After all, *Cready?*

"Would you want to kiss me, Cready?"

The young man hunched his shoulders, suddenly uncomfortable with the way Erin was watching him. "I dunno . . . well, maybe . . ."

Erin's lips thinned with impatience. "Bejesus, make up your mind!" She crossed her arms in front of her, embarrassment creeping into her tone as she spoke. "It won't mean anything, of course, but I could use some practice. I haven't been a girl very long. I mean . . ." she began hastily. An exasperated sigh came out in lieu of the explanation that would not take shape. "Hell, you know what I mean."

The corner of Cready's lips twitched into a lopsided grin. The boys would never believe this. He wasn't sure he did. He wasn't exactly used to anyone like Erin, at least not in the capacity he was considering at the moment. She'd always been like a little brother, something she definitely did not look or act like now. While this wasn't what he was here for, for it was out of a brotherly affection that he'd come to warn her of Horsey's plan, there was a certain curiosity that demanded to be satisfied.

"Sure I do, Wart." Again his hands rested on her shoulders, his finger drifting far enough from the chintz to touch the satiny skin revealed by her ruffled neckline. Who'd have ever believed Erin was so soft? He moistened his lips with his tongue and bent over.

"You try anything funny, Cready, and I'll bite your lip off," Erin warned, halting his progress temporarily. She wasn't sure she could trust Cready. It wouldn't surprise her if he threw her on the carpet

212

and ground her face into it if she let down her guard.

"On Ma's Bible! And girls I kiss can call me Michael," he added lowly.

In frustration, for she was already having second thoughts, Erin wondered what it was about a first name that seemed so important to men when they kissed. Shrugging the concern off, she stiffly raised on tiptoe to meet the puckered kiss that descended on her mouth, her eyes half closed in wary anticipation.

The first thing that occurred to her was that it was inordinately wet and Cready's unwashed teeth, rivaling a cross between the taste of sour milk and wild onions, did not make it any more enjoyable. Her disappointment, however, had no chance to register, for the explosion of the cabin door striking the wall behind it drove the couple apart with a simultaneous gasp of astonishment.

"J . . . Jackson!" Erin, the first to recover, stammered. The black look on her guardian's face placed her protectively between him and Cready, the time when her friend had abandoned her to Black Jack Tyler forgotten. "What are you doing?"

"Getting this ruffian off my ship!" Jackson Tyler growled, reaching past her to catch the cornered Cready by the shirt with a fist. "And just in time, from the looks of it!"

While talking to J.P. Stevens on the upper deck and inviting him to the wedding, he'd caught a glimpse of the scoundrel boarding the ship. He was on his way down to throw him off when the sheriff and a sleazy attorney representing Coleman Horsey interrupted him to demand he bring Erin to the sheriff's office to settle the affair of her guardianship. At that moment, Jackson wasn't sure which set off his temper more, the idea of Erin in the hands of the likes of Horsey or in the arms of the likes of her former partner in crime. All he knew was that it wouldn't take much to vent his frustration and the

213

MacCready boy was a pure temptation.

"I didn't do nothin'!" the lad cried out as Jackson shoved Erin aside and the distance between him and the silver-eyed demon that had charged in on them closed dangerously.

"And you're not going to get the chance!"

"He's my guest!" Erin protested, her shock thawing enough to permit indignation to infuse her voice. She followed frantically as Jackson hauled Cready out into the corridor. "I can have my own friends, can't I?"

As they burst through the hatch leading to the open deck, Jackson sent Cready sprawling onto the planking at the feet of two off-duty deck stewards who were enjoying a smoke at the rail in the bright sunshine. "Throw him off the ship and give orders that he's not allowed back on under any circumstances!"

Grabbing at the tail of Jackson's coat, Erin yanked him around as the men picked up a relieved Cready, who had fully expected to be pitched off the second level of the ship into the shallow water or worse. "How dare you!"

Jackson whirled so quickly that Erin jumped back. His finger jerked authoritatively toward the direction in which they'd just come. "To your room."

"Cready is . . ."

"Now," he said, so softly that it sent chills up Erin's spine.

She gathered her courage and lifted her chin haughtily. "Fine!" With an angry swish of her skirts, she stomped into the corridor to her cabin and slammed the door just as the man on her heels reached it.

Jackson caught it and halted, taking in a deep breath to calm his raw and abused temper. He was in no humor for a shouting match, nor for the inevitable trip to the washstand that would follow, for already he could hear a few choice words being mumbled under his ward's breath. If he could control himself enough to treat her like a lady, perhaps, just perhaps, she might respond accordingly. God help him, what was it Mariette had said about patience?

"Maybe no one has told you that young ladies do not entertain men alone in their cabin, let alone permit them to kiss them like some wanton trollop."

"I slept in your cabin the night before last and *we* have been alone in it many times," Erin rallied indignantly. Jackson had insulted her friend and humiliated her in front of the crew and, while her example was not exactly the same, she was prepared to defend it until she choked.

"That is different. I am your guardian."

"And Lord knows, you've been kissing me at every turn!"

Jackson clenched his fists white. He wanted to throttle her for her belligerence. He wasn't accustomed to it from anyone. However, the truth of her words struck him down with a sword of guilt, making further argument difficult without further recrimination. He ran his fingers through his dark hair in exasperation.

"Don't push me, Erin! It would be easy at this moment to simply step aside and let that weasel of an attorney Horsey has produced put you in Horsey's custody. He arrived with the sheriff on the heels of your partner in crime. As it is, I am going to hire representation to fight it. Until we can get a hearing before the magistrate, you remain in my custody and, by thunder, you will do as I say!"

Erin couldn't help the undermining shudder that broke through her rebellious front at the mention of the grim threat underscored by Jackson's words. Hearing it from her guardian made it seem all the more ominous. "Cready said they had a good chance." Furious as Tyler could make her, she didn't

215

want to leave him. That he might give her up willingly had an icy effect on her fiery temperament.

The bolt of fear that streaked across her sobering face managed to take some of the edge off Jackson's bad humor, inflicting a conscience-riddling guilt in the process. "The sheriff wants me to bring you to his office in an hour and identify the handwriting."

Fearing her knees would fail her, Erin sat down. "I saw it, Tyler," she murmured miserably. "It . . . it did look like her hand, but I know she didn't write it!"

Jackson hid his concern behind an impassive mask for the sake of the girl who had gone white before him. He certainly wasn't going to tell her that Horsey had produced ledgers kept by Giselle Devareau with a matching hand to that of the document with which he intended to take control of Erin's affairs. Even if he wasn't so gut set against Horsey taking Erin, he also had a more practical reason to fight the man—a reason more easily understood than the other. He did not want John's half of the Delta "O" Line in the control of Coleman Horsey.

Leaning on the dressing table, Jackson met Erin's panic-filled eyes in the mirror. "It's going to be all right, kid. If I can't fight Horsey above the table, I'll beat him on his own level." He brought her face around with a crooked finger. "Trust me. I didn't earn the name of Black Jack Tyler for surviving up on the bluff."

Erin nodded silently, wishing more than anything that she could believe him. As angry as he could make her, when Jackson softened the steel set of his eyes and looked at her the way he was now, she seemed to fall under a strange and wonderful spell.

Yet, as she later sat in the sheriff's office and read the letter Horsey claimed to be his right to act as her guardian and manage her affairs until she was twenty-one, its aftereffect quickly faded. The sheriff

216

had to ask her four times if the document was written in her mother's hand before he finally narrowed his question down to one that required a simple yes or no answer.

After a plaintive look at Jackson, who prompted her to tell the truth with a barely perceptible nod, Erin still avoided a defined affirmative by stating that it looked like her mother's handwriting to her. She went on to tell the sheriff how Coleman Horsey had blackmailed her mother into working for him over the years and how much she hated the man, only to be cross-examined by the attorney with Coleman Horsey.

Before the man was through, he had slandered her mother and Jackson. It looked as if her mother, not only had loved Horsey and left Erin in his custody, but that Jackson had seduced her into wanting to remain with him with the intention of gaining control of an alleged inheritance.

It was Erin who lost control first and flew into the attorney, sending his glasses flying across the room before Jackson and the sheriff could intervene. But for Jackson taking her out when he did, she might have ended up in jail for assault. However, there was a dangerous glitter in the silver eyes that silenced any protest of his intentions to take her back to the *Delta Moon* until a magistrate could make a decision based on the facts.

Erin was in such a state of despair that she declined to take Jackson's invitation to catch lunch at the salon. She wanted to get away from people, from anything that threatened to take her away.

As if reading her mind, Jackson tugged at her arm and pointed to a young black boy trying to sell his morning catch on the street to passersby. "How about going fishing then?" he suggested lightly. "I could use a lazy afternoon myself."

Amazed and touched by his dedication to bring a smile to her face, Erin readily agreed. Jackson paid the boy for his pole and leftover bait and, after securing some food for a picnic, mainly pralines, they walked along the riverbank to a small grove where they could watch the tugboat that was taking the place of the ferry on dry dock to move barges of wagons and people across to Vidalia on the opposite bank.

Erin found herself chattering freely about her life at Under the Hill, the good parts that held a special place in her memory while Jackson watched her bait the line with practiced fingers, not the least put off by the wriggling earthworm she skewered on the hook. She told him about all her jobs, from digging worms and selling them to the gentry to shoveling coal on O'Neil's barge and coming home black as Old Annie.

When he laughed, it was a lighthearted sound that made Erin's heart melt with an adoration that showed on her face. Now this was a Jackson any woman could love—even if he didn't see fit to introduce her to his family and invite her to the big wedding planned at Retreat.

The sun, the relaxation after what had been a stressful interrogation, left Erin sleepy and she found herself yawning as Jackson walked her back to the *Delta Moon* later that afternoon and proceeded to get ready to visit his family home. Thinking to rest for just a moment, she lay down on her bed and basked in the breeze blowing through the portals across the cabin, satisfied to think over the lovely time she and Jackson had spent together.

When the dinner bell sounded on the lower deck, Erin stirred. Reluctantly, she opened her eyes and tried to shake off the sleep that had taken her over. Her crinolines, still tied with some twine she'd found in her fishing box and lying at the foot of her bed where she'd dropped them, nearly tripped her as she peeped out the portal at the water now glazed by the sunset.

Cready! she thought, distressed that she'd over-slept. She was supposed to meet him at sundown! Her mind instantly cleared as she searched for her slippers. She'd returned so exhausted from the lazy and delightful time she'd spent with Jackson Tyler that she'd nearly forgotten Horsey's plans and her own to thwart them. She hurried to the door and opened it, listening for movement in the cabin opposite hers.

Encouraged by the silence, she slipped across the hall and used her maids' key to enter Jackson Tyler's cabin. If she were to do any climbing, a dress was out of the question. Since Tyler had burned her clothes, she'd have to borrow some of his. She dug to the bottom of his trunk and found a pair of trousers that looked the most worn of his expensive wardrobe along with a shirt that had a tear on the sleeve. She was about to close the lid of the trunk when she caught sight of a small derringer. Upon examina-tion, she found it was loaded. After a moment's hesitation, she tucked that in the trouser pocket and returned to her own cabin to dress.

The shirt could be tied at the waist and the trousers rolled up and held in place with the same twine that had served to tie up her crinolines earlier. The real challenge was going to be getting off the ship without drawing attention. Jackson had made it clear that she was not to leave the ship unattended, let alone after dark.

She paused in front of the mirror, taking time to examine the hot pink tip of her nose that had suffered as a result of the lack of a proper hat. Her cheeks looked as if they'd been rouged, and they had been—naturally, by the sun. But she'd had much worse and wasn't the sort to get in a tizzy over a little sunburn. In fact, it looked a lot healthier than ghostly white skin with traces of rouge for color and it was cheaper, too.

She supposed she could go over the side and swim around to the bank under the cover of the docks. Erin studied the clothes she'd laid out on the bed. She could tie them up and hold them over her head to keep them dry and swim in her underwear. A shiver ran through her at the thought. That afternoon, the water had been cool, so much so that Jackson had thought her crazy to roll up her skirt and wade in to grab a fish that had nearly escaped his hook. But she'd bathed often enough in the fall water, returning home completely invigorated and refreshed in spite of her blue lips.

The leeward side of the ship was almost deserted with the exception of a couple of firemen playing checkers on a cotton bale near the forward rail. Erin made it a point to descend by the stern steps and used the cover of the cotton that would be transferred to the *Delta Laurel*, a Delta "O" ship due in from St. Joseph that evening, to shed her dress. After tucking it between two bales of the dry musty smelling southern gold, she tied her bundle of dry clothing to her head like a comic bonnet and gradually lowered herself into the cold water.

There was no time to contemplate her discomfort, however, for the current would not allow it. Reaching out with firm even strokes, she began to swim for the wharf boat, its offices now closed for the evening. She reached it and stopped to rest before continuing toward the riverbank where she had sneaked ashore the day Jackson Tyler had chased her into one of the warehouses.

Upon emerging in the shadows of the tree branches hanging low over the continually moving water, Erin quickly divested herself of her wet clothing and wrung them out. Jackson's clothes were dry for the most part and a welcome relief from the bone-chilling cold that shook her. The fall days were warmed by the sun, but the moon was not as merciful. Her slippers filled with water as she hung out her wet clothing to be picked up on the way back and she grimaced. Bejesus, but wouldn't a hot bath in Jackson's tub on Decatur Street be an incentive to get this shady business over with, she mused, checking the trouser pockets for the derringer she'd placed there earlier.

Natchez Under the Hill was beginning to yawn with excitement of a different nature from that one viewed during the day. Like New Orleans, as soon as one part of it was put to bed, the other part came to life. Already saloon music could be heard, competing from both sides of Silver Street. Places to eat, for Erin could hardly call them restaurants after having dined with Jackson in New Orleans, beckoned to visitors with tempting smells that made her stomach growl. She'd skipped lunch and, stuffed with Annie's pralines and some wine and cheese Jackson procured from Rumble and Wensel, had slept too long to consider supper.

A wistful smile graced her lips as her mind drifted once more to the lazy afternoon. It might as well have been a feast where Erin was concerned, for she'd never enjoyed anything more. It wasn't the fare, of course, but the charming company. They'd laughed together and shared childhood secrets that were astonishingly similar, which intrigued Erin all the more with the multifaceted character of her handsome companion. More than ever, she wanted to please him, to be like him, to be able to be at home in the richest house on the bluff or wading with rolled-up trousers in the Mississippi mud. Her hand brushed the bulge of the gun in her pocket and her smile hardened. And so help her, she would. If she had to risk killing Coleman Horsey to do so.

Of course, she hoped it wouldn't come to that. Cready's plan was a good one. Without the letter, Horsey was just full of puff. Her frozen heart reassured, she started up the hill toward a cluster of buildings that flanked those lining Silver Street.

Cready was nervous when she arrived at the outbuilding in back of the saloon. From the smell of his breath, he'd already fortified himself. Erin might have been angry, except that she knew the risk he was taking to help her. It could cost his dad his job and possibly result in Cready's showing up as fish bait further downriver. Erin placed a calming hand on his arm.

"I'm sorry for this afternoon."

"I'm beginning to wonder if living with that bastard is worth it," Cready mumbled irritably. "I think he could kill a man without even blinking."

Erin chuckled. She'd once thought the same thing. "You have to get to know him."

Cready gave her a skeptical glance and turned his attention to the window of the clapboard back of the saloon. The tin roof that covered the supply room in the back posed no problem. Stacked barrels against the outside wall would make easy work of climbing up on it. Even the window to the room adjoining Horsey's suite was open, which was a good sign. No one would have left it so, if the tin bathing rub was in use, for the air was crisp enough to chill a wet naked body. "Ready?"

Erin nodded, her thoughts running close to those of her companion. With a grace that could not be belittled by her oversized clothing and a prowess developed over years of climbing in and out of the shanties and buildings that made up Natchez Under the Hill, she easily scaled the barrels, ignoring Cready's offered hand. When he joined her, his bulky form causing him considerably more trouble, she was prying at the window to enlarge the opening.

"It's jammed," she grunted, struggling with the immovable sash.

"Here, let me try." Erin moved aside, but Cready

could not seem to budge the window either. "Must be nailed," he grumbled, his face darkening with a combination of strain and embarrassment at having failed to impress the determined young lady at his side.

Erin sized up the opening. The width was no problem and, if she didn't mind a tight squeeze, maybe the height would not be either. "I'm going to give it a try," she whispered, turning her head to the side to work it between the sash and the sill.

Encouraged, she began to wriggle her arms and shoulders through. Her bosom felt as if what there was of it was being painfully scraped off, but she persisted, helped along by Cready's obliging pair of hands planted firmly on her buttocks. Hanging half in and half out, she paused to catch her breath and blink the tears from her eyes.

"What's the holdup?"

"Just wait a minute!" Erin rasped irritably at Cready's impatience. She stared into the galvanized tin tub that stood ready to catch her and groaned. Was that water she saw glistening in the moonlight shafting in over her head? "Bejesus! There's water in . . ."

The sound of the door opening in the other room made Erin's voice catch in her throat. There was a sharp click of booted heels on the floor that became muffled as their owner moved on to a carpet. The slash of a match preceded the sudden illumination of the room. The light from the lamp poured in through the half open door.

"Bejesus!"

Erin felt the abrupt chill left by the hands that vacated her derriere and heard the scrambling retreat of her companion on the tin roof. A few seconds later, a barrel fell over, thudding against the side of the building. Instinct bade her to curse Cready for his cowardice, for leaving her stranded, but the sudden

223

cessation of movement in the other room stilled her voice as well as her heart. God in heaven, had Horsey—for there was no doubt from the scent of cigar smoke that the intruder in the other room was Coleman Horsey—heard Cready?

Ever so carefully, Erin began to squirm backward, but the creak of floorboards announcing Horsey's approach made her abandon caution and resort to panic. In her frenzy, her elbow struck the small stick that held the window up and it closed like a dull guillotine across the small of her back, pinning her in place. Her muscles cramped as she tried to reach behind her, a multitude of curses coming to mind for Michael Augustus Cready.

# MORE PASSION AND ADVENTURE AWAIT... YOUR TRIP TO A BIG ADVENTUROUS WORLD BEGINS WHEN YOU ACCEPT YOUR FIRST 4 NOVELS ABSOLUTELY *FREE*
## (AN $18.00 VALUE)

Accept your Free gift and start to experience more of the passion and adventure you like in a historical romance novel. Each Zebra novel is filled with proud men, spirited women and tempestuous love that you'll remember long after you turn the last page.

Zebra Historical Romances are the finest novels of their kind. They are written by authors who really know how to weave tales of romance and adventure in the historical settings you love. You'll feel like you've actually gone back in time with the thrilling stories that each Zebra novel offers.

## GET YOUR FREE GIFT WITH THE START OF YOUR HOME SUBSCRIPTION

Our readers tell us that these books sell out very fast in book stores and often they miss the newest titles. So Zebra has made arrangements for you to receive the four newest novels published each month.

You'll be guaranteed that you'll never miss a title, and home delivery is so convenient. And to show you just how easy it is to get Zebra Historical Romances, we'll send you your first 4 books absolutely FREE! Our gift to you just for trying our home subscription service.

## BIG SAVINGS AND FREE HOME DELIVERY

Each month, you'll receive the four newest titles as soon as they are published. You'll probably receive them even before the bookstores do. What's more, you may preview these exciting novels free for 10 days. If you like them as much as we think you will, just pay the low preferred subscriber's price of just $3.75 each. *You'll save $3.00 each month off the publisher's price.* AND, your savings are even greater because there are never any shipping, handling or other hidden charges—FREE Home Delivery. Of course you can return any shipment within 10 days for full credit, no questions asked. There is no minimum number of books you must buy.

# 4 FREE BOOKS

## TO GET YOUR 4 FREE BOOKS WORTH $18.00 — MAIL IN THE FREE BOOK CERTIFICATE T O D A Y

Fill in the Free Book Certificate below, and we'll send your FREE BOOKS to you as soon as we receive it.

If the certificate is missing below, write to: Zebra Home Subscription Service, Inc., P.O. Box 5214, 120 Brighton Road, Clifton, New Jersey 07015-5214.

## FREE BOOK CERTIFICATE

# 4 FREE BOOKS

### ZEBRA HOME SUBSCRIPTION SERVICE, INC.

**YES!** Please start my subscription to Zebra Historical Romances and send me my first 4 books absolutely FREE. I understand that each month I may preview four new Zebra Historical Romances free for 10 days. If I'm not satisfied with them, I may return the four books within 10 days and owe nothing. Otherwise, I will pay the low preferred subscriber's price of just $3.75 each; a total of $15.00, *a savings off the publisher's price of $3.00.* I may return any shipment and I may cancel this subscription at any time. There is no obligation to buy any shipment and there are no shipping, handling or other hidden charges. Regardless of what I decide, the four free books are mine to keep.

NAME

ADDRESS _____ APT _____

CITY _____ STATE ____ ZIP _____

TELEPHONE
( )

SIGNATURE _____ (if under 18, parent or guardian must sign)

Terms, offer and prices subject to change without notice. Subscription subject to acceptance by Zebra Books. Zebra Books reserves the right to reject any order or cancel any subscription.

GET
FOUR
FREE
BOOKS
(AN $18.00 VALUE)

ZEBRA HOME SUBSCRIPTION
SERVICE, INC.
P.O. Box 5214
120 BRIGHTON ROAD
CLIFTON, NEW JERSEY 07015-5214

# Chapter Fifteen

Suddenly light flooded her face from the open door and she froze. "Well, well, what have we here? A thief, perhaps?" Erin winced as he cupped her chin and lifted her face to his. "Why, it's my dear ward come home!" Horsey chuckled in such a way as to raise the hairs on the nape of Erin's neck. "You could have used the door, my dear."

"Are you going to let me hang here, or invite me in?" Erin responded with equal sarcasm. One thing she'd learned long ago. Never let an adversary know you were afraid, no matter how close your limbs were to turning to jelly or your stomach was to heaving. The pressure on her stomach at that moment could have posed a serious threat, but for the fact that it was empty. Instead it growled, reminding Erin of Cready's mutt's pups fighting for a position at their mother's teats.

"I am not only going to invite you in, my dear, but insist that you have dinner with me. It sounds like you could use a meal," he remarked, pulling the nail out over the sash that had kept her from a smooth and comfortable entry.

Erin poised to shove backward and escape the moment the sash was lifted from her waist, but Horsey firmly entrenched his fingers into her hair and urged her inside. The gun still lodged in her pocket scraped against her hip as she cleared the windowsill, reminding her that her situation was not hopeless after all. She tried to avoid accepting the man's assistance and, in the process, went to her knees in the tub, soaking Jackson's trousers quite thoroughly.

"You may not have your mother's grace and poise, Erin, but you've inherited her stubborn streak," Horsey grimaced, seizing her elbows and lifting her dripping from her wet landing onto the dry floor. "Might I ask to what I owe the honor of this visit?"

Erin's nose wrinkled in distaste at the smell of cheap cigar smoke and whiskey that always followed Coleman Horsey. "I came to find out why, after years of mutual hatred, you want to take care of me, Horsey."

"Through the window?" He lowered the sash and put the nail in a previously made hole, sealing out any hope of Cready coming to her rescue.

Not that she'd expect it, Erin thought grudgingly. She avoided Horsey's mocking gaze and seized a towel to dry the legs of Jackson's trousers.

With an amused grunt, Horsey turned and walked into the other room, bellowing loudly for one of the girls. Erin considered the window for a moment, but escape would not produce what she wanted—the letter and a reason for Horsey's interest for her. This, she thought, her hand going to the gun in her pocket, would.

She could hear Horsey speaking to someone, issuing orders in the swaggering way she so detested, particularly when it had been used on her mother and fought the well of hatred that threatened her control. Instead, she took advantage of his preoccupation and opened the door to the washstand and finding, to her relief, that Horsey had not changed his hiding place for his strongbox. A brief examination of the box told her, her purpose would have been futile, for she couldn't have lifted it through the window and she surely couldn't have broken it open without arousing attention.

She sighed. Her mother, who remained ironically as devout as the hypocrites in the church on the bluff allowed her to be, had always said that sometimes God used the worst of circumstances to work out for the best. She prayed Giselle Devareau had been right. At the sound of Horsey's approaching footfall, she closed the doors and turned back to her drying with renewed fervor.

"Here, put this on. It may not fit, but it'll do as well as what you have on and it's dry."

Erin caught the dress tossed at her and looked at it, her mind working furiously. Perhaps this was the way to get him to talk, another avenue that might avoid violence. After all, Jackson had driven it into her that if she acted the lady, she might be treated like one. One dubious brow raised above its mate. Although she wasn't exactly dealing with a gentleman, no matter how much Horsey aspired to that image. Her fingers went to the fastens of her shirt, now littered with flakes of paint that had peeled off the rotting window sill. But the dress was dry, she conceded, shrugging away her doubts.

There was no problem in restoring her hair to some order. A brush and comb, as well as other feminine trappings littered a dressing table crowded between the door and the corner on the opposite wall of the washstand. Although she had no lamp, there was sufficient light to tell her she'd done a reasonable job of making herself presentable.

The derringer in the slash pocket of her borrowed dress helped calm her nerves as she stepped into the combination of parlor and bedroom that was

227

Coleman Horsey's lair. A table for two had been set with mismatched tableware and a decanter of wine graced the center of the table. But it was the bed that was nearly Erin's undoing, for it had been turned back. She avoided the sardonic gaze of her host and marched with a regal possession she did not feel to the table.

"You do justice to that dress."

The compliment startled her enough to draw her eyes to her host and her stomach lurched at what she saw. In that one matter all men were alike. There was no class distinction where lust was concerned. Suddenly Erin was sorry she had changed clothes.

"Don't even think it, Horsey," she challenged, forcing bravado into her voice. "I'd rather slop hogs for the rest of my life than consider what you're thinking." She walked over to the bed and made it up.

"Don't flatter yourself, girl. Like your mama, you might look all spit and fire, but under all that is a nature as cold as ice. I'd 'a got more pleasure making love to a damned statue than Giselle Devareau."

Again Erin felt sick . . . sick at the thought of such a snake with her mother and sick with unrequited rage. She reached for the glass of wine already poured and waiting and took a healthy swig. She'd find out what Horsey was up to . . . then she'd shoot him.

"Then what do you want with me, Horsey?"

Coleman Horsey pulled out her chair and motioned for her to sit. Since it was apparent that he was going to answer her in his own good time, Erin took it.

"You really don't know?"

Erin shook her head as a knock sounded on the door. At Horsey's bidding, it opened to admit one of the saloon girls carrying a tray with their supper. The girl placed the food on the table, her eyes flickering over Erin in such a way as to remove all doubt as to the identity of the owner of the dress she wore. No doubt Horsey had given it to the barmaid in exchange for services which the girl obviously thought Erin was going to take over.

Erin tried to think of some way to let the girl know nothing was farther from the truth, for she felt sorry for some of the women who worked the saloons and whorehouses. They weren't all there because they wanted to be. Fate, bad husbands, and cruel betrayals just seemed to hem them into such a life. Why she couldn't be any older than Erin herself.

"So Tyler hasn't told you that you're an heiress," Horsey commented when the girl left them alone.

Erin's attention switched completely to the man opposite her. "An heiress?" she echoed doubtfully.

"That old woman you charmed away from her home has left her estate to you. Wrote up a new will, short and simple, withdrew a goodly sum of cash and took off with you to see the river. No doubt you got a warm reception from her family after that. The only trouble is, no one seems to know where it is." Horsey looked at Erin over the rim of his glass. "You wouldn't by any chance have any ideas?"

Too shocked to form a reply, Erin shook her head. An heiress? Grandma had left her a fortune? If it was true, it explained so many things—the way the Lafons treated her, their relief that her only request was that her mother be moved into the family crypt, the fact that her belongings had been repacked, obviously from being searched, when they were returned to the *Delta Moon*, not to mention her room all but ransacked . . . but had the Lafons gotten into her room on the boat? Or was that some of Sturgis's perverted work and totally unrelated?

"Then Tyler must have it. That is the only explanation!"

"He would have told me," Erin disagreed, coming

to her guardian's defense. "How do you know about the will?"

Horsey smiled the smile of a cat, smug and knowing. "I have contacts in New Orleans, contacts who have kept an eye on you since I got the word of your dear mother's death. You see, I knew your mother's family was rich and always hoped that there would be a reconciliation, that there was a chance of her inheriting part of the Asante estate. I thought that when she returned to New Orleans that it would happen."

Lust, Erin thought cynically. Lust of a different nature, a greedy one that served as the lifeblood of men like Coleman Horsey. So that was why, after a while, he'd left her mother alone physically, but kept her under his control. She was like an investment, nothing more. Now Erin was to take her place.

"And you want to control my inheritance," she finished aloud. She cut her eyes at Horsey thoughtfully. He had to have a plan. All she needed to do was get the details. "And if I cooperate, what's in it for me?"

Horsey leaned back against his chair. "I've known you were a natural swindler since you were knee high. Your mama was too transparent, too honest, but you've got her beauty and wit and your father's talents. It's definitely a winning combination."

Erin hoped so. She took up her fork and toyed with the steaming plate of gumbo and rice, food the farthest thing from her mind. She'd get him drunk, let him talk on about his grandiose scheme, for men like Horsey loved to boast of their accomplishments, intended or otherwise. And when he was properly inebriated, she'd pull out her gun, force him to open the trunk, and burn the incriminating letter right before his eyes.

As the level in the decanter dwindled, she discovered that Horsey was willing to allow her a generous allowance from her grandmother's estate. The rest he intended to invest for her, investments she was certain would fatten his pocketbook and most likely leave her penniless at twenty-one. Surely, he didn't think she was stupid enough to go along with him! But as the man spoke, she realized he was too absorbed in his own genius to expect a simple girl to question him.

The hands on the clock seemed to labor in their effort to report the passage of time. Erin sipped her own wine judiciously, wanting a clear head to confront her adversary. When the barmaid finally served dessert, a dried-out cake with excessively sweet liqueur poured over it, she breathed a mixed sigh of relief and apprehension.

Her nerves would take no more of his gloating dissertation, particularly as he ran down Jackson Tyler. The very idea that Jackson knew of her inheritance, that he might possess the will, was absurd. He'd never betray her like that. She was ready to trust him with all her money, if there really was an inheritance, and her love. That was why she had to do this.

"We could make quite a team, you and I, Erin," Horsey was saying as she slipped the gun out of her pocket and pulled back the hammer. The sound echoed loudly in the room, bringing a quick halt to her companion's speech. She watched bewilderment change to shock as she produced the weapon in clear sight. "Wha . . . what the hell do you think you're doing?"

"Ending our partnership," Erin answered simply. She steeled her hand. She couldn't let him know she was shaking to the core inside. To distract her frayed nerves, she pushed away from the table, keeping the gun leveled ominously, and rose to her feet. "You're

231

going to open that strongbox and burn that letter, Horsey."

"And if I don't you'll shoot me."

"Absolutely."

Eyes as hard as the jewel they resembled returned his assessing look coldly. Not even the sudden opening of the door from the balcony overlooking the saloon below swayed them. The barmaid, who had unexpectedly returned for the dirty dishes screamed at the sight of her employer being held at gunpoint, but Horsey did not move, for he faced a more serious opponent than Giselle Devareau had been.

Nevertheless, he thought to test Erin's mettle in another way. "I don't think you want to shoot me, Erin. Should I die, your inheritance will do you little good in prison for my murder."

"It won't do you wonders in a grave either, so it's best that you cooperate."

Horsey held up his hand to halt the two men that answered the barmaid's call for help. "Stay back, gentlemen. I'm sure the lady and I can come to a suitable compromise here without your help." Like Erin, he did not afford them so much as a glance, for his full attention was on her pistol. "Prison will also keep you away from Jackson Tyler and, since you knew nothing of your inheritance until tonight, I'm beginning to think that there is more than a guardian's relationship involved between the two of you."

Erin's facade wavered temporarily, her color confirming a truth even she had not yet fully acknowledged.

"There is a more equitable way to decide this thing for both of us . . . if you're willing to gamble."

"Stay still!" Erin warned, stepping backward as he started to get up from his chair. So help her, she would shoot him, she thought, trying to convince herself. She'd seen men shot, the gore erupt from their chest. No matter how often in her eighteen years she'd witnessed such things, they still managed to make her queasy. Death had been a very real reality, but she'd never grown immune to it. After her mother's and grandmother's loss, she was even less so. "What is it you have in mind?"

"A card game. Two out of three hands win."

"Win what?" Erin asked warily. Getting involved in a card game with Horsey was like swimming with a cottonmouth.

"If you win, I give you the letter, you get to keep your inheritance and remain with Tyler, and I am out of your life."

Erin drew a shaky breath. "And if you win."

"I become your guardian with the letter, administer your estate . . ." he hesitated, his eyes narrowing, "and you will willingly spend tonight in my bed, obedient to my command." For a moment, Horsey thought he'd pushed too far. The will it took Erin to control the finger trying to tighten on the trigger, her nostrils flaring with outrage, came close to losing the battle. "At least that way, one of us would win. Your way, we both lose," he rejoined quickly.

As he watched the struggle taking place on the girl's face, he knew he'd won. She would be easy prey at the table and easier yet, afterward. Not that he was consumed with lust for her body in a physical sense. No, he intended to make her pay for this affront, for her slanderous accusations, for that haughty lift of her chin. Before the night was over, he would break Erin Devareau's spirit and have her groveling at his feet.

She wasn't so different from her mother after all. She had a weakness and he had found it. Giselle's had been her love for Erin. Erin's was her affection for

Jackson Tyler—as if a man of Tyler's station would return it, he thought laconically.

Auralee Tyler quietly closed the door to the study and turned to admire the handsome figure of her son as he sorted the mail on his desk. A smile that time had etched on her face, in spite of the loss of her dear husband and the trials of running a plantation alone until her son could offer support, graced her lips. He was a good son, devoted to her, if not entirely to Retreat. He just possessed a certain wanderlust that she was beginning to think he would never outgrow.

"Jackson, dear, I want you to tell me all about Erin Devareau!" she said, excitement creeping into her voice in spite of herself.

Tom and Myra Allen had told her about the new ward her son had acquired at the bequest of her departed mother. It was such a sad story that Auralee had been moved to tears. And from the way Gina had talked about her, she would be willing to bet, were she a gambling woman, that Erin Devareau was a Creole beauty in the most noble sense. Still, it was Jackson's opinion that she wanted.

"I thought we slipped away to discuss wedding plans," Jackson answered with that mischievous quirk that reminded her of the impish boy who had grown up under her loving care.

Auralee heaved a whisper of a sigh, her eyes sparkling with equal mischief. "You've found me out, I know, but surely a mother has a right to know if a certain young lady has caught her son's interest."

"I am her guardian, Mother."

"I've heard she's absolutely lovely and charming."
Did she dare to think, to hope that this might be the girl to conquer her son's wanderlust? She watched his guarded features and cursed that exasperating

trait he'd inherited from his father with a degree of guilt for her sacrilege.

"I will bring her to Retreat when she is ready so that you might judge that for yourself."

"I'm sure she could use a woman's touch, poor thing. What about tomorrow?"

"She's not quite ready to meet our family and friends, Mother."

Auralee's brow furrowed in confusion. "Whatever does she have to do to get ready?" she asked innocently.

Jackson tried to think of a way to describe Erin without frightening his mother into a faint, when he caught sight of an envelope addressed to him in a feminine hand—a hand he did not recognize. It was posted from St. Francisville.

"Jackson . . ." his mother prompted gently.

Jackson was saved the effort of reply by a polite knock on the study door. He gave his mother a wink as she threw up her hands in exasperation and called for the servant to enter.

"Excuse me, sir, but dere is a white boy out back that say he has to see you. Dat it's an emergency."

"Thank you, Silas."

Tucking the missive in his pocket, Jackson followed the servant to the back of the house to the door of the warming kitchen, his mother in his trail, skirts rustling with the hasty steps she made to keep up with his longer stride. The moon shining through the trellised walkway that connected the out kitchen to the main house cast shadows over the visitor's face, making it difficult to identify him until Jackson lifted the lantern Silas handed him.

"You!" he snorted in astonishment. "What the devil are you up to?"

Cready took a retreating step as Jackson came down off the steps and swallowed hard. "It's Erin, sir.

Coleman Horsey has her."

Jackson's gaze narrowed. Although he'd not suspected that his charge would try anything crazy, he'd warned the watch not to let her leave the ship for any reason. He'd actually enjoyed the dinner party with peace of mind, knowing Erin was probably still sleeping off the wine and sunny day in her room. "How?" he challenged.

Cready nervously walked over to one of the columns supporting the terrace, trying to summon his nerve. "She . . . we," he admitted, "had a plan to steal that paper from Horsey. She . . . she didn't want him to take her from you."

Jackson could feel the blood drain from his face. "And . . ." he prompted dryly.

"She got stuck in the window . . ."

"And you left her?" Jackson exploded, his long reach catching him and nailing the boy to the column before he could escape.

"I . . . I . . . I . . . couldn't help her!" Cready stammered, his voice rising to hysteria. "I come for help!"

"Jackson, for the love of God, you're choking the child!" Auralee Tyler protested, tugging at her son's sleeve. "He's come for help. I'll send Silas for the sheriff!"

"No!" Jackson loosened his hold on Cready's shirt. "I'll take care of this myself."

"But . . ."

"Mother, there are some people who know their way around the law and Coleman Horsey is one of them. I have to deal with him in my own way. Silas, fetch me my horse!"

"Yes, sir!"

Auralee studied the firm set of her son's jaw and knew there was no point in argument. That was something else he'd inherited from his father. "Be careful, son."

Jackson bussed his mother's cheek. "Tell J.P. that one of the servants will drive him back to the boat and return Rex on the way home."

"Maybe he should go with you."

"I can handle it, Mother. I promise. Wait here, boy, while I get my cloak," he called to Cready, who stood observing the affectionate exchange in wonder, considering the same man who was so gentle with his mother had nearly choked the wind out of him only a moment earlier. He was surprised a man like Black Jack Tyler even had a mother!

# Chapter Sixteen

Erin stared at the cards on the table in front of her, her courage wavering in the face of defeat. What had gone wrong? She'd had a good hand. She'd checked the cards to be certain they were not marked in any way. She'd even dealt them. Had she wanted to win so badly it had influenced her judgment?

"I do believe, Miss Devareau, that that is two out of two," Coleman Horsey announced in a smug tone.

"Don't touch those cards!" Erin shouted as he started to gather them up. "I want to check the deck again."

Horsey looked around at the group of men and saloon girls that had come up for the show and grinned. "I've killed men for less than that, but considering the reward," his gaze slithered over Erin meaningfully, "I'd be biting off my nose to spite my face."

Erin burned with humiliation as laughter erupted, but nonetheless, went through the deck once more, checking for marks, for shaved edges, for extra cards. Nothing. Nothing! Her chin quivered, but she forced it to be still before it betrayed her absolute wretchedness. She'd lost everything—her inheritance, Jackson, her pride . . .

"I believe this . . ." Horsey picked up the document she'd attempted to wrest from his possession and folded it. ". . . is mine and so, my dear, are you." He waved his hand, dismissing the smirking crowd. "Out of here, all of you."

Leaving the victor to his spoils, the murmuring gallery began to move toward the door, but was stopped by the sight of the polished steel-eyed devil who lounged in it unconcerned. "I wouldn't rush off so soon, ladies and gents, the show might not be over."

Black Jack Tyler never looked so good to anyone as he did to Erin. He stood like a black knight, a legend in his sparkling silver vest with his diamond breast pin and silver-tipped cane catching the light of the lamps and scattering it about the room. As he removed his black beaver hat in deference to her and approached, she opened her heart in welcome through her eyes, only to be knifed by the flash of contempt that met it.

"Oh, it's over, Tyler," Horsey gloated. "I have everything I want, don't I, Erin, including you in my bed tonight."

Erin shriveled in her chair. She could feel Jackson's eyes upon her, but could not bring herself to go back for further abuse. Not that she didn't deserve it. If Jackson could ever forgive her for this, for not trusting him to take care of her, she'd worship the ground he walked on.

"Was that part of the stakes, Erin?" Jackson asked tersely.

She strangled on her own bile and nodded miserably. She wished he hadn't come. She wished she had killed Horsey and then killed herself. She wished . . .

"Like I said, Tyler, everything a man could want," Horsey taunted.

Jackson lifted the tip of his cane to his cheek thoughtfully and hid his attempt to recover from the shock of Erin's confirmation. Damnation, what had possessed the girl to do such a thing! "I don't think you do, Horsey. You don't have the *Delta Moon*." He struck a raw nerve. It showed in the way Horsey's veins strained against his temples, the same way they had the night he'd won the boat from him in New Orleans. "One hand, winner take all . . . or did you learn your lesson the last time we played," he finished with a cynical challenge.

There was a prolonged silence, broken only by the piano music from downstairs. Erin could almost hear her heart beat.

Suddenly Horsey took up the gauntlet, slapping the cards he'd just gathered up back on the table. "One hand," he agreed, "winner take all. Since I was challenged, I choose the game . . . draw poker."

"Done, sir." Jackson placed a hand on the back of Erin's chair. "If you don't mind," he prodded sourly.

Erin hastily abandoned her seat to her coldly chivalrous knight and took a place behind him. She longed to touch the shoulders that stretched the expensive material of his coat as he extended his arms and adjusted his diamond-studded cuffs, to tell him somehow that she would forever be indebted for his saving her, for it did not occur to her that he would do anything else. Black Jack Tyler never lost.

"I already checked the cards," she told him as Horsey shoved them toward him to cut the deck. "They're clean."

"I can see that," Jackson replied testily. "Perhaps we should send Miss Devareau to another room . . ."

"I prefer to see the stakes," his opponent objected, taking some pleasure in Jackson's fleeting show of irritation. "And it is her fate, we are deciding."

Without acknowledgment, Jackson picked up the cards he was swiftly dealt and spread them for observation when a distressed whimper sounded from behind him. He cast a withering look over his shoulder at the pale-faced girl who met his gaze and then turned back to Horsey. "I think we should deal again and place Miss Devareau on the other side of the room," he grated out through clenched teeth.

"One hand, winner take all. Was that not what the man said?" Horsey asked, looking around at the gallery of observers for support. "I don't think another deal is necessary."

Jackson let out his breath slowly, his brow furrowed in consternation and exchanged two of his cards.

"Only two?" his opponent drawled, tongue in cheek. It appeared that he was going to manage, not only to get to Jackson Tyler, but to regain the ship he'd recklessly lost in New Orleans.

Jackson answered with the tap of two fingers on the table. With a show of disinterest, he placed the new cards in his hand. The draw could have been better, but it could also have been worse. "Well?" He cast an expectant look at Horsey who glanced once more at his hand and gestured magnanimously.

"Be my guest, sir."

"Full house, aces high." To illustrate, Jackson spread the cards for all to see on the table.

Erin nearly squealed with relief as Coleman Horsey stared in obvious disbelief, but maintained a show of innocence. Her ploy had worked. He'd fallen for her dismayed act upon seeing Jackson's cards. "You cheat, sir!" the man snarled, tossing down two pair with disparagement. "I'm beginning to see that I was set up all along. Nice little act, young lady. I admit, I fell for it completely."

Jackson sat unmoved and met the accusing glare cast his way. *"I've killed men for less than that,"* he quoted calmly, *"but considering my reward, I'd be biting my nose off to spite my face.* I'd much rather see you rot here and stew over your losses."

"You won't live to, Tyler." Horsey snapped his

241

fingers and the two men reached for the guns strapped at their hips.

"That would be a mighty unhealthy move, boys."

Erin's mouth fell open in surprise to see the engineer from the *Delta Moon* step into the room, a lethal sawed-off shotgun in his hands. He was flanked by two of his firemen, equally well armed.

"You don't think I'd be fool enough to come in here again without my back protected, do you?" Jackson inquired sarcastically of the apoplectic man opposite him, whose brow was beaded with sweat that he dared not risk moving his hand to mop away. "Now I'll have that letter."

A look of pure hatred glowered from Coleman Horsey's face as he reached inside his jacket where he'd smugly placed the letter earlier. Gone was all trace of his premature satisfaction. Erin could not take her eyes off the fingers that fumbled for the fake document. Sheer relief made her weak in the knees, but there was something about the delay that sparked an instictive thread of suspicion that quickly shored them up with alarm.

"Jackson!" she gasped, knowing Horsey had a gun before she saw it emerge from his vest.

A blur of silver slashed across her line of vision. There was a snap and a thud of metal striking the floor as it cut back just as rapidly. Coleman Horsey cried out like a scalded hound, his hand flying to his cheek where an ugly gash was beginning to seep red. "You cut me, you sonova . . ." The blade that suddenly appeared from within the silver cap pressed against his throat, silencing him.

"Count yourself lucky that a scar is the worst you'll suffer this night, you conniving scoundrel."

Erin was shaking, literally shaking when Jackson, after kicking the pistol out of reach, turned his attention to her. So close. So close to losing everything. She went eagerly under the arm that was

242

extended to her, too anxious for its safety to pay heed to the iron mask of her protector.

She never saw Cready, who hovered near the back door of the saloon to watch the triumphant procession move out into the street, nor did she notice the loud laughter and music that competed with a belligerent domestic quarrel in one of the alleys. Mounted in front of Jackson on the prancing chestnut stallion, she chose to retreat into the warm concave of his body, as if to absorb some of his much needed strength.

The trip to the landing only took a matter of minutes. The *Delta Moon* waited like a fat mother hen nestled low in her muddy water bed for her chicks to come home. There were several off-duty members of the crew lazing about the gangway as Jackson helped her off the sleek racehorse that had won him a good share of fortune on the tracks—a prize he had risked riding at breakneck speed from Retreat, frightening the boy behind him into a stricken silence. The watchmen avoided their employer's gaze as he ushered Erin aboard.

"I'll be biddin' ya good night, sir," Reds spoke up, breaking the strained silence as they reached the steps leading to the texas. "If the engines start early tomorrow, don't go into a panic. I'm fixin' to try that new part that comes in on the Laurel."

"I'll keep that in mind," Jackson replied flatly. "Good night, men."

Erin went ahead of him quietly, unable to muster the courage to bid a good evening to her new friends. They knew, she thought, her feet becoming leaden as she trudged up to the next deck. They knew what a fool she was and she had no one to blame but herself. At least they knew she'd run away. By tomorrow they'd know everything. But she'd only done it to stay with them, part of her argued in her defense.

Upon reaching her cabin door, she put a hand on

243

the latch she'd failed to lock earlier and started to turn it.

"Where do you think you're going?"

Erin glanced up sheepishly. "To my room?"

"I think not."

She stood in dumb obedience as Jackson opened his own room and stood back to let her precede him inside. Feeling uncommonly awkward, she waited while he helped himself to one brandy and then a second. "I'm sorry."

Silver eyes snapped up at her. "You'll even be more so when you realize the gravity of your escapade tonight." He took another glass off the tray. "Will you have a drink?"

A drink. Yes, that was a good idea. She needed something to stop her knees from wobbling. "Thank you . . . and thank you for helping me," she added as he handed her a full glass. She drank it down straight, without thinking and then licked her lips thoughtfully. "And understanding."

"Understanding? Hah!"

Erin started at the humorless boom of laughter, nearly toppling the glass she set back on the desk. He was angry and she couldn't blame him. She commanded the corners of her mouth to tilt up in an attempt at a smile. "We made a pretty good team, didn't we? I mean, you could have gotten a worse hand if Horsey had dealt the cards over."

The diabolical curve of Jackson's mouth slackened. "You did that on purpose?"

"I wanted him to get cocksure of himself."

"I have gambled for years without your help, Erin."

"But three aces up front was nothing to turn your nose up at," Erin retorted quickly.

Jackson groaned silently. She was incorrigible. "What would you have done if I hadn't shown up?"

"Shot him." To illustrate, Erin withdrew the

small derringer from her skirt pocket and laid it on the desk.

The sight of the gun was concrete evidence at how close she had come to harm, something that had ripped at his insides as he'd ridden his thoroughbred with total disregard down the steep incline from the bluff, tore away the last shred of his control.

"You . . . are . . . hopeless!" He seized the pistol and disarmed it before slinging it against the wall in a fit of fury. It dinged the paneling and bounced across the room. "You're stupid, putting yourself up as stakes like some seasoned whore . . . damn you, Erin, have you no pride? Didn't you have any idea what you were doing?"

Erin surveyed the outburst with a degree of trepidation, but she'd seen Jackson lose his temper before and had come to learn that he was more thunder than lightning. "I'll discuss this with you in the morning when you're in a better humor. Things will be clearer then," she announced calmly.

Her prim facade was the last thing Jackson expected or wanted to see. Blood pounded to his temples at an alarming rate. Damn her, she wasn't going to walk off this easy, not after what she'd put him through tonight. He'd make her see the error of her recklessness or die trying.

"The hell you will," he growled, placing a hand on the door to keep her from opening it. "I won you fair and square . . . and I always claim what I win." He reached around her and slammed the bolt into its keeper. All the nights he'd lain awake, fighting this mad desire she could arouse with a chaste kiss or an impish smile, by God, she was going to pay . . . or at least think she was. "I've been waiting for you in my bed long enough and by thunder, lady, that is where you'll spend this night. Since you've decided to play the whore, it's time you knew what it's really like."

Erin held her ground, her stomach doing flip-flops

over what she was hearing. He was bluffing. She knew he was. Tilting her chin defiantly, she rose to the challenge. "What makes you so damned sure I don't know what it's like?" Moving him aside with more ease than she anticipated, she marched across the room, hips swaying provocatively. "After all, I was raised in Under the Hill and *everybody*," she drawled, "on the bluff knows there's no such thing as a virgin under ten years of age down there." She turned and drilled him with a *come hither* look that ran straight from his wary gaze to his loins. "I mean," she went on, helping herself to a healthy swig of the brandy straight from the decanter, "I kind of thought a man of your experience would have caught on to me by now, but, what the hell? You're not hard to look at and word is among the gals on the ship that at least you're not boring between the sheets."

Her heart thudded to a stop as Jackson moved away from the door and strode purposefully toward her, his face a study of undeniable interest. "Then by all means, let me entertain you."

He claimed Erin's mouth fiercely, his tongue invading with a vengeance as she gasped in surprise. Part of him screamed for revenge against the stinging jabs at his ego, while another simply demanded primitive satisfaction. Before the night was out, he would either call her hand or find out the truth.

He moved closer, grinding his hips against her as she yielded backward over the edge of the bunk until there could be little doubt in her mind that he was not playing games. With her scant layering of petticoats, she couldn't help but feel the throbbing need straining against his trousers.

Conversely, Jackson could not ignore the feminine body crushed between him and the mattress that struggled halfheartedly, as if uncertain that it really wanted him to stop. That alone sent the blood catapulting through his veins, his body reacting like a boiler about ready to explode. The softness of her thighs yielding against his more powerful ones made thought impossible, another less practical part of him taking over as she squirmed with faint resistance. And then he could take no more.

"Erin!" he rasped hoarsely, breaking away from his punishing kiss to tug her under him in a frenzied, crushing assault. Rampant release coursed through his loins, ignoring the outraged protest of his mind, and then it was over. He filled his lungs slowly with the breath it had denied him, remaining perfectly motionless otherwise as the shock of what had transpired penetrated his desire-infested brain. Not since his first visit to a New Orleans cathouse had this happened.

"T . . . Tyler, if we're going to do this, I have to be on top."

Jackson swore silently in the aftermath of an unfamiliar shame until her words registered completely. Thunderstruck, he drew away. Were he not so damnably angry at himself, he might have laughed at the stubborn face turned up at him. She honest to God didn't know! At least, he thought, somewhat assuaged by this discovery, he'd narrowed her experience down to limited . . . or none at all.

He pushed away from the bed and let Erin up before reaching for the decanter of brandy. This time it was he who drank without the accommodation of a glass. And he'd bought himself some time and a ticket to restraint, something he'd never dreamed he'd find himself so lacking in with a woman. He'd prided himself on his ability to guarantee pleasure to the fairer sex before taking his own. But that, like so much else of his once orderly life seemed to have been turned around since meeting his unpredictable charge.

"I won't do it unless I can be on top," Erin insisted,

regaining his attention. "That's the only way."

A dark brow shot up as the substance of her demand struck home. He was about to tell her she'd damned well do what he wanted, any way he wanted, when he sensed, more than witnessed, a definable fear in his adamant companion. It obviously wasn't consternation over the act itself, for she was acting as though it were nothing new. It was the manner that peaked his curiosity. "Might I ask why?"

The blood poured into Erin's face in spite of her resolve to remain aloof. Although she'd felt his fierce and urgent kiss at the very center of her being, a half crazed panic had nearly taken her over. All she could see was the man astraddle one of her *aunts*, whipping the woman with a riding crop. She turned her back to the unfathomable silver gaze and busied herself with turning back the bed. "I won't be beaten."

The answer was whispered in such a way as to tear at Jackson's conscience. So she wasn't innocent, at least not in a purely physical sense. He ignored the odd regret surfacing in his thoughts and concentrated on the possible circumstances that would have led her to such a corrupted view of what to expect. Had she been forced? The very idea made him ill with revulsion and instilled a sense of helpless rage. No wonder she'd pretended to be a boy!

Moved by a sweep of compassion, he stepped up behind her and slipped his arms about her waist, inhaling the scent of the soap she'd washed her hair with that morning, slightly tainted by the faint remains of Coleman Horsey's cigar smoke. Damn the bastard, had he been the one to taint her body as well? Is that the reason for her unadulterated hatred of the man?

"The last thing I would do is beat you, Erin," he assured her fervently. His lips brushed the tip of her ear as she whipped around with a dubious look that reminded him of an earlier confrontation. "Unless you go on a swearing rampage and break every bowl and pitcher on the ship," he stipulated, his mouth curling up rakishly at one corner. "And then I promise, that only your derriere would suffer."

Erin's insides quivered as bold hands cupped the cheeks of her buttocks in an expressive apology. She could think of no quick response aside from that she tried to hide. "Do you want me to undress you?" she asked, steeling her gaze from his secret-revealing mercurial one. Her voice was almost flippant with desperation rather than low and sultry as she'd intended.

Yet its business as usual overtone arrived at the same goal, for an irritated Jackson was much easier to deal with than this tender one. Prodded back into his own charade by her unexpected reply, Jackson opened his arms wide and shrugged with a mocking, "Be my guest, madame."

# Chapter Seventeen

Erin prayed the battle royal going on inside her would not show as she slipped Jackson's jacket and vest off and hung them over the back of the desk chair. Of course, he was bluffing, but if he wasn't, was she prepared to see this hand through? Her breasts grazed the front of his shirt as she reached up on tiptoe to remove his tie and false shirt front and her breath caught in her throat at the resurgence of reaction that ran unbridled through her body to converge warmly at the apex of her thighs. Undeniably, there was a part of her that was ready and it was that that made her all the more nervous.

She wished she'd had the time to read more of that book Mariette had given her. She wished she'd found out exactly what a man liked in a woman, because, if this was going to be, she didn't want to appear the total fool. Her thoughts raced furiously as she attacked the buttons on his trousers, aware of the intense scrutiny focused on her. What had the girls at the Palace said, she wondered anxiously. Heaven knows, she'd heard them bragging time and again of their techniques for giving pleasure. The front of the trousers fell away from her hands. Regardless, Erin stopped and willed her gaze to remain downward, rather than risk a certain blood-rushing eye contact.

She could feel her skin burning from the crown of her head to the tips of her toes.

"I think I can finish here, although," Jackson suggested, inducing a crooning quality into his voice that seemed to caress her all over at once, "we do have all night." Heedless of his loose trousers, he dropped into his desk chair and, paradoxically reverting back to his social graces, leisurely helped himself to more liquor. "Why don't we make things a little more interesting?" Erin was wary as he downed the full glass, the tendons in his neck straining as he tilted back his head to get the last drop. "Besides . . ." he went on, drilling her with a diabolical gaze that ran from her muddied slippers to her scantily cut bodice, "I like my women to undress for me."

Somehow Erin found her voice. "No problem," she quipped, her fingers going to the laces at the back of her gown.

"Slowly," Jackson told her, halting them in the midst of untying the bow at the small of her back. "Over a bottle of wine and a few hands of poker." Shock pervaded Erin's assembled features as she observed him reaching into his desk drawer and producing a pack of cards. "For each hand I win, you take off an item of clothing, starting from the outside in. The reverse applies to me." Sensing her reluctance, he roughed up the crisps of dark hair on his chest with his hand and chuckled, taking immense satisfaction that he'd finally found a breach in her show of bravado. "I've already spotted you my jacket, shirt, and vest."

The brunt of his humor not settling well on her shoulders, Erin rallied. "Why not? Cards are decidedly less boring than some pursuits, regardless of a man's reputed prowess," she added with a malicious overtone that erased the offensive gratification from Jackson's features for an instant. She had no doubt she was over her head and about to sink further, but

251

she would be damned before she let him make a mockery of her inexperience. Somewhere within that disconcertingly handsome body was a weakness and if she could find it . . . She refilled his glass and handed it to him with a sweet, "To your health, sir." There was always the possibility that she could get him drunk. He might forget their purpose or at least not find out how protected a life she'd actually led in the field of love.

Jackson promptly returned the gesture. "To the night and all its promise." He finished his glass and looked at Erin expectantly. "I like a woman who can keep up with me in cards, in drinking, and in bed."

"In other words, you don't really prefer ladies."

"Only for the marriage bed and bearing legitimate heirs. Since you have chosen an alternate life from that I'd hoped, I see no reason why I should lament. Indeed," he chuckled, giving her a perfectly avaricious appraisal, "I intend to make the most of it."

Erin glared over her glass. Damn his soul, she'd outfox him if it was the last thing she did, which it might well be, considering the full glass in her hand. She hadn't counted on having to match him drink for drink. Taking a deep breath, she raised it to her lips.

It had not improved in taste since the night John had tried to calm her over the death of her grandmother. The swallow she'd taken earlier had told her that. Her stomach rebelled at the idea of a whole glass, but she quelled the uprising and downed the liquor as smoothly as her companion, at least as far as show was concerned. What it was doing to her insides was purely another matter.

She slammed her emptied glass next to his. "Deal," she said, exhaling long and deliberately to keep from choking. Why on earth had she ever taken such risks to remain in the custody of a man like Jackson Beauregard Tyler?

Less than one hour later, her slippers, borrowed

gown, and shabby petticoats lay on the floor by her chair and Erin was ready to give up gambling forever. Jackson's boots, the only sign of loss on his part, had been tossed with great show across the room, landing askew by the cabin door. Although it had been her victory, it was hard to feel victorious. That smug grin that had been on his face since the first hand had promised misery and his luck and expertise were delivering it most adequately.

The only gratifying thing she had managed to do was to dump most of the liquor he'd poured for her under her chair when he wasn't looking. If she hadn't she would have been reduced to incoherence by now . . . or worse. The carpet was soaked, her bare feet taking a chill from the overflow as she tried to work it in, but at least her head was still clear.

As for Jackson's, Erin wasn't quite sure. His dealing had become more cautious, as if he had to take pains not to flip a card, and his concentration on his hand had grown more intense, allowing her deceit with the brandy to escape his notice more easily than at first.

"'Tis time to pay the piper, Erin," Jackson announced with a fiendish glint as he showed his winning hand. "Now what shall you remove next?"

Erin squirmed in her chair disconcerted by the way he kept looking at her. There was hardly any point in worrying about removing one of her two remaining garments. Jackson had been undressing her with his eyes since this nerve-wracking game had started.

Nonetheless, she chose her cotton and lace drawers. Without getting up, she slipped them over her hips to drop around her ankles under the cover of the table, all the while the victim of a mildly amused gaze that grew hungrier by the moment. Leaving Jackson to deal another hand, she snatched them up and deposited them primly in her lap, daring him with a glower to object. After all, they were off . . . technically.

This round, it was she who topped his two pair with a straight flush. Instead of the discretion she had used, her opponent stood and removed his trousers, revealing not only the remainder of the muscular torso that had proved most distracting all evening, but his ardor as well. Erin fumbled with the cards as he resumed his place at the desk, her breath becoming more labored. Although out of view, the image was burned into her mind, lighting a fuse of excitement that sizzled through her veins.

In the midst of her dilemma, a loud growl rose above the shuffling of the cards to remind her that she had not eaten. The startled look that flashed across her face promptly changed to embarrassment.

"I take it you did not have supper?"

"I . . . I didn't have time," she told him in a small voice. It was absurd to be abashed by something so simple when she was sitting all but naked in a room with a completely naked man, but she couldn't help herself.

Jackson opened the bottom desk drawer and withdrew a tin of thick crackers or biscuits. "I certainly don't want you fainting from weakness. Try these to take the edge off." He tossed the tin on the desktop and proceeded to refill the glasses, emptying the remaining contents of the bottle equitably.

Erin eagerly snatched a handful up and began to munch on them hungrily. Perhaps they would help thwart the sluggish effects the glass or so of liquor that she'd not been able to dump under her chair. While she ate, Jackson took out another bottle, an imported champagne like that Mariette and the railroad broker had shared, and worked the cork free with a loud pop that made her start. He caught the excess that foamed over with his tongue and Erin

254

nearly strangled, the muscles in her throat constricting at the sensual way he lapped at the bottle neck, his kindling gaze never leaving her.

Hair rose on the back of her neck while her breasts, slightly chilled by the night air that slipped in through a half open portal, hardened, Bejesus, she was being seduced without being touched! Surely nothing had ever been written the likes of this!

"I myself had a hearty supper at Retreat before I was called to come to your rescue," he told her as a matter of record, resuming his seat. He lifted his glass to her, peering over its edge as he went on to describe the meal with in an almost lusty fashion. "Thick slices of rare beef and raw oysters on the half shell . . . of course, mother isn't happy unless one goes back for thirds. I had no idea how timely such a meal could be. Do you like oysters?"

Bejesus, Erin groaned silently, recognizing the appetite of a man who craved a boon to his nocturnal pursuit of pleasure. A man like Jackson Tyler would know such things. The mouthful of crackers lodged in the back of her throat and she hurriedly washed them down with the tiny remnant of brandy, neither able or caring to give him an answer.

"More crackers?"

She cleared her throat huskily. "N . . . no, thank you."

"Good! Then we'll get on with the game. If you win, you get to take off your camisole and, if I do, I get to take it off."

"It doesn't appear that I win either way," Erin pointed out grudgingly.

"My dear girl, you lost the moment you agreed to become the stakes in a card game with Coleman Horsey. Time has been the only variable."

Erin could not concentrate on her cards. Her hands shook as she traded in three without even looking at them. There was little point. The inevitable was coming in a matter of minutes, no matter what cards she received or how she chose to play them. Jackson had set out to prove a point and he had done so most effectively. The shame that swept over her was totally foreign. She felt so . . . cheap.

"Aren't you even going to try?"

The sarcasm in his voice stung, bringing a glaze to her eyes. Damn him and his fancy card playing! "Why bother? Like you said, I've already lost." She tossed her cards on the table and rose to her feet, the scant cover of her drawers slipping away. "And I've always paid my debts." Her heart screeched to a halt as she walked over to where Jackson leaned back in his chair. "So help yourself."

The vee front of the lace-edged camisole drew Jackson's gaze like a powerful magnet to the dark triangle it pointed to and a blood thrusting life charged into his manhood, shocking him as much as Erin's beguiling defiance. Damnation, what sort of witchery was she working on him?

"You take it off . . . slowly so that I can savor the sight of you," he told her, his voice growing thick with a resurgence of what he'd thought was a satiated desire. "After all, we can't have this champagne go to waste, can we?"

Jackson chugged the bubbling liquor, hoping for some cooling aftereffect in his inflamed body, but the delicate shaking fingers tugging at the laces of the camisole had far more influence, casting an erotic spell that held him transfixed.

The camisole slid off white shoulders and fell to the floor. His heart thudded as the garment struck in a crush of lace and cotton until hot blood, damned by its seizure barged through and shot to his brain. She was breathtaking, more so than he'd imagined. His gaze followed the slender hands that went to work on the ribbon holding up the pert upsweep of raven locks. Freed, they tumbled in fetching disarray about her neck and face. Alabaster, Jackson decided in his awed musings, as his hungry gaze devoured her naked perfection—small in proportion, but nevertheless ripe with womanhood.

He rose and ran his hands over her shoulders and down to cover her youthful and upthrust breasts. The tiny gasp of pleasure as he cupped them, their hardened tips caught between his thumb and forefinger, acted like a bellows in the forge of his desire and suddenly, he had to know her, flesh against flesh, man against woman.

All thought of punishment and lessons to be driven home vanished at the stirring contact. He could feel her trembling, in spite of the detached manner she tried to maintain and he wanted to ease her fears, to teach her that what transpired between a man and a woman need not be feared, but enjoyed, reveled in.

A pang of guilt at the way he'd toyed with her mind and prolonged her anxiety, briefly surfaced. He'd thought to have some fun with her after following his instinct and searching out the true nature of that ridiculous book she kept hidden under her mattress. Now it had backfired, just as his making her shed the frail defense of her clothing over the course of the night had done. Erin Devareau deserved worship, not abuse.

He proceeded to do exactly that, to make up for his shameful manipulation. Lifting her up, he set her on the edge of the wide berth and dropped to his knees.

Astonished and half frightened by the way Jackson was acting, Erin snatched her ankle from his hand as he poured the champagne he'd picked up from the desk over her feet. "What the hell do you think you're doing?"

"Drinking in your loveliness, my sweet, and enjoying a good vintage at the same time."

Erin stared at him in openmouthed disbelief as he

257

seized the foot and brought it up to his lips. All she could think about was that she'd been wading in mud, but the hour soaking her feet in brandy on the Turkish carpet had left them as pink and well scrubbed as if she'd just climbed out of a tub. The warmth of his breath against her toes, the sensual plunder of his tongue fired a frisson of desire that raced along the lines of her senses to explode at the core of her femininity and all thoughts of his possible perversity disintegrated into a wicked pleasure.

"It tickles!" she cried out in feeble protest, an adequate description for what she actually was experiencing eluding her. "Tyler, plee . . . zz!" Her voice rose to a shriek as the lips that had abandoned her feet moved to the inside of her ankles . . . "Pleeez!" . . . and to a sensitive spot behind her knees. Erin tried to be still, half afraid of what he was going to do next and half in anticipation of it, but the mind-blowing trail of kisses that skimmed along the inside of her thighs made it impossible to do anything but feel and react accordingly.

The closer he came to the juncture where a terrible gnawing need consumed her, the harder it became for Erin to breathe. Her heart pounded so loudly, she hardly heard her own voice when she shoved his head away with a mortified, "Bejesus, Tyler!"

Jackson, his balance somewhat impaired by the considerable liquor he'd consumed, caught himself as Erin scrambled across the mattress, wide green eyes looking at him as if he had horns. He was narrowing down her experience bit by bit, he mused, a half-cocked grin revealing his extreme satisfaction. A woman's past love life had never much mattered to him until now, but somehow, he found himself wishing he was Erin's first, instead of having to content himself with showing her her first intimate pleasure.

At the sight of her oversized eyes and the pillow

clutched defensively to her breast, he turned out the lamp on the desk to afford her a belated degree of modesty and climbed onto the bed to join her.

"What are you doing?" Erin asked, drawing against the wall as he sought her out in the sudden darkness.

"Holding you, Erin. You're chilled and covered with gooseflesh."

Chilled hardly described what she was feeling at all, but Erin slowly let go the pillow and permitted herself to be drawn into the strong arms that enveloped her. His body was warm, infecting her own tenfold with the molding of his masculine proportions against her feminine curves.

"D . . . don't forget, I have to be . . ."

"On top," Jackson crooned against her temple. "You shall, I promise."

He ran his hands over the soft round of her buttocks and tugged her closer so that his hard and aching passion probed the quivering flesh of her stomach. Erin struggled with conflicting reactions to fight its inflammatory spell. It had been a heady experience to feel it straining through the fabric of his trousers, but proud, bold, and unencumbered, it generated a veritable volcano of emotions and feelings that banished all doubts that this was what she'd wanted since the night she'd all but swooned in Tyler's arms. Except that she was the one who was supposed to do the pleasing, she remembered suddenly.

"Let me," she murmured feverishly, rising up on her elbow to push him over on his back.

None of the techniques she'd heard described by the girls who had worked for her mother came to Erin's mind. She reacted purely out of an instinct older than time itself, instinct and a desirous curiosity to know this virile body next to her in the most intimate of manner.

Her fingers splayed as she ran them across the muscled plain of his chest, taking time to catch the taut nipples and circle them before following the long lines of his torso over his hips and down to hard thighs. Although she could not bring herself to become familiar with the masculinity that fluttered each time her hand passed near it, she could not help but notice its eagerness and found a similar urgency developing within.

This strange and wicked fascination became a study in discovery until a desperate hand closed over hers and drew it to where his passion throbbed. Erin seized her bottom lip as her fingers were gently, but firmly, closed about it. The initial obstacle out of the way, she began a shy, tentative examination.

A moan of pleasure rumbled in Jackson's throat, the contact bringing him close to the brink of lost control. "Erin!"

Erin sensed, felt his urgency and knew the nature of his plea. Driven by her own fiery devils, she leaned over and met his kiss with a matching ardor. Tongue curled against tongue in a pagan mating dance that rumbled deep within them as Jackson manipulated her into position, the nest of coarse silk that hailed his goal taunting his manhood to unbearable proportion. He shifted again, breaking away from the breath-robbing kiss to brush the top of her head as she found the thundering pulse in his neck with her lips.

He poised at the warm moist gateway to heaven and waited, giving her the chance to protest, but instead of recoiling, she closed her legs around his hips tightly and uttered a plaintive, "Bejesus, Tyler, don't stop now!"

The words cut through the last shred of his control. Grasping her hips firmly, he drove upward and pulled her frantically wriggling body down. The brief resistance of her innocence was no match for his demanding entry, but it was only when Erin froze, her face stricken with disillusionment, that he realized its source.

"Liar!"

Erin winced at the disparaging accusation, but it could not overcome the sweet fulfillment spreading through her loins from this new and wonderful possession. Already the initial discomfort was receding beneath a cresting wave of need. "It doesn't matter," she responded, tightening her muscles as the male body beneath her threatened withdrawal. "It's too late now, Tyler." She ground her hips against Jackson and heard his breath halt abruptly.

"Jackson, damn it!" Jackson growled, heaving upward and knocking her forward against his chest. "If we're going to do this," he quoted irritably, "I have to be called by my first name!"

He hadn't meant to be funny, but the idea that he was worried about what she called him at a time like this struck Erin that way. Her spontaneous giggle turned into a shriek as he suddenly rolled over, pinning her with his powerful frame to the mattress. But before panic could set in, he claimed her mouth in a soul-searing kiss that eradicated all thought of protest over the change in position. The limbs that started to resist instead enveloped him, hands running up the ridges of his back while legs locked about his waist.

What started out as a slow and sensuous bombardment soon increased in intensity. Each breath Erin took was driven from her quaking breast by Jackson's fierce and rhythmic possession. Blood pumped hot through her body, running riot with shivers of pleasure that threatened to drown her consciousness in wantonness. She called out Jackson's name over and over, until the pitch of his own fever reached its ultimate crescendo, deafening him to all but the thunder of the passion that rocked through him.

"Bejesus!" he croaked huskily, unwittingly resorting to Erin's favorite expression. He was actually trembling, weak with the ferocity of his spent desire. It took all his effort to force himself up on his elbows and roll over on his back, his head still whirling as the last flames of lust were banked by the return of reason.

Yet, already a different kind of warmth was seeping into his system, a tender, more affectionate type that made him reach for the girl he'd abandoned and draw her gently against him. He planted a kiss on the top of her head as she made a pillow of his shoulder and basked in the sweet afterglow of their lovemaking. "What am I going to do with you, Erin?" he sighed heavily as guilt tried to rear its sobering head above the tenacious sea of lethargy that engulfed him.

Drunk, not from the brandy, but from this new and heady intimacy, Erin grinned and ran playful fingers across his chest. "It seems to me you've got that figured out pretty good . . . Jackson," she murmured dreamily against his skin, unaware of the somber expression that troubled her lover's face as she closed her eyes in contented bliss.

## Chapter Eighteen

When the first light of day streamed in through the portal, Erin slipped from sleep nestled in Jackson's embrace to instant wakefulness. The deck was vibrating beneath her and at first she thought they were underway until she recalled Reds saying something about testing out a new part on the engines and relaxed. The brief tensing of her body conveyed itself to Jackson, who stirred briefly enough to buss her on the neck before settling down again to resume his steady breathing, warm against her skin.

Erin smiled as its effect spread through her. She was a woman now and knew the secrets that had sent her to her cabin to read about a subject few women would discuss openly. No longer would she have to ask embarrassing questions and show her naïveté.

Taking in Jackson's boyish face, shadowed by a night's growth of stubble, she decided that this was something she could easily grow accustomed to. She longed to wake him and tell him just how she felt, except that there were no words for it in her inadequate vocabulary. It had been as wonderful as anything Mariette had spoken off and certainly more preferable to acting the starched and stiff lady he'd tried to make of her. She knew now it simply wasn't in her nature.

Nor had it been in her mother's, Erin decided, overriding the shadow of guilt her mother's memory imparted . . . or Grandma's. Her mother had left to escape the very straits Marie Asante had waited a lifetime to abandon. And God forbid she become like her Aunt Lydia, she thought with a shudder of revulsion.

No, she would be a lady of choice, like Mariette. She glanced over at Jackson and sighed. And Jackson Tyler was definitely a good choice. All she had to do was convince him that life on the river was a better alternative than breeding children in a manor house and sewing most of the day while the men had all the fun. The fact that he was a confirmed bachelor ought to help him understand her aversion to such restraints. Combined with last night's eye-opening experience, she was certain he would see the error of his judgment. Then the ladies of quality up on the bluff could go to hell.

Bursting with exuberance, Erin could not remain in the bed a moment longer. If what they had done last night had the debilitating impact on Jackson likened to the loss of blood she'd read about in Mariette's book, he'd be lucky to be up and walking by tomorrow.

Taking great pains to disentangle herself from her companion's arms and legs, she gradually wormed her way free and replaced her body with her pillow as she had done as a child when Giselle Devareau had joined her to coerce her into an afternoon nap. As she lightly landed on the floor, she tucked the edge of the sheet up over a bare shoulder tenderly, her heart swelling in her chest. The idea of a lifetime in Jackson's arms, bearing his children, was not altogether distasteful.

Shoving the conflicting second thought from her mind altogether, Erin slipped her dress over her head and retreated to her own cabin to dress for the day. Her stomach rumbled hungrily as the smell of frying bacon drifted up from the ship's galley and she hurriedly pulled on her apricot day dress to join the crew for the morning meal.

As she did, the jingle of coins she'd left in its pocket from the last time she'd worn it caught her attention and a brilliant idea lit upon her face. It would only be a token of course, but it was a way of showing Jackson some appreciation for his blood-stirring attentions. Hastily, she scribbled a short, "A small token of thanks for a wonderful night," on a piece of paper and wrapped the coins in it. After stealing into his cabin to deposit it on his desk, she blew him a parting kiss and tiptoed out into the hall.

The passageways were now free of the cotton bales that had been transferred to the *Delta Laurel* overnight and the guards were well above the muddy water level. Erin spotted the sister ship, a much newer vessel, docked at O'Neils', where workers brought on cartloads of coal to make up a journey's supply of fuel for the engines. She'd heard Jackson and Reds talking about taking the *Delta Moon* to dry dock over the winter and replacing her antiquated boilers with modern, more efficient ones that would utilize fuel more economically. While she hated to see the ship choke a stump during the dull season—a season not so dull to her thinking considering the tourists that took to the river at that time to go to Mardi Gras—she supposed it would be worth it in the long run.

Many of the crew had already eaten and were finishing a last cup of coffee before meeting the roustabouts on the wharf to reload the *Delta Moon* with freight to go south to New Orleans. Two of the younger stewards moved aside to make room for her and filled her plate with a stack of hotcakes that made her mouth water.

"You're looking mighty peachy this mornin', kid," Mariette observed from the next table. "We thought Jackson would'a had your hide hung on the side of the boat after last night."

"We settled our differences," Erin answered, the color suffusing her cheeks undermining her nonchalance. Realizing by the prolonged silence that curiosities had not been sufficiently satisfied, she looked up from spearing up a thick chunk of spicy sage sausage. "I was wrong and he forgave me." She popped the sausage in her mouth and instantly reached for the water glass at the head of her plate in an effort to blame her heat-reddened skin on the food. Determined not to protest overmuch, she concentrated eagerly on the honey-soaked pancakes. As jubilant as she felt, what was between her and Jackson wasn't everybody's business and she would tell Mariette that when she got the chance.

"Ryan and I were going to walk up to town shortly," the steward at her side spoke up. "If you aren't in any trouble with the boss man, maybe you'd like to go up with us. That way you can stock up on hard candy to pay me back."

Erin grinned, well aware that the young man was not referring to satisfying her sweet tooth. She and some of the crew had played a few hands of blackjack and she'd won a pocket full of the candy they'd used as chips. Since Jackson would be in bed for a while, she saw no reason not to go. After all, she was escorted.

"Sure, I . . ." She was interrupted by the shrill shriek of the harbor tug, several sharp blasts sounding an alarm everyone who lived on the riverfront recognized. "There's a ship in trouble!"

The room erupted in the frantic scraping of chairs and benches across the foor as the crew bounded out of the door and to the leeward rail. Roustabouts abandoned their labors and gathered on the bank watching as the *O'Brien* cast off its lines and began a straight line for the channel where a red and white ship Erin recognized as the *Kara Louise* of Bayou Sara tilted threateningly in the current.

"What happened?" she shouted, recognizing the engineer who ran up the gangway by the suspenders that had earned him his name.

His face was the same color from the exertion as Reds answered. "Look's like she's takin' on water. C'mon, boys, I told the captain of the *O'Brien* we'd back 'er up. Get them lines away!"

Erin scampered up to the hurricane deck, flushed with excitement and stood at the rail, observing the ship struggling against the current that was keeping her from reaching the shore. At least there wasn't a fire, she thought, recalling the disaster that happened a few months earlier when an Anchor line vessel burned to the waterline in fifteen minutes. Although it was right at the dock, ten people died as a result.

The deck shuddered beneath her feet as the large paddle wheel bit into the water and pulled the stage away from the dock almost before the men on the bow had lifted it clear. A few curious passengers who had arrived the afternoon before gathered on the deck, but one of the hands quickly ushered them out of the way. "If you want to look, git up to the boiler deck!"

Ropes, Erin thought as she watched the men hurriedly coil the lines. They would need lots of ropes if anyone went overboard. Springing into action, she commandeered Ryan and two other porters to scrounge up any lines they could find. Running into Hannah in the corridor, she sent the maid to get blankets to take the chill off any passengers they might have to fish out of the water. As she rushed back up to the hurricane, she ran into the captain, his usual impeccably parted hair mussed from having risen without brushing it. He was ordering the lifeboats readied for lowering as soon as they reached the *Kara Louise*.

"I've got the crew collecting ropes and blankets," she informed him, unaware that she'd hopped to attention to make her report.

"Good thinking, Erin. Now you go on up to the pilothouse and tell the boys I'm on my way as soon as we get this pulley unfroze."

"Yes, sir!"

Thrilled to be part of the *Delta Moon*'s valiant rescue, Erin spun on her toes and ran smack into a disgruntled and thoroughly disheveled Jackson Tyler. Still her heart took time from its excited beat to sigh. Even with his shirttail out, hanging below the cut of his jacket, and his trousers half buttoned, he was rakishly handsome. She pressed her hands against his broad chest and met his red-eyed gaze mischievously. "Are you sure you ought to be on your feet?" She was wholly unprepared for his antagonistic response.

Jackson's nostrils flared as he jerked the note and coins up in front of her face and shouted above the din, "What in the hell is this all about and what . . ." He broke off, realizing for the first time that they were moving. He pushed Erin aside abruptly. "What's going on?"

The captain pointed upriver at the *Kara Louise*. "She's takin' on water by the looks of her and we're going out to help." He squinted in the bright morning sun and took in Jackson's rough appearance. "Everything's under control, sir."

Jackson ran his tongue across the roof of his dry mouth and grimaced at the acrid aftertaste of his drinking. His head throbbed unmercifully and his stomach was none too settled. With a cautious nod of dismissal, he grabbed Erin by the arm and ushered her back to his cabin, out of earshot and all the noise.

Having awakened to the jar of the paddle wheel, he'd found a pillow in his embrace instead of the warm-blooded girl he'd remembered falling asleep in his arms. Shaking the stupor from his liquor-dulled brain, he stumbled over to his desk to fetch his clothes when he discovered her note and the coins. At first he didn't believe what was there in front of his eyes in plain black and white. His disbelief, however, was instantly usurped by a rage that his aching head did not improve.

Inside the room, he yanked the spare chair away from the desk and motioned her to it. "Sit!"

Erin obeyed, wishing she'd never left such a pittance. Of course he'd been insulted. "I didn't mean to offend you, Tyler . . ."

"Jackson, damn it!"

"Jackson," she conceded quickly, "but I said it was just a token." His lip curling into a snarl, she added quickly, "It was all I had and I thought you'd be pleased!"

"Pleased!" he shouted, catching his head between his hands to silence the abusive thunder of his own voice. "You actually think I'd be pleased to be paid like a filthy whore for . . ." He threw up his hands as if seeking help from heaven and stepped in front of her. As he opened his mouth to speak, he jumped back and stared at the spot where her chair had been the night before. "The damned floor's wet!" he echoed, thoroughly bemused.

Erin's heart sunk. "I think we should go topside. We must be close and they might need . . ." She didn't think it possible that Jackson's face could become more mottled than it already was, but it did. No longer was it red, but a strained shade of purple. "You promised me last night you wouldn't beat me," she reminded him as his fists clenched white at his side.

"You are hopeless!" Jackson muttered through

clenched teeth, realizing for the first time that while he suffered immensely from the previous night's game of nerves, she had weathered the mix of hard liquor and champagne with no apparent ill effect. His wet feet revealed the cunning deceit that set no better with his current disposition than any of the rest of her outrageous behavior and his ego demanded revenge. "You'll never make a lady! You couldn't if you tried!"

Although Erin had come to a similar conclusion earlier, coming from Jackson the words stung. She'd only wanted to please him, to stay with him. That was what had started the whole thing. But she would not accept the entire blame. "You don't want me to. You keep saying you want me to be one thing and act like you want me to be another!" she argued back. "I don't think you know what you do want, Jackson Tyler, but I know what I *don't* want. I *don't* want to be a lady, stuck with a boring man and his brood of younguns! I've got my own ambitions and I'm tired of trying to please you! You don't appreciate anything!" Erin blinked furiously, fighting tears of frustration and anger. "I'm sorry I even gave you what I did!" She leapt from her chair to escape, to grab some fresh air to quell the misery and confusion overwhelming her.

"Erin!"

"Don't you touch me!" Erin growled as she shoved the hand that reached for her arm away.

Jackson caught her wrists and wrestled them behind her as she attempted to pound him away. "Damn it, Erin, be still!" he grunted, pressing her against the wall with his weight. "I don't want to hurt you!"

With little choice but to obey, Erin's defenses crumbled, battered by the mixed emotions tearing at them. "I t . . . tried," she sobbed, leaning forward to mop her tears on his shirt. "I only wanted to let you know how much I'd enjoyed what happened . . ." She raised her gaze to his in despair. With a shudder, she went on raggedly. "I wish it . . . it was like I'd thought instead of s . . . so wonderful."

Jackson's arms tightened around her, pressing her face against him, his fury fading fast at the candid and heartfelt confession that only Erin could make so effectively. This hurt and vulnerable side of her was a new discovery, one that mustn't be dealt with in anger. What was he going to do with her? he lamented in confusion. He was in over his head. Erin Devareau was beyond any of his worldly experience. "Yes, Erin, it was wonderful . . . but it was also wrong. We need to forget it ever happened."

Even as he uttered the words, his body protested. Stirrings of arousal kindled at the soft crush of her breasts against his chest, her hips against his. She'd spoken the truth about one thing. What he wanted to do and what he said he wanted to do were not necessarily the same. What manner of enticement had she worked on him, that he could want her so— especially in view of his decided satisfaction last night? The ship jarred with a sudden groan, announcing its arrival by scraping alongside the *Kara Louise*, and his embrace tightened as he braced himself in instinctive response.

"We might be able to help up above," Erin suggested flatly, her body suddenly rigid. She had to escape those arms before she was humiliated by the horrible torture his statement inflicted. *Forget?* The idea left a bitter taste in her mouth. Last night was a memory only death would erase. She'd thought her pleasure had been shared, but apparently that was not the case. If so, he wouldn't make such an outlandish suggestion.

The validity of her statement offered reprieve. Jackson broke away with a reluctance Erin was too distraught to notice. "Stay out of the way," he told her, pinching a pale cheek in an ineffective attempt to bring a smile to her desolate face. "We'll work this little problem out."

*Little*, Erin mused, watching as Jackson splashed his face with cold water at the washstand before leaving her to her misery. She could hardly consider this terrible hurt that swelled within her chest little, nor would she ever forget. Her earlier spirit flailing, she abandoned the cabin, trying to leave it and its memories behind for the time being.

Jackson threw himself into the rescue effort, his aching head clearing in the fresh air as he did so. Passengers first, and then cargo were transferred across the stage that bound the two ships together while both crews worked furiously to keep the traffic moving smoothly as possible. Meanwhile one of the tugs moved both ships toward a bar where he hoped the *Kara Louise*, and only the *Kara Louise*, would beach to keep from sinking. There the shipbuilders would work on her to repair the hole torn in her side by a piece of floating rubble from upriver.

His disposition improved, he withdrew from the effort as the *Delta Moon* announced with a shrill whistle her departure to return the transferred passengers and cargo to shore. Retreating to the top deck, he watched the muddy water churn around the ship as she moved away with a slow purposeful motion. Yet it wasn't the water he saw, but the vibrant and lovely image of Erin as she'd reported dutifully to the captain came to his mind and a corner of his mouth tried to curl with humor.

It was possible with the pain diminished to a bearable level to see things in a different light. The little devil had outfoxed him at his own game. Him! Black Jack Tyler with all his worldly knowledge! Maybe he'd met his match.

The idea brought him to an abrupt halt, but before he could ponder it further, a noise from inside one of the cabins drew his notice. What would anyone be doing in John Davenport's cabin? Tension steeled through his body as he approached it cautiously. No one had used the cabin since his partner's departure. There were still a few of John's belongings there that Jackson had not had the time or the inclination to remove. Certain that he was about to discover another clue to the mystery surrounding the bizarre occurrences of late, he drew his hand into a fist and barged through the door.

A man dressed in roustabout's clothing straightened in surprise, but the fist Jackson launched at him halted in midair, weakened by the blood that drained from his face at the sight of his late partner. "John?" he echoed uncertainly. Aside from henna red hair and the smudges of dirt that camouflaged his features, the man was the image of John Davenport.

"Top of the morning to you, partner!" The seemingly healthy *ghost* motioned to the door behind him. "Wedge that damned thing to, would you?"

Jackson was at a loss to do anything more than obey. He leaned against it for support. If his eyes were deceiving him, he swore he'd give up drinking forever. Yet his other senses supported the man's presence. He'd heard him and recognized that damnably jaunty note in his voice. "I just buried you last week!" he muttered, taken back by the grudging quality of his words. If his friend were alive, which he appeared heartily so, he should hardly begrudge him that.

"So you did, and a fitting job." John hauled a small chest out from under his bed. "In my haste to leave the ship, I left one of my trunks," he explained. He glanced up at Jackson. "You don't believe I had anything to do with the old woman's death, do you?"

"Of course not, but . . . damn it, John, what the hell is going on?" he demanded, losing patience over the fact that he was arguing with a man who had caused him considerable grief.

John Davenport sobered. "I'm not precisely sure. Someone not only saw fit to frame me for murder, but tried to do me in when I reached New Orleans. The only thing that I am certain of, is that I am dealing with more than one person. It's too much a coincidence that someone should have been waiting for me when I stepped off the boat."

"Who?"

"Elena Cadiz is one of them. I recognized her perfume and voice as she ordered me bound and tossed into the river after her thugs had knocked me senseless in back of the office. Someone had to have tipped her off that I was aboard the *Delta Star*."

"Elena!" Jackson's brow furrowed. Why would the woman he'd dismissed from the *Delta Moon* go after John? More likely, he himself would have been the target for revenge, since he'd been the one to send her to another ship. He said as much.

"Don't flatter yourself overmuch, my friend. This has nothing to do with you, but it does concern Erin."

Jackson rolled his eyes toward the ceiling. "Why doesn't that surprise me?"

The other man's gaze sharpened. "I take it you're having problems with your ward?"

"You couldn't imagine the half of it," Jackson moaned, his fingers going to his temples to assuage them.

"You haven't . . ." John hesitated, his countenance darkening. "God's breath, man, you haven't harmed her!"

"Actually, she's as hail and hearty as you are, none the worse for last night, I can tell you that!" Jackson replied sourly, so absorbed in his own thoughts that he failed to see the fist that sent him sprawling back on the bunk. He sprang back up in a semicrouched position, head reeling as he spied his partner holding the abusive hand against his stomach in obvious pain from his uncharacteristic and far from ghostly punch.

"I'm getting too old for this sort of nonsense," John mumbled, flexing his slender fingers as if to test them. "I'll be black and blue from this!"

"What the hell was that all about?" the younger man exploded in bewilderment as he rubbed his jaw tenderly to check out his own damage. He'd never seen John violent since he'd known him. Usually the derringer he was known to carry discouraged the possibility of the need for violence.

"I just don't want to see Erin hurt. She's . . . one of a kind," he evaded with a wry twist of his lips.

"On that I could not agree more." Jackson squared his jaw and found it in working order. "So now that that is out of your system, what about Elena and Erin?" The two didn't seem to belong in the same sentence, let alone involved in any other way.

"Guess who showed up at Lydia Lafon's to do her hair the day of her mother's funeral?"

Jackson digested this. "So you think Elena is working for the Lafons." It didn't make sense. "Do you really think Lydia Lafon would have her own mother poisoned? And how do *you* fit into all this?"

John opened the case and began to go through an assortment of wigs and what appeared to be makeup. "Maybe not Lydia, but I wouldn't put it past her husband. As for me, I stumbled in as the perfect scapegoat by admitting that I'd taken her tea the night before. You saw what happened when they found me dead in the alley. The mystery of Marie Asante's death was solved, the murderer punished, and the Lafons were free to inherit the old girl's fortune . . . provided Erin was out of the way. Think a moment, if you will. If the Lafons wired ahead of my impending arrival, Elena would have had ample time to plan my demise."

As he picked some items selectively from the trunk, John told Jackson how he'd gone to the office to change into fresh clothing and that he'd no sooner stepped out on the street when the lights went out. He came to, hands bound behind his back in time to recognize the perfume and voice he knew to belong to Elena Cadiz as she ordered that he be thrown into the river. Once he'd struck the cold water, his head cleared enough for him to slip free of the bonds and hide under the docks until his would-be murderers were gone. "I'm double jointed," he explained, folding his hands to demonstrate how he'd compressed them to escape the ropes. "The fact that the wet ropes expanded only made it easier."

"And who was that poor devil in the alley?"

"He'd already met his Maker when I found him. I switched clothes with him and would have dumped him in the water, but someone was coming, so I had to leave him where I found him. Actually," he laughed, "I was hoping my would-be murderers would at least be confounded by my being discovered blocks away from the watery grave to which they'd abandoned me."

Jackson rolled his head around on his shoulders, loosening the tightening muscles in his neck. It was an incredible tale, but logical. "So Erin isn't at risk, now that she's under my care and the Lafons think they have gotten rid of her."

"I wouldn't go that far," John advised. "Something caused them to panic to have risked killing the old woman . . . like word of a new will. That has to be it! Otherwise, they wouldn't have invited Erin to stay with them. They must have thought she had it on her."

"Coleman Horsey must think the girl's going to inherit some money as well," Jackson inserted in agreement. He proceeded to tell his partner of the fake letter he'd used to try to get Erin's custody and Erin's reckless scheme to get it back. "So help me God, I'm damned if I know what to do with her!" he finished, his exasperation coming through to an extent that won sympathy from his companion. "She actually left money with a note to thank me for a wonderful night! Some stupid notion she picked up from Mariette. And you should see this book she's been reading!" Jackson snorted disparagingly. "I've never seen such nonsense!" He ran his fingers through his straight dark hair. "Damn it, John, I only meant to scare the devil out of her and make her realize the seriousness of what she'd done and . . . she called my bluff." He sighed heavily. "Things just went to hell from there."

"Do I detect remorse?"

Jackson disregarded the sarcastic ring of his companion's question. "Damnation, I'm supposed to be protecting her, not seducing her, although I'm still not certain who seduced whom."

"My word, you are in trouble."

"It won't happen again," Jackson promised vehemently, as if trying to convince himself first. "Maybe I'll send her to one of those finishing schools."

"She definitely needs to be around ladies, not casino girls and gamblers," John agreed. "But I wouldn't send her away . . . at least not until we're certain she's out of danger."

"I could take her to Retreat," Jackson ventured slowly, uncertain that his mother was prepared to deal with a girl like Erin. After all, Jennifer had always been such a sweet and mannerly child, eagerly obedient to her elders' wishes. He couldn't ever remember seeing his sister's starched and ruffled dresses in disarray or anything more than a smudge of chocolate on her face. She'd been a model child.

John tapped him on the chest. "Now there's the

right idea."

The rattle of paper inside his coat pocket caught Jackson's attention and he withdrew the missive that had been stuffed there unopened upon hearing of Erin's misfortune the night before. He'd forgotten all about it.

"And I shall go to Retreat to keep an eye on her, since you can work more freely here on the river," John went on as Jackson opened the envelope and scanned its contents. "I'll show up as that Uncle Charlie of your father's who lived in St. Louis. He's too old to be coming to the wedding, isn't he?"

"I'll be damned!" Jackson murmured in disbelief.

"I was an actor in another life, so we should be able to pull it off. Then we can come up with a plan to flush out the Lafons, although it could take some time."

"She was a genius!"

John broke off with a quizzical glance. "Who? One of your ex-lovers?"

Jackson tapped the two sheets of paper, one a femininely scrawled note giving Marie Asante's admittedly reserved blessing to her daughter's choice of Jackson as Erin's guardian and the other a notarized and sealed last will and testament dated the day they'd left New Orleans. If he'd only gone home sooner, Horsey could have been dismissed without any effort.

"I knew it!" John exclaimed gleefully, handing back the documents. "Those high and mighty swine are after Giselle Devareau's share of the Asante estate. We have a little heiress on our hands."

"It seems Erin has inherited a cunning wit from the old girl as well," Jackson observed, noting the letter had been mailed from St. Francisville. "Mrs. Asante must have been afraid that her son-in-law might try to intervene and sent the will directly to me. It's been in my office at Retreat the whole time."

"I kind of liked the old fox." The nostalgic note in John's voice drew Jackson's notice. "Wish I'd gotten to know her sooner."

"What, so you could have married her for her money?" Jackson teased.

John failed to rise to the jest, his usual sense of humor suppressed by a strange melancholy. "No, but you know how it is when you think you have someone figured out and find out that you were completely wrong?"

"The thought has occurred to me more than a few times in this last week about you."

This time John emerged from his uncharacteristic mood. "I can imagine it has," he grinned. "By the by, what does Uncle Charlie call you?" Jackson looked at him blankly and he explained his plan once more, in greater detail. "Of course we'll have to let your mother and sister in on this."

Jackson nodded reluctantly. Explaining Erin was going to be difficult enough, without explaining her irascible watchdog. But John's point that Erin would be in danger until the Lafon's located the will and had it destroyed was valid, as was the fact that he was still wanted for a murder he had not committed and could neither clear his name, nor Erin of her danger as himself.

Uncle Charlie! The prospect was so absurd, Jackson burst into laughter, an excellent medicine for the morning he'd spent. As outlandish as the plan was, he'd gained back his partner and found a solution for Erin. At least she'd see that ladies weren't all boring snobs and he would have a chance to sort out his feelings away from her. In the meantime, now that he had a villain, he would have the Lafons watched and wait for them to make a move. Only by exposing them would Erin be safe and John be a free man again.

# Chapter Nineteen

The willow-lined drive that swept to the front portico of the octagonal mansion moved gracefully in the river breeze. Terraced plantings of boxwood and untold varieties of flowers that managed to always be in bloom for the better part of the year sloped away from the two layers of balconies that surrounded the main and second floors. Hand-carved colonnades and rails of local cypress gave the impression of intricate lacework.

As the carriage that she and Jackson had taken from the dock came to a halt, Erin blinked widely at the massive structure before her. Her soft, "Bejesus!" put a smile on her companion's lips as he stole a glance at her wonder-struck face.

What she had heard about Retreat hardly did justice to what she was seeing with her own eyes, Erin mused, so caught up with the sight that she failed to notice the coachman waiting for her to exit. It didn't look as if it even belonged of this world with its onion-shaped dome sitting like a crown supported by a glorious display of arched windows on the roof of the third floor. And how many sides did it have?

The gentle pressure of Jackson's hand at her elbow lending a degree of reality to the fairy-tale setting, she broke away from the mansion's spell and gathered her skirts daintily to step down from the carriage. She wasn't sure why Jackson had suddenly changed his mind about her attending his sister's wedding and acted as if nothing had ever happened between them. All she knew was that Mariette's sly comment over his taking her home to introduce her to his family was based on all the wrong assumptions. He acted as if nothing had happened. Like he'd said, it was of *little* consequence.

The hurt and confusion that dominated Erin's emotions, however, were momentarily overridden by the sheer majesty of the place. A woman appeared on the spacious veranda swathed in a gown that reminded Erin of the pink and green hard candy at the general store. Her tailored jacket was a mint green with a pink false blouse beneath that fastened with a bow at its ruffled collar. The skirt, draped across a flat stomach that belied the age betrayed by touches of silver in her chestnut gold hair, was the same green as the jacket, layered over a pink and green pinstriped underskirt. Like the confection Erin was reminded of, the woman's face could not be described as anything other than sweet.

"You *must* be Erin!" Auralee Tyler exclaimed, taking Erin's hand after having floated down the steps and folding it between her own with a fond squeeze. "I have so wanted to meet you. I'm Auralee Tyler, Jackson's mother," she went on, preempting Jackson's introduction enthusiastically. "Jackson has told us of your sad, sad story and I want you to know you have my deepest sympathies." Taking Erin under her wing, she herded her up the steps like a long lost sheep come home to the fold. "I'm sure you'll want to freshen up from your long ride up from the river, so I'll show you to your very own room."

Erin glanced uncertainly over her shoulder, dumbfounded by the warm and sincere reception, to see

Jackson give her a cock-eyed grin and a nod of assurance. Ushered into an elongated octagonal hall, resplendent with a round and richly upholstered sofa in the center under a chandelier with shimmering teardrops of crystal that caught the light from yet another room beyond, Erin nearly stumbled over her dragging feet. Through a round central room, she could see yet another room.

"I want you to think of Retreat as your home, Erin, and I hope, once you come to know us, that you will think of us as your family now."

"Thank you, ma'am," Erin managed politely, holding back long enough to peek into the center room, the likes of which was beyond her imagination.

It was a rotunda, a tall shaft through the middle of the house that rose all the way to the dome she'd seen outside. Mirrors and the tall arched windows that supported it let in natural sunlight that filtered down to where she stood. Who ever heard of sunlight *inside* a house!

"That was my Robert's pride," Auralee, unable to miss Erin's fascination and accustomed to it from new guests to Retreat, told her in a drawl that was thick and sweet as honey. "There's even light in the center of the basement coming through those thick glass sections of the floor there."

Sleep was now the last thing on her mind, but Erin, after examining the glass in the beautiful mosaic design of the floor to see if she could see through it to the basement, allowed herself to be escorted up the curving walnut steps to the second floor to her room. Never in all her wildest imaginings could she dream up a place like this! She wondered what it must have been like to have lived in such luxury all one's life, for this even overshadowed the elegance of her mother's childhood home. She decided to ask Jackson to show it to her later—every room and every nook and cranny.

They passed through no corridors to reach her bedchamber. The rotunda and front and back halls provided the access to all the rooms surrounding the open center. After stealing a quick look over the rail at the mosaic floor she'd examined below, Erin followed Auralee Tyler through one spacious bedchamber, complete with its private veranda, into another, decorated in shades of rose and ivory.

"This is somewhat smaller than the interior bedroom, but it's not as much of a walk-through," her hostess explained, adding with a twinkle in her butternut brown eyes, "My own on the south wall matches it, except that I have chosen lavenders for my colors."

"This is fine," Erin assured her, trying not to act too overwhelmed. "I like corners." If the house had any corners. She tried to get a mental picture of its layout in her mind. Heaven's, she'd be lost!

"Since the noonday meal is already over, I'll send one of the servants up with a snack to tide you over until supper." The woman heaved a regretful sigh. "As much as I'd love to talk to you, you look like you need a good nap. There's something about being on the water that always makes me tired."

Erin might have protested, but for the yawn that tugged insistently at her jaw. Torn between a desire to see the rest of Retreat and the invitation of the plump iron-laced bed that domineered one wall of the room, she acquiesced to her hostess' will. "That would be lovely, Mrs. Tyler."

"Auralee," the woman insisted sweetly. "Now you just make yourself at home and look around, we've a lovely view of the gardens from your balcony—those are *my* pride," she injected with a twitch of her lips, "and the servants will be up with your trunk. If you want anything, you just ring this bell"—she pointed to a small chain with a porcelain knob painted with roses—"and one of the servants will come to assist you."

"Miss Auralee . . ." Erin stopped the woman as she moved to the door. Although she had leave to call her by her first name, a woman like Auralee Tyler demanded some proper address. "Do all the rooms have bells?" The house had to have at least twenty rooms and she could envision the chaos.

"Almost all . . . and each bell has its own tone, so the servants will know where their help is needed," the woman explained patiently. "I'll have Jackson show you the house later. Right now, he's probably dug in in his office. There are some affairs that force me to depend on his business sense. He's such a good son."

Picturing Jackson Tyler as a good son was a challenge to Erin. Picturing Auralee Tyler, who didn't seem to have a malicious bone in her body, as Jackson's mother was yet another. Perhaps he'd inherited his darker side from his father. Determined to seek out a portrait of the patriarch of the Tyler family, Erin chose her reply carefully. "I'd love to see the house, although, from what I've seen so far, I'm not sure my eyes can stand so much elegance in one day."

Auralee Tyler chuckled, a lighthearted titter that reminded Erin more of a young girl than a woman better than her mother's age. It was a pleasant sound and not at all offensive. "You are a dear, Erin Devareau! I'm beginning to see why my son is so charmed by you." She blew Erin a kiss and left with a motherly, "Rest well, dear," that managed to touch the girl's heart. But for her previous statement, its resulting melancholy might have taken her over.

*Charmed?* That was what the woman had said, Erin questioned her senses skeptically. Jackson was charmed by her? Before she could ponder the anomaly further, a knock announced the arrival of her trunk. As it was placed against the wall, one of the female servants who introduced herself as Mary, insisted that Miss Auralee would have her hide if she didn't unpack Erin's things in quick order.

So it was, that when the light snack Auralee Tyler had ordered for her arrived, Erin took it on her balcony to give the maid free rein inside. The royal treatment was a heady experience for her, considering her less than gracious reception at her family home. The fresh fruit and milk were a temptation to the appetite that had dwindled upon finding out Jackson was taking her to Retreat, and the delicious iced torte that accompanied it left her so full and content that, when she was left to her own devices, the bed was as enticing as her urge to explore.

Erin hadn't realized how tired she actually was, for sleep claimed her so hastily and completely that she hadn't heard the maid come in and take the dress that hung, freshly pressed, on the back of the door when she awakened. Her lips pursed with a degree of irritation, partly from having just awakened and partly with the guess that Jackson Tyler had gone so far as to choose her attire for the evening.

Rebelliously, she tossed back the coverlet and went straight to the closet. She'd had in mind to wear her favorite gown and, saints be damned, she'd wear it. After all, she wanted to make the best impression. Examining the garment for wrinkles, Erin pressed it out on the bed with her hands and decided it would do just fine. It was so pretty, who would notice a few creases here and there, she thought, stripping down to her undergarments to bathe.

Taking extra care for fear of an accident, Erin poured water out of the lovely hand-painted pitcher and into its matching washbowl and proceeded to bathe with the scented soap she found resting in yet another matching dish. It was the same scent that seemed to linger in Auralee Tyler's wake, a pleasant flowery one that reminded Erin of roses. She liked it almost as much as the orange blossom soap Jackson had furnished her and didn't mind at all using it in lieu of that which she'd left on the ship. In the few short moments she'd known Auralee Tyler, she knew she had finally met a lady she could like.

As she struggled into her gown, taking pains to arrange its voluminous skirts over her bulkiest crinolines, another knock sounded at the door. This time, instead of a servant entering when Erin bade them do so, a pretty young woman who resembled Auralee Tyler entered the room. Erin could not help but guess her identity, even before the girl introduced herself.

"I do hope you'll forgive me, Miss Devareau, but Mary said that you were awake and I couldn't wait a moment longer to meet you. I'm Jennifer Tyler, Jackson's sister, and I hope you'll call me Jennifer."

Erin held out a hand. "Pleased to meet you, Miss Jennifer."

"Jennifer," the girl insisted. "After all, we're almost sisters . . . your being Jackson's ward and all," she hastily added. "I always did want a sister and wouldn't you know, Jackson waited until I was leaving the house before finding me one!"

A grin broke out on Erin's face to match that of her impish visitor. "I don't think he planned it that way. The fact is, he was stuck with me, sort of honor bound to my mother's last wish."

Jennifer Tyler gave her a chiding look. "I don't think honor has the least little biddy thing to do with it. I know my brother and somebody has flustered his neatly planned little world. I think I'm looking at her." Brown eyes swept over the dress Erin arranged on her shoulders. "What a lovely gown! Are you going to wear it tonight?"

There was a note of hesitancy in the girl's voice that made Erin turn away from the mirror uncertainly. "I'd thought to," she answered slowly. "Why?"

Jennifer marched past Erin to the closet. "Well, I just thought that as pretty as you look in that that you would save it for my wedding. After all, tonight is just a little family affair to welcome you to Retreat. What's wrong with this one?"

Erin's chin set stubbornly as Jennifer held up the yellow dress. Had Jackson sent her to make certain she wore his choice? "Your brother picked it out without even asking me and I'll go stark naked before I'll wear it!"

To her amazement, instead of trying to sell her on the idea of the yellow dress, Jennifer laughed outright. "No wonder Jackson acts like he's walking on firecrackers! Oh, Erin, I only wish I was going to be around longer! My big brother isn't used to women who don't fall over at his beck and call. And mother and I have both spoiled him dreadfully, I fear," she explained with a rueful expression.

"So I'll wear this tonight *and* to the wedding."

Jennifer sobered and placed a hand on either of Erin's shoulders. "Erin, I hope you won't take offense at this, but I'm only telling you because I don't want any of the others to think poorly of your taste. This is a lovely ball gown, but far too overdressed to wear to dinner. It's perfect for the wedding though."

Recalling the startled looks the dress had earned at her grandmother's funeral, Erin saw the validity of Jennifer's advice. So it wasn't just that she hadn't worn black that caused them. She also was aware of the sincerity on her face. There was no malice on her pert features, merely genuine concern. Had Jackson chosen the gown to keep her from making a fool of herself? She sighed heavily. There was so much to know in order to fit in Jackson Tyler's other life on the bluff.

"I suppose you're right. I guess the yellow is a better choice."

"And have you given in to that tyrannical brother of mine?" Jennifer objected, bringing Erin's head up in bewilderment. "You'll wear one of mine! We're about the same size and I have just the thing! Stay put until I get back." At the door, she stopped and looked over her shoulder. "This is called a little sisterly revenge!" she whispered in a positively devilish manner.

If the unsolicited support from Jennifer Tyler was not enough to boost Erin's spirit, the beautiful dress she loaned her was. Its princess lines and striped faille of creme and violet skimmed over Erin's figure, enhancing her tiny waist. Crisscrossed scarves of solid violet formed an overskirt secured by fringed crepe de chine bows. The bodice, cut square and lined with gathered lace made a perfect frame for the solitary silver locket that had once contained her baby picture.

"I can't wait to see Jackson's face when you sweep into the parlor in this," Jennifer whispered excitedly as she placed the finishing touch on Erin's hair—a comb adorned with a bow made of violet crepe de chine and edged with tiny seed pearls. "You look divine!"

Her image in the mirror was pleasing to the eye, but Erin's stomach quivered at the thought of going downstairs to have supper with the family. Auralee and Jennifer Tyler had been nothing like the women from the bluff that Erin had come into contact with during her school years. In fact, she felt as if she'd known the vivacious and friendly Jennifer all her life. As for Jackson, there was little she could do to make him more distant. So what was wrong with her?

The sight of the vision in rose silk clinging to Jackson's arm as she and Jackson entered the parlor revealed the source of Erin's anxiety instantly. As usual, Gina Allen was perfection itself and well aware of it, situated in the midst of Jackson and two gentleman whom she did not recognize. The younger immediately broke away from the group to come to Jennifer's side.

"And who is *this?*" he prompted the girl in a teasing manner that earned him a slap from her folded fan.

*"This,"* Jennifer began.

"Is my ward, Miss Erin Devareau," Jackson filled in smoothly, stepping to Erin's other side. "Erin, since you have obviously already met my sister," he said, his gaze dropping meaningfully over her borrowed attire in such a way that a small giggle hung in Jennifer's throat, "Permit me to introduce you to her fiancé, Chase Allen."

"I am charmed, Miss Devareau. Retreat seems to have an endless source of beauty." He reached for her hand and for one awkward moment, Erin was uncertain whether to give it to him or hold it out for a handshake. She was grateful when he solved her dilemma by catching it and lifting it to his lips gallantly.

"Nor does it lack its share of handsome devils," Erin quipped, falling into the mold of coquette with such brilliance as to raise a single dark brow on her guardian's forehead.

This time, neither Jennifer, nor the others present could hold back their amusement at her quick retort. "Why I do believe she has found you out, gentlemen!"

"I hope I might be included in that unsavory group." The older man who had remained in the background stepped forward and, taking Erin's hand with no less gallantry than his younger companion, introduced himself. "I am Charles Tyler, uncle to one of these devils and to the beautiful bride-to-be. Can I get you a glass of sherry or champagne? We were waiting for Jennifer to arrive so that we might toast this up and coming affair properly."

"I believe Erin likes the creme sherry . . ."

Erin cut Jackson off with a laugh. "But the champagne is kinder to my disposition, sir." With an impish beguiling wrinkle of her nose, she turned back to his uncle. "Champagne would be perfect."

The bubbly liquor helped to quell her nervous stomach. After polite inquiries as to her welfare were made by the Allens, Jackson made an eloquent toast to the future of his sister and her fiancé and the conversation turned to the wedding. As Erin watched Jennifer and Chase, an odd twinge of envy struck her, for the pair had eyes only for each other as they were fondly teased by loving relatives.

"Oh, oh," Jackson's uncle chuckled lowly at her elbow. "I think I detect the look of a woman setting her sights on the institution of matrimony."

Embarrassed, Erin brushed the notion away with a wave of her hand. "Don't be absurd, Uncle Charlie! I'm just happy for them. My ambitions do not include marriage. Being a wife just doesn't mix with business, if you know what I mean."

Jackson Tyler, who'd been listening with half an ear to the light prattle between Jennifer and the young blonde on his arm, strained to hear the side conversation between his partner and the breathtakingly lovely girl at his side. It seemed the unspoken truce between them had been a false assurance. Instead, their differences were being settled in a trying battle of nerves, oblivious to all but the combatants. The gown she wore and the sparkling drink in her hand, Jackson realized, were just beginning skirmishes.

"Oh, but I fear I must differ with your opinion, dear," Auralee Tyler objected softly. Jackson hardly heard what Gina was saying, for he was anxious to see just how his mother would handle Erin. "I have combined my wifely and motherly obligations with business for years with satisfactory success. I helped my Robert with his ledgers and together we discussed decisions concerning Retreat. Such experience stood me in well, for at his passing, I was able to carry on until Jackson was in a position to take over.''

"Don't let her mislead you, Erin," Jackson asserted strongly. "She still runs Retreat with an iron hand and a sharp wit."

"And I would like to retire its reins to my offspring, should he ever conquer this malady of bachelorhood.''

Erin could have giggled at the smooth reprimand that flushed Jackson's face with awkward color. She was coming to like and respect Auralee Tyler more and more by the moment.

"Maybe you should listen to your mother," Gina whispered in a conspiratory tone, having abandoned her conversation for the one that had cornered her escort's interest.

Jackson pulled a wry face. "And throw her into shock after all these years?" His tone was light, but his mood was not at the turn in the conversation. His mother was supposed to be helping him, not putting him on the spot. Thankfully, the appearance of a servant announcing that dinner was served, ended his misery.

As the group moved in unison through the rotunda to the dining room, he heard his *uncle* inquire as to the sort of ambitions Erin had in mind and cringed. Perhaps if he could not overhear them, neither would anyone else. Piloting a riverboat, running a casino, owning stock in a railroad would set society tongues wagging against the girl before his mother ever got the chance to exercise her influence. And, as angry as Erin could make him, Jackson didn't want to see her hurt.

# Chapter Twenty

Life at Retreat was not at all like Erin expected, at least where Auralee Tyler was concerned. Dawn found the plantation mistress up and planning the meals with the cook, after which foodstuffs and staples were inventoried. She presided over breakfast like royalty, infecting those at the table with her effervescent personality. Naturally the conversation was monopolized by the plans for the guests who would begin arriving at midweek. Not the least flustered at the prospect, but more like a general taking an account from her troops, Auralee Tyler ran through a mental checklist with each officer, bestowing a satisfied smile over each affirmation of a duty complete and a concerned lift of one golden brown eyebrow at the opposite.

Only Jackson was spared extra duties. The matron seemed so pleased to have her son in residence, that his only wedding responsibility was to give away the bride. That did, however leave him time to see to the plantation ledgers, formulate the plans for marketing the current cotton harvest, and to look ahead to the spring planting season.

While Erin was hardly needed, Miss Auralee enlisted her to help her remember the things still left to be done. Each morning after breakfast they retired to the plantation office while Jackson rode the fields to jot items and tasks down before they slipped her mind. "I am so afraid I shall forget something and be caught unawares the day of the wedding," she'd told the girl with a heavy sigh. "You shall be my second, if you will, and help me see that things go smoothly."

Erin eagerly agreed, for she liked Jackson's mother and sister immensely. Like a shadow, she followed in the wake of Auralee Tyler's footsteps, checking to be certain the servants had properly seen to each bedroom, overseeing the laundry that was hung out in the sunshine to dry, keeping a written account of every expenditure and disbursing it correctly in a journal. The list went on and on. Not once did the woman even act like she was going to pick up a needle until the end of the second day.

"This is my relaxation," she explained to Erin as she moved closer to the fireplace to enjoy the warmth it afforded on the crisp fall evening. "I can keep my hands busy and let my mind rest for a while."

Erin grinned sheepishly. "If I did that with a needle in my hand, I'd be bleeding like a stuck pig."

Auralee Tyler's laughter rang like a bell, a soprano version of her son's deeper baritone amusement. "My dear Erin, when you have wielded the needle as long as I . . ." The woman sobered abruptly. "You do sew, don't you?"

Put on the spot by her foolish observation, Erin hesitantly nodded. She was certainly better with thimble rigging than sewing. "I can manage well enough, but it isn't one of my favorite pastimes. I'd rather read or . . ." Something told Erin not to mention the casino. "Or act as hostess in the salon for the guests on the ship. One meets so many interesting people on the river."

"That is what Jackson is always telling me . . . and I have no reason to doubt it," Auralee added quickly, reluctant to voice any criticism where her son was concerned. "I certainly enjoy a trip to New Orleans now and then." She ran her needle through the material, her thoughts temporarily claiming her. "What do you think of children?"

Erin glanced up from the copy of *Home Journal* in her hand in surprise. "I love them! I used to help Miss Molly, the lady that took care of me when Mama worked, with the smaller children she took in."

"Well, if you think we've been busy lately, having small children in the house seems to double the work and shorten the hours in the day. They'll also make one mighty handy with a needle." A smile lighted on the lady's lips to match the warm twinkle in her eyes. "But it would be worth it to have little ones laughing and running through the house again."

Auralee Tyler's wishful comment came true with the arrival of the first of many guests to follow. Some of Jackson's cousins came en force with their little ones and the busy schedule Erin had kept with the mistress of Retreat became chaotic at best. The adults wanted to visit and the servants had their hands full dealing with the overexcited youngsters, who kept the dessert plates emptied and found an endless source of energy with which to make an equally limitless amount of noise as they played with distant relations of the same age.

Consequently, Jackson spent more and more time either on outings with Gina and the prospective bride and groom or locked in his study. If that was difficult for Erin to take, the fact that Gina Marie Allen had been assigned to share her room with her was impossible. The older girl hardly spoke to Erin at all except to complain, spending most of her time with the group of cousins sharing the adjoining room.

The night before the wedding, Erin had been so overwhelmed with the number of strangers surrounding her and eyeing her with polite curiosity that she'd retired early with the excuse of a headache. She was still awake when the young ladies sharing the next room burst in to chatter the rest of the night away and could not help but overhear them.

The subject mostly on their minds was the list of eligible young bachelors expected to attend the affair, but eventually it came to Erin and speculation about her past. Were it not so revealing, she might have been tempted to shut it out. But she couldn't.

That Gina Allen vowed that she was a thief from Under the Hill didn't surprise her. However, the story of a man named Devareau who shot one of Natchez's leading citizens in a duel for cheating and fled before charges of murder could be pressed left her stunned. Her mother had said nothing about her father being a murderer or a duel of any sort. She'd said he left to join the war effort and never returned.

Her morale was helped no further as the course of the conversation was changed tactfully by the future bride, who stalwartly came to Erin's defense by pointing out that the charges were only allegations, not fact. She skillfully impressed the others with the fact that Erin was a direct descendant of the casket girls of New Orleans, a fact echoed by oohs and ahhs through the thin door.

But Gina, having gained the complete attention of the gossip-hungry audience, was not about to let the stage go. She proceeded to enlist the help of the other girls to help her relieve Jackson of his burden by introducing Erin to the other young men.

"After all, that's Jackson's plans for her. It would be a relief for him, I imagine, to leave for the North with her comfortably wedded and bedded and would save Miss Auralee no end of headache, I imagine."

This time Jennifer Tyler refused to let Gina's vindictive manner pass. She challenged her guest to say another word, letting them all know that her mother was delighted at the prospect of having Erin spend the next few months with her.

Erin, however, no longer heard the girl, or any of the others for that matter. The headache that had been a ruse became a reality, compounding the terrible anguish she felt within her chest born of fear and hurt. Jackson was leaving her. Such was her anxiety that when she finally did fall asleep, she was oblivious to the scraping sounds of wood against wood outside. Nor did she hear the hastily retreating footsteps spurred by the inconsiderate light that suddenly flooded the room as Gina Allen entered to retire at last from her gossip.

The next morning in behind the closed doors of the library, John Davenport expressed his own opinion of the farce that had just taken place. His face turned an outraged shade of scarlet that clashed with the wig that he knocked askew as he smacked his hand to his forehead in exasperation.

"Things haven't changed a bit in eighteen years!" he ranted, stopping his pace from one end of the room to the other to make his denouncement. "Convenience rather than justice still seems to be the order of the day where our honorable enforcers of the peace are concerned. Wedding prank, my foot!"

Jackson sat in silence and let his friend ramble on. His eyes were reddened from lack of sleep. He shuddered to think what might have happened if something hadn't frightened away the intruders who had put a ladder up to the balcony of Erin's room. John had stepped outside before retiring for a smoke and discovered the abandoned ladder.

Consequently, Jackson had spent the remainder of the night on the veranda below Erin's, just in case the men decided to return. His muscles ached from the fall chill that settled in his bones, in spite of the extra blankets his mother had brought him and his mind was weary from trying to figure out the reason for such an attempt.

In spite of what the sheriff, who had been summoned that morning, thought, there was no doubt in Jackson's mind that Erin was the reason for the ladder being there. Unless it had been an impromptu wedding prank planned by the bachelors who had been imbibing overmuch, he wavered wearily. No, it was too much coincidence. The Lafons had received his telegram. They would have had time to arrange for some nefarious fate to befall the girl that stood between them and the Asante inheritance.

Or the men could have been some of Horsey's thugs, although harming Erin would hardly insure the man of anything but a jail sentence—if the law got to Horsey before he did. The first thing he'd done was make certain Horsey knew of his possession of the will and the additional confirmation of Marie Asante's letter that he was the chosen executor and guardian of Erin's affairs. It was a matter of record in the courthouse in Natchez as well as in New Orleans.

"How the bloody blazes am I to be absolved of this travesty of injustice with such incompetents in power?" John ranted on. "I ought to go to New Orleans and flush out Elena Cadiz. I'd lay money that she'd lead us to the culprit."

"I think Uncle Charlie should stay on until after Christmas," Jackson answered tiredly, earning an incredulous look. "That will give me time to take care of my business in Philadelphia and come up with some sort of plan to force their hand and you can protect Erin."

"Whose hand?"

"Whoever is behind this!" Jackson's frustration told in his tone. "Cadiz, Horsey, the Lafons . . . ?"

"All the aforementioned?"

Jackson considered the possibility. "Maybe. At any rate, I want you to move into the room adjoining

297

Erin's after the wedding guests have departed."

"I think we ought to tell the girl what's going on. Forewarned is forearmed. Besides, the way she keeps looking at me, it's just a matter of time before she sees through this disguise."

Nodding reluctantly, for telling Erin she was an heiress posed untold possibilities of more unpredictable behavior, Jackson forced himself out of the chair and walked over to the window, stretching to ease the tension that seemed ever present of late. Only his mother knew of the intended intrusion. They hadn't wanted to frighten the girls or their guests.

"I suppose you're . . ." Jackson halted in midspeech at the sight of the subject in question slipping out through the garden with a large bundle slung over her back. "Damnation, now what!" he exploded, his frazzled nerves coming undone.

By the time Jackson made his way through the mass of servants setting up tables in the hall and ran out onto the side veranda, Erin was nowhere in sight. Swearing profusely, he started in a run for the stables. On horseback, he could cover more territory and, if she was running away, head her off at the main road that led to Natchez Under the Hill.

He should have been comforted when he came upon the road to town. Aside from early arriving guests, it was empty. A gnawing panic ate at his insides that perhaps Erin had lost her way or had fallen and was hurt—or worse yet, that the men who had been on the property last night had come across her. So help him, if Coleman Horsey was behind this, he would kill the man with his bare hands.

After making two passes along each thoroughfare that led down the bluff and explaining his untimely ride as an escape from the prewedding madness, he cut back along the bluff toward the opposite direction. Fall wildflowers dotted the hills that fought to retain their green color as the stallion cut across the pastures where Retreat's thoroughbreds grazed in the warm afternoon sun. He usually took time to identify them, to admire their sleek lines and shiny coats, but today he shot through their midst without the least notice. Ahead lay the more earthy cotton fields, now cut to stubble and waiting for the spring planting.

Riding parallel to the small creek that divided them, he urged the stallion back toward the manor, certain that Erin could not have come this far on foot. As he moved along the edge of the forest that boasted a plentiful supply of game, he caught a glimpse of white near a cluster of trees at the bottom of the grassy slope that led down from them and reined in the stallion in utter amazement.

Unaware that there was anyone else in the world, his ward stood knee deep in the cold water and was vigorously soaping her bare arms and legs. Nearby, laid out on the blanket in which she'd bundled her things, were fresh clothes warming in the rays of the sun. A familiar ballad drifted his way in short and sometimes shaky snatches indicating the chill of the creek as he gave the stallion its rein and started down toward her.

Halfway down the slope, the horse whinnied and the song stopped abruptly. After a moment's hesitation, the girl abandoned the shallows of the creek and scrambled up on the bank to the blanket. Jackson nudged the stallion into a trot as she turned abruptly, a croquet stick brandished threateningly in her hands.

"And I foolishly thought you might need protection," Jackson called out to her as, upon recognizing him, she lowered it. Shoving back the wet raven ringlets that tumbled down on her forehead with her free hand, Erin tossed her weapon aside.

A relief of great proportion quickly dissolved Jackson's prolonged anxiety as the realization that she wasn't running away sunk in completely. He had to exert restraint not to nervously laugh away some of his tension. Judging from the linens and clothing she'd brought along, the cold water bath had been her sole intent.

Erin stood motionless as the stallion stopped in front of her and its rider, rakish without the formal velvet-trimmed riding coat and cravat that usually accompanied his pleated shirt and fawn breeches, slid off easily. A chill tripped over the surface of her skin, not from her wet and decidedly translucent clothing, but from the disconcerting way he was looking at her.

She bent over and, taking up a towel, briskly began to dry herself, as if to rub away his effect on her. "I can't imagine why you bothered, since all you want to do is get rid of me anyway."

No matter how she'd tried to put it out of her mind to get some rest, Erin had not been able to escape the things she'd overheard the girls in the next room talking about. She'd already made up her mind to confront Jackson about them, but this was hardly under the circumstances she'd planned. He had a casual way of undressing her with his eyes. Not that she needed much undressing, she realized, belatedly covering the taut brown nipples that seemed to take delight in his attention with a towel.

"Where did you get that idea?"

"That's why you brought me here, isn't it?" she defied him, aware that without even touching her, the initial chill was changing into a disturbing warmth that seemed to ignite wherever those mercurial eyes lighted. "To marry me off so that you can get on with your bachelor life?" She sniffed and lifted her chin haughtily. "Well, don't delude yourself, Jackson Tyler, that I have the slightest plans to interfere with your bachelor life. Any female dumb enough to entertain that idea is a fool. Believe me, I shared a room with one last night and I know!"

Jackson's sudden peal of laughter brought a scowl to the girl's delicate features as he began to understand the nature of the unexpected assault on his intentions. "So Gina is at the bottom of all this."

"No, you are, you back-stabbing polecat! Damnation, Tyler, I've tried my best to do what you want and I don't know why you're going to leave me here while you go away. I'll die here! I belong on the river . . . on the *Delta Moon*. I was good in the casino and you know it! We could be partners and you can bachelor your life away for all I care!" She turned away to regain control of the emotion that trembled in her voice, presenting a bewitching view of silk, clinging like second skin to nicely rounded buttocks where the towel had fallen away. "I could make you money, Tyler. All I need is a little more experience."

Jackson tried to ignore the stirrings the very sight of her ignited and maintained the short distance between them. To touch her now would be a step from which there would be no return. "I couldn't agree more," he managed huskily. "But I already have a partner."

"What?" Erin turned so quickly, her feet twisted in the blanket and pitched her forward. The towel dropped as she fell into Jackson's arms. Her skin was like ice and yet the contact was inflammatory. "W . . . who?" she asked, reluctantly giving up his warmth and backing away to stare in dismay at where she'd wet his clothing.

Jackson bent over and picked up the lacy change of underwear she'd brought along. "Put on some dry clothes before you catch your death," he suggested gruffly, handing them to her, "and I'll explain."

Erin took the clothing and stared at him expectantly until he politely turned his back. She worked quickly to rid herself of the wet clothing and pull on the dry while he began to tell her the incredible story of John Davenport, who was not dead, but posing as his Uncle Charlie; how John had been framed for her grandmother's murder and dared not show his face until he could prove his innocence; and how everything that had happened, even the fact that there had been prowlers about the house the night before, hinged on her inheritance.

"You mean my *supposed* inheritance," Erin corrected, caught up in the intrigue. She awkwardly fumbled with the fastens of the blue dress she would change for her green gown upon returning to the house.

Hearing the struggle in her voice, Jackson looked over his shoulder to see that she'd attained decency and came to her aid. He turned her around and refastened the mismatched hooks. *"Your inheritance,"* he averred, drawing a surprised glance. "I've had your grandmother's will since . . . since the night I hauled you out of Horsey's and . . ."

Erin stood speechless. How had her grandmother done it? Was that why she was so long in the bank. Unfamiliar with such things, Erin had assumed it took that long to get one's money out of the hands of the austere and decidedly stingy-looking men who controlled it. An inheritance! Who would have thought it? She'd had money all along and didn't even have to worry about how she was going to pay Jackson Tyler back or make investments in her future . . .

"You sonovabitch!" Snatching away, Erin met Jackson with an accusing glare. "Why in the hell didn't you tell me? Here I've been feeling like a kept woman . . ."

"A kept woman!" Jackson echoed in amazement.

Erin's look was deadly. "You know what I mean! I always earned my way the best I could."

Her reaction hardly the joyous one he'd expected, Jackson tried to reason with her. "Erin, you are my responsibility, inheritance or no. I was honor bound to . . ."

"Oh, let's not bring honor into this, Jackson Tyler. I know about your kind of honor!" she derided venomously. "And to think I was beginning to trust you! You not only hid my inheritance from me, but plan to abandon me to choke a stump."

Jackson's patience was fading fast. "For the love of God, Erin, you're not a riverboat being put to dry dock! You'll learn a lot from living at Retreat. I have business in Philadelphia and . . ."

"Why can't I go back to the *Delta Moon*?"

"It's not safe on the river until we find out who is behind all this dirty business with your inheritance."

"Then take me with you."

"I can't."

The answer came so quickly and vehemently that Erin lost the momentum of her tirade. Confusion surfaced in the swimming waters of her eyes as she folded her arms in front of her as if to fend off the bitter assault of his rejection. "You could, Tyler. You just don't want to." She jerked the corners of the blanket over to bundle up her belongings and wiped angrily at a tear that had slipped down one cheek. Bejesus, what was wrong with her? All Tyler had to do was say boo to her and she wanted to cry. Thank God Cready couldn't see her now. She'd be labeled a baby for sure.

"I said I can't and I meant I can't, Erin."

"Why?" she demanded, straightening in sudden defiance.

"Because of this."

Jackson gathered her into his arms and claimed the trembling lips he longed to assuage. Their startled resistance turned into a hungry response that started a wildfire in his veins, threatening his very sanity, for it was madness, this craving to know more intimately the body molding to the lean contours of his own. Of

303

their own accord, his fingers made quick work of loosening the fastens he'd just secured and sought the satiny feel of her flesh. Demonstration becoming obsession, his tongue began a fiery exploration of her mouth, initiating a possession that would not be complete until he knew all of her.

"And this," he whispered urgently as he stripped down her bodice and cupped the fullness of her breast in his hand.

"Bejesus, Tyler!" Erin nearly collapsed against the strong arm that braced her at the small of her back as a frisson of sensation started from the masterful play of his forefinger and thumb and ran straight to the inner core of her womanhood, exploding with a primitive need that would not be denied. She went with him as he dropped to his knees and found his lips with her own as he lowered against the half-folded blanket.

Hands rushed down the length of the slender leg that drew up to embrace his sturdy thigh, savoring its smoothness, encouraging it to seize his waist so that he might access the fastens of the drawers still warm from their exposure to the sun. He rolled aside long enough strip them away, his gaze falling to the raven triangle at the apex of her thighs as he started on the fastens of his trousers.

"Let me."

The breathless offer told Jackson that the fever infecting him had been contagious. As the buttons gave way, he met Erin's gaze and caught his breath at the passion smoldering beneath the dark fringes of her eyelashes. She was quivering, not with cold, but with anticipation as he kicked away his trousers and covered her body with his own. He tried to concentrate on pleasuring her, but her soft and yielding flesh, her moans of ecstasy, were like fuel to a fire already out of control.

He took her swiftly, driving the breath from her

lips in his fervent desperation. Erin lay still for a moment, reveling in the pounding sensation of this still new intimacy. Yet one need had no sooner been satisfied than another found its way to prominence, one as demanding as that which drove Jackson to such abandon. Her urge to explore his body with her hands as he had so masterfully done to her gave way to a dire one to pull him closer, to climb his muscled torso and weld her flesh to his with the intense heat of the moment. And when they could move no closer, when they were as much one as two bodies could be, the welling tide of desire crashed over them, sending them churning in its white-capped tumult of emotions and feelings until they lay drained in love's languorous embrace.

As she listened to Jackson's ragged breathing slow to a more civilized rate, Erin struggled to reason out this madness that had overtaken them. It was almost frightening how quickly their quarrel was forgotten in the heat of his touch. Yet she could not find fault with this contented aftermath—the warmth of his lips still pressed against her neck, the adhesion of their perspiration-damp skin, the prickly fur of his chest against her breasts, his physical occupation of her.

"What am I going to do with you?"

Erin could not help but smile at his hoarse question. There was one thing Jackson Tyler certainly knew to do with her. "Take me with you?" she suggested in a kittenish tone that ran him through and conveyed its effect through their union.

He lifted his face above hers and raked away the straight dark hair that had fallen on his forehead with his free hand. "I can't, love." He pressed a finger to her lips as she started to protest. "Because I can't keep from doing this."

"But . . ."

"Erin, can't you see what you're doing to me? I

can't be your guardian and lover."

"Because ladies don't have lovers?" she challenged grudgingly.

"In a manner of speaking." He brushed her lips and when he drew away Erin basked in the tenderness of his gaze. "I promise we will resolve this dilemma to our satisfaction when I return from Philadelphia. In the meantime, I want you and John to look out for each other. You see, John needs us."

Erin wanted to believe him, but she also wanted to go with him now more than ever. So what if it meant not being all a lady should be? It didn't matter as much to her as it seemed to matter to him; and as long as John continued to play Jackson's Uncle Charlie at Retreat, she couldn't see how her being there would improve his situation. All she had to do was find a way to get Jackson to take her, something that ought to prove easier now that she knew he wanted her as a woman.

Her spirits renewed beyond her expectations by his declaration of his desire for her, Erin returned to the mansion seated in front of Jackson on the beautiful chestnut—after winning the argument that she would ride astride instead of agreeing to Jackson's suicidal proposal that she sit sideways. Her ears ringing with promises to teach her to ride properly when he returned, she fairly bounced into the house with her bundle of belongings. That was hardly the suggestion of a man who wanted to get rid of her anymore than the wonderful hour they'd spent in each other's embrace had been an indication of the same intent.

Not even Gina's demanding manner could daunt Erin's humor as they hurriedly applied the finishing touches to their appearance. The older girl kept Mary busy arranging and rearranging the coral silk blossoms in her mass of golden curls while Erin chose to remain with the simple gather of locks tied up with a green ribbon that matched the trim on her gown. Her cheeks still pink with the afterglow of Jackson's lovemaking, she left the maid of honor complaining over a certain ringlet that would not hang just right and made her way down the stairs.

The basement and main floors of Retreat were filled with guests awaiting the wedding party's descent into the front hall. The ceremony itself was to take place in the drawing room where only the closest of friends and relatives would witness it. Making her way through a sea of strange faces, Erin wandered from room to room admiring the lovely decorations and searching for John Davenport.

She found him just at the appointed hour, giving him an exuberant hug and a delighted buss on the cheek as a hush fell over the house. The musical notes of the pump organ played by Auralee Tyler's sister echoed from the rotunda throughout the adjoining rooms. Erin slipped her arm through the fake Uncle Charlie's and strained to see over the mass of heads as the groom entered with the minister from the adjoining reception room.

Auralee Tyler, lovely in a gown of dusty pink and green floral design presided over the occasion from her position near the mantel which, like the entire main floor, was draped with garlands of roses, dried bridal wreath, and boxwood. Erin could tell by the way the matron's face seemed to take on a certain glow that the bride had entered the room on the arm of Jackson Tyler. Above the crowd she could see the top of Jackson's head, his wind-tousled hair now brushed into place and curling over his starched collar. As they moved closer, the crown of satin flowers and pearls that held Jennifer's veil in place came into view and eventually Erin could see both brother and sister.

It was no wonder their mother looked as if she would burst with pride. Her children were striking.

Jackson's dark and rugged good looks contrasted Jennifer's fairer beauty, yet there were similarities. They shared the same smile, the same aristocratic bone structure and carriage. Jackson was the epitome of Southern nobility in a pearl-gray evening suit trimmed in the same shade of satin as his cummerbund, while Jennifer's white on white gown with yards of imported lace draped around her petite figure was no less royal in appearance. The house, the people . . . it all reminded Erin of a dream world, too beautiful to be real.

The ceremony was short and with its end, the formality of the occasion lifted to permit the onslaught of well-wishers who filed into the room to greet the bride and groom. The banquet tables in the dining room were heaped with food of every description and servants stood ready to dish it out when the hostess gave the sign. In another room a bar had been set up finer than those in any saloon Erin had ever seen as well as tables containing a delicious-looking pink punch ready to be served in the crystal cups that matched the silver and crystal bowl containing it.

The sound of strings tuning in the rotunda announced the readiness of the string quintet that had been engaged to provide dance music, although their beginning numbers were of a classical nature more conducive to conversation and dining. Erin tried to find a quiet corner from which she might observe the affair, for Uncle Charlie had taken charge of the bar and the Tylers were entertaining an endless stream of guests. It seemed however, that word of her arrival had spread throughout the Delta and every-one was anxious to meet Jackson Tyler's new ward, rumored to be giving ladies competition for the bachelor's attentions.

The names and faces became a blur as Gina herself, who seemed strangely committed to her declaration to make Erin her best friend, took the girl under tow to introduce her to the guests. Of course, most of them were men who practically fawned over her, insisting that she reserve a dance for them. After an hour of such introductions and invitations, Erin began to see the value of a dance card. She was also faced with the dilemma of how to escape her commitments, for her short practice on the deck of the *Delta Moon* with Jackson Tyler had hardly prepared her for this.

Consequently, she avoided the rooms where the dancing eventually began. Her luck, however, gave out as the evening hours drew near. A young gentleman who had been introduced as one of Jackson's cousins claimed her hand as she tried to draw away and started to pull her toward the hall where couples enjoyed a lively waltz.

Erin panicked, certain of making a fool of herself before all of Jackson's family and friends. "I don't dance for free!" she blurted out, snatching her hand away and holding her ground.

Taken aback, the young man stared at her blankly. "It'll cost you twenty dollars to dance with me."

"Twenty dollars! My word, Miss Erin, it would surely be worth every cent, but . . ."

Her would-be dance partner stammered in shock for a plausible excuse to change his mind and exited so quickly that Erin had to cover her mouth to keep from giggling outright. The tact worked perfectly and she was quite pleased with herself when her sixth admirer stood blubbering before her. One thing was certain. Bachelors never carried as large a purse with them when attending weddings as when they were out on the town.

"Not that I wouldn't pay twenty dollars for a dance with a girl as pretty as you," another suave admirer said hastily, "but . . ."

"Done for twenty dollars."

Erin felt the blood drain from her face as she turned to see the amused face of J.P. Stevens. She hardly noticed the other man slip away as the railroad broker held out his arm to her.

"Shall we?"

"Why, Mr. Stevens, I wasn't aware that you were still in town," she exclaimed, staring at the arm as if it were infected with leprosy. Who would have dreamed any fool would pay twenty dollars for a dance?

"Do you want my money up front or . . ."

Her face betraying her dismay, Erin looked over her shoulder and lowered her voice. "I don't want your money and . . . I don't want to dance. I . . . I don't know how."

A chuckle shook his chest as he caught on to the scheme he had foiled. "Then I shall teach you, my crafty little miss."

He circled Erin's waist with his arm and ushered her toward the back veranda away from the lanterns that lit the gardens for those in need of a breath of fresh air. The music followed them, changing to another waltz in a slower tempo as he placed a gentlemanly hand at the small of her back.

"Perhaps if I keep you moving, you won't take a chill," he remarked, noting the brisk change in temperature the dusky blue blanket of the early evening had made.

Erin stumbled over her own feet, too hot with humiliation to notice the weather, and caught herself against his chest, her face flushing with embarrassment. "I wasn't ready," she mumbled awkwardly as he swept her into a wide circle to the one-two-three beat.

"So how do you like Retreat?"

"It's like living in another world," she managed, concentrating on keeping her feet away from Stevens's and at the same time keeping up with him.

"You know, Lady Luck was certainly smiling on Jackson when she sent you his way. You're the prettiest girl here."

Erin cut her eyes up at her partner and narrowed them skeptically. She knew a flirtation when she saw one and began to get suspicious of the motives behind her partner's insistence on teaching her to dance. Particularly considering his penchant for champagne and women, she thought, recalling the night he'd left the casino with Mariette on the *Delta Moon*.

She stepped back as he guided her firmly with the touch of his hand and executed her first stumble-free turn. Actually, this was not so hard after all. When Jackson had held her in the same manner, she'd hardly been able to think, let alone keep track of her feet. Besides, Erin remembered practically, she'd wanted to speak to Stevens that night on the *Delta Moon* and missed her chance. Now, with the news of her inheritance, there could hardly be a better time.

"That's kind of you to say, Mr. Stevens, but if you don't mind, I'd rather do away with the small talk and discuss that railroad you're building."

The announcement was not what the man expected and it showed briefly on his face. "So you are not only lovely and witty, but a business woman as well, I see," he remarked with a wry twist of his lips.

"No, but I will be," Erin informed him solemnly. "I've just inherited some money and would like to make an investment. Jackson says your looking for people to put up twenty to thirty thousand dollars."

J.P. Stevens was instantly serious. He admired a man who came directly to the point and had seen few females with that capability. It simply was not in their nature. But then Jackson had intimated that Erin Devareau was one surprise after another. "That's right. Can this inheritance finance such a sum?"

311

Erin shrugged. "I don't know. Jackson just told me about it this afternoon. Grandmother was rich, I do know that. I wasn't expecting to run into you again so soon, or I'd have been prepared," she explained apologetically. "But I do want you to keep me in mind."

Somehow Stevens did not doubt that she would be prepared when they spoke again, nor was he about to give up on a prospective investor so easily. "Why don't you come along with Jackson and me to Philadelphia then? You'll get a chance to meet fellow investors and see an example of the product we're talking about. I know my trip would be enhanced by your company and I'm . . .'"

"And why, friend, don't you stop being a broker long enough to enjoy a party." Jackson Tyler stepped through the door, his eyes narrowed as he appraised the situation. "Jennifer has someone she'd like to introduce you to."

"Mr. Stevens was just suggesting that I go with you to Philadelphia since I have money of my own to invest now," Erin told Jackson, a hopeful look brightening her face. Perhaps with Jackson's friend putting in a good word . . .

"Then Mr. Stevens should be discussing those matters with me since I am your legal guardian," Jackson announced tersely.

"But it's my money, isn't it?" Erin questioned, somewhat bewildered.

"Under my control until you are twenty-one."

J.P. Stevens had known Jackson Tyler long enough to recognize a storm brewing when he saw it and quickly accepted the excuse the man offered him to leave. "Well, far be it from me to keep the bride waiting." He started for the door and stopped suddenly, fishing in his trouser pockets for what turned out to be a twenty dollar bill. "It was worth every cent, my dear," he told Erin, braving to fold it in the hand he raised to his lips. "Jackson, my friend, you have a gem here. I envy you."

Aware of the piercing countenance turned on her, Erin followed the railroad man's retreating figure with her gaze until he was swallowed in the crowd. Uncertain as to what had put a burr under Jackson's saddle, she sighed and tried to change the subject. "I'll bet that all the stars will be out tonight. Would you like to walk in the garden and see if we can find the evening star?" Maybe if she could get him in the garden and he would kiss her again and . . .

"And what will that cost?" Jackson slashed at her, the cutting edge of his voice giving her a start.

"Oh that!" Erin's fist tightened on the bill in her hand involuntarily. She'd been so shocked that her inheritance was not hers to spend that she'd accepted the money without thinking. "It was a joke. I told Mr. Stevens that it would cost him twenty dollars to dance with me and he believed me."

"Not to mention half the other men here!" Jackson grabbed her arms roughly and pulled her to him. "Damn your mercenary little heart, Erin, just this afternoon I told you you had an inheritance, not that you needed it, and you still are trying to swindle people out of money . . . my friends and family at that!"

"But . . ."

"God, I wonder why I put up with you!"

Erin gaped incredulously that he could have forgotten so quickly. Couldn't he see how hard she had tried to change for him? Would he never forget her past? "Because you have control of my money and like to make love to me," she blurted out, a wounded rage flaring from his verbal assault.

Jackson's hands tightened on her flesh, bruising the tender skin he'd so tenderly caressed only hours earlier. "You conscienceless little viper!" he sneered, his voice quaking with a boiling rage that threatened to break free at any moment. He glanced around and, seeing that they were alone, started for the winding steps leading up to the second floor veranda, dragging Erin with him.

"What are you doing?" Erin cried out, trying to gather her crinolines to keep them from catching on the rail.

"Putting you somewhere where you will not cause further embarrassment to this family!"

At the top of the steps, Erin grabbed on to one of the vine-wrapped Corinthian columns. "Damn you, Tyler, you won't ever have to worry about me embarrassing you again! Just let me go . . . umph!"

The breath was knocked from her as Jackson seized her waist forcefully and hauled her under his arm like a sack of grain. "You won't leave," he rejoined with acidic certainty. "I have your money."

As the upstairs maid appeared near the servants steps, Erin cut loose with a string of names that caused the young woman to gasp in horror, her answering, "S . . . sir?" strangling in her throat.

Closing a smothering hand over Erin's mouth, Jackson issued a gutteral, "Follow me," and strode into Erin's room.

"Sir!" the maid exclaimed in shock when Jackson threw a cursing Erin on the bed and pinned her down with his body weight.

"Close the bloody door!"

Erin yelped as the lace-edged green ribbon that adorned her hair was yanked free. As her hands went up to be certain that hair had not come with it, Jackson seized and wrapped them securely with the makeshift rope.

"You thieving sonova . . ."

A linen towel was promptly shoved in Erin's mouth, cutting off a fresh onslaught of curses.

"That's fresh, you calling me a thief!" Jackson snorted scornfully.

Another ribbon fetched from the dressing table was used to make certain her gag did not fall out. Infuriated, Erin swung her bound wrists at Jackson, only to have him catch her by the waist and thrust her against the mattress again. Before she knew what he was about, her sash had been removed and he was tying her wrists to the headboard to keep her in place. Another belt was used to stop the flailing feet that had kicked her skirts up over her face and grazed Jackson dangerously close to his groin. Soon Erin had little choice but to lie quietly, lest she roll off the bed and hang by her wrists at her enraged assailant's mercy.

"Now!" Jackson exhaled as he pushed away from the mattress, satisfied that the girl could do no further harm. At least until he untied her, he thought, shoving the prospects that came to mind from that encounter out of his mind until later, after most of the guests had departed. He pushed through into the upstairs hall and called for the maid.

"Mary!"

"Sir?" The maid came away from the wall timidly. Never in her life had she seen such actions from decent folk, although she often thought Mr. Jackson to look like a demon when he was riled.

"You're to come get me if she gives you any trouble. I'll be back to check on her in a little while."

Mary nodded mutely for fear of winding up the same as the girl on the bed if she displeased Retreat's master. Nothing short of the devil himself would make her seek the man out in this humor, no matter what the girl on the bed might say or do.

The bed creaked as Jackson sat on its edge and turned Erin's face toward him. A blaze of green fire flared in the depths of her gaze, unabated and, yet, helpless. Oddly, he felt a sense of helplessness himself, tinged with guilt as he rearranged her skirts to cover the shapely lengths of leg exposed by the

315

ribbon and lace-trimmed pantalets he'd helped her don earlier. He'd never had to treat a woman like this, not even the commonest of harlots that tried to entice him into their beds.

Damnation, what would it take to reach her, to rid her of her mercenary and greed-inspired shenanigans? How could he convince her that he would take care of her and see to her every need when she fought him at every turn and made him so angry that he was tempted to choke the breath out of the slender white throat exposed to him? Would he have to bully her and intimidate her for the rest of his life?

Ignoring the mortified reaction of the maid, who leaned against the balcony doors as if about to swoon, Jackson ran his hands up under Erin's gown and began to untie the layers of crinolines that filled out her skirts fashionably in order to take them off. His strained manner was reflected in his voice as he began to speak lowly.

"You may not like this, Erin, but you are my responsibility. I control your money and I will control you until you are twenty-one. You will do as I say or be treated accordingly. If I hear one rumor of your embarrassing my family while I am gone, I can promise you that you will regret it. Is that understood?" The fact that Erin refused to acknowledge him, but continued to glower at him with sheer contempt was hardly encouraging. He tossed aside the petticoats and went on. "And should you entertain the idea of running away, just remember this. I will hunt you down, bring you back, and put you under lock and key until you turn twenty-one. Then you and your damned inheritance can go to hell for all I care! Is that clear?"

"I hate you!" Erin screamed at him, but the towel reduced her denouncement to an incoherent mumble. Yet somehow she managed to convey her message, for Jackson hovered over her like an ominous thundercloud for a moment and then stormed out of the room, slamming the door behind him.

Aside from the faint music playing downstairs, the room was silent. Even Mary stood motionless near the balcony door, looking at Erin with a dismayed expression that clearly indicated she didn't know what to do. Chagrined, Erin turned on her back and fixed her gaze on the ceiling. A quagmire of emotions worked at her, battering her mind and threatening to erupt in tears, but she would not let it. Not in front of anyone. She'd die first . . . which was a likely possibility if she was sentenced to remain at Retreat until she was twenty-one.

She closed her eyes in despair. Three years! Surely she couldn't live that long away from the river, let alone under the emotional seesaw of Jackson Tyler's tyranny.

# Chapter Twenty-One

Erin would not forgive Jackson for his treatment of her. The morning that he left, she made it a point to stay in bed in order to miss saying goodbye. Yet, the moment his coach disappeared down the willow-lined lane, her heart sank and refused to be consoled. She tried to put up a brave front, for Auralee Tyler and Uncle Charlie went out of their way to include her in the daily routine at Retreat. Jackson's mother even started giving her riding lessons in exchange for Erin's attempt to perfect her abilities with the needle.

From time to time, letters came from Jackson telling of the progress he was making in Philadelphia. Included were polite inquiries as to Erin's health and welfare, leaving her as cold and desolate as her dreams were warm and wonderful. She wondered that she could suffer such torment from two extremes stirred by the same man.

And she missed the river and the *Delta Moon*, so much so that her pining diminished her appetite to the point that her hostess was constantly trying to tempt her with sweets and delicacies from the kitchen. Although she'd have never believed it, Erin was tiring of the rich life and rich food, preferring to spend her time alone in the observatory, seeking out the *Delta Moon*'s berth on the riverfront with the giant telescope and sometimes studying the constellations.

The little peace she found there in her lofty tower, however, was soon disrupted by a telegram informing her of the impending visit of her relatives from New Orleans. While her reaction was one of surprise, tinged with a fear that they too would find a way to threaten the river life she fought so valiantly to return to, her guardians had misgivings of a nature that never occurred to the girl. Auralee simply feared for Erin's welfare, but John Davenport made it abundantly clear that he thought the Lafons were at the bottom of this mystery surrounding her grandmother's death and his attempted murder.

Of this, Erin could not be sure. After all, how could one kill their own mother? Surely, not even Aunt Lydia, for all her faults, was capable of that. Maybe they were coming to apologize for the way they treated her, she suggested to her skeptical companions.

However, after only minutes into the polite welcome that took the guests into the parlor for tea and iced chocolate tortes, the real reason for the visit was revealed. Following Auralee Tyler's instruction to the letter, Erin poured the hot tea while the couple began talking about inviting her to come live with them. Having played enough cards, she knew by their eyes, which refused to meet hers straight on, that they were lying. What she didn't know was how to get at what they were really after.

Changing her tact and going straight toward what Auralee and the disguised John, who had remained with them, suspected, she brought up the will Jackson had told her about. The direct approach was her aunt's undoing. All at once, Erin found herself under hysterical reproach for expecting her own aunt to pay rent in a home that had been hers since birth. No matter how she tried to deny that she knew anything about it, Lydia Lafon would not believe her.

Thankfully, Auralee Tyler took command of the situation with a regal manner that would not be ignored. Erin had never heard anyone so graciously reminded of their upbringing as Jackson's mother addressed her indignant aunt. As the woman stammered for an apology, Uncle Charlie spoke up in Erin's defense, explaining that Jackson had been handling Erin's affairs for her. "The girl didn't know, I assure you."

"And I don't want you to pay rent. I don't even want the house," Erin exclaimed fervently. "I thought Grandma had left me money, not property." Missing the rolled eyes of her aunt, she went on. "I can give it to them, can't I, Uncle Charlie?"

"I think that can be arranged."

With that situation diffused, Erin watched in wonder as her hostess, once again the epitome of southern hospitality, invited the Lafons to spend the night. To Erin's amazement, they accepted, opting for a warm bed in a room with a cozy fire than a cool damp berth on the ship.

"She's quite a lady, isn't she?" John Davenport remarked as Auralee Tyler led her guests to their quarters on the second floor. Erin nodded in agreement as he took her arm in his. "And now that she has so neatly put them in our hands, it's time to formulate a plan. Shall we retire to the office?"

Although she felt guilty for being a part of it, John's idea was as appealing to Erin's adventurous side as it was brilliant. Besides, she rationalized, if the Lafons were guilty, it would certainly stir things up. Not since her first day in New Orleans had Erin been so excited. It was almost like working with Cready, except that what they were about to do was legal. If the Lafons were behind his attempted murder, their plan would certainly shake it out of them.

Erin could hardly wait until the long evening of an elaborate meal and cards in the parlor had come to an end. More to soothe Auralee Tyler's mind than out of fear for herself, she moved into the mistress' bedroom, taking with her the croquet stick that had remained at her bedside since Jackson had mentioned the prowlers. Although she would have preferred to remain dressed for when the fun started, she didn't want to alarm her roommate, whom John and she agreed would be better off not to know of their scheme. Hence, Erin prepared for bed as usual and was already settled in when Auralee Tyler joined her.

"I just can't imagine those people involved in a scheme such as my son and his partner suspect," she told Erin as she turned down the lamp. "I think they might be greedy, but not to the extent of committing the murder of their own relative. It must have been horrible for you, losing your mother and grandmother in such a short time." A hand found Erin's under the quilt and squeezed it in sympathy.

Overwhelmed by the sincere show of affection, Erin managed to get an acknowledgment out past the blade that swelled suddenly in her throat. Although no one could ever fill the void left by Erin's mother, Auralee Tyler had found a place in her heart. Not only did the woman say that she was family, but she made Erin really feel like family. No matter what Jackson did, Erin vowed not to do anything to embarrass her new friend.

"I have grown so fond of you, dear. You're like a second daughter . . ." The woman hesitated, lifting her head from the pillow sharply. "Did you hear something?"

Erin not only heard it, she wondered how anyone could miss the bloodcurdling scream that seemed to echo in the chamber of the tall rotunda gallery. It was followed by another and another.

Both women bolted from the bed, and, seizing their robes that had been left on the chest at its foot, ran for the door. In the dim light of the gallery, Mary, the upstairs maid, appeared in a ghostly white nightgown, her eyes round with fright. She fell dutifully into step behind her mistress and Erin. They had to knock a good many times before Paul Lafon, looking somewhat flustered in a dark velvet robe, answered.

"What is it, sir?" Auralee Tyler inquired, glancing beyond to where Lydia Lafon sat on the bed sobbing hysterically.

"My wife seems to have had a bad dream or hallucination. She thought she saw someone on the veranda outside the room."

"I'll have the servants search the grounds," Auralee Tyler declared, turning to give the order to Mary to fetch some of the men from the servants quarters in the rear of the manor.

"That won't be necessary," the doctor objected. "You see . . ."

"It was a g . . . ghost!" the woman on the bed shrieked over the pillow she clutched to her stomach as she rocked back and forth.

"A hallucination," her husband intervened. "I am certain. I could see no one when I checked."

"It was my mother's murderer, I tell you! God in heaven, he's going to kill us all."

"I'll go get her some warm milk and brandy," Erin offered, desperate to leave the scene before she gave the plan away.

Paul Lafon seized on the idea as he went back to the trembling figure on the bed. "That would be wonderful, Erin. I have some of her headache powder. The milk will wash the taste from her mouth."

Leaving her hostess to see to the guests, Erin descended the winding steps to the back hall in her bare feet and burst through the door to the veranda

322

only to run smack into John Davenport. John caught her as she bounced off his chest.

"Well?"

"You've scared the bloody hell out the woman. Lafon didn't see you," Erin reported with a giggle she could hold back no longer. She made a visible effort to pull a sober face. "I don't think Aunt Lydia is in on this. Anyway, I have to get her some warm milk."

With a mumbled curse, John fell in beside her as she continued down the next flight of steps to the basement floor. He lit a candle kept on a shelf near the door and extended it to the gas fixture overhead. When it caught up and its glow filled the room, Erin removed the heavy slate lid covering the bricked hole in the floor where the fresh food was kept cool.

The fire in the stove was never allowed to go out in the modern appliance, even overnight. Hence, the tile near the large woodstove used for keeping the foods prepared in the out kitchen hot until they were served was warm and welcome to her cold feet. Erin put enough milk for two in a pan and set it on the burner, scuffing her feet and regretting not having taken time to put on a pair of slippers.

"John, what are we going to do now?"

"Watch them, especially Lafon . . . and watch you," he added grimly. "If you were to disappear, it would be mighty convenient for them to be your next of kin."

"For two bits I'd give it all to them. It looks like I've been nothing but trouble to everybody since Grandma wrote that will." Erin poured some honey into the warming liquid and began to stir it, her initial appetite for the midnight nourishment waning fast. As she watched it, her stomach felt as if it were swirling like the surface of the milk. Without thinking she leaned against the stove to break the strangely affecting hypnosis and drew away abruptly with a cry.

"Are you all right?" John jumped up from the table and ran to her side as Erin instinctively sucked the burned flesh of her hand with a whimper.

"It was a dumb thing to . . ." Erin stammered as a wave of nausea broke over her. "I'm going to be sick!" she managed, shoving past John to a large copper basin the cook used for washing vegetables. She felt his hands grasp her arms to steady her as she retched with little result until dizziness posed more of a threat.

"I'll call the doctor."

"Bejesus, no!" Erin gasped, sinking into the chair he slid under her. "I . . . I'm all right. I just need some air."

"Auralee won't let him hurt you."

"I'm okay!" She took a deep breath and forced a smile to her pale features. "See?" The spell was subsiding and, although her knees were shaky, she was determined to dispel the alarm on John Davenport's face. With phenomenal will, Erin forced herself up and returned to the milk which was now steaming. "Now fetch me a cup from the cupboard there."

The last thing she wanted was a doctor. Not that she was afraid of Paul Lafon. She didn't want any doctor to discover what she was almost certain was wrong with her—what, like her love for Jackson, she'd refused to acknowledge until it was becoming impossible.

A girl didn't grow up around brothels all her life and not recognize the early symptoms of pregnancy.


The holidays approached quickly, bringing an onslaught of increased social events and visitors. Familiar Christmas carols rang through the rotunda as the women's choir to which Miss Auralee belonged practiced for the coming Christmas Eve service at the parish church. In addition to the fresh scent of the evergreen garlands decorating the entire house, not to mention the twelve foot high Christmas tree John had found to grace the parlor, the smell of baking shortbread cookies filled the air. The plantation cook rushed back and forth from the out kitchen to the warming kitchen supervising the production of the holiday goodies that would fill the bellies of the gaily clad visitors who had been coming almost daily for a week.

But for her condition, Erin would have been ravenously tempted to try at least one of each type of confection that came from the kitchen. As it was, the very thought of eating rebelled in her. Aside from bread and, oddly enough, sweet potatoes, there was little that agreed with her. She had to force herself to make a decent showing at the supper table. Then, after the meal was over, she would retire to her room to promptly lose it in the French porcelain commode.

She tried valiantly to act enthused over the parties to which she'd been invited and the planning of the annual Twelfth Night Ball to be held at Retreat, but all she felt like doing was locking herself up in her room and sleeping. Her desperation and depression became more and more intense as the week of Jackson's arrival drew near, in spite of the distraction of making Christmas gifts for the family, truly a chore of love on her part, for Erin hated needlework with a passion.

Every night she tried futilely to think of an excuse to leave, yet, even if she could come up with one that Auralee Tyler might accept, she didn't have the means to support herself. Her inheritance, she learned, consisted of properties, investments, and money, all of which were controlled by the man who was due in from Philadelphia any day. There was no one to turn to, no one to trust, not even John. She didn't dare risk him talking her out of her plan again.

But she was going to have to go before the baby started to show. That she knew. She would not disgrace Miss Auralee. To leave before Jackson came back would be easier. Threats be damned, she had no choice. All she had to do was come up with the means for the travel and living expenses until she could get a job. She could tell folks she was a widow and find some respectable place like she and her mother had often dreamed of doing—maybe a cottage with roses around the door.

Her knowledge of numbers would carry her to that end. Auralee Tyler had been most complimentary on the way Erin helped her with the plantation books. She'd been delighted to turn them over to the girl and simply checked them over when Erin was through with her posting and totals. That and her excellent penmanship would provide a good income, now that she had the confidence to seek a clerical job. They would have to, she decided, for three years anyway—until she turned twenty-one. Jackson surely wouldn't keep her inheritance from her then and she would need it to raise her child.

She thought of going to Cready for a stake, but the moment Cready made a dollar or two, he spent it. Shame that it was, she'd even considered taking some of the Tyler silver to the pawnshop and asking the owner to hold it so that Jackson could buy it back out of her inheritance after she was gone. She simply couldn't, however, bring herself to take anything from Miss Auralee, even if it was temporary—a loan of sorts. There had to be another way and she would have to find it.

A box tagged with her name under the Christmas tree in the parlor unexpectedly provided part of her answer. It caught her attention as she was placing some of her handmade presents beside those Miss

Auralee had already put there. Jackson's name was signed to it, although the hand was clearly that of his mother, which irritated Erin. The least he could have done was purchase the gift himself.

At first, she'd put it aside, but her curiosity finally got the best of her. Tiptoeing downstairs in the middle of the night, Erin eased open the wrapping and discovered to her astonishment, an exquisite set of jewels, emeralds set in gold. There was a choker, a bracelet, and earrings, all surely worth a fortune. The fortune she needed, she thought, trying to ignore her guilt as she replaced the jewels with coal and carefully rewrapped the gift to return to its place under the tree.

With the means, all she had to do was find the way to escape the watchful eyes of John Davenport and Auralee Tyler. That came in an even more unexpected and far more devastating manner. Erin was immediately suspicious when Gina Allen sidled up to her after a family dinner and asked if she might have a word with her in private. She was dumbfounded when the older girl asked her help . . . to take her to someone in Under the Hill who would perform an abortion.

Even as the plan they made unfolded, Erin still could not believe it was happening. True, Gina was only being friendly to use her, but then two could practice the same game, so Erin played along with it masterfully. The families were delighted when Gina insisted Erin spend the night at Fairbanks to collaborate on a Christmas gift. No suspicion was even aroused the next day when Gina announced that they had to go into town to buy a few extra necessities and, because of the time of year, no questions were asked concerning the specifics of their needs.

Suddenly they were there, among the buildings so familiar to Erin. She could tell from Gina Allen's expression that she was already having second thoughts, for the boardinghouse next to the River Palace was no more palatial than its neighbor. The older girl's face was white beneath the veiled hat she'd chosen to disguise it from anyone who might recognize her. The handles of her purse were twisted so tightly around her gloved hands that a prospective thief would play the devil wresting it from her.

"We could always go back with the train," Erin suggested as they paused on the patched boardwalk that ran in front of both buildings.

While the plan had helped her get away from Retreat, something in Erin rebelled at what Gina was about to do. No matter how inconvenient her own baby was, she had never entertained the idea of getting rid of it. But then, she didn't possess Gina's fickle nature. The unborn child was in the way, the girl had explained that night in Erin's room after announcing that Erin could have Jackson Tyler all to herself. Gina's sights were now set on one J.P. Stevens of Philadelphia, who had been showering her with gifts and sweet letters since they'd met at the wedding. Love at first sight, the girl had called it.

Erin steeled herself as a myriad of guilts sprang forth to assault her. She couldn't do this to herself. She had to think of what was best for her and her baby. John and Auralee could console each other. Jackson would most likely be relieved. As for Gina, well it was her life. The fact that she led Erin to believe Jackson might be the father of the child had nothing to do with Erin's helping her. Gina was welcome to Jackson Tyler. *She was!* she insisted, shoving the matter from her mind with great deliberation.

"Well?" Erin asked of the indecisive girl staring at the door of the less than reputable-appearing establishment. Maybe Gina would change her mind, part of her hoped in spite of her resolve.

Gina nodded. "Let's go."

Clutching her carpetbag tightly in her hand, as if her life depended on it, Erin opened the door and entered the familiar house where she'd been sent from time to time to fetch a girl who had overslept and was late for work at the palace. Actually, her life did depend on it. The jewels in the lining were her future.

Trying not to leave anything to chance that would jeopardize her plan, Erin had taken a precaution to cool Coleman Horsey's ambition, should she have the unlikely misfortune, considering the early hour, to run into him. Under Gina's pillow, she'd left a will, a letter stating that should anything happen to her that her inheritance go to Lydia Lafon. After their visit, she was convinced the Lafons were innocent of her grandmother's murder. Their only sin was greed and a preoccupation with pretense. Besides, she was heading for the North and her chances of running into her relatives were remote at best.

That early in the morning, there was no one about but the housekeeper who ran the place for Coleman Horsey. The shriveled old woman stopped sweeping the floor and leaned on her broom as the girls approached her, her squinting eyes taking in their fine clothes and the bags they carried. Gina shied away from the walls where ragged paper hung, its adhesive long ago having given way, and hovered close to Erin's elbow.

"We'd like to see Aunt Lil," Erin told the woman when it was plain that she was waiting for them to identify their purpose. She heard Gina's small gasp behind her and could well imagine what the girl must be thinking. It didn't matter now, Erin thought. She could leave all her bridges burning behind her.

The old woman snorted, still eyeing Erin suspiciously. "Thought the two of you was too fancy for any of Horsey's new gals, though *you* look a might familiar," she said to Erin.

"I used to live here a long time ago." Had it only been a few months?

Gina grabbed Erin's arm, pinching her flesh, as the old woman accepted her answer and yelled at the top of her lungs, "Lil! Get up! You got some rich company!" After giving Erin one more close perusal, she pointed to the steps. "Go on up. Lil don't mind."

As if she'd already forgotten them, the housekeeper returned to her task, her rounded back hunched over the broom she wielded. Erin led the way up the steps that were worn to the bare grain of the wood treads. Like them, the banister rail was in need of paint. What little that had not peeled off, making the surface mottled and pitted, had collected grime and dirt that had escaped the housekeeper's failing eyes and smoothed it out to the touch.

Knowing exactly where to go, Erin knocked loudly on the third door from the end of the hall where a misfitted door marked a much used exit to a rickety set of steps outside. She supposed that door had saved many a man from getting caught literally with his pants down by an angry wife, not to mention provided discreet leave for some of Lil's more affluent clients who, like Gina Allen, had taken advantage of her talents to solve their problems.

The fresh whiff of toilet water that greeted the girls before their knock was even answered told Erin that Lil thought her rich company might be of the male gender. The woman's expression confirmed it, her wide toothy smile drawing into a tight line as she gave them the same curious appraisal as the woman downstairs.

"What do you want?"

"Aunt Lil, this is a friend of mine and she needs your help."

At the familiar address, the saloon woman, for the excessive amount of paint she used to hide her age betrayed the fact that she was no longer a girl of any description, stared at Erin more closely. "Aaron?" she echoed in surprise. She motioned with a sweeping gesture, the bell sleeves of her red satin robe swinging in emphasis and stirring the strong scent of her perfume to a proportion that threatened Erin's already nervous stomach. "Come right in, child! I was sorry to hear about your mama."

Although Erin doubted it, she acknowledged the condolence solemnly. Lil was now the undisputed manager of the saloon with all prospects of Giselle Devareau returning dashed. And Erin had not forgotten that Lil had been eager to testify that Horsey was her mother's choice of a guardian.

"This is Gina . . ."

Gina snapped out of the uncharacteristic silence that had engulfed her at the sight of the unkept sitting room with clothes of various description strewn everywhere. "Travis," she hastily injected, her cheeks finding color in spite of her trepidation. "Erin has told me that you help girls in trouble and . . . and I need your help, madame."

"My help don't come cheap, Miss . . . Travis," Lil informed her, a smirk indicating that she had not been fooled. "It'll cost you a hundred dollars, though, by the look of you, you got it."

"I'll write a draft from my bank . . ."

"Cash."

Gina looked at Erin in despair. "I didn't bring that much."

"I'll take the draft to the bank," Erin offered, "if that's all right with you, Lil."

The wide painted smile resumed on Lil's face. "Sure. I trust you, darlin'. Meanwhile, you go on in that room and get out of them fancy clothes. You're gonna be in bed for a while," she told Gina authoritatively, making it clear that social status didn't mean a thing in these circumstances. The high society lady had come down to Lil's level and the woman wasn't about to let the client think otherwise.

Erin was grateful to step out into the street, out of the dingy and musty smelling surroundings that made her stomach queasy. Was it her condition that made what she used to accept as a way of life so distasteful or had living in the world her mother had known as a child and young woman changed her?

The streets were filled with drays and carts carrying freight down to the landing and roustabouts shouted lustily from their heavy work to each other. A few whistles were directed her way, as was always the case when a young lady ventured unescorted in the streets in Under the Hill.

Head held high, as if she hadn't heard them, Erin went straight to the exchange located conveniently for the travelers and businessmen who frequented the river-bottom settlement. The draft was honored with no problem and soon she was on her way back up the hill. As she reached the door of the boardinghouse, a loud whistle split the air above the usual hustle of the street and Erin froze. Like she did most of the boats that regularly stopped at Natchez, she knew the identifying shriek of the *Delta Star*. Jackson Tyler had returned from the north.

She entered the building, as if she risked his spotting her from the ship, and raced up the steps so that she was winded and dizzy when Lil admitted her. "Tarnation, girl, what's got into you?" the woman exclaimed, helping Erin to a chair after she stumbled at the threshold. "Some of them street rascals try to snatch your purse?"

"No, I . . . I just ran too fast up the steps. Carrying a hundred dollars around here will make a body nervous," Erin offered weakly.

"Ain't that the truth! Want some hot tea and

molasses cake? I just brewed some to put my potion in for Miss Persnickety in there and Molly sent in the cake for one of the gals' birthday last night. We got a while to wait a'fore it gits to workin' on her.''

Good old Molly, mother of all, Erin mused wryly. "I don't think I can right now, Aunt Lil, but thank . . .''

Lil cupped Erin's chin and stared at her suspiciously. "You ain't in a family way, are you?''

Ordinarily Erin could have brushed off the truth with some excuse, but disconcerted as she was, her face gave it away. Aware of that, Erin looked for the bag she'd inadvertently left when she ran the errand for Gina and a panic set in. It was gone!

"I put it under the table here to get it out from underfoot," Lil told her, catching on to the source of her obvious dismay. "You gonna run away from that fancy guardian of yours?''

Faced with Lil's formidable intuition, Erin gave up the story she'd concocted to explain her need for the money and nodded. She took the bag in her lap and felt down inside, checking its contents. Lil might be acting friendly and concerned, but she'd steal from her own mother. A breath of relief slipped through her lips as she felt the lump of the jewelry case still in the liner.

"Me n' the gals thought something like this would happen. Men like Tyler tire of their toys after a while. They're just like that," she shrugged, as if it were an undisputed right, ". . . especially with gamblers.''

The loose stitches Erin had sewn the jewels in with gave way easily. "I need some money for these," she said, producing the velvet envelope. "I don't know what they're worth, but I'd say at least a thousand dollars.''

"A thousand!" Lil snorted, prying open the flap to dump them on the tabletop. From the screwed purse of her lips, it was evident that she did not like the tables of demand turned on her in her own domain. "Must be diamonds!" she snorted derisively.

"Emeralds." Erin caught the precious jewels and gently laid them out for examination. She might be selling them, but they were still hers . . . for a while.

"Five hundred," Lil said, greedily eyeing the size of the pendant on the choker. She tried it on, but it would not close around her thick neck.

Erin stuck to her price. "A thousand."

"Eight hundred and not a penny more."

Her future lay on that table and two hundred dollars could come in mighty handy in the unknown future that lay ahead of her and her child. "Never mind," Erin answered, taking up the bracelet and slipping it back into the pouch. "I know I can get more than a thousand at the pawnbroker's up on the bluff."

"Now there ain't no need to rush. Let me see what I can find, startin' with your friend's hundred." Reminded of the money she had stashed recklessly in her purse, Erin handed it over obligingly. "She know about this?" Lil asked, counting it carefully.

"No. As soon as I'm sure she's all right, I'm leaving."

"Aw, she ain't that far gone," Lil assured her. "She might think she's been through an afternoon of hell, but she'll be back doing what got her that way in a few weeks if she takes a notion. Where you goin'?"

"North." Erin was relieved to hear that. She'd heard such nightmarish stories about what happened in that other room, most of them about girls that waited until they were showing before taking care of their condition. "I'm just going to buy a ticket from place to place until I see one I like the looks of."

"You got spunk, kid, I'll give you that."

"How far gone is she?" She had to ask, not that it mattered whether Jackson had fathered Gina's child before or after he'd become involved with her.

"She says she missed three months."

*Before.* It shouldn't have mattered but it did.

"Now how about some of this tea?"

"I want my child," Erin averred strongly.

"Just tea, kid," Lil assured her. "I don't do this for nothing, especially when I got to put out a thousand dollars."

Lil poured the tea from the pot she kept atop the parlor stove and put a sugar bowl on the table. "I ain't got no milk. Aside from tea and coffee and what I bring in already cooked, I got to go downstairs to eat."

Erin was about to answer when Gina Allen screamed in the next room. She started to her feet in alarm, but Lil stayed her with a shake of her head. "We got a crybaby on our hands if she thinks the startin' is that bad. You just stay here. When I can get away, I'll get together your money."

After a while of listening to Gina reveal that ladies not only cursed, but did so quite well, Erin walked over to the front window to shake the sudden sleepiness generated from the cozy warmth of the parlor stove and peered down the street toward the dock where the *Delta Star*'s stage was being lowered. If Jackson followed habit, he would not go to Retreat until late in the day. That would give her time . . .

She blinked as the vision of the riverboat became unfocused and moved aside the yellowed sheer curtain to see if it improved. Instinctively, her fingers tightened about the voile material as her knees lost their ability to support her body. Erin turned, staring through the fog that filled the room at the teacup on the table, the chilling sense of Lil's blatant betrayal battling to the forefront of her consciousness.

She slumped against the wall and took the curtain with her as she fell to the floor. No! she thought wildly. God in heaven, the woman was going to kill her baby! A hand that somehow did not belong to

335

her, appeared near her face, backed by the flowing red robe that Lil had worn earlier.

Why? Erin screamed, unaware that the drug-induced sleep had already claimed her vocal cords as it had the rest of her body. Only her mind struggled to cling to the present, to fight for her baby . . . and Jackson's.

Her heart thudded against her breastbone as the door closed behind John, sealing her fate with a click

# Chapter Twenty-Two

The sun was setting when Jackson finally broke away from business. Its orange glow glazed the top of the water behind him as his carriage moved up Silver Street. Some roustabouts that were not still engaged in loading cargo stood in the open doorway of a saloon, beers in hand, and shouted at two ladies of the evening who hung out a window across the street, presenting a fetching display of their wares. The sight was not missed by a group of salesmen who were gathered on the front porch of one of the cheaper hotels, but coming from sounder upbringing, they chose to admire the view without comment.

Near the top of the hill, Jackson caught sight of old Annie on a corner, trying to sell what was left of her early morning's production of pralines, and stopped to purchase the remainder so that she could go home. If he recalled correctly, Erin had an insatiable taste for Annie's cookies and would be able to stuff herself to her heart's content. After all, he intended to use every charm and trick he knew to regain favor with his intended bride, now that he'd had time to think clearly, something that seemed impossible for him when Erin was around. And there was an old adage about winning hearts through a man's stomach. He couldn't think why that wouldn't work in reverse, recalling Erin's healthy appetite for sweets.

A servant was lighting the outside lamps when the carriage rolled in front of the octagonal mansion. Jackson paid the driver well for the deviation from his customary routine and turned to meet his mother who had come running out on the veranda at the announcement that her son was home. Although Jackson embraced Auralee Tyler, he searched the door beyond for some sign of Erin. When John appeared, alone, he took the time to shake his friend's hand and then asked for the girl.

"She's with Gina Allen," his mother told him brightly. "They were supposed to be working on some project."

"You let her leave here alone?" Jackson demanded of John, alarm penetrating his tone. Hearing Erin was with Gina smacked of trouble.

John shrugged, more pleased with his partner's distress than dismayed at the anger aimed at him. "She left with a coachload of people, your sister and brother-in-law included."

"I should imagine they might be by after supper," Auralee Tyler assured her son calmly. "Now come inside and tell us about your trip."

Trying to ignore his wariness and his admitted disappointment, Jackson followed his mother into the house and into the parlor while the servants took his trunk up the steps. He watched as John saw his mother seated and comfortable before taking a seat himself and noticed the warm smile they exchanged, as if they'd forgotten him for a moment. Could it be this fever that had disrupted his entire world was contagious, he wondered, taken back by the fresh glow on Auralee Tyler's cheeks and the youthful twinkle that sparkled in her honey-brown eyes.

"Well, I might as well get to the point. Since you two are closest to me, you should be the first to know.

I've decided to ask Erin to marry me."

The reaction was spontaneous.

"Oh, Jackson, how wonderful!"

"If that don't beat all! Congratulations, friend!"

"We'll have a toast!" Auralee declared, jumping to her feet to ring the servants bell. "Champagne!"

Jackson stayed her hand. "Wait a minute, mother. I don't think we should toast until Erin has accepted."

"But of couse she will!" his mother declared, as if the idea were preposterous that any woman of sound mind would turn down her handsome son. "Why, she's been moping about here since the day you left, just pining for you. A woman can feel these things."

"I thought you said she was pining for the river."

Undaunted, Auralee replied. "Well, it might as well be the same thing! I only hope the two of you will at least spend some time at Retreat so that I can enjoy my grandchildren. I hardly think a riverboat is the place to raise a family."

"For heaven's sake, Auralee," John laughed, slipping a familiar arm about his euphoric companion's waist. "Why don't we take things one step at a time? Erin's not been exactly thrilled with Jackson."

"Why, Mr. Davenport," the matron exclaimed with a hint of indignation, "what do you men know of such things? If we women seem too eager for your attentions, we are subject to be taken advantage of." She switched her saucy look from John to Jackson and tapped her son on the chest. "So you'd best be prepared for a hard chase, dear. I've trained her well."

"Did you get Grandmother's jewels wrapped?"

"Of course! Although I was afraid to lift my hopes too high that this would be the reason you were going to give them to her."

Jackson grinned as he was promptly smothered in his mother's embrace. He was certain to receive the same sort of treatment when Erin heard about the riverboat and train stock. He could only hope and pray that her reaction to taking him as her husband might be half as warm. "Would you mind fetching it for me? I have something else I want to put inside."

"And you men talk about us women changing our minds!" his mother chided lightly. "It's right here." She found the present under the tree and handed it to him. "Go ahead and unwrap it. I have more paper and ribbon upstairs. Meanwhile, I'll tell cook to send us in some shortbread cookies and milk. Or would you prefer a brandy?"

"Milk will be fine," Jackson answered, enjoying his mother's devotion. Coming home to Retreat was always the same. Except that she was unusually buoyant this time.

"I'll have a brandy and skip the cookies," John called after her.

Jackson took out his knife and cut the ribbon that adorned the box. "What has gotten into her of late? I've never seen her look more . . . younger," he finished for lack of a better term. "It can't be my news. She was that way outside." He glanced up from his work to see a knowing smile settle on John Davenport's lips. "Damn it, John, she's my mother!"

"But I promise not to hold that against her," John quipped glibly, before wiping the smirk from his lips. "And a lady among ladies. Were I given to settle down, I can assure you, my friend, that not even you could keep me from her side."

Jackson nearly dropped the package, its contents rattling loudly as he fumbled to catch it before it struck the floor. "Bejesus!"

"Don't worry. I shall return to the river as soon as this charade comes to its right conclusion. Although, I must admit, Auralee has been like a breath of spring in my life when I had thought that only autumn and winter remained for me to weather."

340

"If you hurt her, I would kill you with my own hands."

"I'd take my life first. I hurt one woman years ago. I vowed never to become seriously involved again. Auralee knows that. We've . . . shared a good many secrets and have become the best of friends . . . just friends," he reiterated. He sighed heavily and made a visible effort to shove the past aside and lighten the tone of the conversation. "And your mother is not the only one who has changed. I like to play bridge!" he laughed, as if the very idea was ludicrous. "Having a female partner is a refreshing change from our cigar-smoking contemporaries. And I'm developing an ear for the parlor music and a taste for . . . milk," he finished disconcertedly. "No, the sooner I return to the river, the better off we both will be."

A few small pieces of coal fell out of the box, the lid which had slipped sideways in Jackson's struggle to catch the gift not being quite righted, and drew Jackson's undivided attention from John to his feet where they'd fallen. John stooped quickly and retrieved one, examining it curiously.

"Now what in the devil . . . I saw your mother wrap this and the gems she placed inside were definitely not . . ."

Jackson tore off the lid and shook out the remainder of the contents until the black fuel lay scattered around him. The nagging feeling that had haunted him about Erin, that she had not really accepted his ultimatum as gracefully as she had led him to believe, flared in his mind, followed by a cold dread that penetrated to his very bones. Would he never be able to trust her? "The little thief isn't at the Allens. With a day's start, God knows where she is by now!"

Slinging the box aside, Jackson raced for the door, his long stride nearly taking him into a head-on collision with his mother who narrowly managed to

341

pull back the tray she carried in time to avoid disaster.

"Jackson, what . . . ?" She recovered in time to see Jackson bolt out the door, leaving it to slam against its jam with a vibrating crash. "John?" she stammered in bewilderment.

"It's Erin. She's taken the jewels and Jackson thinks she's run away." John grabbed the tray as Auralee Tyler stepped back in shock and put it on the hall table. "Oh, John, what have we done?" she cried, her hand pressed against her face in despair.

"*We* haven't done anything. Erin did. It's up to the two young people to straighten this out."

"Go with him!" Auralee pleaded urgently, her wide eyes filled with unspilled tears. "Go with him and help him find her!

The road to Natchez was clearly marked and posed no delay for the sorrel stallion leaving a trail of dust for the bay that followed in its wake. Had one witnessed the spectacle from a distance, it looked as if it had a wild man on its back, the tail of his tawny coat flailing behind him as he hunched over the horse's back and urged it to a speed that was dangerous to them both. His dark hair was plastered against his head and his face was a cold mask that hid a dozen powerful emotions, all straining to rip it away to reveal his anguished soul.

The rider on the bay struggled to keep up with the faster mount, for years on the river had diminished his skill in the saddle. When the red started a headlong run down to Natchez Under the Hill, he would have no choice but to slow down. With a broken neck, he would be of no use to anyone. It was a good piece of advice to give the man in the lead . . . if he could catch up with him.

As they rounded a turn at a forested intersection, the stallion cut across the inside of the clearing marking it when a coach appeared unexpectedly.

The bright light of the setting sun blinded the hell-bent rider to its presence until it was almost too late. With a startled whinny the stallion reared and pivoted on its hindquarters to avoid the matched pair of blacks that John Devareau recognized as belonging to the Allen family, driving the team off the road in the process. John reined in his own steed as Jackson Tyler fought to control his spirited and frightened red with curses unfit for the ears of the lady whose head briefly appeared in the coach window.

As he gained control of his mount, Jackson managed to rein in the temper that flared from the helpless frustration he felt. Afraid to give in to the surge of relief at the sight of the Allen coach, he forced the spirited animal over to where the driver was trying to urge his team back on the road.

"I'm sorry, Master Tyler! I didn't see you comin' till you was on us."

"It's my fault, Sam," Jackson admitted, pulling up against the side of the vehicle to peer inside. "Erin?" In the dim light, only one face emerged from a pile of blankets, a pale and drawn one. "Gina?"

"I'm ill, Jackson. Please leave us be."

Still hoping against hope, Jackson pulled open the door and peered at the floor where his ward might likely hide if she was set on avoiding him. The cab, however, was empty . . . empty of other passengers and empty of packages. Knowing Gina's penchant for shopping, which was where the Allens had told him the girls had gone, it was a certain oddity.

"Where's Erin?"

Gina turned her face away from him. "How should I know? She was supposed to meet me at the hotel and didn't show up on time. I grew tired of waiting and . . ."

"Damn you, Gina, do you ever think of anyone but yourself!" Jackson accused with such vehemence that large crocodile tears spilled from the girl's eyes. "Where did you last see her?"

Gina wiped her cheeks with the rough blanket which surrounded her and sniffed. "I . . . I can't remember. Maybe it was the dry goods store."

Jackson looked over to where John sat patting the lathered neck of his bay. The older man had never seen such pain on his partner's face. But then, he'd never seen Jackson Tyler act the desperate man before either. "I'll get the sheriff. You go to the palace," he suggested calmly. A new concern flickered in the young man's eyes as he thought over the proposition and John smiled. "She's worth the risk," he assured his partner. He, of all people, recognized the chance he took exposing himself, even as Charles Tyler. A scuffle, or even a good close look, might easily unmask him as the murderer everyone assumed dead.

Once Jackson accepted John's proposal, there was no point in trying to hold him back until the law joined them. John would have to get the authorities and catch up with the young man before he tried to take on Coleman Horsey and all his henchmen. And, of course, there was always the possibility that Erin was not there. As he handed Jackson his own pistol, John said as much.

The white hot steel of unrequited rage building in silver eyes that had temporarily lost their infamous ability to hide the thoughts lurking behind them was unnerving as his partner reckoned with the possibility. "If she's not there, then I'll have to assume she's safely aboard one of the steamers." Jackson had already forgotten the presence of the woman inside the coach when he whipped the head of the stallion about sharply. He neither saw the hand that pressed to her chest or heard her relieved sigh as she sank back against the tufted leather seat. "If that be the case, Coleman Horsey will stand a chance of seeing

344

another sunrise," he called back over his shoulder.

True to expectation, the stallion all but scrambled down the steep grade leading to the ramshackle shanties and buildings nested on the riverbank. John held his breath, frozen for a moment, until he could no longer stand the idea of Jackson and the animal taking a debilitating stumble. He might not be able to keep up with his partner, but he could bring help, assuming Jackson would need the sheriff's aid and not a doctor's.

Lanterns hung lighted outside the doors of places that would remain open all night while closed signs hung on those establishments that operated during daylight hours when Jackson reached the front of the White Palace. Instead of stopping, he urged the stallion around the corner and down a narrow alley, disturbing two cats who were enjoying the remains of fish that had been cleaned earlier by the woman who ran the boardinghouse next door.

He was frantic, but he was no fool. If he were going to face Coleman Horsey it would be on his own terms. After checking the pistol tucked in his waistband, he dismounted and tied the red to a slim sassafras sapling that had volunteered from a grove near the necessary in the back. Barrels conveniently stacked in the rear provided all the boost he needed to climb up to the shed roof off the back of the building. He easily scaled the wall and made his way to a window. After listening to be certain the room was empty, he tried the sash and found it open.

The door to Horsey's parlor was closed, making it easy for Jackson's entrance to go undetected. Yet, even before Jackson determined the adjoining rooms were vacant, the same sinking feeling he'd experienced as he looked into the Allen coach swept over him. Erin was not there. But neither was Horsey.

God, was it a wild goose chase, he wondered, leaning against the door to try to think where else they might be. And if she wasn't with Horsey, had she already left Natchez? He racked his mind, trying to think of the ships that were ready to pull out when the *Star* arrived. The *Memphis Princess*, the *James Howard*? Logic told him he'd made a mistake. Instinct told him otherwise.

On the other side of the door, footsteps resounded and suddenly the knob rattled as it was pushed open. Jackson, caught up in his dilemma, stepped to the side quickly and pressed himself against the wall as the woman who ran the saloon walked into the room. She crossed the carpet to the table at the foot of Horsey's bed carrying a wooden box. His hand relaxed on the hammer of his pistol as she dumped it and began to count out the pile of coins it had contained. With a stealth earned from hours spent in the forests of Retreat stalking game, Jackson crept noiselessly up behind her and pressed the barrel of the gun to her back.

"Scream and I'll shoot."

The woman started, her eyes flying to a gilded mirror on the opposite wall to discover the identity of her assailant, but her cry for help hung in her throat judiciously. Lil had seen Black Jack Tyler shoot a man for cheating without so much as blinking an eye and she had no reason to believe she would be any different, considering the heartless gaze that met hers. She knew what he was after. She'd warned Horsey that Tyler would kill them all if they harmed a hair on Erin Devareau's head.

"Mother Mary, I don't have nothin' to do with this!" she blurted out in a hoarse whisper. "I just did what Horsey told me to do. It's only a little syrup of ipecac. She won't die or nothin'."

The unsolicited confession made Jackson weak with concern. He knew of Lil's reputation for performing certain services for soiled doves who found themselves with child. Not that Erin would be . . . A frisson of alarm raced along his spine. Rebelling against the nagging suspicion that surfaced, he hid his confusion behind a ruthless facade and pressed the gun against the excess flesh of the woman's ribs until she whimpered in fear. "Where? Where is she?"

"If . . . if you kill me, you ain't never goin' to find her," Lil ventured boldly.

"No, but I wouldn't kill you. I'd leave you gut shot to suffer while I tear this town apart board by board." Jackson stepped around so that she bore the full brunt of his formidable countenance, the gun leveled at the rounded belly stretching the faded gathered satin of her skirt. He meant it. He meant every word of his threat. If the bitch had hurt Erin in any way, he'd . . . "Have you ever seen a man gut shot," he queried softly, as if he savored the idea.

Lil's loss of color told Jackson she had. "She's in the boardinghouse . . . in the back." She licked her lips and backed against the table. "She ain't gonna die. She just thinks she is."

"Horsey with her?"

Lil nodded mutely.

"Alone?"

She nodded again and flinched as the barrel slipped around to the side to nudge her ahead of the man who held it.

"Then let's go." Jackson put the gun inside his coat pocket so as not to draw attention. "And if you so much as bat your eyelashes, they'll be plucking lead from your back."

Because it was early evening, only a few patrons occupied the tables in the saloon. They were so involved in their conversation that they hardly looked up when Lil led the fine-looking gentleman out the back door. She was always leaving with men for an hour or so and then coming back. Mac MacCready was in the small rear kitchen getting

347

glasses ready for a busy night, the edge of his trousers visible as they passed unseen by the door and stepped out into the back alley.

A set of questionably stable steps wound around the rear corner of the boardinghouse to a small second-floor landing. The escape had been built for Lil's finer customers, like the one she'd had earlier that day, who wanted to slip away undetected. The wood creaked with their weight as they climbed in strained silence, Jackson's gun still aimed at the woman's back.

"I'll be right behind you," Jackson warned lowly when the woman lifted the latch on the ill-fitted door that led into a poorly lit hall.

The hair stood up on the back of his neck as Lil came to a stop at the third door and placed her cheaply jeweled hand on the chipped porcelain knob. He wouldn't put it past her if she'd lied about Horsey being alone. If that were the case, he'd have to stall until John and the sheriff arrived. But whatever the cost, he would see Erin, assure himself that his fears were unfounded and Lil's protest that she was merely sick to her stomach true.

"Knock."

Obedient, the woman did as she was told, raising Horsey's irritated voice from within. "Who is it?"

"It's me, luv. I got my hands full. Could you open the door?"

The moment the door opened, Jackson shoved the woman with all his strength into the thin man. Her weight carried the surprised Horsey backward until they both went down in a heap. Seizing the advantage, Jackson withdrew his pistol and closed the door behind him. "Where is she?"

"Who?" Horsey rasped, shoving the stocky woman aside and righting his toupee.

"I can search these rooms on my own, friend . . . after I shoot you," Jackson informed him threateningly. "But I'd advise you to cooperate."

"Cooperate?" the man sneered, pulling himself stiffly to his feet and rearranging his jacket with indignant snatches. "You seem to think that you have the winning hand in this game."

There were two rooms adjoining the shabby parlor, one on either side. Jackson wanted to shout for Horsey to take him to Erin, but something held him back. He knew how to read a man's eyes and Coleman Horsey truly believed he held the better cards.

"I would say this is a pretty convincing argument that I do," he answered, waving the gun meaningfully. His accuracy with pistols was as well-renowned as his prowess with cards. Horsey knew that, yet the man wasn't showing his cowardly colors.

"Oh, it does. But, you see, if you don't cooperate with me, Erin will die. I have the antidote for the poison she's ingested." Horsey moved over to the table and took a seat, uncommonly relaxed for a man with a gun pointed at him. He motioned to the door on Jackson's left. "Go ahead and look for yourself. She's weak as a kitten now."

Jackson's stomach turned over in his abdomen as he debated his move. Poison? A glance at Lil's smug face did little to reassure him. She hadn't been lying about Horsey being alone, but she had lied about the ipecac. Or were they bluffing? Another time, he might have been able to call them, but his growing concern for Erin made it impossible to tap his inherent gift of reading faces. His own impassive expression was beginning to fray with anxiety.

Keeping his gun on his adversary, Jackson backed to the door and tossed it open. The knob struck the wall with a bang, causing the white-faced girl on the bed to flinch. The room reeked with the smell of bile and her hair clung damply to her face and neck, the bow that had once held it up lying discarded on the bare mattress. Jackson was grateful for the staunch support of the jamb at his back as he fought the urge to run to her.

"Erin?" he managed hoarsely. A soft groan was all the acknowledgment he received. She never opened her clenched eyes or gave up her death grip on the pillow which she curled around, like a child drawn in pain. The sight was more than Jackson could stand. There was a time for bluffing and there was a time for folding and this was a time to throw in the hand. For Erin's sake. "What do you want, Horsey?"

"The gun first."

Jackson released the hammer slowly and tossed the gun. John would be there soon with the authorities. All he had to do was stay alive . . . and insure Erin's life, until they got there. "So give her the antidote!" he muttered with a surly growl.

"In due time, sir." He waved the woman toward Jackson. "Tie him to a chair over there."

The bite of the ribbons and satin sashes Lil used to bind his hands to the chair reminded Jackson of the forceful torture he'd inflicted on Erin and his chest constricted even further. From now on, all she would know was his love, the gentle touch of his care.

Once Horsey checked the knots to be certain they would hold, he handed the gun over to his accomplice. "Time to propose again. I would think she'd see things my way this time."

"Propose!"

The man grinned widely at Jackson. "The girl thought to outwit me as well. You produced letters proclaiming you her executor and wooed her with your charm to cheat me of my due. She's left a will leaving her estate to her aunt in New Orleans. What neither of you considered is the fact that, should she marry, her inheritance becomes common property of her husband . . . me," Horsey mocked with a short bow.

Lil stepped out from behind Jackson, her hands poised on her hips. "Wait a minute, Cole. You said you was gonna marry me!"

"Shuddup, woman! It's not like I could never become a widower after I'm done with her . . . a rich one at that." He raked disdainful eyes over Lil's abundant figure disdainfully. "And you sure as hell aren't going anywhere."

"You said poison, sir," Jackson interrupted impatiently. "Was it the same sort you used on Marie Asante?"

"Me?" Horsey remarked in feigned astonishment. "Why, sir, I was here in Natchez when the old woman met her Maker."

"Brilliant," Jackson derided. He couldn't help the sour note in his voice, but his compliment was seized upon nevertheless.

"Yes, it was, wasn't it?" Horsey started for the door and then turned, his ego unable to resist further temptation. "I'll tell you the whole scheme of things . . . after my sweet accepts my proposal."

Jackson's heart fell silent with the thud of the door that closed behind the man. Where in the hell was John? He glanced toward the window overlooking the street, but all he could see was the slope toward the river, not the bluff from which help might be coming. Although that could be to their advantage . . .

The creaking of the mattress on the iron cot that Erin had rested upon brought his attention to the door again instantly. It was frantic noise, as if she were struggling. A bucket scraped across the wood floor and there was the faint sound of anguished retching, interrupted by heartrending sobs. Jackson clenched his jaw and leaned against the rounded back of the chair. As he did so, he noticed the spindles to which each of his wrists were tied gave where age had loosened them in their mortise.

"You're in love with her, ain't you?"

Jackson pretended to sink against the chair back in despair, an act that came easy as another cry lifted in the other room. "Yes." He doubted the woman knew the meaning of the word, but there were other things she would understand. "And I will see you set up comfortably in a house on the bluff for the rest of your life if you'll help us. You have my word as a gentleman."

Lil snorted and ran fingers through Jackson's thick dark hair. "I take it you don't come with it."

Jackson was tempted to paste on the smile that had warmed his way into more than one bed, but found that it eluded him. He shook his head.

"You do have it bad," Lil observed bluntly, adding with a sneer, "and I heard you was a tough stud!"

Silver eyes pierced Lil's bloodshot ones with murderous contempt. "Could you carry on a flirtation when someone you love more than your own life is being tortured like that?"

Lil's answer fell silent as the door opened and Coleman Horsey emerged from the room with a satisfied look that expanded into a smile for the benefit of his unexpected guest. "Lil, go downstairs and see if the parson's sober while I have me a toast to my new bride-to-be. All he has to say is the main words, nothing fancy. Tell him there's a bottle of whiskey in it for him . . . two, if he hurries."

"What about the antidote?" Jackson reminded him as the woman left the room, unaffected by his proposition.

"There isn't one. She wasn't poisoned, just made to think she was . . . like you."

Cold ice formed in Jackson's veins from the impact of the deception. He was unaccustomed to losing and felt pure rage at his folly. This was no game any longer. It was his life . . . and Erin's.

"The old woman on the other hand was."

"So you were behind her death."

"One of my people was."

"Who?" Jackson demanded. "You're going to kill me anyway. The least you can do is solve this blasted riddle that has robbed me of peace since it all began. Were you behind the kidnaping attempt as well?"

Horsey nodded, pleased with himself. "You don't mind if I have a little champagne, since it's such a special occasion?"

Jackson shifted in his chair, working at the rungs as the man turned his back to take out a green bottle from beneath the hutch jammed against the wall that separated them from Erin.

"Of course, it will be a unique wedding, what with the bride bedridden. I imagine she's too weak to stand."

Twisting his wrists so that he could grasp the chair back, Jackson began to lift with all his might. Whether it was outrage that gave him his strength or whether the chair glue had finally lost its battle with age, the rungs came loose. Horsey turned, two glasses in hand, and walked toward him, his eyes moving to where Jackson's wrists were still tightly bound. Jackson, having eased the rungs back into their mortise, waited.

"How does it feel, Tyler, to be bested for a change. The great Jackson Beauregard Tyler of Retreat, squirming helpless in his chair. The infamous Black Jack Tyler, losing his first important game."

"You should know, Horsey. It's a way of life with you and your kind." Jackson recoiled as cheap champagne splashed against his face and drenched the front of his shirt.

"Yes, I'll put your mind to rest!" his nemesis snarled vindictively. "And then I'll do the same for your soul. That will tidy things up nicely." He drained his champagne and, with a loud belch, proceeded to the hutch to refill his glass. "Just like your partner so graciously did for us to turn up dead in New Orleans. That fool of a sheriff will never know he was an innocent man."

Jackson eyed the pistol next to the hutch on the table with calculation when a movement in the corner of his eye caught his notice. The powder-ridden red wig he knew to belong to his partner bobbed briefly along the roofline of the overhang in front of the boarding house. As it disappeared, so did the hands that were clenched on either side of it. Thinking to distract his host, Jackson decided to bide his time.

"So if John didn't have anything to do with Marie Asante's death, who did?" Jackson exclaimed, loud enough so that the maker of the stealthy footfalls outside the window could hear.

Mistaking Jackson's increased volume as a result of his frustration, Coleman Horsey took extreme delight in revealing his scheme that had almost been foiled until Erin walked straight into his hands. He told how he knew Giselle Devareau was dying and had her watched by his contact in New Orleans, the same one whose lover worked as a clerk in the office where the impulsive will had been drawn for Marie Asante.

It was one of his people who poisoned the woman. After all, the *Delta Moon* had once been Horsey's and he had his contacts on the ship as well. When they hadn't found the missing will, Horsey figured it was just a matter of time for it to show up. In the meantime, gaining the status of Erin's guardian became essential.

"Oh you thought you were so clever when you produced that winning hand and made off with her with your tail covered by your men," Horsey laughed humorlessly. "And I vowed then that if I couldn't

354

have Erin Devareau, you wouldn't."

"You are lower than even I dreamed, sir," Jackson vented distastefully in a raised tone. Someone was outside the window and he wanted to be certain every word was heard. *"You had Marie Asante murdered, framed my partner for it, tried to have my ward kidnapped, and now you plan to kill me and force her into marriage with you! By God, have you no scruples?"*

"None whatsoever, sir," the man replied, pleased with the furious summation. "And to illustrate further . . ." He picked up the gun and walked casually over to Jackson, his glass sloshing champagn on the threadbare carpet. "I shall toast this momentous and gratifying occasion and put a bullet through your temple with the biggest smile I can muster."

Jackson watched the barrel of the gun slacken as his adversary tilted his head back to drain the last of the liquor. With a lunge that pulled the rungs free of the chair seat, he plowed his shoulder into the man's stomach and twisted violently as the gun went off. A terrible burning sensation cut through the flesh of his upper arm as he struck the floor.

"You bastard!"

The curse blended with a crash of glass as a foot kicked through the window, followed by the ball of John Davenport's body. At the same time the door burst open, admitting the sheriff and one of his men, each bearing guns. John pulled himself to his feet and leapt on Horsey's back as the man snatched up the gun he'd dropped. Jackson shook his head to clear the glaze of pain from his eyes, watching as the room seemed to go into slow motion.

The sheriff and deputy pulled up their pistols as Horsey swung John into their firing path. The red wig that fell to the floor next to the dirty blond toupee shocked them into a stillness that seemed to

Jackson to last an eternity. Ignoring the glass that cut into his already bleeding arm, Jackson tried to lunge for his feet, but before he or the authorities could help, John was slammed against the doorjamb leading to the chamber where Erin was imprisoned and brushed off roughly.

The sheriff caught him as he slumped against the wall, his damp brown hair thickening with blood from the nasty blow against the sharp edge of the facing.

"Get away from that door or I'll kill the girl! One more murder won't make much difference now," Horsey warned from inside the room, belatedly realizing the reason for Jackson's loud tone. "Damn you, Davenport, I mean it!" he said, his voice rising to a frenzied pitch. "Those fools might have botched killing you, but I promise you I will not!" They'd heard everything, and now the girl who was to have insured his good fortune was going to insure his life. Horsey reached down and grabbed the back of her dress, hauling her to her feet with his free hand.

Erin swayed precariously in confusion. She and her baby were dying, a preferable fate to that which Horsey proposed. Why couldn't they just leave her alone? She squinted, barely able make out Horsey's face in the light coming in from the other room, but something was different. He was bald, she realized. But he still smelled the same . . . that nauseating odor of stale cigars and unwashed flesh. She started to slump, only to have him hoist her up again.

"Straighten up, gal. You're coming with me. Now get back and give us room. I mean it!" he shouted through the door.

Blinking to see who he was talking to, Erin shuffled her feet ahead of her captor's into Lil's parlor. The lamp hanging over the table cast a dim glow in the room, but all she could see was that they were men. The cold press of steel against the flesh of her throat shocked her tired eyes into wakefulness and she tried again to focus. Her head drooped to one side, finding a face much lower than the others turned toward her . . . a handsome face fraught with anguish and silver eyes that grabbed her attention and shook her as nothing else could.

"J . . . Jackson?" The man slowly rose from his kneeling position so as not to intimidate Erin's captor and let go his bleeding arm.

Erin cried out suddenly as the gun barrel bore into her jugular and Jackson stiffened, like a white marble statue in silent torment. Fear swept a clear path across her face as she was dragged toward the door and into the hall, for the scarlet stain spreading on the tawny jacket registered as blood. Jackson's name lodged in her throat, unable to emerge past the pressure of the gun as she fought to keep from sliding weakly to the floor. He'd come for her, she thought wildly, and now he was hurt. The mingled joy and dismay compounded her confusion as she steadied herself on the ball-crowned banister to make the turn to the steps.

Suddenly a shot pierced the silence that thickened the air and Erin cringed, expecting some sort of pain from the weapon that fell away from her neck. The arm that imprisoned her waist dropped and a heavy thud echoed behind her, followed by the sound of a body sliding against the plastered wall.

"Erin!"

Erin teetered unsteadily on her feet as she turned toward Jackson's voice and raised her arms to reach for him. But as she moved, the floor beneath her seemed to disappear. She grabbed desperately for the arms she knew would take her away from all this, but they were not there. All she found was emptiness, a steep tunnel of sharp jabs and blows that rattled her consciousness. When the thunder of her fall subsided, she heard Jackson's frantic voice above her and thought for a moment that somehow Horsey had sent her to heaven and Jackson was coming downstairs to help her make it the rest of the way.

Except that she hurt. No one was to hurt in heaven. And the steps were wood, not gold. The arms she'd tried to seek found her and she felt herself being lifted into them, but instead of comfort, an excruciating pain wracked her body, overshadowing all the other aches and bruises for her fall, and she screamed in agony.

"A doctor! My God, we've got to get her to a doctor!"

"J . . . Jackson!" she gasped, going limp as the viselike cramp released her.

"I'll find a coach," the sheriff offered, leaving a wounded Coleman Horsey to his deputy. "We'll run down that gal that shot 'im later."

"You're going to be all right, love. I promise," Jackson whispered urgently, oblivious to the pain of the bleeding wound in his arm as he made his way through the hall past the curious boarders who had come out of their rooms to see what the commotion was about. Not that what they saw was anything new to them. It was just some beginning excitement for the night.

"Tyler!"

Jackson paused at the door and turned to see a pale and breathless Coleman Horsey toss down a satin envelope he retrieved from the inside of his coat. It landed with a crash at his feet. Jackson knew it instantly as the one that contained the jewels he'd intended to give Erin as her engagement gift. But it wasn't the gift that held his attention. It was the pool of blood lying on the floor beyond where Erin had landed at the foot of the steps.

"There isn't any need to pay Lil to get rid of your baby, now that she seems to have done it on her own," Horsey taunted vindictively.

Jackson thought he would come apart with the

358

volcanic mixture of emotion that screamed inside him. Wrath, anguish, frustration, and fear formed a formidable force that he was at a loss to deal with. He stumbled out of the boardinghouse and into the street with his precious burden, unaware of the final conscious-robbing wound his stricken expression dealt or of denial that formed on Erin's lips as blessed blackness claimed her. All he knew was a consuming terror that he was about to lose not only his love, but his child as well . . . a child that might take her from him forever.

# Chapter Twenty-Three

Through a myraid of dreams mingled with
brushes of reality, Erin felt a strong warm grasp that
seemingly never left her and clung to it, resisting the
endless tunnel of darkness that sometimes spun to a
whirlwind pitch, threatening to draw her into its
vacuum. There were occasions during the timeless
period when she heard Jackson's voice speaking
wonderful words that inspired her to try harder to
back away from infinity toward the light and its
promise.

Yet she wavered, intimidated by a less identifiable
threat that reared up when she was tempted to bridge
the chasm that separated her from him. All she knew
was that it was something so horrible that it
jeopardized her chances of ever reaching the man she
loved and happiness.

And what happiness awaited her, if only she could
sort out these illusions! He wanted to marry her. He
loved her. He was going to take her home to the river,
to the *Delta Moon*. The ship was going to be theirs,
just like she'd wanted. Partners in life, he'd sworn.
And he'd kissed her. She knew the tender touch of his
lips against hers, sweet and heady. It made her feel as
though she were flying, floating in heavenly bliss
toward him. But before she could reach him, a black

and frightening cloud wedged itself between them and she became lost and afraid. And finally there was rest, absolute and void of any incentive to strive for anything beyond simply existing.

It was into that oblivion that the early morning sun marking the daybreak of Christmas Eve managed to penetrate. Its blinding light came in full force through the curtains that had inadvertently been left open by the man slumped down the chair next to the bed, assaulting Erin's eyes through closed lids. As her senses stirred to the first reality that registered as such during the two days she'd been in her far-off netherworld, she weakly threw an arm across her face and wrinkled her nose in displeasure. The fall of her hand against the pillow was soft, but the movement was sufficient to stir her companion from his despondent pose with a start.

"Erin?"

Her hand was snatched up and the sun once again assailed her. Unable to return it, she tried to withdraw the other from the folds of the coverlet and struggled with them grumpily.

"Erin, wake up! Mother!"

Erin winced at the booming thunder of the voice as she was drawn up from her pillow and shaken roughly. "W . . . what?" she moaned, forcing one eye open to see the bedraggled man hovering over her.

"Come on, love, speak to me," he pleaded with an urgency she was at a loss to understand. "Come on, Erin. Don't leave me now."

Jackson? Erin blinked uncertainly. The voice sounded like Jackson Tyler's . . . sort of. And this man looked something like him, except that he was unkempt and appeared sick and hallow-eyed. And in dire need of a clean shave and bath, she thought as she was hauled against his chest enthusiastically. "Bejesus, I can't breathe!"

Her protest was weak, but it was typically Erin. Jackson loosened his hold on her and shook her with his relieved laughter. "She's awake!" he said to Auralee Tyler, who rushed in the room with cheeks flushed from the exertion of climbing the steps.

"Darling, put her down, for heaven's sake! You'll crush the life out of her!"

Erin found herself being lowered gently to the pillow and was grateful for the intervention of the woman whose smiling face appeared over the broad shoulders of her zealous companion. Recognizing Auralee Tyler, she glanced back at the man in surprise. "Jackson?" she ventured uncertainly. What had happened to him?

"Here, love." He took her hand again and held it to his cheek, his silver eyes glistening in the morning light.

"I'll send for some rice pudding. I fear the broth we've been spooning into her hasn't been too sustaining," Auralee Tyler said from the balcony doors where she drew a drape across to shade Erin's face. "Do you think you could eat some pudding, dear?"

Erin nodded as confusion engulfed her. She was in her room, the one at Retreat with the pretty wallpaper and lovely view of the garden. But how could she be? She closed her eyes and tried to make sense of it. The last thing she remembered . . .

"Erin!"

Her eyes flew open at Jackson's frantic tone. The last thing she remembered was Jackson's face, stricken with the suspicion that she'd intended to rid herself of his child. Their child. A panic of her own ensued. Her hands found their way to her stomach as her eyes sought out Auralee Tyler. "Where's my baby?"

It was a foolish question. Erin knew even as she asked it that the child was gone. Besides the overwhelming emptiness that overtook her, she remembered the pain, a pain like nothing she'd ever known. Lil and Horsey had killed her baby, poisoned it with their damnable potions and herbs. And Jackson believed Horsey's lie . . . it had shown in his eyes, eyes that now were fixed on her, veiled and suddenly emotionless.

No one would ever understand, not even the sympathetic woman who moved to the other side of her bed and sat on the edge of the mattress. "The doctor said you will be able to have other children, dear. You're lucky to be alive, considering the fall you took."

*Lucky!* Erin swallowed with difficulty and stared at the ceiling. Now she knew the monster that had kept her from her dream of Jackson and his sweet promises. She squeezed her eyelids shut, forcing out the tears that welled there and sought to retreat into the darkness again, but it would no longer have her. Instead, it abandoned her to the tormented memories of the nightmare in Lil's apartment.

Dreams, she thought miserably, they were all dreams. A sob caught in her throat and made a tiny strangled sound.

"Erin . . ."

"Go away!" she exploded, venting her anguish. "I don't want to see you! Please . . ." Erin felt the restraining hands on her shoulder as she rolled away to bury her face in her pillow, but Auralee Tyler's plaintive "Jackson!" removed them.

In the background she heard retreating footsteps and the click of the door as it was pulled shut, but remained frozen in her shame. Why hadn't she died with her baby? At least she would have been spared having to face the people she'd betrayed.

The bed swayed with Auralee Tyler's weight and a gentle hand came to rest on her shoulder. "Erin, dear, I know what it is to lose a child. Robert and I lost our first for reasons I will never know or understand. I had to draw on my strength from the Lord and rest in the assurance that it was his will. Had your baby survived that terrible fall, it might have been born with some affliction that God saw fit to spare it and you. I, for one, am most grateful that He has answered our prayers and spared you for my son."

Bewildered, Erin lifted her head. So Jackson hadn't told his mother how she came to lose the baby. Miss Auralee thought it was from the fall. Still, the woman must know about the jewels by now—the jewels she stole and her deceitful plan to run away. Erin longed to say she was sorry, but could not bring the words to her lips.

"I believe that you and Jackson will give me many grandchildren," the matron said with a wistful smile. "And I so look forward to that." A sudden look of dismay settled on Auralee Tyler's face. "Oh, dear," she exclaimed, her hand belatedly flying to her lips. "I do believe I've spoken prematurely."

The truth hit Erin soundly, dulling the excitement that might have been under other circumstances. She'd tried so hard to win Auralee Tyler's approval because she truly liked and respected the woman. "Do you mean that Jackson is going to marry me now?"

In a fluster, her companion jumped to her feet. "You must promise me that you'll not let on I said a word," she implored. "It wasn't my place. It's just that . . ." She gave Erin an impulsive hug. "It's just that I would so love you as a daughter."

"Even after all I've done?" Erin's voice quivered in disbelief.

With characteristic serenity and a sincerity that could not be doubted, Auralee Tyler took Erin's hands in her own and squeezed them tightly. "My dear Erin, I am sure that you had your reasons for your actions. I pray that they are, or will be, resolved between you and Jackson quickly. That is all I ask of you . . . that and, of course, for you to get well," she added brightly. "I'll fetch the pudding and bring it up myself. After you eat, perhaps you'll feel like seeing Mr. Davenport. Like all of us, he's been beside himself with concern over you and will be distressed that he has slept so late this morning."

John, Erin thought, as Auralee Tyler took her leave. Would he be as forgiving as her hostess? Or would he believe the worst of her like Jackson? She pressed her fingers to the ache in her temples and shut her eyes. Since it appeared that she was going to survive, she would find out soon enough, she supposed wearily. In the meanwhile, she'd just rest for a few moments and perhaps gather her strength.

When Erin awakened again, she found she was ravenous for the pudding that had been left on a tray by her bed. To her surprise, her right hand shook so badly from weakness that she had to steady it with the left to feed herself without spilling the deliciously sweet pudding on the coverlet. When the last was finished, she let the bowl rest in her lap and lay exhausted and damp from perspiration.

Mary came in and promptly refilled the small potbellied stove on the corner hearth with coal, opening the damper to raise the heat in the room. All the while she chatted about the holiday activities that were taking place at the surrounding plantations. Erin could hardly believe she'd been unconscious for two days and that it was Christmas Eve. As the maid rattled on about the Twelfth Night Ball being moved to the Allen plantation because of Erin's accident, Erin's shock thawed sufficiently for her to ascertain that an edited version of her illness had been given to the neighbors. They believed she'd taken a fall down the steps and was bedridden with injuries sustained from it.

At least Auralee Tyler had been spared the embarrassment Erin had sought to save her, if not directly by Erin's hand. She should be grateful for that, the girl decided dejectedly. From the way the maid was running on about her head injuries, she wondered just who did know about the baby besides those closely involved. Perhaps the mistress of Retreat had managed to keep it a family secret from the servants as well.

Either that was the case, or the people she'd come to know over the last weeks were going out of their way to hide any knowledge of her shameful situation. When supper was brought up, they used it as an excuse to slip up to her room to wish her a Merry Christmas and tell her how glad they were that she was recovering. Tears came entirely too easy for Erin's liking and she was thankful when Auralee Tyler ran them out so that she might give Erin a bath and help her into a clean night shift and robe.

"I'm sorry you missed your Christman Eve service," she told the woman as she settled back onto the freshly changed bed. "You didn't need to stay here for my sake."

"I wouldn't hear of leaving you after what you've been through! I'm certain the ladies choir is managing well enough without me. Now sit up and let me fix your hair."

"I'm just going to sleep on it again. That seems like all I've done today."

Auralee Tyler perched on the edge of the mattress. "Humor me, child. I used to do this with my own little girl."

Recalling that this was the first Christmas Jennifer Tyler Allen had spent away from home, Erin forced herself upright and submitted to the woman's ministrations. They were not altogether unpleasant and somehow filled a void in her life as well. This was her first Christmas without her mother.

Christmases of the past flitted through Erin's mind as her companion tied up her locks with a white satin bow. Christmas Eve was a slow night in Under the Hill. Only a few fourteen-carat derelicts frequented the saloon and the result was more of a private party among the employees and the patrons who had no family than business as usual. Those who did have relatives close by were home with them.

Horsey let her mother off that night. After reading the story of the nativity to Erin from the Bible, Giselle Devareau would climb into bed beside her and sing her to sleep with Christmas carols.

*"God rest ye merry gentlemen, let nothing you dismay,*

*Remember Christ our Savior was born on Christmas day . . ."*

"What in the world . . .?" Auralee Tyler exclaimed, hopping to her feet to rush to the balcony. A blast of cool air rushed in as she opened the doors and the singing that Erin had first thought echoing her mind, became louder. The carolers launched into the second verse as her hostess turned abruptly in delight. "You must see this!"

At that moment, a knock sounded at the door. Upon Auralee's invitation, Jackson Tyler and John Davenport entered. A smile played on Jackson's freshly shaven face as he walked over to the bed and began to fasten Erin's robe as a father would a child's. "It seems the Christmas service has come to us," he announced wryly, before scooping Erin up in his arms, cover and all.

"But I want to be the first to wish you a Merry Christmas, young lady! By thunder, I'm glad to see you've decided to stop playing the sleeping princess and rejoin us." John planted a loud kiss on her cheek and stepped aside to let them by.

"Merry Christmas to you, John," Erin mumbled awkwardly, too dumbstruck by all that was happening to protest being snatched from her warm bed and too weak to put up much of a struggle if she wanted to. As Jackson carried her out on the balcony, the choir, bundled in blankets and huddled tightly with their respective husbands in six carriages, ended the carol and lifted their voices in greeting.

"Merry Christmas, friends!"

"Glad to see you're recovering, Miss Devareau!"

"God Bless you all!"

"We missed you, Auralee!"

Auralee Tyler leaned over the rail, eyes sparkling with excitement. "You all must come in for refreshments! I insist!" Her encouragement was all the group needed to disembark from the carriages for a chance to warm their feet and hands as well as their stomachs. As Jackson ducked back inside with Erin, she turned to them. "Jackson and John could bring you downstairs, dear, if you feel up to it."

Erin shook her head. "You go see to your guests and . . . thank them for me." Her voice broke. "I'm tired," she managed.

"Go on, Mother. I'll see to Erin."

"I'd be glad to," John offered, affording her a wink that told her all was forgiven between them. A hint of a smile touched her lips in gratitude.

"You help Mother," Jackson insisted. "You always were better at the bar than I."

Erin's eyes widened as she realized that she was being left alone with her guardian. She wasn't ready to face Jackson, not yet. She pleaded silently with John to stay, unaware of the subtle exchange of looks between the two men.

"If they stay overlong, then I'll come up and relieve you so that you can throw them out," John quipped. He gave Erin a buss on the cheek. "Maybe we can play a hand or two of cards later."

Her heart thudded against her breastbone as the door closed behind John, sealing her fate with a click of the latch. She couldn't help but stiffen as Jackson tenderly lowered her onto the bed and proceeded to tuck her in securely.

"Mary said you ate well. I was glad to hear that."

Erin mumbled an acknowledgment, unable to ignore the pungent aroma of pipe tobacco that clung to his indigo velvet smoking jacket. He'd been sequestered in a room with John, for she could not recall having seen Jackson smoke any sort of tobacco. Yet he always possessed that masculine scent of smoke and fine liquor combined with talc and soap. And he certainly had improved in appearance since that morning. Someone had said that he had hardly left her bedside since her confinement. Was it concern for her that accounted for his weary and disheveled presence earlier?

"There's something I'd like to talk to you about, if you're up to it."

Afraid to rely on her reasoning as yet, Erin seized on an excuse to avoid discussing anything with Jackson Tyler. "I'm tired."

"This won't take but a moment," he persisted gently. "Then I promise to sit back and watch you sleep."

As if she could close her eyes with him in the room, she thought frantically. Bejesus, she couldn't talk about what had happened, not yet. She wasn't strong enough to take his inevitable accusations and contempt, nor could she stand his honor-bound proposal.

"Tyler, I . . ."

"I think, since you're going to wear this, that you might learn to call me by my first name." He took a ring out of his pocket, the emerald ring to the set she'd taken, and slipped it on her finger. "Most future brides use their fiancés' first name, I believe."

369

Erin stared at the sparkling emerald on her finger until she could no longer focus, her heart clenching in rebellion over the turmoil stirred by its representation. What was he trying to do to her? Couldn't he see a forced marriage would make her miserable? Or was that the purpose? "I don't want it," she averred, reaching to take it off her free hand. "You don't have to marry me."

Jackson grabbed her hands and held them captive. "No, I don't. That's not why I gave you the ring. If you recall, it was already intended for you before . . ." He broke off, cursing silently for the forbidden turn in the conversation. What in the blazes could he say? "I don't want to upset you, Erin, but I do intend to marry you, if I have to pay court every day between now and the wedding and sweep you off your feet." Watching her chin set stubbornly, he grasped awkwardly for different tact. "And I don't think Mother will be adverse to the idea. We'll tell her together."

"I don't want you or your courtship, *Tyler*," she added in mustered defiance, not about to be taken in by his ploy. "I told you once that I didn't want a husband."

"But you said you wanted a partner. Well, I'm making that proposition, Erin. Many marriages are mergers of a sort. You marry me and we'll throw in our fortunes together. We can invest in the railroad you wanted, you'll own half of my share of every one of the Delta 'O' ships . . ."

Erin turned her face away to hide the anarchy consuming her mind. Forces lead by reason and emotion both plied for domination with equal strength. It was one thing to say that she didn't want Jackson as a husband. It was another to really mean it, especially after all those wonderful dreams.

*But that was all they were.* Jackson didn't love her. He felt duty-bound to marry her. Still, to own part of the Delta "O" Line and a railroad! A lifetime of having nothing came into the mental fray, led by ambition.

"We can be business partners without marriage. You're not married to John." Her head was starting to ache again with the ferocity of the battle going on inside. "Do we have to talk about this now? I don't . . . I don't feel well."

She massaged her temples in demonstration, hoping he'd leave. God help her, she was tempted to accept his proposal and that would be a disaster. It seemed like an eternity of silence broken only by the general noise of the congregation downstairs, a festive sound unfitting for the grave turmoil she was experiencing.

"No," he conceded reluctantly. "You can think about it. Until your mind is made up, just keep the ring."

Upon hearing Jackson rise from the chair by the bedside, Erin relaxed. But instead of leaving as she'd anticipated, he sat on the edge of the mattress and leaned over her. Her eyes widened with anxiety. "I said I wasn't well!"

"Your head aches," he observed clinically, placing his fingers to her temples as she had previously. "Perhaps I might be able to ease your discomfort a bit. I've seen Mother do the same for my father in the past."

It did feel heavenly, but Jackson this close, this tender, was a terrible torture. Erin shut her eyes, but she could not shut out the disconcerting pressure of his thigh against her hip through the folds of the covers. A small sigh escaped her lips at her plight which was instantly misinterpreted.

"You see, there are decided advantages to marriage . . . for both of us," he whispered, diverted from his ministrations long enough to trace the outline of her lips with the tip of a finger.

371

It wasn't his lips, but it might as well have been for the way the seemingly harmless gesture disrupted her pulses and undermined her defenses. Erin didn't dare look at him. It would be so easy to throw caution to the wind and go into his arms, to pretend that everything was fine and that this was a happy ending where she would live with her prince happily ever after. Purposefully, she moved his hand back to her temple and remained silent. There was little use in debating his point. She knew, in spite of herself, there was truth to his words . . . if love, honor, and trust were involved, none of which applied in their case.

Trust was a decided problem . . . on both their accounts. After all, she was not the only one recovering from the loss of her prince's child. Although the circumstances were somewhat different, Jackson Tyler had still been the father of Gina Allen's child and God only knew who else.

No, she decided, unable to resist relaxing under the constantly firm and gentle massage that assuaged one source of pain. Jackson Tyler was the sort who didn't know how to maintain the kind of relationship he expected her to accept. She would be the one bound by it, not him. It wasn't right, but men weren't ostracized for stepping outside the limitations of marriage as women were. She was better off to keep her inheritance and her name, for, as Coleman Horsey had made so clear to her, once she entered the state of matrimony, it was no longer her own.

Nor were the ships or her stock in the railroad, it came to her. Her heart hardened against the caring ministrations that had begun to melt her resolve. So that was the silver-tongued devil's game! He was suckering her into wedlock with things he knew she wanted desperately, just to hog-tie her so that she was totally under his dominion to torment as he pleased for her shameful deceit.

Well, it took two to play and she was not the ignorant little waif from Under the Hill that he thought he was toying with. She'd learned a lot being around Jackson Tyler and his businesses, and as soon as she was on her feet she intended to show Mr. Jackson Beauregard Tyler, with his sweet-talking charms, just what she did know.

# Chapter Twenty-Four

The doctor had warned them that Erin might be subject to depression, but that hardly prepared Jackson for the behavior that followed her return to consciousness. Erin simply used every excuse within her grasp to avoid him. With his mother standing over the girl like a protective hen with her chick, the situation was becoming impossible.

True to character, Auralee Tyler did not attempt to pry after Erin begged not to have to speak to him Christmas Day. On one hand, it had been a relief, for there were some parts of their relationship he was loathe to explain. Yet, because he had not gone out of his way to confide in her, his mother had somehow gotten the opinion that he had committed some odious crime against the girl. At least that's the way she acted. And when he balked at not seeing Erin, he was simply put off by the explanation that he was expected to tolerate without question . . . *women's matters*.

As his frustration grew and Erin was out of danger, Jackson's initial guilt over her mishap dwindled. He had taken her literally off the street, clothed her and provided her an education, tried to make her an honest citizen and a lady and she had fought him at every turn. She had paid him back by stealing from him, running away and aborting his child. Granted, he had contributed somewhat to her dilemma, but not enough to drive her to the extremes she'd sought. If he had one ounce of good sense left, he'd forget her, maybe send her off to a girl's school in the East.

But he didn't possess one sound thought, not where Erin was concerned. His last separation from her had nearly driven him mad. All he wanted to do was settle the unspoken declaration of war between them and tell her how he felt. She'd gotten under his skin and in his blood to where she was all he could think about. Until she was his, body and soul, he would have no peace.

The worst of the matter was, he knew she wasn't as adverse to marrying him as she insisted. All he needed to do was get her alone long enough to prove it to her . . . alone where no one could come to her rescue, except him.

He tugged at the reins of his mount and urged it around the corner of the house toward the stables to the rear. Tempting scents wafted through the crisp cool air as he passed the summer kitchen with its wide stone chimney adorned with ivy and its fence woven with barren vines that would be hanging with fragrant wysteria in the spring. His stomach growled reminding him of the lunch he'd missed and he decided to pause long enough to run in and steal one of the cold muffins or some of the cookies that had always been in the old green painted pie cupboard since he was a child. After all, he was home earlier than usual and he wasn't certain he'd last until the formal supper hour.

However, as he brought the chestnut up short, he caught a glimpse of a blue duck coat in the rose trellis in the side garden. It was the same shade as the coat his mother had given Erin and, unless he missed his guess, Erin was wearing it. A scowl crossed his face as he slipped easily to the ground and tethered his steed to the kitchen fence. But instead of going inside where he could hear the cook's laughing orders being given to one of the helpers, he detoured behind the building and through the boxwood hedge that marked the garden's outer boundary. If Miss Erin was up to a late afternoon stroll, she was certainly up to seeing him.

From inside the cover of the trellis, Erin listened cautiously for the resumption of the hoofbeats that had marked Jackson's unexpected arrival. A few moments more and she would have walked right into his path as she returned from her outing. She knew she'd have to face him sometime, to tell him that she was not going to marry him. She just wasn't prepared to engage in such a formidable confrontation. And, if the truth were admitted, she didn't want to.

She peered through the seemingly dead and decidedly thorny vines woven in the arched wood structure and saw the chestnut tied to the fence of the summer kitchen. He had to have gone inside, she thought, venturing to poke her head out for a clearer look. If so, she might make a dash for the house and up to her room before he came out.

She chewed her bottom lip in indecision. That morning the doctor had pronounced her well enough to climb the stairs on her own once a day and she'd practically jumped from her bed with joy. Her sequester had begun to play on her nerves and she was less and less able to pass the time by sleeping. The moment he was gone, she hurriedly bathed and dressed in the first day clothes she'd worn since her accident and went downstairs to share the noonday meal with the mistress of Retreat at the dining room table. Afterward, she'd been forced to take a little nap, but when she awakened an hour later, she felt refreshed enough to go outside.

The fresh air had been a wonderful treat. She'd taken some stale bread from the kitchen and was feeding the birds in the garden when she saw Jackson's stallion round the corner of the house. Dumping the rest of the crumbs, she'd made a dash for the trellised enclosure where she'd first seen Jennifer and Chase stealing kisses on a warm fall afternoon.

Absently, she brushed away the remnants of the crumbs from the long skirt of her Ulster and peeked around the trellis again at the tethered horse. Whatever Jackson was doing in the kitchen, he was certainly taking his time. But then, when she visited the cook, it was hard to walk away from the treats that were forever on hand. She'd go, she decided, inhaling deeply in preparation for her run.

She gathered her cloak up in her hands and moved forward when her sleeve caught on something. With a dismayed cry, Erin spun about, certain a loosened nail was about to do damage to her new coat, only to come face to face with Jackson Tyler. Her face went white under the pink hue the river breeze had painted on her cheeks and she stumbled backward in an instinctive effort to pull away.

"No!"

"Not so fast, young lady!" Jackson yanked the loose sleeve, bringing her abruptly to him, and captured her about the waist with his free arm. "My, but I'm glad to see that you are up and about now. I was beginning to think you were going to spend the rest of your life in that bed."

"The doctor said I might get up today," Erin explained hastily, her heart lurching against her chest with each frantic beat. She knew from the accusing mercurial eyes fixed on her face that Jackson was aware of her deliberate and cowardly attempts to avoid him, which only compounded her guilty expression.

"Then it's time we finished that conversation I so gallantly let slide in consideration of your earlier frailty." He drew her hand up to his lips. "I see you have not removed the ring. Am I to take that as your answer, Erin?"

"No!" she declared fervently. "That is, I have been giving it some thought." A lot of thought was more like it, she mused. But she didn't want to discuss the matter . . . at least not like this, alone in Jackson's arms.

"So have I," Jackson whispered, his voice deepening to a velvet caress that was carried out against her lips.

Erin tried to move her head away, but a hand came out of nowhere and held it imprisoned, subjecting her to his sweet punishment. Desperately, she grasped for the resolutions she'd made, but the dominating male body that pressed closer to her own, until she was yielding in soft surrender, scattered them to the breeze whipping her curls about her face.

Shocked that her traitorous senses could so easily forget the recent pain that had resulted from similar intoxication, that they could ignore the certainty that he was exploiting her for his own revenge, she shoved against him with less intensity than she actually felt. Was nothing subject to her own will when Jackson worked his way with her? she wondered in exasperation.

"And there will be so much more after the wedding," he promised, brushing her ear with the warmth of his breath.

Erin shivered and managed to draw her arms across her chest. Unfortunately, the same thought played on her mind and haunted her sleep. Reason told her that accepting the proposal was wrong. Her heart and body argued differently.

Watching the confusion swim in the emerald depths of her gaze, Jackson's initial irritation subsided with satisfaction. It was just as well that she was hesitant, for if she responded as heartily as she

378

had in the past, he'd be sorely tempted to take her right there on the white painted bench beneath the winter sky. Although, he'd learned a hard lesson for not controlling the lust so easily prodded by the girl in his arms. The marriage bed would be soon enough.

"I don't want to marry you because you are honor bound to see it through."

"I intended to marry you anyway, if you remember."

"But why?" Erin demanded breathlessly. She had to know, to hear it from his own mouth. This was no dream. It was cold and she was unaccountably frightened. But if he had truly said those wonderful words she recalled, he'd say them again.

"Because, against my better judgement, I am in love with you, Erin Devareau. We'll be married the first week of February and spend our honeymoon at Mardi Gras."

Erin's knees threatened to buckle beneath her. Her crossed arms abandoning their defense, she grasped the stronger ones that tightened about her. This was not what she had expected to hear, and yet it was. At least, it was part of those distant memories. But dare she believe them? What if it was a ruse to lure her into his grasp completely—body, soul, and inheritance? "How can you love someone you cannot trust, sir?" she asked lowly. She found herself hoping against hope that he would have an answer she could accept.

"Oh, Erin!" Jackson exclaimed in frustrated annoyance. He hugged her to him and clasped her head to his chest. "Forget about the past! Whatever has happened doesn't matter. It's the future we need to focus on."

Erin's face fell in disappointment. He was willing to overlook it, but he as much as admitted that he still believed the worst of her. She pulled away, her arms once again folding across her chest in despair. "The future is built upon the past, Jackson. My answer is no."

Not to be put off this time, Jackson sprinted ahead of her, blocking her path through the boxwood entrance. "Damn it, Erin, what would you have me say? Yes, I trust you implicitly? There isn't much future in building on lies, is there? If *I* can overlook what has happened, then you *certainly* should be able to!"

So now it came. This was more like the response she anticipated. "I won't discuss it," Erin declared loftily, rising above her hurt and pain.

"Then it's settled. We'll announce our engagement at the Twelfth Night Ball."

Her eyes flashed in retaliation. "Announce what you will, you will be the fool when you have no bride!"

The muscles in Jackson's jaw bulged threateningly, hailing the wintry frost that hardened his gaze before her. "Oh, you'll marry me, Erin. Even if I would let you out of my sight again, your mercenary little heart will not allow you to do otherwise. I have complete control of your grandmother's estate and I can assure you you will not see a penny of it until you are Mrs. Jackson Tyler. Is that understood?"

"I will when I'm twenty-one."

"Not if it's lost on bad investments."

Erin gasped. It was inconceivable that anyone would lose money on purpose. Her inheritance was hers, even if Tyler was her guardian. He had no right to hold it over her head like a juicy carrot to entice her into the torment of the matrimony he planned. "You wouldn't!"

A sardonic smile twisted Jackson's lips. "Try me, sweet. Now you can fight me, Erin, and make it most unpleasant for all concerned . . . or you can accept my offer and, I think, be pleasantly surprised with the life you will lead. I will expect your answer tonight.''

Green eyes searched his face with a desperation that inflicted guilt upon his conscience, yet Jackson maintained his ruthless bearing. The fact that it was money and not affection that worked its way with Erin shouldn't gall him, but it did. But if money was what the girl craved, so help him she'd have it, all she could spend. He would be satisfied to cultivate love later. The seed was there. He knew it. It just needed to be nurtured and fed, something that could be done when she was securely in his grasp.

"I . . . I vow, I feel faint.'' All too aware of Erin's penchant for deception, Jackson watched with suspicion as Erin placed her hand against her temple and swayed in his arms. "Let me sit, sir.'' As if stricken, she dropped slowly to the seat shaded by the arbor, her hands still clutching the sleeve of his jacket for support.

Nonetheless, alarm infiltrated his wariness as she gently laid her head against his thigh and shuddered. "Erin?'' The gaze that lifted to meet his spilled large tears that seemed to claw at his conscience with a merciless vengeance. This was not Erin. He really had distressed her. He'd done it again, acted the bully when she was not yet fully recovered.

"I've got . . . something in my eyes,'' she stammered wiping her face irritably with the back of her hand. "You don't scare me.''

"God I hope not!'' Jackson fell to his knees and took her into his embrace, squeezing her tightly. "I don't want to scare you, Erin, I want to love you and protect you.''

Because she wanted to believe him, needed to, Erin returned the embrace, conveying her desperation with an urgency that, unwittingly, was her companion's undoing. As he swept her off the bench and climbed to his feet with her in his arms, she cradled her head against his chest and basked in his warmth and strength.

*To love you and protect you.* That was what she craved, at least for the moment. She would deal with his motives and her own terrible guilt later. For now, this was enough.

Auralee Tyler met them in the hall as Jackson started up the steps with his precious burden. "What happened? Is she all right?"

"She's just a bit overtired," he called over his shoulder. "I'll see to her."

As he anticipated, his mother's footsteps echoed behind him when he carried Erin into her room and deposited her on the bed. As he started on the double-breasted row of fastens on her coat, the mistress of Retreat stepped in authoritatively and took over, gently pushing him aside. Jackson clenched his jaw to hold check the spontaneous resentment that surged in his thoughts. After all, it was hardly proper for him to undress the girl, or to be in her room at all without proper chaperone. But he had worn the collar of propriety too long.

"I can take care of her, Jackson. You run along."

About to reply that he had no intention of doing any such thing, Jackson was checked by the unexpected request from the girl on the bed.

"Does he have to go?" Erin sought him out beyond her benefactress. She ignored the rebellion of her sounder nature in favor of the volatile emotions that clamored recklessly to return to his arms. How she'd missed them.

Caught by surprise, the mistress of Retreat glanced from her son to the girl, unable to miss the powerful bond that seemed to hold their gazes locked, smoldering silver against limpid green. "Well, I . . . it is irregular, but . . ."

Jackson saved her the decision by assuming command of the situation. "Leave us, Mother. Erin, was just about to answer my question." He stepped up to the bed and folded Erin's hand in his. "I can assure you, I have no dishonorable intentions."

"Of course, you wouldn't! I . . ." Auralee Tyler broke off with a sigh of resignation. "I'll be close if you should require me," she finished, a delighted twinkle lighting in her eyes at his suggested prospect.

Jackson didn't acknowledge, for he was already busy with the folded coverlet that rested at the foot of the bed. He tossed Erin's coat on the chair and tucked the blanket around her gently, his eyes never leaving hers. There was too much at risk to break the contact he'd finally made through the mysterious defenses she'd erected around her. She wanted him there and propriety be damned, he would have stayed, even if he'd had to physically remove his mother. He thanked God that Auralee Tyler was a free-thinking woman and understood even more why his father had treasured her so.

"I've decided to say yes on two conditions," the girl on the bed spoke up hesitantly, as if she too were afraid of breaking the emotional bond that had so totally engulfed them.

Jackson grinned crookedly. Well, he hadn't expected total capitulation. "What are they, sweet?"

"That you sign papers that guarantee my inheritance will be mine, even though I'm married to you."

"Done." That would dispel any outrageous inkling she might have that he was really interested in her money. Besides, why start worrying with irregularities now? Life with Erin would be full of them, of that Jackson was certain. "And?" he prompted curiously.

"And that we get married on the *Delta Moon.*"

This time Jackson laughed, not at the idea, but with relief. "Done."

Misinterpreting his amusement, the girl on the bed lowered her gaze. "I know it sounds foolish, but I don't want a lot of people lollygagging at us . . . and I was raised on the river. It will seem more real to me down there than up here in this . . ." Erin yawned in spite of herself, ". . . fairy-tale house."

"So that's what you think of Retreat?"

The girl on the bed looked away self-consciously. "I don't know whether I've been living in a nightmare or a dream. It's been both. I . . . I do love your family."

"That's a start," Jackson acknowledged, tongue in cheek.

"And you can be agreeable when you want to be," she conceded cautiously.

"I'll do my best to stay that way, but I will need some cooperation. A kiss to seal the deal would be nice." His dark brow arched expectantly over a perfectly boyish grin that was irresistible. Black Jack Tyler was gone and the Jackson who had spent the afternoon fishing with her stood before her.

Erin's expression betrayed her eagerness. She moistened her lips as Jackson leaned over the bed. When he gently claimed them, her doubts seemed to fade, swept away by the warm tide that flowed through her, melting her heart. It would all work out. The thought rang in her mind over and over, drowning out the last wary protests against her reckless choice.

"Could you just hold me?" she whispered softly as he drew away with a shaky breath. "Just for a while," she added upon seeing his hesitation. It never crossed her mind, the effort she was asking him to make, the restraint he had to exercise. "For a little while *now*," he conceded gently. "And forever, after our wedding."

Erin sighed as she settled into the comfort of his embrace and closed her eyes. If the rest of her life could be spent in Jackson Tyler's arms, doubts and fears wouldn't exist at all.

# Chapter Twenty-Five

The announcement of Jackson and Erin's wedding plans to Auralee Tyler set a whirlwind of preparations into effect. Jennifer Tyler Allen eagerly offered her wedding gown to Erin, since the two wore the same size. Hence, the seamstress who was summoned to Retreat to fit Erin for a trousseau was much relieved for one less burden, not to mention a generous advance, and left to pull three of her best girls off their current projects to complete her assignment in the time frame expected. Invitations were printed and sent to a select few that would attend the riverboat gala that was already the talk of the bluff settlement in spite of the fact that it had not been formally announced. Menus were collaborated on with the *Delta Moon*'s chef, who not only had to prepare for the wedding feast, but the maiden excursion to Mardi Gras for the passengers who had already booked their cabins well in advance.

The day of the wedding, Erin's breath froze within her chest as the whistle of the *Delta Moon* filled the air, announcing its departure. As the deck shifted under her feet she clutched to her chest the red roses that Mariette and Anita, who were as excited as she should have been for her, had given her after she was dressed. The precious note Jackson had sent with them was folded and tucked in her bodice, close to the heart it had touched.

It was a New Orleans custom, it had read, that a dozen roses be presented on Christmas Day to the chosen Mardi Gras queens by members of the krewes that had selected them. Citing that she had been indisposed to the idea of wedlock on that particular occasion, Jackson wrote that he had waited until their wedding day to ask her to be his queen, not only in the upcoming celebration, but for life.

"It's time, honey," Mariette prompted sweetly at her side.

"And don't crush them pretty flowers," Anita fussed, teary-eyed.

Overhead the steam calliope began to play "If Ever I Cease to Love," the song the Grand Duke of Russia had inadvertently made synonymous with Mardi Gras a few years earlier, so that everyone along the river could not doubt the ship's destination. Taking care not to catch the expensive lace or silk of her gown in any of the hatches, Erin made her way down to the boiler deck. The guests were already inside and seated when the calliope started to play the traditional wedding music. Curious passengers gathered near the rail to watch as Jennifer Tyler Allen left her husband's side to rush out to meet her.

"Oh, Erin, you're beautiful! I just want you to know, I couldn't be happier to have anyone for a sister than I am to have you." Jennifer hugged Erin tightly and then readjusted her veil as John Davenport, splendid in a beige frock coat and trousers, offered his arm.

"And I couldn't be happier to have this privilege than if I were your real father," the man told her with misting eyes as Jennifer hurried inside to stand by her mother. "You would make any man proud."

Erin couldn't speak. She needed all her strength and presence of mind not to panic. Everything had happened so quickly, too quickly for her guilt-ridden mind to accept. She'd wanted to tell Jackson the truth, to admit the guilt he knew nothing about, but hadn't been able to find the right time. Now it was too late. Would he change his mind about loving her if he knew about her hand in aborting his and Gina's child?

Grateful for John's reassuring hand on her own, she braced herself for the long march up to the front of the main salon where an arch of flowers that had not been there earlier and a man dressed in black broadcloth and a collar awaited them with Bible in hand. The roses she carried trembled visibly as she moved blindly forward at her companion's urging.

"God bless ye, child," she heard a familiar voice near the front of the small group that had been invited as she neared the striking young man dressed in a wedding suit of pale gray broadcloth with satin lapels and waistcoat. Tearing her eyes away from the glittering silver of the gaze that was only for her, she glanced back to see Molly MacCready and her family standing among the wealthy collection of guests. Standing next to her was Mac MacCready in a new store-bought suit and his son in an equally new and ill-fitted one. Both were grinning like a cat with a belly full of fish, in spite of their obvious discomfort.

Unaware that she'd stopped walking, Erin gave into John's gentle tug and proceeded, her face streaming with tears born of yet another burst of tenderness over Jackson's unerring knack for touching her heart. How had he ever thought to invite the people who had been her family since her mother moved to New Orleans? And how could they have afforded the riverboat trip?

Her bewilderment was interrupted by the clearing of the preacher's throat. Erin glanced away from Jackson Tyler to stare at the man, only to realize that she had come to a stop and was holding up the proceedings. Fortunately, her embarrassment steeled her from making a further fool of her herself as John presented her hand to Jackson and she made her way woodenly through the vows.

No one watching could have guessed the turmoil going on within her from her numb exterior. Only her gaze betrayed the surge of love and wonder that brushed aside her fears as she stood next to Jackson Tyler, pledging her life to him. It only wavered once, when pricked by his vow of love, honor, and *trust* until death. When she repeated her response, her eyes took on a feverish glaze of earnestness, for surely if he meant to love and honor her, by doing the same, perhaps she could win his trust.

She could, she tried to convince herself as a matching band to the emerald engagement ring he'd given her was slipped upon her finger. And when he leaned over and brushed her lips with the blessing of the minister, she tried to show him her sincerity, abandoning her flowers to heartily return his embrace.

"I meant every word, Jackson!" she told him, caught up in her own fervor as their lips parted reluctantly. "I'm going to try so hard, it'll make your head turn."

"It already has, sweet," Jackson chuckled lowly, completely taken by her spontaneous and ardent commitment. For a moment, he begrudged even the few friends they'd invited, for his body and thoughts were consumed with the girl in his arms.

The minister cleared his throat in reproval over the murmurs echoing here and there in the room, earning a scowl from the gentleman who was to pay him. Thus reminded of their circumstances, however, the groom gave the impetuous bride a perfectly rakish grin and resumed the proper stance so that the final announcement of man and wife could be made.

As the guests engulfed them with congratulations,

Erin's fingers bit into Jackson's arm, giving away her insecurity. Consequently, he fought the tide that inevitably separated the groom from his bride at most weddings to remain at her side and refresh her mind as to the identities of some of the people as they shook hands and claimed the right to kiss the bride.

It was only when the last of the guests moved forward that he felt Erin relax. Not only were they the end of the line, but they were the only ones who represented her. Standing close by, he watched as she hugged and kissed each of the MacCready family and discovered how he'd not only invited them, but given them free round trip passage to the next stop where the *Delta Star* would return them to the saloon Mac MacCready now owned.

"But how did you buy it?" Erin insisted, knowing full well that, even run down as the River Palace was, it would cost more than Mac could earn on the pitiful wages Coleman Horsey had paid him.

"I got a loan," the big man answered, glancing gratefully at Jackson Tyler. "The only reason I could come was because we can't open till the paintin' and repairs are done."

"And Ma and me are his partners, with wages and all," Cready spoke up proudly. "She ain't gonna tend youngun's no more, 'cause she's cookin' for the place."

"Mac's divided a section off the big saloon where I can serve food, nothin' fancy, mind ye, just plain cookin' with a choice of two dishes each day," Molly explained timidly with the soft Irish accent inherited from her mother, Erin's namesake. "Maybe some of them roustabouts'll eat and not get fightin' drunk and go to tearin' up as much with a belly full of Molly's cookin'," Mac beamed, drawing his small wife under the thick muscled arm that threatened the seams of his jacket. He looked around the room. "Speakin' of which, got any good drinkin' liquor? It

389

ain't often I get it served up to me."

Miss Molly pulled her attention away from the luxurious setting where servants were hurrying to put out the accoutrements for the sumptuous meal Auralee Tyler had selected and punched him in the side playfully. "Seems to me ye do well enough on your own, Mac MacCready! Now don't go embarrassin' Erin in front of these folks with a blight-eyed drunk. See that ye eat good first."

"Could they sit with us?"

Jackson nodded in answer to his suddenly shy wife's request as Mrs. Jackson Tyler and, with his flushed bride on his arm, walked toward the head table to officiate the beginning of the planned reception. The sooner it was started, the sooner it would be over and the sooner he would have Erin to himself while his friends and family joined the other passengers for the evening's entertainment.

Odd that when his sister had worn the same dress, he hadn't noticed how the lining dipped gracefully in the front, just to the point of immodesty. The imported lace that made the choker collared overblouse had perhaps disguised it then, rather than tantalized as it seemed to now. Nor had he admired before the way it skimmed over the bride's figure, emphasizing the perfect proportion of her feminine curves before layers of silk, draped across the front and drawn to a bow at her lower back to form a train tempted imagination to carry on.

"Did I tear it?" Erin asked, alarmed by the consternation on the face of the man studying the back of her gown.

Caught in his blatant perusal, Jackson chuckled wickedly as he held out her chair. "Just admiring the handiwork."

Although the servants worked furiously to feed the head table first, Jackson constantly had to pull his anxious wife back in her seat to keep her from waiting on the MacCreadys. John and Auralee Tyler were certain to include them in the conversation which gravitated toward Coleman Horsey's fate with the court. It seemed that he had been sentenced to ten years in prison. Lil's sentence of three years as an accomplice to Erin's kidnaping had been suspended for her aid in apprehending the man. She was, however, ordered to leave the state of Mississippi and word had it, she'd moved on to New Orleans.

The conversation moved on to more detail than Erin cared for, in spite of her husband's attempt to divert to another subject. Her dismay was such that she hardly noticed Gina Allen's testy manner at having been abandoned temporarily by her new love over a business deal mellowing suddenly with the paling of her face when Myra Allen demanded to know why on earth Erin had risked going to Under the Hill in the first place. Nor did she pay attention to the terse attitude that developed toward Jackson by John Davenport for having neglected to mention that Coleman Horsey had had a third partner by the name of Woodward, a discovery made while his partner was in New Orleans. She was merely grateful for the meal to pass, bringing the discussion to an end.

In the interim that followed, during which the band set up for the dancing to follow and the tables were removed to accommodate the same, the ladies returned to their cabins to freshen up and the men sought the open deck or casino for a smoke. From the upper deck of the *Delta Moon*, Erin leaned against her husband and watched the sunset glazing the river surface with brilliant orange, red, and gold hues. Although, they'd started for their cabin, an endless stream of people they didn't even know stopped them to offer their congratulations, confirming the off-handed comment made by one of the passengers that the world loved a wedding.

After the last of them moved into the main salon, porters, stewards, and members of the housekeeping staff continually intercepted them until Jackson steered Erin toward the observation deck where the captain and his pilot were hopefully engaged in keeping the boat underway and clear of bars. It was a relief to get away from the numbers, if only for a little while, for the strain was beginning to take its toll on Erin's nerves.

Of course the MacCreadys hadn't meant to make her uncomfortable, nor had anyone, for that matter. But then, aside from Gina, no one knew of the guilt she carried in her heart, not even the thoughtful husband whom she'd betrayed. Would he still love her if he knew? She shivered at the thought.

Jackson removed his jacket and placed it over her shoulders. "I'd take you to our cabin, but I'm afraid we'd miss the rest of the reception," he told her, folding her in his arms with a quick buss on the forehead.

His words were as intoxicating as the setting, yet Erin struggled with her despair. Forcing a smile, she laid her head against him and welcomed his embrace with one of her own. "This is good enough," she murmured wistfully. "If it all goes too quickly, I might forget something and I don't want to miss one special moment of my wedding day."

"Are you happy, Erin?" Jackson inquired quietly, his eyes searching her troubled gaze for the reason behind it.

Erin turned away to stare into the sunset. "Yes." She shouldn't be, she thought guiltily, but she was. "It's like a fairy tale, even here on the river. I only hope . . ."

"There you two are!" John Davenport called out from the hatchway, interrupting the confession on the tip of Erin's tongue. "Everyone is waiting for the bride and groom to start the dancing. But before you go down, I wanted to give this to you." He reached into his jacket pocket and handed an envelope to Jackson.

Jackson opened it and withdrew the note he'd signed obligating him to pay for John's share of the *Delta Moon*. It was marked paid in full and signed and witnessed, complete with a seal of authority. "I don't know what to say!" the young man remarked, overcome by his partner's generosity. "The *Delta Moon* is yours without any encumberment now," he told Erin, showing her the note.

"Thank you will do." John quipped lightly. "Now get below before the party moves up here or we all take a chill."

Applause broke out as the couple entered the room and the music began instantly on cue. Erin's heart fluttered as Jackson bowed gallantly and led her, like a queen, onto the dance floor that had been cleared of the earlier tables. The chandeliers overhead seemed to whirl above them as they fell into step, moving as one to the music. After the couple made one complete circle around the circumference of the cleared area, the other guests fell in with them.

"We've met our obligation," Jackson inferred meaningfully as the waltz came to an end. "There is nothing more required of us now."

"But the night's only just begun, Tyler . . . Jackson," Erin corrected swiftly. "And I hate for all those lessons to have gone to waste," she added, reminding him of the dance lessons that had occupied many evenings in the parlor at Retreat.

Bemused by her unanticipated eagerness to remain part of the celebration, Jackson swept her away again before one of the other gentleman guests came forward to claim her. If he was going to have to dance his wedding night away, it was going to be with Erin in his arms. However, by the fourth dance, he conceded to turn her over to John Davenport and marched with decided frustration to the bar to contemplate a means of prying his bride away from the sudden zeal she'd developed for dancing.

Erin followed Jackson with her gaze and felt a pang of remorse as she moved away with John. The dancing was only an excuse, although she was indeed enjoying it. And she did fully intend to honor the vows she'd made. It was just that Jackson's eagerness to begin their private wedded life left her unnerved, particularly in view of the confession she'd decided to make on the upper deck.

There was no alternative. Jackson had been right in the garden when he'd said they couldn't build their lives on lies. Hers was not a spoken lie, but one of omission. Her mother had chided her as a child for telling only part of a story, saying that omission was just as bad as lying outright. So, she would tell him about his and Gina's child and leave him the choice to annul the marriage before it was consummated under law. If he would still have her afterward, then she would make good the vows she'd made and go with a clear conscience into his arms forever. Believing her would be up to him.

"Hey, kid, look what I found down on the main deck!"

Erin was shaken from her thoughts as she walked to the refreshment table with John after the number ended by the sight of Cready, his jacket shed and sleeves rolled up, with a long roughly dressed plank in hand. "You suppose them gents could play something with a little more kick and holler?"

In his usual gregarious manner, Cready soon took over the room and coaxed Erin into taking a place at the opposite end of the board. Fascinated by the spectacle, the guests gathered around to watch. The band fell in with a lively jig and Erin shook off her troubles as she danced lightly with a swirl of ivory lace and silk to the music.

When she could go no further, she stumbled off the board to let Mac and Molly MacCready take over and made her way to the refreshment table to quench her thirst, leaving Cready to round up more boards for other interested parties. Her grin as she sought out the face of her husband froze however, as she caught sight of him slipping out one of the servants' entrances with Gina Allen tucked cozily under his arm.

Erin blinked furiously, trying to ignore the blade of jealousy that shattered the fun she had started to enjoy. What were they up to? Surely Jackson hadn't been in such a way that he'd sought another woman to warm his bed because Erin had wanted to stay for the dancing! And what about Gina's new love? She helped herself to a glass of champagne and turned to see John Davenport and Auralee Tyler being coaxed onto the board by the MacCreadys. No. She was being silly.

There were six boards, courtesy of Cready and two dapperly attired gentlemen who had gone to the lower deck to take advantage of some supply crates being dismantled by the crew, when Erin's increasingly green curiosity became too much to contain. After considering a freshly uncorked bottle of champagne, still foaming at the neck, she picked it up and started for the door, ignoring the speculative looks that followed. Maybe she'd just help herself to some of Cready's courage and then look for her husband and his charming companion. Whatever she found, she intended to confront it head on. Her time for guilt was over.

Cheeks already rouged by the combination of the champagne, dancing, and mouthful of supper she'd sampled, Erin chose the inner hatchway the crew predominantly used to make her way to the observation deck. With the chill of the night air, she should have some peace to deal with this new dilemma without the pasted-on grin and small talk she'd been forced to exhibit since the wedding. Fuming as she was, a winter storm would play hard to cool her down.

The passageway to the observation deck was quiet as she emerged from the lower level, except for the opening of a door near the opposite end. Erin was so involved in her turmoil that she failed to notice until she heard her name echoed in surprise and looked up to see the source of her anxiety standing half clothed, his jacket and shirt draped over his arm. The sight was so unexpected that for a moment, she remained as still as Jackson, her fingers gripping the neck of the champagne bottle with whitening knuckles.

"I thought you wanted to dance."

"I thought you wanted to go to our room," she blurted out in an equally cryptic tone. It didn't take a genius to see what he was about. To think that she'd actually believed he meant those vows he made, at least the one about *keep you only unto her.* "Bejesus, Tyler!" she accused bitterly, spinning to retreat, not to their room, but to her own.

However, in her haste, she failed to account for the train of her gown and nearly tripped over its ruffles and lace. She caught herself on the rail just as Jackson reached her.

"Erin . . ."

"You lying polecat, don't you ever talk to me about love!" She squirmed in the grip that circled her waist and stomped his foot.

"For the love of God, be still or we'll both go down the steps!"

The bottle clanged against the metal railing as she was hauled up from the first step of her retreat and Erin's eyes gleamed with fury. Thumb firmly entrenched in its neck, she shook it and twisted to let her captor catch the explosion of foam and liquor full in the face.

With an equally explosive curse of astonishment, Jackson loosened his hold only to receive the full force of the bottle in his stomach. As he went backward with the blow, his feet slipped on the wet surface of the step and, instead of catching the fiery lace-bedecked spitfire who pulled away from him, he grabbed at the rail to keep from falling on her.

"Erin, damn it . . . I can explain . . ."

"You ought to have that tongue of yours stuffed and mounted you smooth-talking sonovabitch!"

Jackson cleared his eyes of the champagne in time to duck the bottle that flew past his head and slammed against the bulkhead. As he quickly climbed to his feet, however, the only sight he caught of his bride was a fleeting glimpse of her train as it was snatched inside the door leading to cabins on the texas below. Swearing profusely, he picked up the bottle, which had miraculously not broken and hurled it down the hall, not taking time to see if it smashed or not, for his temper had been pushed to its limit with the damnable set of circumstances, innocent as they were, that set off his new and tempestuous bride.

Behind the bolted door of her old room, Erin listened between gasping breaths as Jackson's booted steps sounded in the hall. It was over, she thought in utter desolation and wounded contempt. There was a saying about the streets that if something sounded too good to be true, it generally was, but fool that she had been, she'd believed in the fairy tale Jackson had so cunningly built around before her. She'd walked in like a wide-eyed innocent, ridden with guilt and he . . .

"Erin!" The door jarred with the impact of Jackson's shoulder. "Open the door or I'll take it down!"

"Go ahead! Maybe you'll break your fool neck!"

Jackson's voice dropped to a semblance of normal

as he struggled for control long enough to let some passengers who had come in from the deck proceed to their cabin. "Things are not as they appear. I'd like a chance to explain, but not from out here in the hall. For the love of God, Erin, there are passengers out here," he uttered urgently after the door closed behind them. He wiped away some of the foam from the champagne that still clung to the damp curls of his chest in distaste. It was no wonder the female looked as if she were about to swoon in shock. He checked his hair which had been just as thoroughly soaked and groaned.

"Things weren't as they appeared when you thought I was stealing your damned silver, but you wouldn't listen to me!" a desolate voice rejoined from the other side of the door. "You believe I went to Lil to get rid of your baby, but you won't hear my side of it. You just say it doesn't matter. Well, I can't ignore things like that. They do matter to me. So why don't you go back to her and leave me alone?"

Jackson rolled his eyes toward the ceiling as a single gentleman strolled into the passageway. Leaning up against the wall, he let the stranger pass. "All right, I was wrong. Let me in and we'll both have our say." The man glanced back over his shoulder and Jackson glared at him, daring him to even wonder what was amiss. At that moment nothing would please him more than to throttle someone, even this unlucky soul.

"You sonovabitch! You *were* with her!" Erin shouted, mistaking his admission for the most immediate of his alleged crimes.

"No!" Jackson slammed the wall with his fist in exasperation, sending the intruder into a swifter pace that carried him out the midship hatch to the deck instead of to his cabin. "Erin, I am going to count to five and if this door is not opened willingly, I am going to go below and get Reds to help me dismantle it so that I will be hail and hearty when I get my hands on you. Now will you have me bring the crew in on this as well, or can we keep this among ourselves and discuss it rationally?"

Silence.

"One, two, three . . ."

"Your word of honor that you'll not touch me."

"Yes!" Jackson hissed, unable to make his tone as convincing as he would have had it. Strangulation had occurred to him as a possibility, were he one to spite himself to satisfy a grudge. More silence. "Four . . ." he resumed threateningly.

The bolt clicked and his fifth count faded on his lips. He straightened as the door opened a crack to reveal eyes reddened with tears and a trembling chin poorly reinforced by the bottom lip firmly clamped between teeth. Jealousy? The dawning of the idea rising about his indignation struck him with wonder as he entered the room at his companion's wary bidding. It was an emotion he hadn't associated with Erin and not altogether annoying now that he considered it in less aggravating circumstances— even if it was unfounded.

He had hurt her, nonetheless. As a rule, Erin was stingy with her tears, not the sort to use them to undermine a man's defenses. And Jackson could see how she had come to her conclusion, erroneous as it was.

"Gina was sick," he told her quietly. "She was upset over J.P. and had too much to drink. I got her out of the main salon just before she embarrassed herself and her family." He rubbed his chest self-consciously "But not before she ruined my jacket and shirt. I'd left her with Hannah and was about to change and rejoin you when we . . . met."

"Is that why you were drinking with her in the casino before the wedding?"

Jackson nodded. "J.P. took off after a prospective

business deal and left her to go to New Orleans without him. But he'll catch up with her there, like me, I think he's met his match.''

Erin looked away from the silver gaze that met hers. It was a plausible explanation, she supposed. Gina had been upset earlier, although Erin was so enrapt in her own quandary she'd hardly paid attention.

"Why don't we go to our room so that I can clean up a bit?"

Erin's eyes widened as she glanced up to see him only a hand's breadth away. "No," she protested, walking to the dressing table to put a comfortable distance between them. "I haven't had my say yet."

"All right. Go ahead."

Erin watched through the mirror as her companion poured water into the washbowl and took out his impatience in scrubbing his chest and arms. It was a harmless enough gesture, yet the soap smeared over the flexing ridges of muscles and sinew was somehow distracting. Until it stopped and she realized that he realized she was staring.

"Well?"

Disgruntled by the knowing gleam that lighted in Jackson's eye, she pretended to examine the inlay on the dressing table. "I admit that before I met you, I had been party to helping Cready in his street work, though I made most of my money thimblerigging." Her voice dropped. "Mama wouldn't have been proud of either." At Jackson's acknowledging silence, she continued. "I earned my keep at the MacCreadys by washing dishes at the saloon and helping Miss Molly with the kids . . . and ever since I've been on this boat I've earned my keep and never stole a cent's worth of anything. That polecat Sturgis put the silver there to make you hate me," she averred, adding miserably, "and it worked, too!"

"Erin, I could never hate you. Why didn't you tell

me before now?"

"You wouldn't have listened."

"I'm sorry I gave you reason to think that." Jackson toweled his chest and leaned over the washbowl to pour the rest of the water over his hair.

How could she not believe him? Her offense wavered further as she became distracted by his ministrations. She had seen many things in Under the Hill, but had never watched a man perform his toilette. She didn't think she'd ever seen bearded Mac MacCready or his son bathe, unless she counted the times she and Cready went buck bathing in the river when they were younger. At any rate, she could hardly compare either of the men she knew to Jackson Tyler. With his skin still faintly bronzed from the summer sun and dark hair tousled by the rough toweling he'd given it, he looked like some pagan prince, untamed and virile.

"Would you care to step into our room, Mrs. Tyler?"

Erin swallowed dryly. "I'm not finished. I . . . I want everything settled between us before we . . . go to our room," she finished, her skin burning with color.

Jackson slung the towel on the washstand in a ball and combed his hair with his fingers in frustration as he dropped on the edge of the mattress that had been her bed. "Well?"

"About the . . . the jewels you gave me for Christmas," she stammered nervously. "Since they had my name on them, I figured they were mine and I meant to use them to run away."

"Because you didn't think I would marry you?"

"I didn't want you to have to." Erin drew in a deep breath to steady her voice against the pain that surged through her mind at the recollection. "And I didn't want to embarrass Miss Auralee after she'd tried so hard to make me a lady."

"So you conspired with Gina to get away, using her own desperate plight to escape us all."

Erin's face went blank in disbelief of what she was hearing. "You know about Gina's baby?"

"I'm afraid she confessed the whole thing to me just before she lost what little dinner she'd consumed. She had no idea she was endangering you by asking you to take her there and was upset afterward when she heard what had happened. I don't blame you, Erin. I was foolish to have listened to Horsey to start with and later, the doctor said not to discuss it . . . that it would upset you."

A sick wave washing over her, Erin buried her face in her arms. "And it didn't bother you? That even though I lost my baby by accident, I helped Gina get rid of hers and they were both yours." A sob erupted, shaking her shoulders. "And then I saw you coming out of her room and I . . . I . . ."

Jackson pulled the distraught girl into his arms. "Erin, Erin," he coaxed gently, "what are you saying?"

"What was I to th . . . think?" she sniffed against his chest. "I know you and she have been . . . that you . . ." Try as she might, Erin could not bring herself to say that Gina and Jackson were lovers. It was too personal, too much an intrusion on what she'd treasured for her and Jackson alone.

"You think *I* was the father of Gina's child?" Jackson wasn't one to apologize for, let alone explain his past, particularly to women, but this called for an exception. "I was not the father of that baby, Erin," he grated out in an attempt to check his irritation. "Gina and I . . . well, whatever was between us ended a long time ago on my part. She has always been a flirtatious sort and I've played her game, but not to the extent we're speaking of here."

"But she said you were the baby's father and . . . and I know you've kissed her . . ."

"We're not talking about kissing here," Jackson countered sharply. "Damnation, Erin, can't you see what she did? She used our relationship to get her way. She obviously knew that if she told you it was mine, you'd help her."

"But I was going to run away anyway," Erin murmured miserably as Jackson's words began to make sense. "How could she do such a thing? I've felt so guilty I couldn't even think about the happiness you were promising. I . . . I was afraid if you ever found out that you would take back all the things you said . . . that you wouldn't love me . . ."

Jackson hugged Erin tightly as she began to cry with all her heart exposed to him. Now it all made sense, the fact that no matter what he did or how he tried, he could not overcome Erin's reticence with him. Not only did she bear her own guilt, but his as well, thinking he was the father of her lost child as well as Gina Allen's. Damn his lovely and calculating neighbor to hell! The feline antics that at one time amused him had gone too far.

"I ought to drag her lying carcass out of that bed and make her tell you the truth."

Erin tightened her embrace as he pulled away. "No! I . . . I believe you." She caught his face between her hands and looked up at him through her tears. "I guess we . . . we're more alike than I thought. I'm j . . . just as stupid as you are."

The fleeting vengeance vanished at the sight of the smile battling to the tear-stained face turned up to him. Her lips trembled a breath from his, begging to be assuaged. Tenderly, he grazed them with his own, persistent until they began to return the little pecks he bestowed, hungry for more. Yet, as she swayed against him, he backed away and captured her hand to his lips.

Eyes glittering with fire, like the diamond displayed in its silver setting on the lapel of his discarded jacket on the floor, reached into hers, seizing Erin's very soul. "I, Jackson," he began in a low and fervently earnest tone, "do take you, Erin, to love, honor, cherish, and *trust*," he said, planting an emphatic kiss on the hand where his ring sparkled in the lamplight, "until death do us part, so help me God."

Words failed her. Enrapt in the magical spell he so fervently cast, Erin whispered a heartfelt, "Me too," as she took possession of the lips that had made her world whole again and imparted her earnest response with all her being.

This time there was no propriety to be honored, no audience to limit the expression of her love for Jackson, love that had been denied long enough. There was only delay sufficient for Jackson to sweep her up in his arms and carry her across the hall to the suite he had designed specifically for them, for the hidden fires that burned in her veins would no longer be ignored.

Their hands could not move fast enough or efficiently enough to remove their clothing, which, after a tedious trial with the fastens of her dress, lay in a reckless pile beside the large brass bed that replaced his old bunk. Such were the sensations of delight stemming from Jackson's urgent worship of her naked body that Erin did not see the beautiful drapes cascading from a large brass coronet that canopied the top third of the bed. Nor did she notice the decorative stove that warmed the cabin against the chilly winter river night, for the heat of a tropical storm consumed her, a storm that grew in intensity as their bodies eagerly joined, flesh against flesh.

Whispers of passionate endearments and moans of ecstasy rose above the gales of desire which carried them spinning wantonly into the heavens of carnal pleasure. Blood-stirring caresses and furtive clutches added fuel to the flames that burst forth with lightning speed until perspiring bodies shuddered with the thunderous explosion of sweet release. Absorbed in the most intimate of embraces they drifted down, bodies entwined, to bask in the afterglow of the storm. The other passengers on the *Delta Moon* danced to the music wafting in the air from the deck below and strolled along the lantern-lit promenade to enjoy the view of the calm river carrying them surely toward their destination. With the silver moon casting its placid spell over the winter night, no one except the lovers knew of the wild tempest that had left them drained and contentedly sleeping in each other's arms.

The same moon filtered its way through the torn curtain of a window on an alley behind the Crescent City's Gallatin Street, casting grotesque shadows across a rusty iron bed, its green paint long having chipped away in all but a few places. A woman lay on it, stripped to the waist, her wrists bound to a headboard above her head. Her eyes were wide with a fear like she'd never known as the man who had kept her there for two days without food approached the bed with the riding crop that had been her torture, even in the scarce times when sleep would take her away from her living nightmare.

"If you try to run away again before I am through with you, my dear, I shall have to kill you." He straightened the lapel of his jacket in the fastidious manner she'd come to despise.

Elena Cadiz had never seen him in anything less than a three-piece suit, no matter what services he required of her. He slapped the whip across her breast and she screamed in agony. No man would ever look at her after what he'd done, she realized through the pain-dulled fog of her mind. She should have just left the city when she'd heard John Davenport was asking around for her, instead of going to Woodward.

But she'd thought him a gentleman then, a gentleman of means who would reward her for the news that the thugs she'd hired had not killed the gambler after all. Now she knew he was a demon from the pits of hell and not a man at all. At least, not in the sense she knew men. Instead of rewarding her, he had beaten her senseless, inflicting the ugly gash across her cheek with his ring. Since then, she'd been kept like an animal. No, she thought bitterly, not even animals were treated as inhumanely.

"Soon I shall have another to replace you, one I can count on to help me get my revenge." Her tormentor smiled, exposing crooked teeth, as if there were too many to fit in the narrow allotment afforded them.

"And you will let . . . let me go?" Elena asked hoarsely. Her lips were dried and cracked from lack of water.

"If you please me. Shall I untie you now?"

She licked her lips. "Yes. I will do anything you wish."

Pleased by her answer, the man unfastened the ropes that had cut into her wrists. "Then you will strip and bathe. I want no part of you in your unkempt state."

Elena drew her wrists to her mouth as they were freed, as if to soothe their burning and curled on her side. The mere weight of her full and badly bruised breasts caused her to wince.

"Now, young lady!"

The leather crop hissed through the air, biting into the flesh of her arm. With a squeal, she leapt from the bed and swayed unsteadily, her legs weak from the confinement. Her hands worked frantically to remove the rest of her blouse and skirts. She shed her garments as if they were on fire and rushed to the washbowl her keeper had meticulously kept full of fresh water. He was adamant about cleanliness if she was expected to touch him.

"And put fresh linens on the bed."

"Will I have food?" Elena applied the scented soap to her abused skin in haste, hoping that he would at least allow her a morsel before he had his vulgar way with her. She forced a smile, unaware that in her effort to appease him she turned his stomach.

The only women who intrigued him at all were those who had spirit. This one had broken, but he would keep her until the *Delta Moon* arrived. He'd waited a lifetime for this revenge and spent most of the money that he'd embezzled from the bank where he'd worked until Coleman Horsey had contacted him. He never guessed the favors he owed the man for providing him the sort of feminine entertainment he did crave from time to time would lead him to discover a nemesis he'd thought killed during the war.

How many lives could a man have? he wondered, adjusting his spectacles up on his nose. His half brother had missed him in that absurd duel over the dark-haired beauty that had captured his fancy. He had escaped the sheriff and apparently emerged unscathed from the war. Once again framed for murder, he slipped easily from the hands of the law and then from the clutches of two of New Orleans' most practiced villains.

Only this time the gambler's luck had run out, the man mused, smacking his fist into his other hand to vent the years of unrequited rage burning in his soul. Jacques Devareau would pay with his life for killing Henry . . . dear fickle Henry whom he'd loved as more than a brother. The bitter taste of betrayal rose in the back of his throat, to think his half brother had lost his life over a useless woman. A damned raven-haired wench with green eyes.

His breath came quick with the anticipation of the

plans he'd made personally this time, to avoid the complications that came with incompetent help. It had cost him dearly, but he had found out all he needed to know about Jackson Tyler's plans to celebrate Mardi Gras with his new bride.

Women, he seethed, an answering smile coming to his lips as Elena turned away in satisfaction, thinking her sustenance guaranteed. They made most men weak. He hated them. Almost as much as the man who had taken Henry from him, the lover who had an irritating fondness for them, especially those with long dark hair and satin smooth skin.

# Chapter Twenty-Six

Erin's gown was new and it made her favorite seem shoddy in comparison. Made of ivory and emerald tulle and *peau de soie*, it made her feel almost as much a queen as the husband who helped her into it. Since their wedding night, Jackson insisted on helping her into and out of her clothing himself, forbidding Mary to enter their private haven. As a consequence, they were frequently late, for his assistance was not without a familiar touch here and there that would lead to a playful romp on the big brass bed. Although no one said anything, there were sly looks Erin could not help but notice. However, when she pointed that out to her irascible mate, he merely shrugged it off as jealousy.

"I don't think it's fair that you know what I am going to look like, but I won't know you," she grumbled peevishly, adjusting the shoulders of the dress he'd pulled disgracefully low to reveal her corseted breasts. Jackson and John were members of the krewe and hence, to be costumed and in the parade itself. "Jackson, you'll squash the flowers!" She slapped his hand away from the edging of silk petals adorning her neckline, her pout quirking threateningly toward a smile.

"Why not, I intend to pick them later," he quipped deviously.

"Not if I dance away with some complete stranger, thinking he's my husband."

Upon seeing the genuine concern on his wife's face, Jackson finished the last of the fastens and circled her waist with his hands. It fascinated him that his fingers could almost touch on either side. "All right, I'll be dressed as a pirate. Our krewe is honoring Jean and Pierre Lafite and their part in the Battle of New Orleans. I'll have a black-bearded papier-mâché mask and be wearing red balloon trousers. The mask is rather unbecoming, but . . ."

A brisk knock interrupted him followed by John Davenport's, "Come on, Tyler. We'll be late for the warehouse!"

"I'd love to take you with me, sweet, but this is for men only," he commiserated at Erin's fallen face. "I promise to reclaim your hand at the ball. In the meantime, I entrust you to my family's care." Taking her in his arms, he laid claim to her lips, his hands slipping familiarly over the curve of her breast to free it from its flowery bed.

"Bejesus, Tyler!" she gasped as he pulled away and planted a loud kiss on its budding tip. While his mischievous familiarity never ceased to delight her, she doubted she would ever become accustomed to it.

"That's exactly what I say, you devil! Will you let your wife dress and get out here?" John bellowed from the hall to Erin's mortification.

But after Jackson grabbed his coat and ducked through the door, a giggle escaped, ending with a wistful sigh. Happy? What went beyond happy, Erin wondered, trying to find a description suitable for what she had shared with her husband the past few days. If she were to draw her last breath that very moment, she knew what it was to love with every fiber of her being and be loved in the same way.

Behind the door of their suite—for now the cabin had been expanded to contain the little room that

410

had been hers for a while, allowing room for some parlor furniture at one end—they had both disregarded their inhibitions and been themselves. Sometimes they were like children, laughing and teasing as they discovered each other again and again. At others, passion would flare up to engulf them until they were lost in a world of the senses, savoring the sweet torment of the moment.

And the book that Mariette had given her, Erin found out firsthand, was no more than pure hogwash! If she and Jackson were weak-minded as a result of the frequent lovemaking that marked their downriver sojourn, then it was with love. And Jackson had disproved the myth that coupling for the male was equivalent to the loss of fourteen ounces of blood. If that were the case, he'd have been bone dry and dead by the time they reached St. Francisville!

A naughty smile played on her lips as Erin resumed her preparations for the parade, recalling his howling laughter when she'd timidly confessed how Mariette had led her to believe she ought to pay him for the first time he'd made love to her—that she'd meant it as a compliment, not an insult. The fact was, it was a good thing she didn't have to pay for his attentions, for she'd not have a penny of her inheritance left by now.

The parade was a spectacular sight, one Erin wished she could have shared with her husband at her side. She had heard the grand celebration described as too magnificent for words—the marching bands, the elaborate costumes and imaginative floats—and now she knew why. Not even the showboats and circuses that came through Natchez from time to time could compare to this grandeur.

Floats depicting the Battle of New Orleans made their way down Royal Street past the balcony of the St. Louis from which she and her companions viewed the proceedings. The streets were thick with costumed people, some in elaborate trappings and others having donned outdated clothes and a mask. There were British soldiers who were booed, rough-shod colonials who where cheered as they waited beyond stacks of cotton bales with their muskets, and then there were the bands of pirates moving in and out of the elaborate floats stealing kisses and handing out candies and cheap jewelry to the adoring populace.

Those who took to the streets often stopped long enough to brush off a dusting of flour or dirt tossed out by urchins in the trees hanging over the parade route. Police moved back and forth in the chaos trying to catch the young scoundrels who always seemed to be on the opposite side of the street. By the time they made it through the marching bands and parade participants, their quarry had moved to another block.

Over the sound of a band marching to the notes of "If Ever I Cease to Love," a small cannon fired from the deck of a massive pirate ship that crept up the street with the King and Queen of the krewe to mark the end of the parade. Erin drew her attention from some British costumed acrobats in front of them who were in hilarious retreat to watch with baited breath.

As the ship drew near, drawn by six horses, a rollicking fight ensued, live with the clash of steel and the discharges of unloaded muskets. Smoke drifted up from the street amid the howls of delight from the observers while pirates of every size and shape scaled riggings and dueled on deck.

Anxiously, Erin scanned the unsavory-looking crew for the handsome pirate who had stolen her heart. There were three men who had red balloon trousers like the eastern pirates of the Red Sea, but only one could have been Jackson. The one clinging to the rigging as if his life depended on it was too stout, straining the stitches the costume-maker had made to their limit, while the other waving a threatening cutlass at the crowd, was too thin. His voluminous drawers were pressed by the brisk river breeze around scrawny calves that looked like the peg legs belonging to some of the most notorious of the swashbucklers of Bayou Barataria.

Her pirate was the man dueling furiously at the main mast, his sturdy legs, equally well defined by the playful breeze, drawing more than one pair of admiring feminine eyes as he danced about with catlike grace, just a step ahead of his opponent's flashing blade. That both men were schooled in the art of fencing was apparent and the show was greatly appreciated by all. However, as the ship came abreast of them, Jackson sent his partner sprawling against the deck with a flying kick and scampered up the main mast, his cutlass in his teeth.

The other pirate bellowed in rage and, picking himself up, started after Jackson to the encouraging shouts of the onlookers. Just as it appeared that he was to be caught, Jackson grabbed a line and swung away, landing, not on the deck, but on the street beyond. Erin peered over the edge of the balcony to see him climbing up a drainpipe covered in ivy, a fearsome spectacle had she not known who he was. As the crowd below cheered ecstatically, he grabbed the rail and swung over to the balcony.

Reaching into his shirt, he pulled out a long medallion and placed it over Erin's head. "Booty for the laidee!" he shouted, before enchanting his audience and his bride by seizing her and stealing a kiss through the stiff mask.

Erin was still laughing and wiping some of the paint that had flaked off his red paper mâché lips as he took to the drainpipe and returned to his ship.

"Well, I don't have to guess who that was," Jennifer Tyler Allen teased as her new sister-in-law examined the medallion made of tin and stamped with a heart. "I never knew Jackson was so romantic and . . ."

"Wild," Auralee Tyler finished, clutching her chest in relief to see he was safely back on the ship and dueling once more. "But then, love does strange things to people, I suppose."

"You could learn something from your friend," Gina Allen remarked petulantly to J.P. Stevens, who had joined them as promised a day later.

"Yes, I'll buy you a cheap medallion for pennies instead of that ten dollar bonnet," Stevens countered jauntily, threatening to remove the conciliatory offering he'd made the moment he'd set foot in New Orleans.

Gina smacked his hand away. "Don't you dare, you naughty boy! Although you needn't think you are totally forgiven . . . at least not yet," she added with a perfect moue of disapproval. "You're just lucky that Jackson agreed to get you an invitation to the ball after missing his wedding like that."

"I don't think he missed me overmuch," the railroad man rejoined, giving Erin a devilish wink.

"I wonder which of the pirates was John?" Erin asked, turning the embarrassing subject away from her.

"He was the cannoneer, dear," Auralee Tyler informed her. All eyes turned upon Jackson's mother. Her tastefully rouged cheeks heightened in color to reach a natural shade that matched that of her daughter-in-law's.

Gina, not about to let the faux pas escape, gasped in mock astonishment. "Why, Miss Auralee, I didn't think the men were allowed to give away their identities!" A general amusement took over the entire assembly, for the teasing was meant purely in fun. If Auralee Tyler had ever made an enemy, it was not known to anyone in Natchez.

After a lavish buffet at the St. Louis, the Tyler-Allen entourage refreshed their appearance before taking a covered coach to the auditorium at Beauregarde Square. Upon presenting their engraved invitations, they were led into the large ballroom. Erin thought it had to be at least four times greater than that at the Allen mansion as she observed the massive steps ahead of them that flared to the left and right from a landing midway to a balcony above. The gallery, reserved for observers only, was supported by a series of arches and columns, giving it a regal and fitting appearance.

"What sort of ball is this where we have to sit and watch?" J.P. Stevens complained in disgruntled surprise as Gina pointed to the seats above.

"Darling, we are only guests to observe the proceedings. The ball is strictly for the krewe and its ladies. To watch alone is an honor," his escort explained gaily. "Once, I was given a call-out card to sit below there with the women and I thought I had reached the very highest honor next to being chosen queen herself. Jackson had just been invited to join the krewe and . . ." Gina stopped herself and glanced at Erin self-consciously.

Erin, however, was too fascinated by the glorious decorations that glittered from every column and arch in the massive ballroom to notice, let alone comment. A miniature of the parade ship dominated the scene at the opposite end, bearing upon it the gilded thrones of the King and Queen as well as the chairs of their court. Jennifer had explained that the court would enter first, followed by the remaining members of the krewe. Partially hidden beyond the ship were two giant open doors where a flurry of activity marked the arrival of the parade participants. From the sounds of singing and laughter, they had already begun their celebration.

"Excuse me, Mrs. Tyler, but I have call-out cards

for you."

Auralee Tyler stopped at the foot of the stairs, her mouth dropping open in astonishment. Suddenly she laughed. "He must mean you, dear," she told Erin fondly.

"Actually, madame, I have cards for two of you . . . a Mrs. Robert Tyler and a Mrs. Jackson Tyler."

"Why, Mother, you sly devil!" Jennifer Tyler Allen razzed, her eyes twinkling in delight. She gave her mother a big hug.

"I thought there was more than friendship between you and that partner of Jackson's," Myra Allen chimed in heartily. "Although, you'll pardon me if my complexion hints of green."

The elder Mrs. Tyler stared at the cards handed her in utter amazement, as if some mistake had been made. "Now, Myra," she drawled, recovering with an inborn poise Erin often admired, "I am certain that Jackson and John must have been concerned, leaving Erin down there alone. You well know that Mr. Davenport and I are merely friends."

"Humph!" Myra Allen sniffed knowingly. "If I were in your shoes . . ."

"But you're not," her husband grumbled irritably. "Now move on up the steps, Mother. We're holding up the folks."

"If you ladies will come with me . . ."

The gentleman who presented their cards started to usher them toward the chairs on the floor itself when someone called Erin's name out above the murmur of the arriving guests. Glancing up at the gallery, Erin saw an elegantly gowned woman waving a sequined mask at her and recognized Lydia Lafon. At her side was her husband, just as formally attired. After they'd sent apologies for not attending the wedding, Erin was shocked that the woman would even acknowledge her, even though

416

Jackson had agreed to signing the Royal Street residence over to them. She lifted her hand to return the greeting.

"Mrs. Tyler."

At the floorman's prompt, she joined him and Miss Auralee to go to their places of honor. "Are the Lafons members of this krewe?" Jackson's mother asked curiously.

"Indeed not, madame. Ours is a newer organization. As this year's captain of the Mystic krewe of Comus, the good doctor does us honor to acknowledge us. He and his wife will be recognized officially by our king and queen later and invited to preside over the ball with them."

"No wonder they couldn't come to your wedding, child!" Auralee Tyler remarked meaningfully. "Your family belongs to New Orleans' oldest and most prestigious krewe, and with the doctor as captain, I would imagine they've been frantic with entertaining and last minute work since Christmas! My daughter-in-law is an Asante, Mrs. Lafon's niece," she explained sweetly to their escort.

The comment must have made an impression, for instead of giving them seats on the second row where the committee member had stopped, he reconsidered and moved them to the first. "Please listen attentively for your names to be called, ladies. Once the music and dancing begins, it's very difficult to hear our announcements and misunderstandings can be embarrassing for us all."

Intrigued by this new concept in parties, Erin forgot her aunt for the moment and studied her engraved card. *Mrs. Jackson Tyler.* That meant much more to her than her lineage. A girl couldn't chose her relatives, that was God's doing, Miss Molly used to say. Her friends, or husband in this case, were a different matter.

It still seemed like a dream, less real than their

make-believe surroundings. Yet the emeralds glistening on her hand reflecting the brilliant light of the chandeliers tinkling overhead in the breeze were proof positive.

A loud burst of trumpets from the orchestra seated on a raised platform to their left heralded the entrance of the royalty. A page standing at the foot of the steps leading to the ship stage announced the majesties of the krewe, who according to Auralee Tyler still were not to know each other's identities until later in the night. The king appeared to be much older than his queen. Still, he was a striking figure in tight-fitting black breeches and large cuffed boots. His gold brocade frock coat parted to reveal pistols strapped across his broad chest as he escorted his young queen to her throne and seated her.

"Their identities are kept secret until the unveiling at midnight, which only adds to the mystique of it all," Jackson's mother whispered in Erin's ear. "But you can be sure the queen is beautiful. It's a position saved for only the most cultivated of southern flowers . . . and that girl will keep that gown forever. She'd rather give up her life than get rid of it."

The queen's polonaise costume was made of royal blue damask over a white ruffled silk underskirt that ballooned so wide with crinolines that it required care to sit on the velvet throne prepared for her. Her ladies in waiting were dressed in similiar period costumes, wearing wreaths of flowers as opposed to her ostrich-plumed headdress. Surely real royalty could not have appeared more regal, Erin mused in open admiration.

Once the entire krewe was inside the auditorium the music began with the king and queen, and then the court, leading off the dancing. Members of the floor committee marched up and down in front of the selected ladies seated at the edge of the dance floor calling out names. Once the lady acknowledged her name, she was presented to the masked krewe member who had submitted her card in advance and whisked away to the romantically portrayed Orleans of 1812.

When Mrs. Robert Tyler's name was called, Jackson's mother reminded Erin of some of the younger girls smiling brilliantly on the front row. She strained to see the surly-looking pirate making his way toward the woman, amazed that the same man could be the polished and charming John Davenport. Although he approached with a limp, it disappeared the moment he waltzed away with his prize in his arms.

Women from all around were called as Erin scanned the crowd for her handsome rogue in the red trousers. When John returned Auralee Tyler to her seat in order to claim a dance with one of the wives of a fellow krewe member to whom he owed a favor, she questioned him as to Jackson's whereabouts.

"He got a message from the boat and slipped out back to see what it was. He'll be along," John assured her.

"Nothing serious, I hope."

"He didn't seem to think so. He said . . . there he is now."

Erin looked over to where one of the announcers took a card from her pirate and called out, "Mrs. Jackson Tyler!"

Eagerly, she rose and waited for him to claim her hand. She laughed as he bowed lowly and pointed to the crowded dance floor. "How long will you wear that mask? It must be hot!"

Jackson nodded emphatically and slipped his hand behind her. The moment they fell in with the circling crowd, however, Erin knew something was amiss. Her partner wasn't as tall as Jackson. The mask lent him some height, but his shoulder height and breadth could not be disguised.

419

And there was no hesitation at all when Jackson led her. Erin knew instinctively which way he wanted her to go. This man was more awkward, with jerky movements rather than the smooth ones so typical of her husband. The corner of her mouth tugging into a smile, she stepped closer and looked dreamily into his eyes.

"This is the most lovely moment of my life," she sighed, playing along with her husband's trick. She was certain Jackson was watching them from somewhere in the room to see what she'd do. That's what she got for putting the notion in his head with her fretting. "Thank you for marrying me, Mr. Tyler." Impulsively, she bussed the papier-mâché face on the cheek.

"You know I am not your husband, Miss Deva-reau, so please refrain from your antics," a familiar voice snapped from inside the mask.

Erin nearly stumbled in shock. "Sturgis?"

"You've very perceptive. Now I am going to dance over toward the doors. You'll come with me . . ."

"No!"

Hands jerked tight at her waist as she started to pull away. "If you want to see your father alive, you will come with me."

"My father?" she gasped. Her mind staggered with the blow of his statement. "But my father is dead . . . and *where is Jackson?*" she demanded, fear giving way to alarm. She couldn't imagine Jackson handing his costume over to Sturgis.

"Your husband is nursing a nasty crack on the head, but he was not seriously injured. It's you I'm after. Your father, who is very much alive, wishes to see you. Wouldn't you like to meet him?"

"Where is Jackson?" Erin insisted stubbornly.

"He is safe as long as you do as I say. Shall we go?"

Although they'd stopped dancing and made a hasty exit through the open doors, Erin's head was still spinning, almost as fast as the rapid beating of her heart. Jackson had to have been hurt worse than Sturgis indicated. *Her* Jackson!

Without hesitation, she climbed into a waiting coach on the back street and leaned against the seat, trying to collect her thoughts. She had to remain calm, she told herself, wishing she had but a portion of Auralee Tyler's self-command.

"Where is my husband?" she persisted with more calm than she felt.

"I told you he is safe." Roderick Sturgis pulled off the cumbersome mask and put it on the seat beside him.

"Where?"

"Even as we speak, we leave him behind. I'm certain members of his organization will find him, neatly trussed and gagged on his float, tomorrow when the festivities are over. It's you and your father that concern me."

"So he is safe." Erin closed her eyes in relief.

"Safe," her captor assured her. "My retaliation for the rough way he put me off his ship will be to let him live, wondering what happened to his wife. Believe me, living with a lost love is a torment worse than death."

"And my father? You say he is alive?" The coach turned and Erin tried to read the sign that passed too quickly, hoping to gain an idea of their destination. "Is that where we're going . . . to see him?"

Her feelings were mixed on that matter. Dead, he'd been a hero. Alive, he was the man who had left her and her mother in Under the Hill to the mercy of a man like Coleman Horsey. And if he chose friends like Roderick Sturgis, he couldn't be a man she'd want to meet. And why would he suddenly take an interest in meeting her now, let alone go to the dire extent he had to do so.

"A note would have sufficed," she spoke up. "You

needn't have assaulted my husband and kidnapped me. I would have agreed to meet my father anyway."

"You're not afraid." It was an observation more than a question.

Erin lifted her chin. "Not of the likes of you . . . and if my father is a similar bird, not of him either."

"Take off your dress."

Erin's front faltered. "What!"

"Take off your dress. It's much too fancy, not to mention cumbersome . . . and it will draw suspicion where we're going," he explained at the stubborn set of lips that sent his pulses pounding with anticipation. "There's a plain dress under there."

Reaching under the seat where Sturgis indicated, Erin found a package containing a freshly laundered and pressed dress of faded calico. So her father wasn't at all what she had hoped he'd be, she thought, ignoring her companion's blatant perusal as she set about unfastening her gown. Nor was he the gentleman her mother had longingly spoken of. If he was, he certainly wouldn't have left them.

Her arms ached from the awkward strain, but she would sooner spit than have Sturgis assist her with the fastens Jackson had playfully done up earlier. *Oh, Jackson!* How could her father be party to something like this? In the corner of her eye, she could see that Roderick Sturgis had withdrawn a small pocket knife and was at least pretending to scrape his nails with it. When she shed her gown and three of her four petticoats, however, he snapped it shut and dropped it in the baggy pocket of his trousers.

And he thought *she* was going to draw attention, she thought in disgust as an idea came to mind. She pulled the plain dress over her head and rose to her feet to straighten the skirt.

"What are you doing?"

"Fixing my skirts!" Erin answered with equal

sharpness. She judged the uneasy sway of the vehicle as it made its way through the narrow streets and when it leaned at the right angle, she gasped and fell against her captor.

Instinctively he caught her and even took some deviated pleasure in trying to hold her in spite of her frantic pushes to get away. When he finally let go, she scrambled to the opposite seat and drew to the farthest distance she could manage, the pocket knife securely in her hand. It wasn't much, but her captor wasn't nearly as intimidating now. Deftly, she slipped it into the slashed pocket of the dress to make her escape . . . after she met Jacques Devareau.

"My father lives here?"

Erin stared in disbelief at the ramshackle house that was separated from its equally dilapidated neighbors by a space barely wide enough for a man to walk through on either side. It was a story and a half, appearing to be a single room wide and deep from the glimpse she got as she crossed the muddy yard with Roderick Sturgis's fingers biting into the bare arm exposed by her summer dress.

The first-story windows were boarded up, indicating to Erin that no one lived there. But then, the house on either side boasted dim lights through the louvered shutters covering their windows and a woman's boisterous laugh echoed from inside one of them. The River Palace *was* a palace compared to the places in this back alley neighborhood. All thought that Natchez Under the Hill did not have a counterpart vanished in Erin's mind.

"Devareau does not live here, but he will die here."

Erin dug in at the startling statement, but was unceremoniously hurled into the room with more strength than she would have given the scrawny Roderick Sturgis credit for. The door was closed and a lock clicked ominously with the turn of a key, shutting off all light but the precious bit of moonlight seeping in through the spaces left by a missing louver in the shutters. It was, however sufficient for her captor to find a lamp and light it.

Gradually the room took shape. A steep and narrow staircase rose only a few feet from the front door, the thick newel post explaining the hard object that struck Erin's shoulder as she fell to the floor beyond. Two unmatched chairs were shoved under the round table bearing the only lamp and a threadbare settee rested against the stairwell. An equally worn round carpet covered the floor under the table in the center of the room, just short of the wide bare planks that had cushioned her fall. Although it was seedy in appearance, Erin could not help but notice that it was clean. No sand or dirt grated into her elbow as she picked herself up and rubbed her arms with a grudging look.

"You said my father wanted to meet me. Now you're telling me you plan to kill him. Just what do you intend to do, Sturgis?" She studied a closed door, wondering if that led to the back of the house or if it was a closet. As spotless as the place appeared, there was a faint stench coming from somewhere. Perhaps garbage in the backyard.

Her captor intercepted her thoughts. "There is no way out of this house except by this key. The shutters and windows are nailed to, as is that door. Should you make a nuisance of yourself, I shall have to bind you. Otherwise, you will remain free and do as I say."

"And just what is that? Sit back and watch you kill someone?"

"Torture first, then kill," he admitted with complete candor. "And I shall expect you to participate, my dear."

"You're crazy!" Erin's incredulity gave way to the realization that she was absolutely right. That made the affair more frightening, for she might deal with a rational man. An insane one was less predictable.

"That was an unkind thing to say," Sturgis tutted in disapproval. "And I'd tried so hard to make you a lady. I told you you would never make one . . . my tempestuous *Kate*."

Erin's gaze sharpened, but she let the name pass. She had to find out what he was up to before she could figure a way out of this mess. "Obviously, you've given this matter a lot of thought."

"Even since the moment I discovered Jacques Devareau had survived the war."

"So you knew him before the war?"

"I knew him," Sturgis muttered, contempt infiltrating his superior tone. "And I knew your mother. Imagine my shock to find the girl Coleman Horsey wanted me to watch for him was her very image. Even if your name had changed, I'd have known you. Your father and I both left the past behind us in Natchez as a result of his cowardice, but I never forgot the face of the woman who was our undoing."

Erin paled. "You work for Horsey?"

"Actually I used him. He wanted your money. I wanted your father."

"How . . . how do you know my father is alive?"

"I've seen him." Sturgis laughed and a chill ran up Erin's spine at the sound. "He didn't know me. No one ever paid attention to me except Henry."

"Henry?"

"My dear departed half brother. Jacques Devareau killed him in cold blood in a duel over your mother. She was so beautiful, she even tempted my Henry. Just as, I must admit, you tempt me, Kate."

"Stop calling me that!" Erin snapped scornfully. She recalled the way he'd chased her about the cabin, stopped only by her threats; and then they hadn't stopped him. Rubbing her hands over her hips against the reassuring bulge of the pocket knife, she took a seat at the table opposite her captor, all too aware of the flare of interest that had leapt to his weasellike gaze.

"Do you suppose I can tame you, Miss Devareau?"

"My name is *Mrs. Tyler* and I'll thank you to use it, you persnickety polecat." She hadn't gotten used to her new name, but somehow just saying it gave her courage. She prayed Jackson was all right, but Sturgis had lied about so many things . . .

"Starvation and a sound beating worked with . . . *Kate.*"

Erin glared across the table, but checked the additional names that came to her mind for her repugnant companion upon realizing that he was baiting her. There was almost an excited expectation in his beady gaze. "If my father is alive," she returned to the original subject primly, as if carrying on over tea and cake, "what makes you think he will come for me? After all, he abandoned my mother." It worked. She could almost see Sturgis's disappointment.

"He had to leave your mother or face a hangman's noose for the murder of my Henry. He cheated during the duel and fired before the count was up."

Giselle Devareau had never mentioned a duel. She said her husband had gone off to fight the war and died on some distant battlefield. She also said he was a gentleman with good family in Paris, although, admittedly, the black sheep of the family for his love of gambling. That explained his residence in New Orleans when they met and fell in love.

"I don't believe you. My father was a gentleman which, obviously was more than this Henry of yours was or he wouldn't have insulted a married woman." Her mother hadn't lied. Erin knew in her heart. "Were there witnesses?"

"Only me, I'm afraid. It was rather a spontaneous thing. Devareau caught Henry following his wife and called him out then and there. He sent her to await him at their rented room and went straight with us to the edge of town. He was so cocksure of himself, he didn't even seek a second. And well he didn't, since he fully intended to murder my brother."

"More than likely, your brother was as poor a shot as he was a fool."

Sturgis studied her quietly. "Henry knew he was a poor shot . . . but my brother was no fool. That's why he fired first."

"But you said . . ."

"I had forgotten that it doesn't matter whether you know what really happened or not. Actually, it was your father who was the fool. He had no friendly witnesses and hence, when I swore that he had fired prematurely, who were the authorities going to believe? The gambler or the sole survivor of one of Natchez's founding families. Yes, my dear girl," he told Erin upon seeing her amazed expression, "my blood is just as blue as yours, even though Henry mismanaged our money until all we had was our name and the townhouse. The name was enough to discredit your father's story. Gamblers were frowned upon on the bluff."

"Where is he now?"

"Why, celebrating the Mardi Gras, where else? I doubt that he will get my message about you until morning, so we've a long night ahead of us."

Too close to the answer of a question that had repeated itself in her mind for most of her eighteen years, Erin missed the suggestion of his words. "Who is he?"

"You'll see soon enough," Sturgis taunted, enjoying the masterful edge he had achieved. "I've heard it said that history repeats itself. Isn't it ironic that I was able to discredit your father as well as you?"

Erin's thoughts came to an abrupt stop, jarred by the still painful reminder of the travail caused by the stolen silver Jackson had found under her mattress— the peace and happiness it had robbed her and

Jackson of . . . just as he had robbed her father and her mother.

"You sneaking sonovabitch!"

The green fire that flared in her gaze was exactly what her companion had counted on, but the table that suddenly was flipped against him was not. Seeing the kerosene lamp sliding perilously toward the floor, he lunged for it as the chimney flipped off its base and broke into smithereens just ahead of him. Holding it up to keep the part containing the flammable fuel and fire from breaking, he fell full force on the glass, the table's edge cutting into his stomach.

Erin watched for a moment, uncertain of approaching him with the flaming lantern in his hand. He had the key. She fumbled for the knife in her pocket as he threw the table aside and rolled away from the glass. Unless there was a way out upstairs, she thought in desperation. Shaking the imaginary weights from her legs, she darted for the staircase and up the steps as her captor climbed unsteadily to his feet.

"You won't like it up there!" he shouted as he stumbled after her. "I haven't cleaned! You can't get away, Kate!"

Erin ducked as her head brushed the slanted ceiling of the upper room and groped toward the light shafting in through the dormer. Behind her, she could hear Sturgis's pursuing footsteps and plunged ahead. Her legs struck the edge of a bed and before she could catch herself, she sprawled across it, the knife in her hand clattering to the floor on the other side.

Cold fingers seemed to creep up her spine, raising the hair on the nape of her neck as she realized that there was something or someone, on the mattress beside her. The stench that she had assumed to be garbage in the back filled her nostrils full force as she reluctantly ventured to explore the nature of it when

428

the light from Roderick Sturgis's lamp cast its glow over them. Blinking her eyes, Erin stared into the wide lifeless gaze of Elena Cadiz, or a woman that might have been her. A scream mingled with bile in the back of her throat as she slowly drew away.

"I told you I hadn't cleaned."

"She . . . she's dead!" Erin gasped, raising her arm to cover her nostrils.

"I don't know if it was the lack of food or the beatings," the man behind her puzzled aloud.

Stricken with disbelief, Erin turned slowly.

"But you're a survivor, aren't you, Kate?"

Before Erin could even think of an answer to the bloodcurdling inquiry, a blow struck the side of her face. She fell backward, twisting frantically to avoid the bed as the light from the lamp flickering above her exploded into tiny fragments of pain and quickly disintegrated into darkness . . . darkness that swallowed her up and gently cushioned the hard landing on the floor beneath her.

# Chapter Twenty-Seven

"Damn it, why the bloody hell didn't you tell me about this before now?" Jackson Tyler shouted at John Davenport above the ache of his pounding head.

"Jackson, please!" his mother fretted, her hands wringing as she stepped between the two men. "Anger will not help this dreadful situation."

Jackson glared at his partner over her head, fists clenched in frustration, and swung away to pace over to the window of the Decatur Street office. He knew she was right, but somehow his pent-up rage had to find some vent and John Davenport certainly deserved his portion.

"I admit to being a coward, if that is what you mean to say, sir," John spoke up quietly. "Would you have wanted your daughter to know you were the man who abandoned her mother to that hellacious life in Under the Hill?"

"But you said you thought your wife had returned to her family in New Orleans," Auralee Tyler pointed out, not wanting to believe John Davenport, or Jacques Devareau the scoundrel he admitted to be. "How could you have known her family had lied about her death when you tried to find her after the war?"

"Madame, I knew the moment I saw Erin that she was my daughter. I should have told her then."

"Or at least told me!" Jackson boomed over his shoulder sardonically. "For the love of God, John, I knew you were no saint, but to risk Erin's life to hide your past . . ."

"I thought the whole affair over with Horsey behind bars," Davenport commiserated dejectedly. "It wasn't until you mentioned the name Woodward that I knew I was involved . . . and I had thought the man dead!"

"You should have said something then!" Jackson insisted hoarsely. "I might have been on guard."

"I put people to work the minute I set foot in the city to find Henry Woodward. Could you have done more?"

"I wouldn't have left Erin's side for a moment, let alone fallen for such an obvious trick to get me out of the way!"

Jackson's partner didn't answer, because there was no excuse. Instead he sank in the chair behind his desk. The office grew silent, invaded only by the sounds of the bustling city outside. Jackson might have felt some of the compassion his mother showed for the man, if he weren't so consumed himself with self-directed anger.

He had known from Lil's admission that Horsey had an accomplice, but the fruition of his wedding plans with Erin had overridden his usually cautious nature. Worse, he'd walked blindly into the alley without the slightest hint that anything was amiss until he came to, bound and gagged on the float.

At first, he'd deluded himself to think that he had been the victim of someone desperate to participate in the ball. Such things had been known to happen when someone became peeved over not being invited to the private affair. But whoever his assailant was, he had been so eager to get inside that he'd neglected

431

to take Jackson's cutlass. While it proved to Jackson's advantage, for he was able to use it to cut himself free, it also alarmed him. Someone who was intent just on attending the affair would likely have paid more attention to appearance than someone bent on simply gaining access.

The moment he stormed into the ballroom wearing a pair of borrowed trousers he'd found in the back and seen his mother sitting alone among the women anxiously awaiting the call of their names, he'd felt as if someone had stabbed his heart with an icy dagger of fear. He knew, even as he scanned the dance floor, that he would not see his new bride.

The waiting while the authorities tried to follow up on every possible lead that might take them to Woodward's lair, had not served to thaw the frozen dread that afflicted him. They'd questioned everyone who might have seen Erin and her abductor leave, but the festivities had been too great a distraction for anyone to notice. His mother, who had tried to watch them across the crowded dance floor, saw them duck behind the stage, but thought little of it, considering their newlywed status.

Their only hope was that, since Woodward hoped to do away with Jacques Devareau, that he would use Erin to do so. Left with little alternative but to wait for the man to make the next move, they returned to the Decatur Street headquarters to spend the remainder of a sleepless night in hopes that the authorities might find something, anything to give them a clue as to where Woodward or Elena Cadiz, whom Lil had said worked with the man, might be.

"You fled town before you found out if the man was dead?" Jackson questioned suddenly, something in his partner's story not quite fitting. "How could a dead man accuse you of murder?"

"It wasn't Henry Woodward, it was that little wimp of a boy who came with him to the dueling ground . . . some relative, as I recall."

"What did he look like? Maybe we've given the police a description of the wrong man."

John Davenport's face lit up at the possibility, but as he reached back in time to retrieve the information they needed, he could recall little more than he'd already said. "I didn't pay that much attention to him. After all, it was Woodward who had the gun. He was not much more than sixteen," he ventured slowly, "and almost effeminate . . . like that schoolmaster you hired for Erin . . ." Even as he said it, the startling revelation struck home. "Oh, God!"

Jackson was already rushing for the door. Everyone was looking for the wrong man. The man they wanted was the one he'd put off at the landing upriver, one Roderick Sturgis. He seized the latch and yanked open the door, only to run headlong into a startled young boy who stood about to knock with a package in hand.

Smothering a curse, Jackson stopped long enough to haul the raggedly dressed youth to his feet. "What the devil do you want?"

Withering under the demonic glare of the man, the boy held out a package hesitantly. "I was told to deliver this to a John Davenport at this office."

Jackson took the unmarked package in one hand and, catching the youth by the collar, ushered him inside. "Who gave it to you?" he demanded, tossing the bundle to his partner.

"I . . . I don't know, he just gave me two bits and told me to bring it here."

"Where—" Jackson broke off as he saw a blanched John Davenport unfold the exquisite gown Erin had worn to the ball. His voice dropped perceptibly, drawing an alarmed look from his mother. "Where did he give it to you?"

"At the marketplace."

"What did he look like?"

433

"I don't . . ." The boy yelped as Jackson grabbed his shirt front and threw him against the wall.

"Think, lad! What did he look like?"

"Jackson!"

The boy sought out the sympathetic woman who rushed to her son's side to stay his hand with a frantic look. As the dark-haired demon lowered his feet to the floor, still keeping him within his clutches, he swallowed dryly and tried to find his voice.

"Sh . . . short, I think . . . compared to you, sir," he added nervously. "And he wore spectacles."

"Mustached?"

"Yes . . . I think so . . . and he corrected the way I talked."

"There's a note." All eyes turned to where John Davenport held up a neatly penned message. "I'm to meet him at the corner of St. Phillip and Bourbon in—" he glanced at the clock on the wall—"a half hour." He added somberly. "And I am to come alone."

"Isn't there a parade scheduled for this morning along Bourbon?" Jackson reflected aloud. The grand parade of the Mystic krewe of Comus would be that night, followed by that of the krewe of the fair-haired son of Mardi Gras on Fat Tuesday, Rex. Smaller organizations worked their events in whenever possible.

"The man has planned this out well," Davenport concurred. "Even a small parade will make it difficult to follow us."

"Well, you sure as hell are not leaving me out this time," Jackson decreed vehemently as he snatched on his jacket.

"Shouldn't we contact the police?"

"And tell them what, Mother? We don't even know where we're going, only that we have a short time to get there." Jackson paused as Auralee Tyler covered her face with her hands in fearful despair and his tone softened. "I'll send for help as soon as we locate him," he assured her, "but I won't do anything to jeopardize Erin's life."

"Or yours?"

"I won't be any good to her if I up and get myself killed, will I?"

"Nor will you be of any use either, if you continue to talk," John Davenport told him, gently moving the lady aside so that he might pass. "Madame, you will have my eternal gratitude for remaining staunch in my defense, even though I do not deserve it." He brushed Auralee Tyler's hand softly with his lips and dashed out the door before she could reply with the feeling that welled in her honey-brown eyes.

"And take care of him, too," she called out to Jackson, who did the same to her cheek and ran after him. As he rounded the corner, she caught sight of the pistol he'd tucked in his waistband and shuddered. "God be with you all," she whispered brokenly, sinking against the open door, eyes closed in fervent prayer.

With the coming of daylight, the nightmare of the darkness became no less intimidating. Yet, in spite of the sheer terror that threatened to overtake her as she listened to Roderick Sturgis's mad plan for revenge against her father, Erin clung stubbornly to her instinct for survival and concentrated on a plan of her own.

She'd awakened from her brief interlude of unconsciousness to find herself bound and gagged on the same bed with the stiff and deteriorating corpse of her predecessor. She couldn't help the cry of horror that strangled in her throat, inadvertently giving the man who held the kerosene lamp over her face no end of delight. She'd thought her heart would never start beating again, but it did, frantically and

435

painfully, as if it were going to burst from her chest.

Try as she might, Erin could not keep her fear from showing as Sturgis went on to tell her of the hellish torture Elena Cadiz had suffered at his hand. As he did, he touched her and spoke with such illustration that she could almost feel the agony the Hispanic girl had finally escaped from in death. Yet, Erin remained unscathed, at least, physically. Her suffering was to be saved for the eyes of her father in Sturgis's demented plan.

When he finally left, satisfied that her initial torment be the company of the corpse he accused her of seeking out, she was almost relieved. Struggling with her panic and the terrifying and nauseating presence of the deteriorating body sharing the bed, she tried to collect her wits as she listened to the movements of the man downstairs and the loud celebration next door that had run nonstop since her arrival.

It sounded as if Sturgis were moving furniture, and on occasion making it, from the hammering noises that drifted up the stairs. Whatever preparations he was about, at least he was no longer menacing her. When Erin finally resumed control of her senses, she remembered the pocket knife that had fallen on the floor beyond the bed and set about trying to reach it without drawing overmuch attention.

It seemed to take an eternity to gather enough nerve to roll over the top of the blank staring remains of Elena Cadiz. As she came face to face with her, Erin thought surely she would strangle on the nausea that rose in the back of her throat. At that point, the death would have been welcome, but for the single image she conjured in her beleaguered mind—that of a dark-haired man with a dancing silver gaze that could read her very soul. She echoed Jackson's name over and over, like a cheer to encourage her weary and cramped muscles onward.

With the corpse's forced possession of the headrail, Sturgis had fortunately not taken the time to secure Erin to the bed. Perhaps he'd counted on her fear rendering her completely helpless. Whatever the reason, Erin was grateful. Using extreme caution, she eased with painful slowness to the floor, praying that the noise from next door, combined with Sturgis's own ministrations, would camouflage her movements.

When Sturgis's voice drifted up from the steps telling her he would return soon, Erin's movements came to an instant stop. She held her breath, fearful that he would come up the steps and find her, not where he left her, but on the floor with the knife in her hand. Closing her eyes, she listened and prayed until the opening click of the key in the lock told her her prayers had been answered.

She lay still for several minutes after she heard him lock the door behind him, her agonized moment of expectation having left her physically and emotionally spent. Tears fell unrestrained down her cheeks as she sawed away awkwardly at the thick jute. Sometimes a sob of frustration exploded behind the starched handkerchief her kidnapper had stuffed in her mouth when the knife would drop and she'd have to carefully reposition it again.

Then her hands were free. Ignoring the stinging of her raw wrists, she removed the gag and sawed through the bonds on her feet, her head bent over her task to keep from noticing her grotesque companion. Yet, as she climbed to her feet and tested her cramped legs, Erin's gaze seemed drawn to the lifeless body scarred with ugly marks of degradation from the red-hot irons and the whip Sturgis had described. Her repugnance and fear gaining the upper hand, however, she hurriedly covered the dead woman with a blanket and stumbled down the steps.

The door, for all its years, was as sturdy as the day it

had been installed. Secure in its jamb, it would not give under the weight Erin threw against it. Discouraged, she set about trying the windows, only to find them equally well fixed. Sturgis had not exaggerated. Even free, she could not force her way out of her prison.

As she reluctantly made up her mind to return to the second floor, hoping the windows might not be as sure as those below, she realized that Sturgis had been changing things around. Instead of a sparsely furnished parlor, the room looked more like one of Byron's dungeons. Manacles and leg irons had been fastened to the wall under the stairwell and where the table had been, four spikes were driven into the floor through the round threadbare carpet, each with a length of rope tied to it.

On the table, which had been moved close to a small potbellied stove attached to a chimney in the back corner where it had previously gone unnoticed, an assortment of instruments that she could only guess the use of had been placed, laid out like a surgeon might the tools of his profession. Shuddering, Erin checked the ominous wanderings of her imagination and, seizing one of the irons to use as a tool, raced up the steps to what now seemed the less frightening place in the house.

It only took a matter of seconds to knock the glass out of the windowpanes of the dormer. The cypress louvers, however, were more resilient. When she was at last able to pull away a section of them, she could see the boards nailed over them that had rendered her attack ineffective. Anger and frustration flaring at her helplessness, she started banging on them and shouting for help.

Finally, she leaned exhausted against the wall and stared through tear-glazed eyes at the results of her tantrum. Most of the louvers lay scattered at her feet. Only the shutter frames and the tightly nailed boards

438

separated her from her freedom. Her shouting had had less effect, for it seemed that the participants in the all-night party had either left or fallen into a deaf sleep.

If the iron weren't so big at the end, she could slip it between the boards where sunlight streamed into the room and loosen them. *But there were smaller ones!* she recalled. Taking heart, she started toward the steps again when the sound of a key in the lock made her draw back against the wall in trepidation. Sturgis was back!

Clutching the iron to her chest, Erin closed her eyes and listened as the door swung open and, not one, but two sets of footsteps sounded on the floor. Was one of the men her father? she wondered.

"All right, Sturgis, you have me. Now where is Erin?"

"Your daughter is upstairs . . . in bed where I left her."

"By God, if you've . . ."

"Now, now, Davenport," Roderick Sturgis chuckled, the threatening click of a pistol hammer cutting off the outraged outburst. "Or should I say *Devareau?*"

Erin's eyes flew open with the confirmation of the image of her husband's partner that she had uncertainly matched with the voice below. John Davenport? She was almost tempted to peep around the corner, still mistrustful of her ears, but common sense prevailed. Was that why he'd taken her necklace and kept the pictures . . . because he was Jacques Devareau? She'd never confronted him about it, preferring to think it the act of a desperate man escaping the law, a man she chose to remain fond of in spite of that. The multitude of other questions that began to consume her thoughts were silenced as her father spoke.

"This is between you and me, Sturgis. You have

me, now let Erin go.''

"Actually, Devareau, I have both of you.'' He laughed again, a spine-tingling sound. "Oh, I have waited for this ever since I saw you on the *Delta Moon* . . . and you didn't recognize me,'' he mockingly chided.

"There are people who are worth recognizing and others who are not. You fall into the latter category, sir.''

"Enough! Get over to the stairs and slip those manacles on,'' the other man snapped, his delight disintegrating.

"What if I refuse?''

"Then I shall shoot you and put you in them myself.''

"From the looks of things in here, shooting might be preferable.''

"But then you'll leave your daughter in my grasp. Now put on the irons.''

Erin glanced around the corner and caught a glimpse of John Davenport as he stepped up to the chains fastened under the staircase and began to examine them. Iron in hand, she stepped out so that he could see her and motioned for him to lure Sturgis over to the stairwell. Their eyes only met briefly, the urgency of the situation forbidding more, yet Erin could not doubt the sincere apology her father sent her. Again the questions stirred, but this was not the time to dwell on them.

"I don't mean to set off your temper, sir, but I don't see how these blasted things work!'' he exclaimed, with a convincing rattle of the chains.

It seemed an eternity before Sturgis rose to the bait. He approached the gambler with caution, his pistol brandished threateningly as his troublesome prisoner stepped aside, placing him back to the head of the steps. Erin cautiously took her first step, the iron raised with the intent of smashing the man over

440

the head before he noticed her. A second step and both breath and pulse came to a stop.

"There's nothing wrong with these any simpleton can't figure out," Sturgis expelled irritably. "Just put your wrists in them and clamp them shut."

Her father grunted as the pistol was jabbed into his abdomen, prodding his hands up.

"I warn you, if I even think those hands might stray from their course, I—"

The tread on the third step creaked loudly, splitting the air like the wild screech of the peacocks in Jackson Square. The pistol swung up to where Erin froze, white-faced. Although she'd failed to render Sturgis unconscious, the distraction was enough for Davenport to seize the pistol. Moving out of its range as a scuffle ensued, she dashed down the steps, to assist him. However, upon reaching the tussling men as they fell to the floor and rolled toward the stove, a clear swing was almost impossible.

As if to join the fray, some of the loud neighbors who had partied so boisterously all night came alive, their earlier good humor soured no doubt by hangovers, and began what sounded like as violent a confrontation as was taking place in front of Erin. The loud crash of furniture breaking above a woman's outraged shrieks and a man's furious bellows seemed almost as if it were in the same room with the grunting struggling men as Erin ignored her father's breathless warnings to get away from them and tried to get close enough to land the iron on Roderick Sturgis's balding head.

Suddenly an explosion deafened her and the entire scene before Erin went into slow motion. She watched in fascinated horror as the man rolled once more and John Davenport raised up, smashing his fist into the face of his opponent. Then, just as relief began to thaw the ice that had, but a second before, encased her beating heart, he fell aside, his other arm clasped across his abdomen.

"No!" she screamed, knocking the pistol from the hand of a panting Roderick Sturgis. She caught him full across the face with her back swing, ripping his cheek open to draw blood . . . like the blood that flowed through her father's fingers as he tried to rise. She struck the man again, this time knocking him senseless as the scrambling motions he'd made to escape her hysterical assault collapsed into stillness.

"Erin . . ."

Upon seeing John Davenport trying to shove himself upright, Erin dropped her weapon and rushed to his side. "Let me see," she insisted, prying away his jacket. She'd seen Miss Molly and her mother tend plenty of gunshot wounds until the doctor could be summoned from up the hill and had long since conquered growing squeamish at the sight of blood.

Another crash of splintering wood from next door sounded as if the roof were coming off. In spite of the start it gave her, Erin gently pulled the shirttail out of her father's trousers and lifted it to expose the dark hole the ball had torn through his side. Freed of the material and John's clasping pressure, it seeped red faster than she cared to see.

"I've got to get you to a doctor."

"Erin, I didn't know you existed until the day I first saw you on the *Delta Moon*."

"Mama said you didn't know about me," she answered matter-of-factly, intent of ripping off the hem of her gown to bind the wound so that John could be moved safely.

"And after the war, when I went back to New Orleans where I'd told Giselle to go, her family had spread the news that she had died of childbirth in Natchez. As long as I traveled on the river, I wouldn't get off there. Besides, I was a wanted man there."

442

*So that was why he hadn't come back for them.*
"Sturgis told me the truth about the duel, how he set you up because you'd killed his lover. Now try to sit up."

"His lover!" Davenport winced and looked up at the ceiling as Erin reached around him to wrap the length of bandage she had improvised.

"It was revenge he wanted against you. He'd planned it from the moment he saw you on the *Delta Moon* and decided to use me to get you personally when the thugs he and Elena hired failed.

"Speaking of which, where is the wench?"
Erin met her father's gaze and her composure faltered. "Upstairs . . . dead."

Another crash, a ripping sound, made Erin wish the neighbors were in Sturgis's house. If she'd had them on her side, she could have gotten help, she thought wryly as she helped Davenport to his feet. Remembering the only way out was the front door, and that Roderick Sturgis kept the key on his person, she left her father leaning heavily on the high back of the settee and turned to where she'd left the man. Except that he was not there. He'd dragged himself over to the stove, leaving a trail of blood from his bludgeoned face.

"I . . . underestimated you, Kate," he gasped as he tossed the key into the open door to land among the glowing red-gold coals. "I thought . . . Elena would keep you entertained until my return. Obviously, you found her as boring as I."

Erin ran to the place where she'd dropped the iron, thinking to fish the key out with it, but as she straightened, she heard Sturgis cackling. Bemused, she looked at him and paled. In his hand was a powder flask.

"But you underestimated me as well," he said, holding it dangerously close to the open door of the stove. "I would never let you live, Devareau. Never

443

while I drew . . ."

"Erin!" Above the loud thunder of her heart, Erin heard Jackson's voice booming from the upstairs room.

"Get back, boy!" her father warned behind her as Jackson Tyler thundered down the steps, unaware of his danger.

"Jackson, no! Go back!"

Erin lunged toward the stairwell, only to be caught by the waist. The room erupted first in motion, rolling a circle around her and the body dragging her over the back of the sofa. Then as it seemed to swallow them both, a hysterical shriek pierced the darkness followed by a deafening thunder that seemed to lift them off the floor and hurl them through space.

The impact left her stunned, numb to all but the strange crackling sound surrounding her and an unbearable heat. Erin coughed and groaned as the darkness that had covered her was hurled away.

"Erin!"

The weight that was on top of her was lifted and a hand seized her arm. "We've got to get out of here!"

"Jackson?" she whispered hoarsely. She blinked her eyes and, as they came into focus on the man drawing her to her feet, she became aware of the room blazing with fire beyond there where Roderick Sturgis had been.

"But he had the key," she mumbled brokenly as she was hauled toward the front door.

She heard Jackson curse as he tried the lock. "Get back," he warned, moving her aside. In a daze, she barely heard him, but moved back instinctively when her foot struck something. She looked down and felt, rather than saw through the thick smoke filling the room, John Davenport lying still in the pile of rubble from which Jackson had plucked her and realized that her father had covered her with his body to protect her.

"Father!"

A panel of the door split with the force of Jackson's fierce kick as she dropped to the fallen man's side and moved the smoking cushions from the settee away from him just as they too burst into flames. Upon seeing that the frame which had protected them from the brunt of the blast was about to do the same, she slung it away with all her might.

"Erin get . . ." Jackson erupted in a fit of coughing as he staggered back to her. "Get out!"

"Not without John!"

"I'll get him. Now go!"

"We'll both get him."

Not to be moved, Erin helped Jackson drag her father toward the open door from which the bottom two panels and the center stile had been kicked away. The fire that was rapidly eating up what was left of the room seemed to catch in her lungs with each breath she took as she struggled with his feet.

"You go through first and I'll hand him to you!"

Nodding, she climbed onto the warped wooden step, only to be dragged away. "No!"

"Get back, miss. We'll get 'em out!"

People were shouting and running around, adding to the confusion that enveloped Erin as she was ushered out into the street struggling frantically. She tried to see beyond those who manhandled her, to assure herself that the man had told the truth . . . that Jackson and her father were being pulled free of the inferno as promised.

John Davenport's limp body was pulled down the steps by two men, who stopped long enough to grasp him under the shoulders and legs, before proceeding with him to where Erin was being held.

"Lord, he's been shot!"

"Is he dead?" she asked, not tearing her gaze from

the broken door where Jackson Tyler stumbled out, an arm around each of his two rescuers.

"Naw, he's breathin' but he ain't none too good."

"A doctor," she whispered, her voice too choked to do more.

"Somebody's already gone for one . . . and the police, too."

"Are you all right?"

The man who had fought his way through the crowd toward her, caught her in his arms. It was only then that Erin felt relief and knew for certain that she was truly out of danger. After all, in Jackson's arms nothing could harm her. Not Sturgis, not anything. She nodded dizzily, but just as she thought the swirling dark cloud hovering just beyond her vision would claim her, she caught sight of his tattered shirt and jacket, stained scarlet with blood.

"Jackson!" she gasped, inadvertently inflicting additional pain as she clung to him unsteadily in her attempt to examine him. His clothes had been ripped from across his chest and one shoulder of his jacket was missing as if something with great teeth had torn it away to expose the raw flesh.

"It's just a splinter," he assured her, forcing a laugh to assuage the terror floating in the emerald eyes he'd nearly despaired of ever seeing open again as he had blindly dug through the rubble trying to find her. He didn't even feel where the large splinter of banister railing had grazed him, knocking him backward on the step with a staggering blow. All he felt was Erin, living and breathing in his arms.

A cough at their feet, drew the couple's attention to where John Davenport literally clawed his way to consciousness, his flailing arm knocking over one of the women who had stuffed a petticoat under the bandage Erin had applied earlier.

"Father!" Pulling away from her husband, Erin dropped to the invalid's side as he opened his eyes and sought her out.

"Erin!" He smiled weakly as she seized his hand and held it to her cheek. "We can't be in heaven," he observed, wincing as he shifted to see the smoke rising above the rooflines. "So I must assume from the way I hurt that we have survived. Are you all right?"

Erin laughed, her pent-up emotions giving way with tears of relief. "Thanks to you and Jackson, I'm fine. Jackson kicked down the door and got us out."

"You damned fool, you were to keep him talking while I broke in upstairs, not get yourself shot," Jackson derided good-naturedly.

John peered over Erin's shoulder at the bedraggled young man grinning at him. "I'm surprised you didn't just leave me, after all I've done."

"What?" his partner exclaimed in mock incredulity. "And be left to account to my wife and mother?"

"I don't deserve the respect of either of them."

Erin squeezed his hand. "There are a lot of things in life you didn't deserve, Father. Why don't you just accept the good ones," she suggested, her lips curling in a way that struck Jackson as pure Davenport . . . or Devareau, he corrected himself. Why hadn't he seen it before? he wondered incredulously. He should have suspected John's interest in Erin to be more than ordinary. He'd reminded Jackson of an outraged father on more than one occasion, but lovestruck dolt that he was, Jackson failed to see the way the cards were falling. Although they didn't look alike, they were like two peas in a pod. They shared the same sense of humor, the same penchant for trouble . . .

"Here's a wagon we kin haul your friend to the doctor's in," someone called out.

"We'll go with you," Erin promised as two men picked John Davenport up gently to put him in the back of a produce wagon that had been rapidly

447

emptied to accommodate him. She linked her arm in her husband's. "You need some attention, too."

Jackson pulled her to him and lifted her soot-smudged face with the crook of his finger. "This is the only attention I need," he told her softly, his tender gaze embracing her soul as he lowered his lips to hers and captured them with an urgency that told her of the tortuous anxiety he'd suffered on her account.

Erin's knees buckled, but her husband's strong arm held her pressed against him, unwilling to give her up just yet. A warm giddiness filled her head as she returned his kiss, all trace of the nightmare of terror she'd lived through vanishing in the sunshine that refused to be daunted by the smoke rising from the burning house. Even when Jackson hadn't been there in person, he'd come to her rescue. His love had inspired her to a strength she didn't suspect she possessed, a love that would not be denied . . . a love born *under the Delta Moon*.